CIRCULAR

MOTION

CIRCULAR MOTION

ALEX FOSTER

A
NOVEL

Grove Press
New York

FIRST EDITION

Published simultaneously in Canada
Printed in the United States of America

The interior of this book was designed by Norman E. Tuttle
at Alpha Design & Composition.
This book was set in 11.25-pt. Janson Text by Alpha Design & Composition
in Pittsfield, NH.

First Grove Atlantic hardcover edition: May 2025

Library of Congress Cataloging-in-Publication data is available for this title.

ISBN 978-0-8021-6448-3
eISBN 978-0-8021-6449-0

Grove Press
an imprint of Grove Atlantic
154 West 14th Street
New York, NY 10011

Distributed by Publishers Group West

groveatlantic.com

25 26 27 28   10 9 8 7 6 5 4 3 2 1

CONTENTS

PART I

Part II

Part III

PART I

Arctic Lemmings

It was still early. The northern lights hung like creamed angels, and my sister went out alone to feed the pigs. As the snow crunched beneath her boots, she repeated the Lord's Prayer to herself, trying to remember what came after deliverance. She was nine and already accustomed to the occasional feeling that her world was spinning out of control.

She found the pigs hiding in the corner of their pen, away from their space heater. They hadn't touched yesterday's feed. She didn't know why. For several minutes, she tried to scrape the old pellets from their trough, but they were frozen solid. In the woodland wind with the stars all falling westward, she grew vaguely afraid.

Something creaked in the dark, and she looked up toward our house. The sound seemed to be coming from underneath the snow. She stepped toward it, the pigs silent at her back, and for a moment, the yard seemed perfectly still.

Then she screamed. Across the yard and into the street, the snow erupted with thousands of rodents. They were like maggots bursting from a carcass, zigzagging and trampling one another. One scrambled up her leg. She kicked it away. They seemed to have no idea where they were. The pigs barked at them, and they dashed for the tree line, following one another blindly. By the time she reached the front door, cold air burning her lungs, no sign of them remained but rough, white scarring in the earth.

DAYS OF 23 HOURS AND 59 MINUTES

I wasn't home to see my sister come in panting, exclaiming how the apocalypse had arrived and it was starting on our lawn. I didn't witness my parents' reaction. I can only imagine it. I imagine that had my sister borne testimony to a revelation of doom on any morning other than that one, our father would have encouraged her. "Damn right," he would have said, barely listening, and then he might have cited the biblical plague of rats at Ekron, consoling her with the admonition that judgment ought only be feared by sinners, socialists, and queers. On any other morning, our mom might have tried to pacify her with promises of red Jell-O or a trip into town to play at the entertainment annex. But my parents' mood on that particular morning is difficult to guess for the same reason that I am limited to guessing: For on that morning they were preoccupied by the discovery that I, their other child, was gone. In the middle of the night, I had finally run away.

I was twenty and had lived in Keber Creek, Alaska, pop. 900, all my life. My father moved us out there the year I was born, after getting a job in the town's opencast gold mine. He charged holes for blasting. I remember walking to and from the mine with him as a kid, long walks that he spent excoriating me for not appreciating this opportunity to live out in the boondocks, or as he put it, "amidst Creation." I remember the mine's looming concrete walls and how the aspens quaked each time the blasts went off. During my teens, his job was abruptly automated, and the week before my sixteenth birthday he received his pink slip.

He was encouraged to move to an A-O Company town outside Eugene for retraining. I wanted us to go, to leave Alaska. But we stayed. My father was sick of relying on corporate caprice; he appreciated his frontier liberties and said he would find gig work. He never did. Instead, he retreated into bitterness and religion. He had always had a survivalist streak, and this grew inflamed in the want of employment's civilizing influence. My father was a Mormon who believed even his own Church's leadership in Salt Lake City was infiltrated by Jews—you can imagine how he felt about, for example, the government. He obsessed over eschatology. For as long as I can remember, he was forecasting society's spectacular collapse. Violent scripture was his favorite. I feared him. Unlike some other mine workers, he didn't imbibe, and for that alone I'm inclined to thank his God, but there really wasn't much difference between an impatience for annihilation expressed by drinking oneself into oblivion and one expressed through his particular brand of piety. While technology-driven unemployment led many men of his generation to pine for the past, he just prayed all the more fervently for a hastening of the End.

I, by that time, did have a job: doing custodial work at our town's largest church, a crummy little bethel held up by wood glue and blind prayer. Suddenly my family's primary breadwinner, I drew our livelihood from the building's lightbulb sockets and clogged drains. Attached to the narthex was a small arcade, Keber Creek's only recreational facility, stocked with Old Testament–themed video games for the betterment of the youth—*Frogger: Red Sea Crossing, Balaam's Donkey Kong*; the machines sat unlit most days, like tree trunks after a forest fire. I spent many afternoons climbing up the narrow wooden ladder to the church's belfry and there, above the haggard white pines, I would smoke Natural American Spirits and scroll social media on my little 1600p, watching other kids thousands of miles away dance in

Eastern ruin bars, kiss astride mopeds, or drink champagne on observation decks above the Champs-Élysées. Sometimes I posted videos of my own. They were nothing better than what any teenager posted in those days (thirty-second clips of me calling Democrats idiots, and later, when I grew uneasy with my father's politics, deepfake videos of celebrities dancing), but I took to social media with a seriousness certainly enhanced by the fact that the world online seemed to me more important—realer, even—than my backwater hometown.

It was my minor addiction to social media that led me to contact Victor Bickle and earned me the ticket that would end up freeing me from Alaska, not quite for good but for a very long time. Afraid of my overture being lost among ordinary fan messages, I refrained from fawning over Bickle's videos. In truth, I didn't really understand a lot of his Scroller content. Bickle, a professor of mechanical engineering at Columbia University in New York, had garnered attention online the year before with a ten-minute video about the structural instability of the Queensboro Bridge—released six months before the bridge's shocking collapse. In the six months before the accident, his post had garnered fewer than eight hundred views, and then, overnight, eight hundred people were dead, and the video was trending on CNN's homepage. The earnest forty-year-old professor was suddenly a media go-to. Since then, it was common for his videos to be picked up by mainstream outlets. "Professor Victor Bickle, who predicted the Queensboro Catastrophe, releases his latest warning." He railed against corrupt regulators, becoming a champion of transparency and of the public's understanding of the world around them. His videos were technical—too technical for me to follow—but I admired his success. He was handsome, in a lanky, brainiac sort of way. And while I didn't understand him, I hoped he might understand me, for Victor Bickle, the sudden minor celebrity, had been born and raised in Keber Creek.

I sent him a private message saying that I admired him for getting out of KC and said that I, like him, aspired to make something of myself. I wanted to learn how the world really was. I asked if he might share any advice, or perhaps even take me under his wing, as an aspiring content creator.

When three months passed and Bickle didn't reply, I feared I'd overstepped in presuming a kinship between us. I read that he'd left Keber Creek on his own at seventeen for university; I, a twenty-year-old church custodian, probably resembled the very thing he'd rejected. Admittedly, I had spent most of my life in Keber Creek trying to fit in. I'd grown from a church youth so desperate for the counselor's favor that I volunteered for testimony every month, to a middle schooler who threw rocks through my teacher's windows in the hopes of winning acceptance from my peers. When the other boys in my school groped Rebekah Hamsley after she blacked out at Winter Dance, I fearfully joined in, but then snitched on them the next day. I followed my classmates in ridiculing Brian K., the "fag," but apparently that made me no less "faggy" myself. I'd wanted to fit in desperately; I just never figured out how. As a kid I cowered at everyone's disapproval, which to me were correlates to, if not strange incarnations of, the primary disapproval—my father's—which I fought and fought through adolescence before finally emerging disaffected only in my late teens. I recognize the sour grapes element to this account—I only resolved to ditch Keber Creek after it repeatedly rejected me. But I had other catalysts too for disillusionment during my teenage years. The world changed. The westward circuit normalized flights between the lower forty-eight and the capitals of Europe and Asia that took barely an hour, making our isolated Alaskan town seem to me increasingly irrelevant. Unemployed, my father hoarded his welfare checks while cursing government largesse (he was the type never to forgive someone for doing him a favor). He turned our moldy prefab house into his pulpit, and as one prophesized apocalypse after another failed to pass, his aggression grew. So did the rift between us. And all the while, the screens around me presented with increasing persistence and allure all the things in the world I was missing.

It seemed obvious to me that our town was already suffering its apocalypse as the mine automated, job after job, and the only thing to do was move on already. I thought maybe Victor Bickle, a man of the world and of prestige by way of science, could rescue me. I had no real evidence for this, no history to draw on. Just another kind of faith.

When Bickle finally replied, his message was brief.

Dear Tanner, it said. *Apologies for the delay. Been a hectic time for me. I would love to meet you and help however I can. You say you want to "get out" of Keber Creek. That's something I can understand! Would you like to meet me for lunch in New York? How about Ronan's Grill on 37th at A.H. 973,839? You will love Ronan's. I'm sure I can refer you to a job in the city if you're interested. I've attached a credit for circuit flights, on me. But if this isn't of interest, no need to explain. – VB*

I turned the message over and over in my mind as I showered that night, using all the hot water. Sitting down at dinner with hair still wet, my heart raced. *To meet for lunch tomorrow.* So casually proposed, as if New York City were just down the street. I obsessed in particular over the closing line, "no need to explain," intimidated by its cool indifference. (It didn't occur to me to interpret it the other way, as a preemptive defense against rejection; I wasn't yet trained to see in things their opposites.)

But Bickle should have known that even just making use of circuit passes would be impossible for me. The closest pod station, in Fairbanks, was eight hours' drive on unplowed roads. Our snow machine didn't have that range. I sat at the table, rolling dirt between my toes. The only option was my father's pickup truck. I knew he'd never let me take it, but as my mother slid misshapen trout cakes onto our plates, I worked up the nerve to ask.

"What do you need my truck for?" he said. He sat on the couch in the adjoining room, watching news about migrants at the border three thousand miles away.

"To get to work tomorrow morning," I lied. "The snow machine is empty."

He told me to go across the street and borrow a shot of propane from the Tumeskys, mix it with corn oil. The dogs wrestled in the hall.

"The engine isn't working," I said.

He looked over. "You fucked up the engine? What'd you do?"

"I didn't do anything."

"Well, fix it." He turned up the TV.

Cold seeped into the house through cracks in the carbon fiber siding, and little moths tapped on the windows, fighting to get in front of one another as if each thought its own warning was more important than the rest. Across the table, my mom ate with her fingers.

"Busy day at work?" she asked me.

I shook my head.

"Answer your mother," shouted my dad.

"He did," said my mom.

"He ought to speak to his family in complete sentences." He beckoned my younger sister Ashtyn, who brought him another can of nonalcoholic apple beer and collected his empties. My mom drew plasticky trout bones from between her teeth. I had a headache and craved a cigarette. I kept imagining myself walking out the door and never coming back. I glared at my father, at the truck keys carabinered to his belt loop.

"Your brother doesn't know how the real world works," he said to Ashtyn.

She looked at me, her overgrown hair the same shade of red as his, and mine. His gaze didn't leave the TV. I watched him, smarting.

"Hypocrite," I murmured.

"What did you just say?" demanded my mother.

My father looked over. The TV was blaring about Christian values so loud that there was a chance he hadn't heard me. I looked at Ashtyn. Her eyes were pleading, wishing to be left out of it.

"Come here," said my father.

I stayed where I was, frozen between the immaturity of refusing and the emasculation of giving in.

"I said come here."

I took my last bite but held on to my knife. It was he who finally stood. Hunched, he walked over. He was a man who'd spent adolescence waiting for relief from his family's bank debts to come in the form of widespread calamity. A man (I now believe) tormented by the mounting possibility that his life might not be a labor of preparation for the world's climactic end, but rather a labor of endurance through countless small disappointments. He moved very close to me, so close I could smell his Ocean Breeze bodywash, which was the same as my own. Neither of us, father or son, had ever stepped foot in an ocean.

So quietly that not even my mom would hear, he said, "I've tried to create a good life for you, boy. It's up to you whether you deserve it."

That night I tossed and turned. Owls hooted to one another over our property. After three hours, I gave up on sleeping. The clocks flashed A.H. 973,826:02. I crawled out of bed and began packing for New York.

I emptied my "luau pack" of all my father's survivalist shit no one would ever need (the tent, the unloaded rifle) and stuffed it with clothes, stashing at the bottom all the money I had managed to steal from the church over the years. Three hundred dollars. I looked out the window. A circuit vessel's blue light streaked across the moon.

"Tanner," Ashtyn whispered. "Is something wrong?"

"Everything is fine," I said. "Don't worry about me."

I found my father asleep on the couch, changing colors as pundits disagreed. I stood so close that I believed I could feel the warmth of his body. His breath was strained. I reached down and unhooked the Dodge keys from his hip. He stirred. As I left the room, seeing him for the final time, I heard a woman on TV saying her offer wouldn't last forever and him mumbling, "Amen."

*   *   *

The drive was quiet. I put on the electronic music I liked but, feeling anxious, soon turned it off. I drove through to morning, along endless chain-link fences, escaping the Arctic Circle to find the sun. Its rise over the highway tundra was freer than anything I'd ever seen. Route 2 bridged the Chatanika, and rush hour traffic began to collect. I'd never been so far from home before. I pressed my phone against the pickup's windows, taking photos of the big animated billboards. At the end of a mountain tunnel, in low light, Fairbanks appeared. The river was incredibly bright, as if filled with fire, strapped down by bridges, squirming between blue roofs. The city seemed so much hungrier for inhabitants than Keber Creek, so much larger not only in space but in spirit. Yet even as capacious as the city was, I soon hit gridlock. And construction: Even as big as it was, it was being built bigger. Cranes fed on Fairbanks from above. Sawhorses blocked every other road, and men with jackhammers were tearing up the detours. There was no snow. The directions off my phone kept rerouting. My truck seemed to be the only one around that wasn't driving itself, and nearing the pod station I was taken by lights and arrows, loudspeaker announcements, and the mineral breeze of industry. It took effort to keep my focus on the road in front of me. I parked in the open-air long-term lot and hardly had my duffle out of the truck bed when a passing car honked at me to move. I turned to see the car was empty. It wheeled around into the passenger pickup line as a circuit vessel popped overhead, and I darted across the street toward VISA HELP, DUNKIN' DONUTS, and PODS—ALL DESTINATIONS.

In the pod station's domed lobby, a few dozen travelers rested on wooden benches, drinking coffee and staring at their phones. I stood by the door to my platform, anxiously rechecking that I had mapped the right route. There were a dozen circuit vessels crossing over Fairbanks every hour, and you had to be sure to board the pod that would shuttle you up to the vessel you wanted. The pods went up and down, but the vessels never landed—they orbited the Earth, again and again and again. On clear mornings in Keber Creek, I would look up and see their contrails crisscross. Their paths inclined northward or southward to varying degrees, but as a rule, all circuit vessels orbited roughly from east to west. That was the model drawn up by the world's oldest and largest circuit vessel carrier, the Circumglobal Westward Circuit Group, or CWC, upon whose dreams of commercial empire the westward circuit had first taken its way. It was for CWC flights that Victor Bickle had bought me a day pass, good for arrival and departure at any of CWC's tens of thousands of pod destinations in fifty-eight countries (even more for US citizens who added special visas to their passports). I knew there were people who viewed circuit travel as a basic necessity (and a single-day pass didn't cost so much by most people's standards: around fifty New Dollars for regular users and even less for first-time users off-peak), but I couldn't imagine ever losing the sense of wonder I presently felt at possessing one.

The platform door to my pod slid open to reveal a revolving door through which several passengers emerged. Some popped their ears. After the last woman exited, I attempted to enter, swinging my duffle ahead of me. I hit the revolving door like a wall.

The woman who'd just depodded called me honey and said, "You gotta scan your ticket to unlock the turnstile."

She pressed my phone against a small blue panel, the two screens kissing teeth to teeth.

Once through, I found myself alone in a round cabin about three yards across, encircled by a low bench. It wasn't heated, and I saw no place for luggage. The only compartment I could find was stocked with barf bags.

"Welcome to CWC," said a female voice from a speaker above. The wall across from me, which was a screen—all the pod walls were screens—played a promotional montage. It showed people stepping out of pods into various city centers and festivals. I recognized Paris and Hong Kong. A blond kid and his mother were shown exiting a pod in the center of Times Square, and the camera panned up to a bright sky with a circuit vessel approaching—all fuselage, no wings—getting closer and closer until it reached the depth of the screen and burst right out. It was aiming straight for my head. I ducked as the hologram entered the screen behind me with a digital shiver.

Everything was bluer than blue, and the voice said, "Welcome to the world."

The turnstile locked.

"Excuse me," I said to no one. "Are there seatbelts or . . ."

As the floor and ceiling began to vibrate, I felt myself growing lighter, rising off the bench. I groped for a handle. Then I noticed my duffle sliding off the bench's edge. I reached out to it and was knocked forward by an invisible force. I screamed. But my hands didn't hit the floor. I was weightless. The pod had taken flight.

Victor Bickle, Ph.D., was not quite so attractive IRL. Ejected from the protective frame of the screen, his rangy height, at six-foot-one, seemed to put his head at constant risk. He was balding—you never saw that in the videos, how his brown hair folded over in capitulation and frizzed out in alarm around his ears, which were truly humongous, like a child's drawing of ears, rounding out his physiognomy in the videos, but here, in the physical world, looking bony and appendant. He waved me over to his booth, and I made my way around young finance bros wearing fleece pants with the names of their employers stitched across the seat. Steaks sizzled in the wet New York City air. I was starving.

My parents had called. I hadn't answered.

"Tanner," said Victor Bickle, extending his hand. "You're late, but that's okay."

He wore a mustache, which intimidated me then, though later I wouldn't be able to help imagining him shaping it alone in his bathroom, and it endeared him to me.

Sitting down, I explained that I'd actually arrived early and had waited at the door to meet him.

"Why would you wait there?" He laughed. "The food is *inside* the restaurant." He said I would love the food here at Ronan's. "I come to Ronan's whenever I'm stuck in Midtown. Everyone I take loves it here."

"It seems really lively," I said.

He replied, "Well. It's not *that* lively."

We ordered lobster.

"So you're from Keber Creek too, huh?" he said. "My condolences."

"It's surreal," I said, "being here in New York."

"Yeah. It's almost half as good as the pictures."

I laughed. In truth, I had feared New York might offer nothing more than what I'd seen online, but on the contrary, the things I saw astonished me precisely *because* I recognized them so well. The dripping AC units. The flags at half-mast. The Empire State Building penetrating low clouds. To see New York was to step into my own personal dream, uncannily realized.

Bickle asked where I'd landed.

"Thirty-fourth Street," I said. "I expected there'd be a station like in Fairbanks, but the pod just fell down onto a platform in the middle of Herald Square. There were like a hundred people waiting around it to board."

"They've got a station in Fairbanks now?" Bickle said.

"Yeah."

"Wow. You know, since leaving Alaska twenty-odd years ago, I've never returned."

"That's amazing," I said. "Did you leave family behind?"

Bickle looked at me. The air was warm and oily, redolent of seafood and rubber. "I left for college. My dad was a surveyor for the gold mine. I apprenticed there, and the company got me a scholarship."

"My dad worked at the gold mine too," I said. I told Bickle that I didn't know much about engineering but I loved his online videos. "I might have mentioned, I make videos myself. Nothing serious."

Our lobsters arrived. They were more like crayfish.

Bickle said, "That Queensboro Bridge video changed my life. Now, I can film a five-minute rant and a stadium gets renovated. No one wants to risk a lawsuit for having ignored my warnings. The truth is, it's funny, but I don't even need another prediction to come true. If I say an ugly mall is going to collapse, these pathetic little commissioners all scramble to tear it down and rebuild it before we can ever find out if I was right. That's impact. You know I have two million followers on Scroller now? And I've gotten offers. I'm actually considering changing jobs. I've been butting heads at Columbia. I'm sick of it. I want to do something real."

I waited for him to begin eating, while he waited on more butter. If he noticed me waiting, he chose not to release me. As he spoke, he kept waving—with both arms—at our server. An elderly man fell down across the bar, causing a minor stir. When we finally ate, my food had a chalky bitterness, almost what I imagined poison would taste like, but Bickle ate the same thing and didn't mention it.

More than halfway through the meal, he finally stopped talking about himself. "Tell me, Tanner," he said. "What are *you* looking for?"

Although in his message he'd already offered to find me a job, I feared that to ask for one outright would seem too forward. Instead I said euphemistically that I'd be grateful for any advice about making a career outside Keber Creek.

"Well, are you willing to run errands?" he asked.

"Sure."

"Shovel shit?"

I told him I was a janitor before.

"Do you have any moral stipulations?"

I thought about it. "Probably," I said.

"Okay," said Bickle. "That's good, I guess."

He asked how I liked to be managed. Having no experience working under different managers, I wasn't sure how to answer. I considered saying I liked to be given the opportunity to do work that would make a real impact, since this seemed to be something he valued, but it occurred to me that if he cared about impact, people like him might want to hire others who would do the more thankless grunt work. Ultimately, I just answered, "I don't mind it," hoping that was funny.

He smiled. He did seem to like me. He said there were lots of jobs out there.

"This is actually quite an exciting time for me," he said. "I got contacted the other day by the CWC group."

"Wow," I said.

"Yeah, they're looking for a spokesperson. They want the company to have a familiar face. Someone who people see as being on their side. We'll see. I think of myself more as an independent voice. It's important that I retain my independence, right?"

"Totally," I said, realizing to my disappointment that for the rest of the meal, we would be talking about him again. As he went on about his own options, my gaze wandered. I noticed two homosexuals holding hands. One smiled at me (I thought of the cephalopodic creatures of the gruesome *Sodom Striker* game in Keber Creek's church arcade). When I returned my focus to Bickle, he was talking with food in his mouth.

"Circuit travel isn't the flashiest thing to become the spokesperson for," he said. "I mean, it's glorified airplanes. But then, it's more important than bridges. And any collaboration with a company as big as CWC would really grow my platform. I'm a little concerned about this day contraction stuff that's come out lately, but, you know, the agencies putting out that research are the same ones who got Queensboro wrong."

"What's day contraction?"

"You haven't heard about day contraction?"

I made some excuse for my education, but he didn't seem to care. He kept rattling off the pros and cons of his own career opportunities. I grew doubtful that he had any jobs to connect me with at all. Outside, smoke poured up from the sidewalk, ignored by passersby. I wondered what it was. I'd been awake for thirty hours.

"I thought CWC already had a guy in their commercials," I said. "Captain Sam? 'Welcome aboard, I'm Captain Sam.'"

"Pederast."

"Oh."

"And sure, I'm ready to be making real money," he said.

For the rest of the meal, he talked about how you can't live in New York on a professor's salary, you'd be better off in Keber Creek.

"Anyway, my advice for you," he said. "Stay out of academia."

He stood. Following him from the restaurant, I stepped out into the full light of Midtown and within fifteen seconds was almost struck by a scooterist. "Goddamn one-wheels," said an Indian man with a holographic chess game open on his tablet. "Oughta be illegal." It was January, and New Yorkers ate on park benches, greedily, like squirrels.

"Well," said Bickle. "I've gotta run. But it was nice meeting you. You seem like a good kid. I'm going to be in touch about jobs. Give me like one week."

"Thank you so much," I said, wishing I could believe him.

"Of course," he said magnanimously. "And hey. What did you think of Ronan's?"

I wandered around New York a few hours, but soon got scared and searched my phone for places to spend the night. In a motel in Jackson Heights, Queens, I got a room by the icemaker. Even Queens prices were lethal. I knew I had to call my parents, but I put it off, watching random videos about how prebiotics work, trying to pretend I hadn't traveled three thousand miles with no concrete plan. I watched a video about curb stomping while the motel heating unit wheezed out aromas of soaked dog.

My phone rang.

My parents were calling me.

I stood, walked to the wall (which wasn't far) and back, and without fully considering my actions, I answered.

"Tanner, oh my goodness, where—" It was my mom.

"I'm in New York," I said.

For the next five minutes, I explained everything, clearly and calmly, and when I finished, my mom said she didn't understand what the hell I was saying.

"Where will you sleep?"

"A motel."

"Did your sister know?"

"No."

"But when will you come home?"

I told her I didn't know.

She began to cry, and I realized my dad was on the line too, his breath rapid. I imagined him hunching over the phone. When he spoke, his voice trembled.

"You never think about anyone outside of yourself," he said.

I told him I just needed to get away.

"Do you hear what you've done to your mother?"

"I'm sorry."

"No, you aren't. You don't care."

"Dad."

"I've had enough of this. You stole my goddamn truck."

"I'll bring it back."

"No, you won't."

"I promise I will."

"You're not ever coming back here, Tanner," he said. My mom moaned. "If you do," he said, "I'll kill you."

And the line went dead.

I sat in the same place for a long time after that. He didn't mean it, I thought. I considered calling back. I stared at a yellow stain, while a couple in the next room fucked verbosely. Sometime after A.H. 973,847, I put on my windbreaker and stepped outside.

At a Citgo station, I bought American Spirits and smoked half a pack right there. A bread truck passed, wafting warm wheaty smells.

People were laughing on a stoop, speaking a language I didn't recognize. I watched the blue light of a circuit vessel climb through eastern clouds. It reached apogee overhead, where it emitted a faint pop—the sound of a distant sonic boom—and then descended over the Manhattan skyline, the city not sleeping, afraid of its dreams. Instead of calling my parents back, I turned off my phone. I was alone and scared, like everyone else, but I was free.

The next morning I got woken early by construction. I checked my phone to see if Bickle had called. Nothing. So for the rest of the day, I explored New York (my CWC day pass had expired, so I couldn't go anywhere else). I took a video of the dancers in Times Square and posted it to my Scroller page, slightly disheartened to find that everyone around me seemed to be doing the same thing. In Greenwich Village, I saw people my age eating twenty-nine-dollar brunch and talking loudly about how "we all know America sucks." I watched screens alongside the buildings. The Dow was up six points. I looked at a lot of menus and didn't know how anyone could afford any of it. Everyone in New York seemed to be dissipating unthinkable fortunes daily. I held out until dinner, then ate one-dollar pizza near my motel, folding my slice two times over like I thought I'd seen people do on TV. There was still no word from Bickle.

The next day was the same, and I began to feel I'd made a terrible mistake. I had spent half of my three hundred dollars already. I considered setting aside money for a CWC single-ride back to Alaska.

The day after that was Sunday. I went down to a church in Woodside and prayed for benevolent intercession. They gave me a job as the janitor's shadow. I cleared roach traps from the chancel and scrubbed bomb threats off Sunday-school desks. At the day's end, they paid me sixty bucks, barely enough to cover my motel. Again that night, I watched my phone. The woman in the next room performed her midnight vocal exercises, moaning "Please, please, please"—she was very polite. I held my breath, afraid that if I sneezed she'd shout God bless you.

A week after my lunch with Bickle, I got a message.

I've taken the job at CWC, Bickle wrote. *And I was given the budget for an assistant.* He made a point of saying that he'd offered the job first to his RAs at Columbia. *They didn't see how it would help them get into graduate school. It won't. It's a boring job, mostly. Scheduling meetings, running errands, handling admin (details attached). Even you're probably overqualified. But the pay is idiotically high, and look, I just want someone I can trust. This is new to me too. I think I can trust you. Anyway, someone's got to give a kid from Keber Creek a shot. No pressure, but if you'd like the job, let's meet at my office on campus and we'll fly to London together. I think it could be a great opportunity for you.*

I responded immediately and took the subway straight to Morningside Heights, where I weaved as quickly as I could around students in backpacks, as if they were all racing to steal my offer. I was like a New Yorker. Circuit vessels cut contrails over the library. A little plaque honored the memory of the Lenape People, and landscapers unrolled fresh rugs of sod. A student let me into Kent Hall where I found Bickle's office door. I considered waiting outside, but remembering my error at Ronan's and wanting to prove a quick learner, I instead walked right in.

"Don't look for me again. I just want to be alone," said a woman seated on Bickle's desk.

Under pale hair she seemed to be crying. There were boxes everywhere, and an unopened champagne bottle had rolled to a stop against a plastic wastebin. Bickle glanced over her at me.

"Excuse me," he said. "Could you wait outside?"

"Of course."

I shut the door.

I retucked my shirt. Eventually the woman exited. Our eyes met.

"What?" she said.

"Nothing," I said, and she ran down the stairs.

A few minutes later, Bickle emerged with his anorak rolled under his arm.

"I'm sorry for barging in," I said. "I—"

He put up his hand. He didn't seem angry. If anything, he seemed slightly embarrassed, but he managed to smile.

"You got here quick," he said, closing his office door. "Shall we head to the pod?"

We boarded at Riverside Park, sitting next to each other on the circular bench. It was a large pod, it could have fit at least thirty people, but it wasn't very crowded. The panorama of screens advertised *Cats! Back on Broadway*, creepy and lame.

Bickle told me more about what we'd be doing at CWC. The more he talked about it, the more he relaxed.

"As I understand it," he said, "I'll be representing the company in select press appearances and starring in commercials. We'll also be making posts most days. Your social media experience will help."

"I'm excited to help however I can," I said.

The pod hummed, its contraccelerator plates firing up to counteract the impulse of takeoff. Without them, the release of the spring in the pod platform would turn passengers to pancakes when the pod launched into the air. (The first times in New York that I saw a pod take off from the outside, I was amazed at the launch's abruptness— blink and it was gone.) Inside the pod, I felt myself rise an inch or two off my seat. I hovered there, realizing that our pod was airborne only because the humming died down: The contraccelerators didn't need to keep running after we were launched. We were floating in tandem with the pod now, hurtling thirty thousand feet straight up.

I asked if Bickle would keep his post at Columbia too.

"No," he said. He didn't hold the pole, so neither did I. "This is a full-time thing, they say, or at least they're paying me like it is. Paying me *more* than that. They don't want me publishing other content simultaneously that could dilute my brand, and they need me available at all times to make content for them when events unfold, so . . ."

The pod lurched left—a gust of wind—and the pulsejets on the left side kicked us back on course, with a boom and the momentary suspension of the Rum Tum Tugger, mid-somersault, behind Bickle's head. The contraccelerators revved back up. We were nearing the top of our ascent.

"Truthfully, I don't expect to work more than twenty hours a week," Bickle said. "You should, though. Being the person who answers the emails just tends to be that way." He said this with neither cruelty nor contrition.

In spite of the contraccelerators, there was a little bump as our pod was caught at its apex by the orbiting circuit vessel that it latched onto. My shoulder hit the wall, or the wall hit my shoulder, and Bickle glanced up from his bag with, touchingly, a look of concern. I told him I was fine, and he nodded. The turnstile unlocked with a click. He led the way out of the pod.

We were still weightless as we pulled ourselves through the circuit vessel's docking cabin and into Standard Economy. Circuit vessels stayed aloft by orbiting the planet—in a sense, they were weightless too, which was how they conserved fuel. Horizontally we climbed the hand rungs up the aisle, our legs trailing behind us. I felt nauseous, as I had on my first circuit ride, and I fell behind Bickle, fearing I might be sick.

Bickle said, "They're going to start me in commercials in March. I've read the scripts. The idea is that I stand for trust and transparency, responsible development, that sort of thing, but what they really like is that I've also got the Alaska angle. CWC's chief of communications says mobility is the westward circuit's 'key brand pillar,' and I've got it in my personal story: a man from the woods who's become a hero of modern industry or whatever."

I nodded along. My stomach settled once we found seats. The cabin was crowded, but every seat had its own "socket," a little stall, divided from the next by a half-wall, like the partitions between urinals. I was kept in my seat by a synthetic graviton field maintained by contraccelerator plates in the ceilings and floors, activated by a button on the socket wall. It ran on a timer to save energy. An elderly woman reached a vacant socket opposite mine, slowly positioned herself, and then pressed the button and fell into her seat with a grunt.

Spanning the cabin walls, "windowvision" screens showed the Pacific Ocean as it might have appeared out a real window but with visual enhancements and CWC watermarks. I pictured myself sitting in midair and was struck by the underlying rationale of circuit travel: to maximize efficiency through perpetual motion (or, when some movement needed stopping, to stop it against springs, preserving as much energy as possible). All of that motion—whether you were taking a pod up, orbiting across in a vessel, or taking a new pod back down—was technically freefall. But it didn't occur to me that the sensation of freefall had anything to do with circuit travel's rationale. That aimless feeling in your gut, characteristic of the whole experience—that, I thought, was merely incidental.

Bickle addressed me over the top of the partition. "CWC's chief of communications promised me I could retain a lot of autonomy in this role. He's a very generous man. He says my independence is part of my appeal. He wants audiences to know the content I'm creating comes directly from me."

I said, "That's great."

The screens blinked: SOON DISEMBARKING FOR LONDON, UNITED KINGDOM. I followed Bickle back into the docking cabin, suppressing a bout of queasiness, and waited, our bodies two skew lines, beside the portal marked PICCADILLY CIRCUS PLATFORM I, until the vessel's sliding door gave way to the turnstile for our pod.

"I just want to say," I said, as we entered the pod and positioned ourselves above the circular bench, "I'm really grateful for this opportunity."

Bickle said, "Yeah, I mean, whatever your opinion of CWC, they are one of the great companies of our time."

Our pod sprung backward, dropping out of orbit, and we plummeted thirty thousand feet.

* * *

We were met in Piccadilly Circus beneath a giant crotch for GAP Teen underwear by a man my age with a shaved head and a Mexican accent.

"Miguel Oriol," he said.

"Miguel is the comms department coordinator," said Bickle. "He'll be onboarding you."

His cheeks were poreless, and his brown eyebrows, the only hair he had, perched lightly on their ledge. I looked him up and down. He was the sort of put-together man that I admired online growing up, the sort of man I'd always secretly wanted to be.

"I'm Tanner," I said.

He gave a nod and a smile.

We proceeded down Great Windmill Street. As Miguel congratulated Bickle on the new job, I soaked in London, which felt understated after New York, but still an eyeful with its lorries and double-decker buses and the iconic glass skyscrapers of Soho. Bickle and Miguel spoke chummily, their gaze fixed on the sidewalk ahead (watching, I would later learn the hard way, for dogshit). They seemed unfazed even as we turned onto Broadwick Street, the south perimeter of CWC's headquarters, to find a crowd of protesters.

Few but fiery, the protesters paced between orange cones, carrying signs—some cardboard, some thin pocket projectors—with messages like FIGHT DAY CONTRACTION! FIGHT CWC! and NO TIME IN THE DAY FOR INJUSTICE. One man cast a GIF of an elderly woman (perhaps a CWC executive? I didn't recognize her) photoshopped into a polka-dot clown ruff, balancing atop a ball made to resemble the Earth. The ball rolled backward while she ran forward in oversized red shoes. A local reporter took notes. Scotland Yard sat on one-wheels across the street, vaping and watching traffic.

"Just keep walking," said Miguel. "Hey. Hi." He nodded to the protesters as he cut a path to the atrium door. "Yesterday a few of them got inside," he told Bickle. "Six arrests and major scuffing of the tile floor. Poor custodians, they had to work overtime."

Inside, the entire back wall of the lobby was a screen, three stories high. It depicted circuit vessels streaming past the shimmering letters of the building's name: AVIATION TOWER. I watched it, transfixed, until our elevator doors closed. We rode up to floor 118. There, in the reception area of the comms department, I was taken by the view: fog rolling out to the horizon, a field of white pierced by strong, sudden spires.

Bickle went off to see the chief of comms, and Miguel gave me a tour. The kitchen. The printer room. The "loo." Harried people popped in and out of offices, trying to find one another. I was brought to a conference room lined by screens and, for the remainder of the English workday, was initiated into the communications department of CWC. I was told things like, "three quarters of communications spend is wasted, the trouble is knowing which three quarters," and (wanting to seem attentive) I copied every word into my company-issue holographic tablet. Miguel left and was replaced by a waddling events coordinator, who was in turn replaced by two gorgeous social media managers. "So, Bickle hired you?" they said in near unison. I kept quiet, hoping they would mistake my timidity for Arctic laconism, like a lumberjack. They talked about their CWCxBickle Scroller campaign. They wanted me filming Bickle any time he got on or off a pod. "And have him say things like, 'I love flying with CWC. CWC: Moving the World.'"

I said, "Maybe sometimes he should mention CWC more casually? So it's not like he's just getting paid to say things?"

"What?" The girls exchanged looks. "I thought you had experience with content creation," said one. "Welcome to hour 970,000, dude. Anti-consumerism and image-envy have converged." "Yeah, the fact that the content creator's getting paid is how we know they're famous enough to be worth our attention."

By A.H. 974,004, as the sun set over London, I had ten pages of notes that, when read back, were total gibberish, plus a tome from HR on company policies. "The only thing there that matters," advised one of the social media girls, "is the instructions for activating your CWC unlimited pass." "The best reason to work here," said her friend, texting.

Unlimited travel! "Can I use it tonight?" I asked. "I need to get back to New York."

They looked at me like I was stupid. "Just expense a hotel."

After work, I smoked a cigarette while walking beside the Thames, drawing validation from the company of other businesspeople while trying not to get in their way. Men in wheelchairs shouted at lorries speeding by. Big Ben struck six. It was strange to think that people used to keep time that way, cycling back every twelve hours as if time, rather than progressing forward, just kept starting over; the thought was almost depressing. Not until then, though, did I fully appreciate the simplicity of A.H. timekeeping, the same in London as in New York as in Keber Creek. I realized that the system was designed to benefit the jet-setting generation, a generation in whose ranks I could now count myself.

After retrieving my duffle in Queens and checking out of the motel, I returned to London so it'd be dark enough to sleep. I got a room in the Oxford Street Hilton. I still couldn't sleep though. I was too jet-lagged, too anxious about work, and too distracted by my new tablet whose holograms cast Scroller nearly to the ceiling. An article posted by the *Times* science section claimed days were getting shorter. I followed Miguel Oriol and the social media managers. Miguel had told me that they were all going dancing the next day, and when I looked up the club he'd mentioned, I found that it was in Berlin. I wondered if people spoke English in Berlin and considered what I might wear if I were to join them. I knew I should close my eyes, but the whole world felt too strange to trust through the night. In the back of my mind, I was prepared for someone to burst through the door, declare a mix-up, and return me to Alaska. I suppose I literally couldn't believe my luck.

I reported to work the next morning on two hours' sleep, my red bangs sagging across my brow. It shouldn't have been an eventful day; all I had to do was unpack Bickle's office. I unloaded boxes of diplomas, old books, and stress balls. Bickle came and went, bringing me a boxed salad for lunch. At the day's end, I heard my coworkers gathering in the hall, but I stayed hidden in Bickle's office with the door closed until Miguel popped in.

"¿Listo?"

I told him I was too jet-lagged to join. The girls behind him were whispering.

"Besides," I said, "I still have a box to unpack here."

He told me to come later if I changed my mind, and I waited until he and the others disappeared into the elevator before I shut the door again. *Next week*, I told myself, with a tinge of regret. This week I'd finish my work and get some rest.

I turned to my last box.

It was in that box that I found the folder labeled: COLUMBIA PROCEEDINGS. I opened it.

The first document in the folder was a printed summons for Victor Bickle to a Columbia University disciplinary hearing in regards to the events of A.H. 962,784.

The second document was a request for paid administrative leave. Approved.

The third document was a union pamphlet informing faculty of their rights under Columbia's AAUP contract, including the right to the confidentiality of all disciplinary action as permitted by law.

The fourth, fifth, and sixth documents were revised notices of proposed disciplinary action from the Office of the Associate Provost.

The seventh document was a hearing committee report recommending in the case of Victor Bickle dismissal for cause, having registered clear and convincing evidence of (1) theft and misuse of university data, (2) use of professional authority to exploit others, and (3) violation of state and federal laws.

The eighth document was a minority report, finding evidence of wrongdoing but not of a grave order and recommending suspension with pay.

The ninth document was an email suggesting that Bickle tender his resignation before a public dismissal notice need be issued.

The final document was a letter of resignation signed A.H. 973,956. Three days ago.

These were splayed across the floor when Bickle walked in, picking at his mustache and speaking to himself about where he might have left his good stylus. He saw the files, then me.

"What are you doing with those?" he said.

I said, "I was unpacking."

He looked around. "You're unpacking my files from their folders?"

"Those just fell out."

A building custodian peeked in, saw us, and pushed his cart to the next office.

"You're lying," said Bickle. "I can't stand lying."

"I'm sorry."

"These are private."

"Sorry."

He picked up one of the documents, his face red. He said this wasn't anyone else's business, his life was his own. He asked if I was dishonest.

"No," I said.

"Are you?"

"No."

"If I wanted a crooked assistant, I could have gotten one from Columbia," he said. "I thought if I stayed away from those little New York bloodsuckers I might find an assistant I could trust."

"You can trust me."

"What?"

I wiped my nose on the sleeve of my Target button-down.

"Alright, get out of here," he said.

"Like, for the weekend?"

"I'll have to think about it."

I walked to the door. "I'm really sorry."

"Just leave."

Grapes may cause cancer. Dow up another five points. Scrolling on my phone, I rode CWC line 831, a circuit vessel whose geodesic route crossed the equator above Quito, continued to New Zealand, and arced northwestward over Australia. I transferred (riding a pod down and right back up) in Sumatra (a hub), which adjusted my course slightly before the next vessel took me over the Bay of Bengal, the contested Indo-Pakistani border, and Eastern Europe. It was lengthy routes such as these—taking you around the world and still beating by half an hour traditional aviation from Heathrow to Berlin—that made the westward circuit so efficient.

Speed was less appealing, however, when you had no place to go. I was kicking myself for opening Bickle's folder. I wondered if he would fire me. A part of me expected him to, the part of me that believed I was a fake, pretending I belonged in London when I'd never managed to fit in anywhere in my life. I sat on the plane and scrolled social media: Greta Yusef applying face cream, Miguel taking shots with a bartender at Petra Dance Haus.

In a fuck-all mood, I had looked up directions to the club. I knew if I returned to the Hilton, I wouldn't sleep anyway; I'd waste my Friday night in self-recrimination. Trying to forget work, I swallowed fear, rallying my nerve, thinking in circles about excuses to bail, but the circuit moved faster than thinking. I checked my hair in the shiny doors to the pod to SCHNÜRSENKEL KREUZUNG, BERLIN, and before I could fully clear my mind of anxiety, I was there.

The moon was high outside Petra Dance Haus, and the line I joined stretched halfway down Hirsestrasse. People didn't seem to

mind the wait; they relished the opportunity to livestream from a
real industrial neighborhood. The club (a small, concrete warehouse
nestled beneath the Autobahn) was supposedly one of the last spots
in Berlin that still lay beyond the tidemark of shiny neo-Deutsch
developers' sprawl, which is to say, it was practically in Poland. Musi-
cally, Petra wasn't exactly modern bleep-bloop. As far as I could
piece together from the website, it championed a sort of pre-A.H.
krautrock, "real" music, albeit heavily remixed in the bleep-bloop
metronomic style. I looked for my coworkers. Ahead of me in line,
a group of underaged Russians in see-through Sarandex pants said
Berlin was their second-favorite city for clubbing, after New Delhi,
Jaipur, and Agra, which had consolidated into one megacity back
when each grew so distended as to blur their boundaries. Big New
Delhi, as it was known, claimed their highest affections on account
of its tolerant culture toward public urination, which kept bathroom
lines down, giving people an open place to go when they wanted
privacy to trade blowjobs and cocaine. They offered me a swig of
Jäger, which I declined.

The club was dark, and after fighting my way to the bar for a
Pepsi, just to have something in my hands, I found myself pushed
toward the center of the floor. Everyone was jumping—leaping—as if
to dodge the snares that ricocheted between the mylar walls and the
big No Bowie sign on the ceiling. (The sign was meant to discourage
foreign tourists but seemed to have the opposite effect, instead assur-
ing them they had found a real local spot to recommend to all their
friends back home.) Almost immediately, I wished I hadn't come.

I bounced on my toes, but the bass and the heat had a sedative
effect. My button-down was wet. My whole body was baggage. I was
so tired.

Then someone crashed into me.

It took me a moment to recognize Miguel. I carried him out of
the vortex, awkwardly clutching his elastic shirt. Neither of us spoke

until we were standing a safe distance from the dance floor, behind a coat compactor.

"What'd I hit?" he said. Blood trickled from his nose.

"Oh god. I'm so sorry."

"No te preocupes, I'm fine. Hey—it's you!" he said, seizing my cup of Pepsi, which I'd somehow managed to hold on to through the collision (a late-capitalist instinct, I suppose—I'd paid ten euro for that drink). He sipped, then made a face of disgust and dumped it on the floor. "Pure sugar."

"I don't drink alcohol."

"You should try. Might teach you how to dance." He sat, touching the sticky ground with his bare hands. His pleated trousers bunched at the knees.

"Are your friends here?" I asked.

"Nah. Cannot stand those pinches mamones."

"Your nose is bleeding."

"Pinch it!"

He tilted his head up, wincing in the disco lights. Embarrassed, I looked around for something clean to wrap my hand in and finding nothing, I used my sleeve.

"Not so hard!"

His nose was short and fleshy. Snot seeped out. A bubble rose in my throat. "Higher," he said, basking like a cat. Other clubbers kept eyeing us. I wanted so badly to disappear.

"What's wrong?"

"I'm sorry," I sobbed. I didn't know why.

"Are you crying?"

I shook my head. I couldn't breathe well and couldn't talk well.

He asked me to let go of his nose now.

"Sorry," I said, sitting down.

He kept saying my name and telling me I was alright. He said to take deep breaths. I did. With a shriek, the next song started.

He said, "You want to tell me what's the matter?"

I didn't think I wanted to, and I could only manage to speak in fragments, saying things like, "It's too hard," and "I don't know any-one." After a while, though, he seemed to understand.

"You know *me*," he said. "Hey, I've been there too. You'll fit in fine, I promise. You were getting on great with everyone yesterday. I liked your vintage headphones."

I sniffled and wiped my eyes, annoyed to have blown it with him now too. The crowd was singing to some song I didn't know. An older couple, laughing with abandon, snuck around the corner but then saw us and backed off in apology.

"It's a good place to work," said Miguel. "You're not going to quit, are you?"

I considered explaining to him about the Columbia files, but I decided to keep Bickle's confidence. In that moment, among the many thoughts spinning through my head was the sudden feeling that losing my job would be letting Miguel down. He was staring at me too intensely for comfort. Staring through me, probably high on something.

"Stop looking around," he said. "What are you looking for?"

Our eyes met. On silent motorik ones and threes, my heart pounded.

"You're really drunk, dude," I said.

He shrugged.

I rubbed my eyes and said I wouldn't quit.

A wave of glitter from the dance floor reached us. Miguel was smiling, dabbing his nose.

"Shit, so you're, like, from Alaska," he said. He leaned back against the coat compactor. "Welcome to the world."

Like heavens in time-lapse, the planes of the westward circuit crossed the sky in a continuous wave, each plane a blinking sapphire against the black midnight, which was actually more like gray on account of light pollution over San Francisco. Fifteen-year-old Winnie Pines in boxy plastic glasses and blue jeans sat on the beach, gazing up. She didn't know me yet, and I didn't know her. We didn't know we were bound together on a world spinning out of control. She listened as each plane popped and fell toward the Pacific. Though the waves scared her, she liked the ocean. It reminded her of late nights on the beach with her mom, back when they lived together. Her mom would wear short skirts or leggings—she always was, Winnie thought, very pretty—while Winnie wore jeans, letting the cuffs get damp and sandy as the two of them strained to see the black-on-gray horizon. They tried to figure out if the world really was round. Her mom said it was, but for a long time Winnie didn't believe it. For some reason, she had felt the need to see it for herself.

"Hey, Winnie, look alive," whispered her cousin.

For the past eighteen months, since her mom's first suicide attempt, Winnie had lived with her aunt, uncle, and nine-year-old cousin—the Wwlliamses—in a second-floor apartment in San Francisco's Sunset District. It was supposed to be a temporary arrangement, but sometimes "temporary" takes on a long-lived frame of reference. Even before tonight, it had become clear to Winnie that her mom wouldn't be taking her back.

Then tonight, the first warm one of April, her Aunt Carsie had sat her down in the sofa room and said her mom was in a coma.

"Did she do it to herself?"

Her aunt nodded. Above her a clock ticked. '12:59. '13:00 . . .

"Is she going to wake up?"

The doctors weren't optimistic. Carsie touched Winnie's wrist. It seemed Carsie wanted to communicate that she was upset too, though Winnie knew that Carsie and her mom, eight years apart, had never been close. At Carsie's touch, Winnie hated her a little.

"I'm so sorry, sweetheart," she said.

"It's fine," said Winnie. "This just means I won't have to move again."

Winnie had moved often living with her mom. She was born in her mom's hometown, in the sticks of Alaska, a place she remembered little of except the name—Keber Creek. Then they lived in Chicago, St. Louis, New Orleans, and minor cities in between, sometimes with indifferent boyfriends, sometimes with employers. They lived in a mansion once, where Winnie's mom nannied two boys who stole Winnie's tampons. They moved in with the Wwlliamses for a few months when Winnie was ten, but Carsie and Winnie's mom couldn't make it work. Winnie had never liked moving. She liked nights of sitting still and letting the waves go in and out.

The waves seethed. Winnie faced them, sitting on the lowest step of the stone beach-access stairs. Nearer the shoreline, her cousin Juju approached an empty pod platform. Carsie believed that Juju was getting ice cream, and she'd made her take Winnie along for supervision—she never had any idea what her daughter was up to. As soon as they left the house, Juju had cut for the beach, ordering Winnie to be the lookout. The light from Juju's phone passed over an orange sign: POD DOCKING PLATFORM ELECTRIFIED. DO NOT TOUCH. She piled sand against the side of the platform and climbed atop.

It was about three yards in diameter, the same as the pods that landed on it, and five feet tall. Glancing over her shoulder, Juju started placing pennies along the platform's edge.

A concrete groin charged into the sea and crumbled. On its other side, Winnie heard the coughs of some teenagers she didn't know. She pushed her palms against her ears for quiet and focused on the offing. For a moment, she saw the concavity she was looking for, but then it seemed like maybe the horizon slanted uniformly to the left, or teetered to the right; then she could have sworn that if anything, it sagged in the center, as if the ocean were folding in on itself. Her eyes watered from staring too long.

With one minute until the next pod would land, Juju jumped off the platform and scrambled up to Winnie. She pointed at a blue light rising over the promenade wall. "There it is," she said. When directly above them the circuit vessel popped, Winnie let out a little sigh.

The pod appeared, a metal can tumbling from the clouds. For a moment, it looked like it might miss the platform, but of course it didn't. It struck and, with a screech, fully compressed the platform's springs, so that its doors halted at ground level. Sand spilled into the turnstile vestibule. No one exited. No one boarded, and after a minute the pod launched again, straight up, upon the springs' release, a nearly lossless redeployment of energy. It would latch on to the next passing vessel only to fall again someplace west. Juju ran to the vacated platform and screamed with delight, lifting a flattened penny wider than her head.

Snap!

Two weeks later, Winnie was alone in the apartment bathroom, electrocuting herself. The jolt like an ice-cold worm spiraled up her tibia. She'd torn apart her home hairdresser, dropping chunks of plastic machinery in a pile beside her rubber bathmat. It was the black wire she wanted. She folded it, and it girdled. She tugged; the other wires tightened. Avoiding her body in her bathroom mirror, she touched the copper to her palm. This was her Friday night.

It had started in school with a nine-volt battery. She sat in the back of the classroom, and when she thought about her mom, she soothed herself with little shocks to the thumb. Attainment Academy Charter School occupied the top floor of a shopping mall, a school located above a Whole Foods Delivery Locker, a stocking facility for children. She didn't like school. She dreaded computerized tests, during which she could never focus. Her teachers depressed her. The mere thought of lunch period had the power to knot her insides. Lunch had to be taken in the cafeteria, and finding someone to sit with was a daily trial. She generally succeeded only by cornering a classmate with a canned question ("Was there any Chinese homework?" or "What'd you get for lab run three?") and then planting herself at their table uninvited. She would spend the next forty-two minutes scrambling to keep up conversation, exploiting her classmates' patience and feigning obliviousness to their irritation. *Yes, I know*, she thought, *I irritate myself too*. She'd long given up hope that someone might actually want to sit with her. She just wanted to be seen talking to people so that she wouldn't appear so desperate when she tried someone else the next day. She could live without making friends at Attainment Academy. It was the idea of everyone knowing she had no friends that terrorized her. She heard her mom's voice saying, *Just give it up*.

The coma having been designated "indefinite," Winnie's mom was being kept alive by machines in a nursing facility outside Alamo, Nevada. Winnie's aunt Carsie visited the facility last week and encouraged Winnie to come (she didn't want Winnie going alone). Although Winnie wanted to see her mom, accompanying Carsie on a trip to Alamo, with all its emotional presumptions, felt like too much.

"Are you sure you don't want to come, sweetheart?" Carsie had pressed. "It could be good for you. A good step." There seemed to be more she wanted to say, but then Juju came whining about her dad, and Winnie slipped into the other room.

Her aunt and uncle's apartment hadn't become home. "Winnie's room" was still clearly a guest room, country floral with a rocking chair and a closet of extra linens. She never bothered to adorn the neutral pistachio walls. It seemed at first premature, then needless. Last night while she did homework on her clunky old Macpad Air, she heard Juju and her friend talking in the hall.

"She spends all her time in her room because she has depression," Juju said. "Her mom did too. It's genetic."

"I heard her mom killed herself."

"She tried. She couldn't even do it."

Then Carsie: "What are you girls saying?"

For some reason, Winnie feared that Carsie would make them come in and apologize to her, so she dimmed her lights and pretended to be asleep. Her sheets were itchy. It had been unusually humid in San Francisco, exacerbating her torpor. She couldn't tell if she was de- or overhydrated, her thighs and belly full of either salt buildup or water weight. She hardly ever slept. Her lime-green eyes sat deep in wells bruised by the trauma of prolonged consciousness. Her pale hair was always frayed. Like the hair of a corpse, she thought.

Aware yet unaware, lost to daydreams, she was in the back of her physics class bringing the nine-volt battery to her mouth. Later she would ask herself why she did this, and she would have no answer, but she'd remember the jitter dancing across her lips even before contact. Her two fingers slipping over the battery's far end and her tongue peeking out of her to taste metal. An instant of electricity that ran from her ears all the way down her front.

"Oh my god," said the student next to her. "Are you eating a battery?"

"No," she said. She put it down. There was a ferric taste, like blood, in the air between her tongue and the roof of her mouth. *You idiot, Winnie.*

"She's so weird."

The next thing she knew, she was walking out of the room. A flight reflex. *Where are you going??* she heard her mom say, but by then it was too late to turn back. Her teacher asked if she was okay. Someone said, "Winnie ate a battery."

She hurried down the hall, trying not to cry, or at least not to be seen crying. Stupid. Why was she so impulsive? She was trying to block out her mom's voice when a girl stopped her.

"Would you like to eat lunch with us?" the girl asked.

She should have kept walking, but she made the mistake of looking up. Mentally she scanned her own face. She wasn't crying. She held it together. The girl had soft, brown skin and amber eyes and something pinned in her earlobe, a triangular yellow tag. Winnie had seen her in the cafeteria before. She sat in the back corner, apart from kids her age.

"I'm Nat Agarwal, fifteen years vegan." She stood by a classroom door whose screen read THURSDAY A.H. 976,287:30–85:30 FUTURE'S ADVOCATES MEETING.

"Come in."

Inside there was one other girl, another upperclassman. Her uniform blouse was unbuttoned, and underneath she wore a scary shirt that read ASSIVE ATTAC.

"Luna Tsiang. Ten months," she introduced herself, pushing her short black hair out of her face. "What about you?"

"What?" said Winnie. "I'm not anything. I mean, I'm Winnie, but I eat normal stuff."

"That's okay," said Nat. "We're all at different points in our journey. Anyway, we're glad you're here to check out our club."

She straddled a chair and pulled from her backpack a tinfoiled loaf of banana bread, which she explained was free of dairy, eggs, gluten, soy, sugar, nuts, and apportionments—she and Luna tore handfuls off with a degree of abandon that to Winnie suggested sexual familiarity.

Nat explained that Future's Advocates was a club committed to waking up Attainment Academy's student body to the important issues of the day. "Students here are so absorbed in their own little bubble of *Who has the latest nipdip* and *Whose MateMe page has the most swipes*— they don't understand that there are real problems in the world. Like, there are children starving in Canada! So we're trying to bring people together around different issues each month, issues that matter. This month, we've been focusing on issues related to the westward circuit. The westward circuit is really bad, and people don't get it."

She tossed her fishtail braid over her plump shoulder and started dictating objectives, which appeared on the classroom wall (REGULATE CIRCUIT VESSELS!). She was confident and pretty. Pretty enough, almost, to pull off wearing her earring, which—Winnie realized with a mix of awe and disgust—was a livestock tag.

"Sorry," said Winnie. "I'm actually supposed to be in class right now."

Nat stopped. "Oh. Okay."

"Yeah," said Winnie, knowing they thought she was a liar. She said it was nice to meet them.

"We're meeting again tomorrow after school," said Luna. "At Whole Foods, if you want to join."

Winnie wasn't sure what to say. She said, "I don't really like Whole Foods."

"Good," said Luna. "Neither do we. We hate it!"

"No pressure, Winnie," Nat said, powering down the wall mid-bullet point and returning to her seat. "Thank you for checking us out. If you feel like coming tomorrow, we would really love for you to join us. We'll be spreading the truth about CWC."

That night Winnie woke up from a dream about her mother hurtling into space, and for a moment, in her unadorned room, she thought that she was there. Nowhere. In space. She lay awhile, knowing she wouldn't be able to fall asleep again, and eventually got up to use the bathroom. She found it remarkable how much more dramatic her feelings were than their outward signs. Outside in the city light, rain fell like buckshot through the marine layer, creating exit wounds that spontaneously healed. Weird weather. They said sea levels were rising too. The apartment smelled of bleach and twinkled with digital blips: outlet pilot lights, a printer display, a flickering power strip—she crossed the kitchen, picking up her pace—oven and microwave clocks, intercom buttons, phone chargers, and thermostats. The lights seemed to be proliferating before her eyes, and for some reason, a shiver of fear traveled up her spine. She hurried down the hall and did not look back until she held the knob of the bathroom door. Behind her, all she saw was a smoke detector's patient blink.

*   *   *

The next day transpired in a daze of anxiety like every Friday as
school buzzed with anticipation for the weekend. Winnie compul-
sively thumbed her nine-volt battery secretly in her pocket, watching
gulls peck at the anti-roosting spikes along the windowsill. The roofs
of the Sunset District beyond were all different colors, all washed out
and crisscrossed with cables and loomed over by the twin tridents of
Little and Big Sutro Towers. She nodded off. She shocked herself.
She had every intention of spending the whole weekend in her room.

When the bell finally rang at A.H. 976,314:17, she rushed out
of class, hoping to evade the assemblage of kids negotiating groups
for Friday plans. But as she stepped onto the escalator out of school,
someone tugged her backpack.

It was Juju. She needed to be called an Uber.

"I thought your mom is picking you up," said Winnie.

They got to the bottom of the escalator and stood outside Whole
Foods. A donation box managed by the mall said PRAY FOR MADRID.
Juju wore her PINK cap, arms akimbo.

"Mom has to work late again. I told her I'm going to Ruthie's."

She and Ruthie were too young to call their own ride. She wanted
Winnie to call it—and then Winnie would need to wait for it with
them and let them in, since the driverless car wouldn't unlock without a
fingerprint match. In other words, she'd have to stand in the rideshare
lot with two fourth-graders, while all the other kids her age witnessed
her friendless Friday night.

"Can't Ruthie's mom pick you up?"

"Ruthie's parents think Mom is getting us. We need a ride to Club
Proma. We're gonna get freaked up on energy drinks."

An Auntie Anne's employee, on break, shouted at her boyfriend
through the phone. She said she loved him but she couldn't do this
anymore.

Winnie said, "I don't think they let fourth-graders into the club."

"At Proma they do. If you get there early."

Winnie spotted a group of her classmates on the landing above the escalator. It was the popular girls, Mia Poe and Sammie Gutierrez, and the boys they moved with, whom Winnie hated and always feared would catch her stealing glances. The boys were into drugs and played on the e-sports team—weird, aggressive potheads, constantly posting pictures of girls on MateMe and adjusting erections in their waistbands. For some reason, they thought it was hilarious to call Winnie "Bunny Royale," a character in some game they all played. Winnie had looked the character up. It was a one-titted rabbit.

Mia Poe was the one who had caught her licking the battery. Winnie didn't want to be around when they came down the escalator.

"I'm busy," she told Juju.

"No, you're not. Who are you busy with?"

"A friend. See?" Winnie waved up the escalator to no one, then turned around to leave.

"You're so annoying."

Then someone called Winnie's name.

Between her and the popular kids, Nat and Luna were coming down the escalator, returning her wave. They carried trifold posterboards that said BOYCOTT CWC.

"Yay, Winnie," said Nat. "You're here to pamphleteer with us, right?"

Juju looked at Winnie.

"Yeah," Winnie said.

Juju groaned, "Why are you so *weird*?"

Nat showed Winnie a stack of pamphlets she'd printed out. They were all about the evils of circuit travel. There was a panel on the discriminatory nature of the visa system, and one about CWC's participation in the forced displacement of ethnic minorities. There was a panel on the famous pod collision of A.H. 901,968 and on cancer risks from contraccelerators. The centerfold was about "day contraction"—the theory that Earth's rotation was speeding up. Though climatologists, even those who agreed about the measurements, didn't agree about day contraction's cause, and plenty blamed natural phenomena like a bad hurricane season and fluctuations in atmospheric pressure, Nat's pamphlets proudly blamed the westward circuit, claiming that all the cargo being shipped around the world was, in the process of propelling itself forward, pushing the Earth very slightly back, like a tiny runner on a floating log (or, more precisely, thousands of tiny log-runners—the thousands of circuit vessels—all moving roughly west and spinning the Earth eastward beneath them). The pamphlets said Earth's period of rotation was twenty-three hours, fifty-eight minutes, and forty seconds—eighty seconds too fast.

"They're great, right?" Nat said.

Winnie nodded, having barely taken in the information. She had nothing bad to say about the pamphlets. She was just trying to figure out what response would get her out of there before Mia Poe and her friends came down the escalator.

She said, "I'm all for this, but I've never pamphleteered before, so maybe to start I'll stand on the side, just over here, and I'll just watch."

But Nat prodded, saying it was easy and forcing a stack of pamphlets into Winnie's hands.

"Freak this," said Juju, leaving. "We're better off walking to the club."

Nat said to Winnie, "Don't get overwhelmed. The thing about pamphleteering is that the pamphlets do the work, you just need to get people to take them. It's that simple. Okay, try that old lady."

She nudged Winnie in front of a woman heading into the Whole Foods Delivery Locker.

Winnie's tongue grew heavy. "Excuse me," she said. "Are you—I don't mean to bother, but if you have a minute—would you like to learn about—" she looked at her pamphlets. "A corporate abomination?"

The woman walked past.

Luna gave a thumbs-up, and Winnie started praying. She prayed both that no one notice her and at the same time that some curious stranger take all her pamphlets so she might leave immediately. It soon became clear that both prayers would be frustrated by Nat and Luna, who stood in the middle of the landing loudly accusing everyone of ecocide and shoving pamphlets into their hands before Winnie could possibly unload any of her own.

A mother with three kids was telling Nat she didn't have time right now for a "little talk."

Nat persisted: "Did you know that days are eighty, or maybe even one hundred twenty seconds shorter than they used to be?"

"Then I especially don't have time."

Luna told a couple that when they used the Westward Circuit, they lined the pockets of warlords.

"Aren't days getting *longer*?" asked Nat's next victim. He was trying to reason with her, showing her his weather app. He said, "Last night the sunset was at A.H. 976,294:04, and tonight it's at A.H. 976,318:05. So actually if you calculate the difference, that's twenty-four hours and a minute—"

"That's irrelevant!" Nat was saying. "That's just because—it's spring!"

Eventually he gave up and took a pamphlet.

Nat turned to Winnie.

"You'll get the hang of it," she said. "Everyone has their personal style."

"No, no. I don't have any style."

"You're funny," she said. "Maybe you should try a joke. Like this."

She stepped in front of the escalator just as Mia Poe and Sammie Gutierrez were coming down. To Winnie's horror, Nat didn't even seem to know who they were.

"Question for you, ladies," Nat said. "What do you call a boycott that's both socially just *and* environmentally sustainable?"

"Huh?" said the boys behind them. Mia frowned at Winnie.

Nat said, "Feeding two birds with one scone."

They took the pamphlets, totally confused, and Nat turned around to face Winnie with an immodest look of joy, like a child who'd gotten to perform her magic trick for a fresh audience. "See?" she said.

Winnie felt like throwing up.

Nat tilted her head. "You alright?"

Winnie nodded.

Nat kept studying her. Numerous shoppers walked by unmolested. Finally Nat said, "You'll find a line that works for you." She tossed her braid over her shoulder, turned, and resumed declaiming corporate depravity.

A sixth-grader glanced at Winnie's pamphlets.

"Excuse me," Winnie mumbled, handing him one. "Do you believe in protecting the planet?"

"Sure." He crumpled the pamphlet in a ball. "I believe in recycling."

Snap!

Winnie knew that shocking herself was a bad idea. The black wire of her home hairdresser was completely stripped, and the shocks were leaving red marks. She wasn't even sure that they felt good. But it was Friday night, she was finally home, and she'd had a humiliating fucking day.

No one else was in the apartment. Winnie's phone lay on the sink counter, playing Scroller in gallery mode for background noise. It projected a rotating tower of livestream channels.

"If I could change one thing about myself," said Israeli actress Ayla Amsler, "it would be to be more comfortable in my own skin."

Winnie had found the home hairdresser in a cabinet beneath the sink while looking for batteries. It was a cheap knockoff that she never used. The clunky plastic bowl groaned and rattled when you placed it on your head. Its only settings were to tug your hair into a ponytail or yank it into a topknot and stab a wire flower through as if it had half a mind to pierce your ear. WARNING! said a little tag with a lightning bolt. CIRCUITRY HAZARD! DO NOT USE NEAR WATERS. GUARANTEED

COMPLIANT WITH ANTI-TAMPERING GUIDELINES FOR THE LIBERAL REPUBLIC OF VIETNAM. NOT FOR USE BY CHILDREN.

Just reading this, she'd felt a jitter, and that was enough to sell her on the idea. She'd plugged it in, flipped it onto its crown, and picked, picked, picked.

Snap!

The shock was no mere nine-volt battery. She tossed the front half and focused on the back panel, tearing away cushioning for better access. Just her pinkie at first. Clenching her teeth, curling her toes into the rubber bathmat . . . The pain evoked wrists sliced open and veins teased out.

Then she'd been shocking herself for fifteen minutes, and the marks went all the way up her arm. She felt weird. She shocked her hip and caught a whiff of burnt hair. Her belly twitched.

She heard her aunt and uncle come home, but she couldn't stop, so she locked the bathroom door and hit the lights. Her phone turned the walls psychedelic. On Scroller, sounds from a police crackdown in Russia. Two of Winnie's classmates sang the *Ironman* song. Juju, filming from a loud restaurant, said she and her friends were going to "get outside" tonight. Ayla Amsler was replaced by Heinz Ketchup.

Snap! Winnie imagined her body skipping over a glassy lake.

Carsie was asking her husband, Mark, where the hell Juju was.

"*You* call her friends' parents this time—"

"To declutter all that junk, we recommend you get at least one Organizizer for each room and then purchase additional Organiziz-ers . . ." "A generous helping of this one food cancels out calories." The two boys who had been singing *Ironman* were now talking about how their English teacher was a fat whore. Winnie peeled off her shirt and shocked her shoulder and the small of her back. She didn't know if it was the electricity itself or just the excitement, but her heart was racing. She heard Mark apologize to Carsie. They were in the hallway now.

Fuck off, Winnie thought, to no one in particular. A late-night comedian blew up a putatively indestructible water bottle, and Winnie acknowledged herself in the mirror and had no choice but to laugh. Shirtless, touching herself with a broken machine. *Fuck off!* she thought again and laughed at her own face—that ugly face that awaited her in every mirror of her life. When she was young, she believed her face was merely incidental. She lifted her right breast with the intention of shocking the sweaty crease of skin underneath. But as she brought the wire nearer, she heard Carsie and Mark arguing just outside the bathroom door.

"Are you sure she's not in the bathroom?"

"That's Winnie, Mark."

"How do you know?"

"Because Winnie is always fucking home."

"What's she doing in there?"

Winnie's hand left her chest and tore for the sink to feign washing. She slipped off the insulating rubber bathmat just as her other hand touched *Snap! Snap!* to her ribs.

The contact was too much. Her arm fell through Scroller ("Pray for Madrid; vote for Walker"), triggering an artificial sizzle that was nothing next to the real thing, which coursed straight through her heart, a stream of destruction that just kept coming as her hand found the perspiring metal faucet and seized.

Claira Lynx

One hundred comatose patients lay quiescent under blue blankets inside glass chambers that didn't fog above their faces, in a hermetically cool gallery off of Interstate 93 outside Alamo, Nevada. They were varying degrees of human and machine. Their lives presented an eerie thought experiment to be avoided by the orderlies on-site, who took shifts scrolling social media, eating, dreaming, ordering clothes, making evening plans, dropping resumes for new jobs, occasionally sneaking in friends and fucking, and generally asserting secular life amidst the quiet, crowded bardo of their comatose wards. A translucent number hung above each patient's bed, so that to walk the aisles was to venture through a numerical arcade. 46. Perhaps the patients communicated like trees. Communication without thought, the sort of affirmation exchanged by numbers out in nature. Eyelidless zeros staring on one another. Now and then, it gave the orderlies a chill for which the recirculated air couldn't account, and they were relieved when their shifts ended and time was real again—had been ticking all along.

They would be relieved by the passage of time even when the Earth's rotation sped up another four minutes. A part of them would unconsciously welcome the tightening circumscriptions of dawn and dusk, because no matter how much the stress of calendar notifications, payment deadlines, delivery windows, and deliverable due dates had them running around, the overwhelming frenetic energy of a life compacted was always preferable to the airless void they felt in the facility of so many braindead, aptly designated "patients."

DAYS OF 23 HOURS AND 55 MINUTES

"There's always been something different about your generation."

An uplifting riff of sustained beeps in C major gains momentum over a wide-angle shot of a circuit vessel bursting like a chariot from the rising sun. The sun's rays collect around it like water pulled up by a leaping whale and then return to uniformity as the vessel breaks free. It tears through creaseless sky. Sky even bluer than sky-blue.

The voiceover says: "You're a generation of explorers, learners, and sharers."

A young woman on a scooter negotiates a hairpin turn in Barcelona's Gothic Quarter to discover a market with booths extending far as the eye can see. Docking pods disappear into night, as we cut to a bubbly rooftop toast in Zurich, backlit by firecrackers reflected off the shimmering Limmat while St. Peter rings in the New Year. Arrows trail ceremonial silk tails, chasing airplanes into the potable firmament; they tilt down and seize earth with a thunderous gong. "Your generation values the *experience* of just being present." A young person in designer sunglasses enjoys a compost beer in a convertible in Cuba.

It all dissolves, back into that trademarked hue. Title card:

CWC

Moving the World!

This was perfectly familiar to the viewer. But then someone new came on . . .

He said, "Where in the world am I?"

Victor Bickle wore a safari hat carefully positioned to thrust forward his distinctive ears. His nose was plastered with sunscreen.

"This West African capital," he said, "was connected to the circuit back in A.H. 880,000, and ever since, it has exported its cocoa to processors in Switzerland for sale at your local grocery. Did you know CWC's engineers invented special cargo pods for cocoa beans? Refrigerated and vacuum sealed, they not only economize chocolate production—keeping your wallet heavy—but also minimize the synthesis of free fatty acids—to keep your ass light!" Between his teeth he snapped a square of dark chocolate from a bar wrapped in gold foil. "Mmm. A wonder of modern science and technology that you can count on. Delivered by CWC. But can you guess from where? Where in the world am I?"

"Here!"

"What?" said Bickle, spitting out the Styrofoam chocolate.

"Not there. Stand *here*," ordered the director. "You've left the frame again."

I watched Bickle apologize. He was on a completely lime-green set in a studio outside London. Peeling the sunscreen sticker off his nose, he asked if he could get a break when it was a good time. The director closed his guide monitor and told everyone to take five.

I greeted him at the snack table with a pat on the back.

"That was great," I said. Bickle just shook his head.

I poured another cup of dark roast from a Starbucks box. It'd been a month since I left Alaska, and while I still didn't drink alcohol, I was learning to imbibe wholesale quantities of coffee (which had been prohibited by my father and unavailable in our home). Starbucks was my favorite. A television in the corner of the studio played the news on silent, talking about reports of day contraction worsening.

The IERS had called for schools to adjust start times according to sunrise calendars each semester. Someone walked by and changed the channel.

"Question," I said. "Have you seen Miguel at the office this week?"

Bickle turned to me.

"To keep your *ass* light," he said. Then he frowned. "Does that sound right to you? Should the emphasis be on 'ass'? Like, *ass* light?"

"Maybe he's sick," I said.

"Please focus," said Bickle. This was our fourth commercial shoot. He had decided that the whole business of reading other people's scripts, rather than presenting his own analysis on camera as he had always done before, disagreed with him. He kept complaining to me about it. I didn't really know what to tell him. "I don't even understand this commercial," he said, shaking his head. "I'm getting all tripped up. Should the emphasis be on 'ass' or 'light'? Your ass *light*. Your ass *light*."

"Just say it like you mean it," I said. "How would you say it to me if we were talking?"

"We are talking," he said.

"Right."

We each waited for the other to talk.

"Like if I said, 'Professor Bickle, what does minimizing the synthesis of free fatty acids do?' What would you say?"

"I've no idea. My Ph.D. is in mechanical engineering."

"You're overthinking," I said. "With respect, I think you should just say the line. Don't worry about the delivery."

"Let CWC worry about deliveries, so you can get on—"

"What?"

He took a deep breath.

"Drink your coffee," I said. He drank his coffee. The television was now talking about a parasite wiping out genetically modified tomatoes. A petite Chilean girl from the makeup crew walked by. She told Bickle that he was positively glowing, and Bickle blushed, though it was hard to tell under all the makeup.

"Standby," called the director.

"Listen," I said. "This is *your* commercial. You're the man here."

"Okay," he said, "yes."

"Okay?"

"Okay," said Bickle.

"Okay then."

"I'm the master."

"Right," I said.

"I *am* the master. I am *the* master."

"Okay," I said. "Sure. Fine."

He returned to his place before the camera, nodding at his shoes, repeating, "ass light."

I topped off my coffee and walked to the edge of the set. Working with Bickle had not turned out quite how I'd expected. The Chilean makeup girl approached me with a Fiji water.

"Your boss is very insecure," she said.

"Yeah," I replied. "I guess he's going through a bit of an adjustment."

Bickle was, it turned out, the most insecure man I'd ever met. Perhaps I should have seen it in our first encounters, the flipside to his narcissism. But who could begrudge him a little self-consciousness in his new circumstances, being suddenly subjected to the perlustration of makeup crews, directors, and script coaches preparing him for an audience twenty times what he was used to.

I was going through an adjustment too, even if it had stopped feeling that way. Instead, to my pleasure, it felt like the world was finally adjusting to me. I loved my job. I was getting paid more per month than my father had ever made in a year. And crucially, I felt valuable to Bickle.

He and I never again discussed his departure from Columbia. I couldn't help wondering about the documents I'd uncovered, and I wondered if they had anything to do with the woman I'd seen crying in his office, but I made the prudent choice not to confront him about it. He was right; it wasn't my place. After that day, a trust developed between us. It was uneasy at first, but in the cracks of uneasiness, intimacy took root. I came to understand that from an assistant Bickle didn't need an administrative crutch so much as an emotional one. It made sense that in hiring me he'd prized loyalty and patience over technical expertise, for what he wanted was never advice, always validation. And I could give it. He got flustered. He blew up. Often. And like an overheated computer, he had to be reset, coaxed back to the camera, or back into a meeting, or even coaxed over the phone back into bed, by earnest, obliging, slightly-out-of-his-depth me.

Less and less out of my depth every day, though. After work, I would return to the Oxford Street Hilton, where I continued to stay in a room on the sixty-seventh floor. I'd begun to exercise, lifting small weights in a secluded corner of the Hilton gym, and to dress more deliberately. Waxed-cotton jackets with flowers inside and slim-fitting collarless Lacoste polos as the weather warmed. With money, scrolling social media became a way of shopping, and shopping became fun. I caught myself paying particular attention to my outfits on days when I might see Miguel.

Curiosity motivated my friendship with Miguel. I learned that he was gay, the sort of boy my father had taught me to loathe, and while I had my apprehensions around him, I told myself that if we could become friends, it would prove something. I stalked him on Scroller. There was a clip of him playing soccer in a muddy jersey. He kicked and whiffed at the same open shot over and over and shouted the same half of the same expletive before suddenly resetting mid-stride. Step; kick; whiff; "¡Chinga tu—!" The clip restarted at the moment of surrender.

When I had free time at the office, I chatted with colleagues by the coffee machine. This was around the corner from Miguel's desk, and I sometimes caught myself laughing louder than necessary and afterward, when I walked past Miguel's desk, feeling disappointed if he wasn't there. On his desktop, he kept styluses of varying thickness lined up in perfect parallel. One time I messed them up to see if he would notice. He must have, but when I saw him next, I couldn't think of any halfway normal way to admit that it was me.

One Friday afternoon, I swung by his desk to find him in a yellow summer shirt.

"Tanner," he said. "¿Qué tal?"

I said, "I was wondering if you wanted to step out for a smoke."

I was smoking more than I ever had. Miguel said I ought to switch to vaping. "What do you do with the butts?" he teased. "You put them in your pocket?"

"Flick 'em."

"Flick 'em!" he echoed, apparently delighted. "Flick 'em."

Which made me smile. The truth, of course, was that memories of teenage liaisons have a way of clinging to the fabric of our hearts, and in the woods of Alaska, I had had my liaisons not with other people but with Natural American Spirits. The moss-green ones. I'd been afraid I wouldn't be able to find them in London, but no, you could buy everything in London.

"You want to come?" I asked.

But Miguel had to make copies for Cromwell Grant, the chief of communications. I still hadn't met Grant, though I had walked by his office and seen him through his frosted glass. I had watched him talking to Bickle, who would sit in a low task chair while Grant's mammoth form encircled him, stirring silent words. Once, while I was standing there, Grant had stopped pacing, and with eyes blurred out, looked straight through the opaque window at me.

I spent that weekend catching up on *Big Life* in my hotel room and exploring London by foot, watching seagulls sweep along the glass facades, and I awoke Monday with a stony pit of an erection to the noise of my phone ringing. I had a premonition that it would be Miguel calling. It was Bickle.

"Cromwell Grant would like to meet," Bickle said. "Could you schedule something for this morning?"

"Yes. You and Grant?"

"You and Grant."

I fumbled my phone getting out of bed.

"Hello?" said Bickle.

"Yes. Me and Grant."

"I'd wear a collar," Bickle said, "thanks," and hung up.

I knew a bit about Grant from Miguel. I knew Grant had started his career at the PR and marketing consultancy Weber Shandwick, then founded his own firm, whose time CWC bought more and more of until Grant expressed concern over client concentration, at which point CWC bought him outright. His agile little firm became CWC's internal comms department, and he still ran it with the personality of a CEO, if not a dictator. Miguel called him a genius. "Totally insane of course," Miguel said. He reported straight to CWC's CEO. I'd asked if Miguel liked working for him. "What to say," Miguel said, laughing. "He's the kind of man who performs so capably in a house on fire that he brings matches everywhere he goes. Yeah, I like him." Miguel said he was "quite English." Over time, I heard histories of Grant's crusades. I learned that the prior year, after a large, well-funded migrant-rights group circulated an online petition against CWC's deportation services, Grant fed reporters racy accounts of the group leader's marital infidelities.

"He's a fighter, but you just need to earn his respect," Miguel told me.

And so it was with that aspiration that I approached his corner office Monday morning in my best collared shirt. Before I touched the door, it swung open, and Cromwell Grant bellowed, "You're late!"

"Oh," I said, stepping back. "I'm sorry, I thought I scheduled us for—"

"*SHeduled*, you mumpsimus!"

I looked up and for the first time beheld Cromwell Grant's full penetrative presence. The man was like Aviation Tower itself: sleek, strong, secure, and rooted in English soil. Six-foot-four vertically and almost the same around his strapping chest—a measure augmented by the protrusion of his nipples, two spikes beneath his English-spread collared shirt—his body tapered down into oak trunk thighs; his head was a rugby ball with a side part.

"I am, famously, a global man," he said, "but a nation's culture is its crown, and language is its crown jewel; it is the one thing we mustn't let be nicked by Johnny Foreigner. Never let it be said that I am deaf to the discomfitures of globalization. I hear the hush where belongs a hearty *shhh*."

"I'm sorry," I said. "What?"

Cromwell Grant clapped me on the shoulder. He was laughing. "Come in, Tanner," he said. "I'm charmed you're here."

Cromwell Grant's office was full of trash. Trash tacked up to the walls and overflowing from crates onto the carpeted floor; placards, posters, tip-ins, billboard mockups, fanned-out brochures, bumper stickers, and advert storyboards. By the door, a heap of buttons flashed *CWC: MOVING THE WORLD!* in every language from Hebrew to Pidgin to nothing but emojis:

As he strode to his desk, he slapped a holographic globe, sending it spinning. The globe was choked by hundreds of circuit vessel route lines all displaying at once. Like a rubber band ball. On his desktop was a framed photo of his wife and two skinny boys. He took his seat and gestured me into mine, asking if I fancied a smoke. I shook my head, and Grant drew one electronic cigarette from a silver-trimmed leather case. He took a long drag. Then he turned his head and exhaled a sickly-sweet strawberry fog.

"So," he said. "How have you found CWC so far?"

"I'm loving it," I replied, shifting in my low chair.

"You like working with Bickle?"

"Very much."

"He seems to trust you." Grant tapped his e-cig against the desktop, which rippled with shallow waves of blue light. "That's important,"
he said. "A man and his employee share a sacred bond. I've come to
trust Bickle, and that's what I'm calling you in to discuss."

"Okay."

"Bickle would like more independence. He's keen to be seen in
a certain light, if you know what I God-save. I think he's dissatisfied
with playacting in our commercials."

Straining to parse his thick English accent, which wasn't quite like
any English I'd ever heard before, I nodded.

"So, we're toying with the idea of giving him his own program. We
want to take his mediagenicism and his credibility with the population,
and let him go back to his roots as an educator on matters of science.
But it will be the science of CWC. He'll make the westward circuit—its
technology, its materials, its design, and its principles of optimization—
into something impassioned and fun. What do you think?"

I said I thought that was a wonderful idea.

"We're going to let Bickle write his own episodes," he said. "I've
trepidations. You'll be closest to him, and there may be times when
it's necessary for you to keep him on track. He's temperamental,
isn't he?"

I nodded.

"If this program flies, it'll be what elevates 'Professor Bickle' to
hoarding-status. We're prepared to give him four-fifth's grasp on content, but I need to know that there's someone around him with a little
finger on things, making sure he doesn't lose his grip."

Grant held his enormous pinkie erect, as if both demonstrating his
request and waiting for me to consummate it. Eventually he smiled
and lowered his hand.

"Tanner, do you know what customers demand from CWC?"

The corner of his desk kept generating news alerts about hurricanes and foreign elections. I tried to focus.

"High-speed transit?" I ventured. "And shipping?"

"Granted they do," he said. "Granted by Grant." He laughed at his own joke. "But what else?" He waited. "I'll give you a hint. This is what customers want when they whinge about things like 'social impact.'"

It seemed as if he were baiting me into criticizing the company. I didn't know what to say. An email appeared on the surface of his desk. Then another. His gaze remained fixed on me.

"I suppose," I said, "they want fair, sustainable business practices, and that's why they choose CWC, because CWC is the brand consumers can trust to—"

"Oh, spare me the pork pies," he said. "This office all too easily becomes a haram feast. No. Every CWC customer demands *two* things. He demands the products and services you alluded to. *And* he demands a clean conscience with which to consume them. All the other departments at CWC are devoted to providing the first thing. Number two—that warm, fuzzy feeling—is supplied by me."

He stood. "The world is small from up here," he said. "You understand? The messages you help Bickle and me craft will ring across the land like God's own bitty bells." Looking out his floor-to-ceiling window, onto the fog wreathing clusters of lesser skyscrapers, Cromwell Grant swelled with pride. "I'm glad you're with us, Tanner. I do believe this department is the greatest church hands ever built. And that's why, from what I've gathered, my employees have taken to calling my office suite 'The Belfry.'"

And so *Professor Bickle's Science Hour* was born.

The twelve-minute pilot episode, available on Disney+ and YouTube Premium, chronicled the launch of CWC's first circuit vessel. Bickle interviewed the now-retired engineers who led the project, reviving the tensions of those heady days. He narrated over archival footage. As the episode reached takeoff's eve, it turned inward: Bickle ("Professor," to the viewers) recalled his own childhood in Alaska, watching the launch on TV and dreaming of an escape from Keber

Creek . . . Back to takeoff. Ground control counting down, and a last-minute burner malfunction (hitherto unreported, since Bickle had made it up for narrative suspense) giving way to climactic plumes of rocket exhaust and the first iconic blue light.

After the second episode (in which Bickle flew on a circuit vessel for twenty hours straight to demonstrate the health benefits of sleeping in freefall), the *Times* wrote: "Victor Bickle, a Columbia professor and breakout Scroller star, brings fresh insight into some of the most familiar elements of our world, reminding us of the wonder all around. A sleek program, much evolved from his angry social media content (while retaining the anorak), *Science Hour* is sure to appeal not only to science buffs but to anyone looking to put their streaming time to more productive and educational use. Watch with your family, and all will rediscover the joy of learning. As the show demystifies sponsor CWC Group's undoubtedly impressive tech, it is the lovably dorky, the macrotous, Professor Bickle himself that has earned our admiration. *Three stars out of four.*"

Bickle's fan mail increased. People who had never followed him on Scroller before he joined CWC started messaging him to say how much they loved his show. They sent videos of their kids doing impressions of his drawl. They made memes of him with his anorak billowing in zero-g.

Naturally, though, not all the attention was positive. As Bickle's click-rates ascended, he began to get noticed by activists.

"What the fuck is this?" Bickle said, showing me an email attachment from osw2z239lk12gsps@vacst.com (which he had mistaken for his CWC-assigned internet security detail, who enthusiastically practiced their own preaching down to their use of the unguessable email address wj54onw7021n.ize@globalsecure.uk).

In the attachment, Bickle's own likeness stared back at him, wide-eyed, sprinting down a Pamplonan street in flight from a bouncing, wrecking-ball-sized globe.

I worked to placate him. "Let me see it," I said. "That's an interesting joke someone sent. Isn't that interesting."

"Is it political?"

"I don't know. Here, I can block them if you want."

He was upset that people could find his email address. I said I'd ask IT to improve his spam filter. While we spoke (we were in the hall of the comms office, where Bickle was already late for a meeting to finalize funding for his next five episodes), I noticed Miguel. He was lingering at the end of the hall, watching me with a bemused smirk.

"I just worry if this is how people see me—" said Bickle.

I assured him people liked his show.

"Alright. Okay." He took a deep breath.

"Think about all the fan mail you're getting."

We went back and forth like this for five minutes. When finally he went into his meeting and I could catch a breath myself, I looked at Miguel. We both laughed.

Miguel and I had started spending more time together. Earlier that month, I'd asked him about Spanish lessons, and while he said teaching me Spanish sounded tedious, he was learning French and thought it'd be good for him to practice by teaching. I wondered how many languages he knew. I also wondered if midday rendezvous to practice French carried for him some special association Spanish lacked. In any case I agreed and had plenty of time as *Science Hour* consumed Bickle's schedule. While Bickle and Grant negotiated production budgets and wrestled for the blue pencil over scripts, Miguel and I did simple greetings, wishing each other "*Bonjour, monsieur*" and "*Très bonne journée.*" While Bickle screen-tested anoraks, we sipped coffee and discussed "*la banane*" and "*le pamplemousse.*"

One day, to teach noun-adjective agreement, Miguel printed out a list of personal traits.

"Use these to describe me," he instructed. "Whichever words you find fitting."

The vocab ranged from "*brillant*" to "*magnifique*." I laughed.

"Make sure you use the right form. I changed some to trick you."

"*Tu es . . .*" I said and wracked my brain for the correct pronuncia-
tion of the masculine version of "*menue*"—slim. But what I produced
was a blundering epithet that came out clearly as "*mon nu . . . minou?*"

My naked pussy. Miguel couldn't have been more delighted. He
pardoned my French and spat back, "*Va te faire foutre!*" Which went
right over my head but struck a passing Haitian custodian like a dirty
bise. I—gleefully apologetic, abashedly confused—buried my face. For
the rest of that day, I couldn't stop smiling.

Issues with Bickle got tougher. In late July, although the EPA held that
day contraction was "transient if existent" and its causes not understood, radical news outlets were reporting that days were short anywhere from four to six minutes. Bickle received a threatening email
with a photo of his old office at Columbia.

"Someone broke into my office!" he said, showing the picture to
Grant.

I got a good look at it. Across his desk was spray-painted: PLANET
KILLER.

"This image is obviously faked," I said, trying to show Grant that
I was in control. "I'm pretty sure. Anyway, you don't even work there
anymore."

"How do they know my old address, though?" Bickle asked.

I said IT had already promised to strengthen the filter on his email.

"Then why haven't they blocked these yet?" said Bickle.

"I'll ask again," I said.

"No, I'm asking you."

I feared if I urged him to calm down in front of Grant, he'd feel
emasculated. Grant sat back in his chair, watching.

Bickle said to him, "They want to hurt me for doing my job."

I opened my mouth to intervene. But to my surprise, Grant said,
"Yes. They do."

He quieted Bickle with a wave. "Now you see, this is what we're
up against," he said. He leaned forward. There was a cold intensity

in his stare, directed entirely at Bickle, as if I were no longer in the room. He said, "These activists don't know the first thing about you, they've never met you. You've gone out of your way to create content that's educational in a media landscape littered with disinformation and obscenity, yet they want to send you for a Burton. There's no reasoning with them. No room for collaborative problem-solving. Because you are an accomplished academic and a popular star who's earned acclaim for speaking truth to power, they want you dead. We can filter what emails you see, but they'll still be out there. I believe you're strong enough to handle knowing that. The real question I invite you to ask yourself is what does this make them, Victor? Eh? And what will it make you?"

"What do you think of all this day contraction stuff?" my colleagues in the Fighting 118th asked one another. I had joined them after work for a night out in Bangkok, my third or fourth time hanging out with them. I'd hoped Miguel would be there, but he had to work late. So I stood awkwardly with them on Sukhumvit 45 Alley, where they'd stepped outside for fresh air (after tiring of the club, where I watched them all roll their shoulders and try to look sexy to songs we were hearing for the third time in an hour). The air outside the club was even more suffocating than inside, but instead of body odor, it was muggy with smells of fish sauce and burnt paper. Passersby in short reflective dresses and long shoes were violently chiaroscuroed by all the neon signs. The Fighting 118th (short for "the 118th Mixed Avia-tion Regiment," their self-appointed nickname, for they all worked with me on the 118th floor of Aviation Tower) played hot potato with a glass bottle of Jameson.

"I'm tired of hearing about day contraction," said Kiko Alexandra, one of the two social media managers I'd met on my first day. "If it turns out to be real, it'll be like a minute a day, a few hours a year—less of an adjustment than daylight savings time used to be. And with A.H. time, the clocks are still accurate."

While she spoke, she braided her friend Fez's velvety-straight hair. Fez said, "Our work schedules will have to change, though."

"You come to the office for like three hours a day and then go clubbing in Asia, what will you notice?"

"I work."

"I haven't seen you do an honest day's work since we were sophomores at Cambridge."

"Don't pull my hair!"

A plastic bag tumbleweeded into a lamppost.

"It is kind of scary, though," said Noah White, Grant's trusted pollster, a data guru in his early thirties. I had seen him in some of Miguel's Scroller posts. He was tall, with a neat V of sweat down the front of his ONCHEK polo. "I'm stocking up on things. It seems like it could become a big issue for, like, supply chains."

"Oh my god, Noah's ready for the apocalypse."

"What are you stocking up on?" Fez asked, a hint of nervousness in her laughter.

"I don't know," he said. "Canned foods. Medicine. Guns."

"Are you serious?"

He laughed. "No guns. But medicine, yeah. Xanax."

"You're such a dope."

Noah shrugged. "When you're all freaking out, wishing you'd prepared, I'm going to be extremely chill."

Imani asked me what I thought. The oldest of the group by several years, she got the drunkest and still tried to play group mom.

"I'm with Kiko Alexandra," I said. "I'm kind of bored of all the talk. No one knows anything for sure anyway."

Fez pulled her tube top higher. "Sorry for boring you."

I laughed.

"We don't have change," said Kiko Alexandra. "*Have a good night. No change.*"

They asked how *Science Hour* was going.

"People are watching it, actually," I said. "Like more than I expected. It was a good idea from Grant."

"He gets those sometimes," said Kiko Alexandra.

"If you can understand them," said Fez.

I was glad to hear I wasn't the only one who had trouble understanding Grant talk. "He's so Oxbridge," I said.

"*Oxbridge?*" Kiko Alexandra snorted. "Sure, that's why me and Fez talk like that too. Right, Fez? When we were in uni we all talked like Cromwell Grant?"

Fez laughed.

"Oxbridge . . . Who said Grant was Oxbridge?"

"Miguel told me that Grant talks like that because he went to Oxford," I said.

"That's probably what *Grant* says. The guy is dialectically demented. Twenty years of international comms has run his tongue in loops, and he clings to the belief that he's the last true Englishman."

"Of course, that's where he heard it, though," said Fez. "From Miguel."

She was talking about me. I asked what she meant, and the rest of the 118th laughed.

"You and Miguel!" said Kiko Alexandra.

Noah wiped Jameson from his cheek. A few yards away, someone pissed on the sidewalk.

"What are you saying about Miguel?" I said.

Fez raised her eyebrows.

"What?"

"You two seem to have taken a liking to each other, is all."

"We're not—no," I said. "I'm not into that."

"You don't fancy guys?"

"Told you," said Noah. "It's only on Miguel's end. He's always trying. I feel bad for you, bro. I sneezed him off, and I guess you caught him."

"No, I totally—" I said, dazed by the light of speeding tuk-tuks, "I mean, ew." Fez asked, "Ew what?" and I said, "Just Miguel, you know, like, coming on to me."

Kiko Alexandra asked if I'd noticed him obsessing over me. My heart raced. The club's music thumped like smothered bombs. I said I hadn't. She advised me to stay away from him.

"He's desperate," she said. "He was always trying to get in Noah's pants."

Noah said, "I rooted him. Big mistake. Not even a good lay."

"Rooted?" I said, blood rushing to my face.

"Rooted; HU'ed; shagged," said Fez, finger-combing the ends of Kiko Alexandra's hair. "Ooh, I bet you have some crazy word for it in Alaska." Kiko Alexandra guessed "elking."

"Ew," I said again.

"Okay, no need for that," said Noah, laughing at me.

I tried to clarify that I just meant it wasn't what I was into.

Noah said to his friends, "That's why Miguel doesn't come out with us anymore. He decided to act too cool for us in order to get my attention so I'd fuck him again."

"And you did!" said Fez.

Noah blushed. "Yeah, I did."

My hands were shaking as I flew home that night, and for the rest of the week I avoided Miguel. There was a heat wave, and that became all anyone talked about. On Scroller, people were saying it had to do with day contraction, but no one really knew how that would be. The air conditioning in my hotel room groaned too loudly to run at night, so I lay with the sheets kicked down to my ankles. Some nights when I was almost asleep, I felt a jolt of excitement; then I remembered who it was about, and I became angry. At myself and at Miguel. He repulsed me. I resented him for tricking me into French lessons; he was giving people in the office the wrong idea. In my room, I watched hetero-sexual porn on the "Hilt-In" pay-per-view, films of women with long, bovine mammillae, succoring huge men—and I came with a heave of relief before even allowing myself time to get fully hard.

Friday evening, heading for the elevator, Miguel caught me.

"There you are," he said. "You've been playing hooky from French class."

The joke seemed nervous, like he sensed something wrong between us. Even the implication that there was something between us that could be wrong irritated me.

I called the elevator. "I've just been busy," I said.

"This heat wave."

"Uh huh."

Miguel asked if I was alright.

"I'm fine," I said.

"You seem off."

"What do you mean?"

"You don't seem like normal Tanner."

What did he know about me? I said that I had other priorities besides learning French. If he loved speaking French, that was his prerogative, but he shouldn't just assume everyone on Earth wanted to learn French. I laughed, not meeting his gaze.

The elevator display counted down. One hundred thirty-nine. One hundred thirty-six. He said, "I thought you wanted to." I said he was incorrect. He said okay.

I felt dizzy. Out of body. I heard myself say, "You know, there's nothing wrong with where I come from," and I buttoned my Thom Sweeney jacket, then unbuttoned it, and then the elevator arrived and we got in. When we were near the roof, where company pods took people home, I regained control of myself and said, "You think everyone wants to be like you."

"What do you mean like me?" he said, to my frustration.

The elevator opened. The roof was hot. The wind was hot too. A security guard, rifle dangling, drank from a big bottle of La Croix. There was a pod waiting, but it wasn't mine.

"I'm sorry," he said. "What did I do wrong?"

He seemed like he might cry, and I scolded myself for being surprised, expelling air quickly from my nose, which I realized was something my father did when annoyed. Miguel boarded the pod but glanced back as if he thought I might follow.

When his pod launched, a violent sensation overcame me, as if a piece of myself were being torn away with it. I watched it get snatched up by an anonymous circuit vessel popping overhead. Nothing catastrophic happened. The world kept turning.

That night, I obsessed over trying to reconstruct our conversation in my mind to figure out which words precisely I had used against him. The AC ran overdrive, and I thought I would never fall asleep. I dreamt that I was screaming at my dogs. I woke with a start, imagining that someone held a gun at the foot of my bed. My heart raced. Dirty sunlight filled the empty room. I lay back, my dread about Miguel returning.

Saturday I sat in bed for hours, considering texting him. My hotel room was a mess: drawers hanging open, empty Nespresso pods overflowing the wastebin. On both walls, *Big Life* played at 100, Gretch saying how pissed she was at Joni for telling everyone that Samuel had a huge cock. Unable to come up with anything to text, I dropped my phone on the nightstand. It landed with a clap, and I lifted it and set it down again, gently, which was something my mother used to make me do, even though the stuff we owned wasn't nice. It wasn't even about checking for damage; as long as I picked the object up and put it down again, I felt resolved. My father used to say this showed respect. He had accused me of "cultural self-loathing" for as long as I could remember.

Sunday the heat wave broke, and I visited the hotel's eighth-floor Zen Garden. Nothing doing. I sat on my bed in waxy boxer shorts, trying to summon the energy to order lunch.

"Those are all perverts, you know," my father used to say, while I, in the kitchen, nine years old, read a list of Hollywood's leading men. I had finally gotten a phone from my mother—the last in my class to get one. She had hoped it might ease the bruisings I was receiving from the other boys in school. My father watched me on that phone, and he saw something my mother didn't. "Why is that what you're looking at?" he berated me when Will Flowers's new music video dropped, and I couldn't stop watching. I thought he wouldn't disapprove of me watching clips from the new live-action *Prince of Egypt*, which we'd been shown in Sunday school, but I was watching Moses wrong, and he saw . . .

In the hotel gym, I took a treadmill. There was an older man next to me, drenched in sweat as if he'd walked a thousand miles. Each of the treadmills had little screens, so that everyone could get exactly what they wanted. The older man watched people talking about college football. I put on "Captivate News" and watched weightlifters in the mirror. I ran and ran and ran.

"What's wrong with you," my father had said. "Taking that phone everywhere. You think you can invite the devil into your house and expect him to leave when the sun goes down?"

As a preteen I had labored to figure out who, in online glamour mags, was a homosexual, thinking if I was learning to identify them then my fascination wasn't a sin. I started picking them out based on the quality of their skin and hair, whether their shirts fit correctly (the way the magazines said they should, with a little poofiness around the shoulders), and whether their shoes were clean. They wore frivolous bracelets. I was obsessed with how different these men were from my father, whose fingernails were always soiled and whose armpits stank of work. Homosexuals, I understood, used their appearance to seduce boys who were weak enough to give in to immature temptations.

So many nights of my childhood ended with my father shouting and me going to bed in tears. Then compelled to probe, harder and harder, the part of me that hurt, I opened my phone and summoned the devil. I wanted to prove that I *was* strong enough to face him.

Eventually came the summer night when I was woken by the report of a rifle. I was fifteen. I leapt out of bed, groping in the dark for my luau pack, but it was gone. My sister Ashtyn screamed.

"Your brother has chosen the image over the word." It was my dad, standing by the window. He'd picked this night on purpose; the moon was full. His AR-15 was pointed at me.

"Dad, what are you doing?"

"I am but one servant of God, trying to save you from the fire," he said, "but they are too many. I've let them into our home, into your room, even into your bed through that device, and they have turned your eyes green like the serpent."

I looked down the barrel of the gun.

My mom pleaded, "Randall, stop it." Ashtyn wailed.

"It's over." With a sigh, he lowered the gun. He rested it against the windowsill and left the room. Ashtyn cried for another hour while our mom tried to calm her and I sat in my bed, embarrassed, looking at the nose of the gun peeking into the moonlight. The next morning, our mom informed us that our father was being furloughed at work and I should see about a job at the church. I understood that it was my fault.

I spent my days in the church, hiding out after my custodial work was done, smoking in the belfry to avoid the entertainment annex, where the screensaver to *Sodom Striker* gave me nightmares. It was only a matter of time before I receded fully into the digital Xanadu of social media, with its algorithms, accepting and charitable, to spare you the distress of confronting your fingers' predilections. And since then—I thought, panting—I had never really emerged.

The Captivate channel showed a family eating fish finger wraps. I powered down the treadmill, walked until it came to a stop, then stood in place until the screen went black and I could see my reflection. I was so tired of myself. I just wanted to be good.

* * *

For the next week, I was afraid to encounter Miguel. I showed up to work early, avoided the coffee machine, and left late. When we crossed paths, he didn't look at me. I took Friday off.

The next Monday morning, tired, I lingered on the roof of Aviation Tower, turned against the wind to light a cigarette. I was afraid to go down the elevator and cross Miguel's desk. I wore my salmon short-sleeve and brown pants, both nice, but they didn't really match. A pod was taking off when behind me Miguel said, "Hey."

"Oh," I said. "Hi."

"How was your weekend?" he asked. His puffy CWC jacket was bunched at the belt so the zipper furrowed.

"Not so great," I said.

"Mine neither."

I gave up on lighting the cigarette. "You going down?"

Miguel said, "In a minute."

He seemed to be collecting his thoughts. I grew nervous.

Just as he said, "I feel exhausted, physically and emotionally," I said, "I feel like you have the wrong idea of me."

We both stopped. A pod snapped into the sky.

"What did you say?"

"I don't know," I said.

"What do you mean I have the wrong idea of you?"

Hair blowing in my face, an inarticulable feeling overcame me: a sense that Miguel was the only person in the world. That not even I myself was real. A voice in my head kept trying to remind me who and where I was, a little voice like a man running across the deck of a ship, desperate to reach the wheelhouse before the captain did something that could not be undone. "I regretted our conversation last Friday," I said.

Miguel's laugh was confused and curious, a little mean-spirited, but I didn't take offense.

"You were really rude to me," he said.

"I'm sorry."

"In fact, you were hurtful."

"I know," I said. "I didn't mean it."

"I didn't think you did."

"I'm not sure how I feel."

"I get that."

"There's all this noise," I said.

"Okay."

Pods rose and fell. Miguel was watching me, waiting. I said, "Sorry, can I start over?"

He thought about it. He answered, "No."

I nodded. "Well, maybe—sorry, it's just, getting to know you has been really meaningful to me, since I don't know anyone here, and I feel like—I mean, I don't want to pity myself. You don't owe me anything."

He put his hands in his pockets.

"What I was hoping is," I said. "Is there any chance you'd want to go out for a drink with me?"

He started walking toward the elevator. People were filing in alongside him, and there were no clouds, the blue was like a closed container. "Maybe," he said. "Maybe I would."

He didn't need to look back to know that I was coming too. The cigarette fell from my fingers, and I saw the wind carry it off the roof to the street below. That day, I quit smoking cold turkey.

○

A nurse examined a jumble of tangled cords and sighed, as in, *this is going to be really tough*. Somehow, Winnie knew even before waking up that the nurse was standing beside her bed. She knew she was in the hospital, and she knew that the beeping on the screen above her was the sound of her heart. When she first opened her eyes, twenty hours after her electrocution, the only thing that surprised her was the dizziness.

It came in awful waves. A sickening confusion of body and mind, as if her brain were unraveled out to her fingers, the world teetering left and right at the same time, her plastic hospital bed swallowing her down and puking her back up into intersecting tunnels, and her aunt Carsie shouting foreign gibberish from behind her ears. The questions didn't scan. Everything smelled like latex.

The nurses gave her vitamins, carbocapsules, and powdered milk, and over the next two days she returned to the stationary world. A woman in the next bed over kept telling her that her nose was running. On her third night in the burn ward, she was weaned off morphine. Her hands and chest were bandaged, and surgery scars stung up and down her arms. A chip had been injected into each of her wrists, and purple nanotech carboxyhemoglobin probes, the size of deer ticks, beat beneath her skin. She remembered that she'd been electrocuted, and she realized with dread that she was going to need to explain herself.

The thing she would remember most about her stay at Zuckerberg San Francisco General, though, was waking up cold in the middle of her final night, to the noise of a terrible storm. She got out of bed, or at least she thought she had, pushed as if by atmospheric pressure to the window. It was dark and streaked with rain. On the vacant street below, power lines swung and trumpet flowers flew horizontally from trees. Thunder's brutality. The ocean tumbled through the air. The gutters backed up, and the waters just kept rising, and there was a clamor among the nurses as the wind seemed to cry that San Francisco was nothing. That the whole enterprise of building a city was foolish and doomed to fail. But then it passed. By the next morning, when Carsie checked her out of the hospital, the sky was clear.

"Did it rain last night?" she asked.

"You really *were* out," said Carsie.

Weak morning rays beamed through the moisture, and the wind was no more than a tired sigh. It rippled puddles through which Pacific Gas & Electric workers were already wading. Circuit vessels hashed the sky. Winnie and Carsie took an Uber home, passing people barefoot on their balconies, sipping coffee and straightening their drying racks. There was a slow feeling that the world was scanning itself, making sure it was all still there.

Winnie's first week out, she hung around the apartment, relaxing more as each day passed without her aunt forcing her to discuss the accident. She was comfortable except when she had to move—then she felt her ribs scrape. And sometimes her arms fell randomly asleep, which concerned her. Her recuperation required that she miss the rest of the school year, though, and that, to her, almost made the whole ordeal worth it. There would be summer school, but she wouldn't know anyone there, and anyway, repeating some material was probably good for her. Carsie offered to take work off for Winnie's first days at home, but Winnie adamantly refused. She was fine alone. It took a long time to get dressed and undressed, but what else did she have to do. Those days, with the apartment to herself, she felt like she was getting away with something. She started a show about the murder of a fictional high school cheerleader, watching mostly for the boyfriend/ lead suspect, who took his shirt off whenever he'd had enough. She memorized the pattern of circuit vessels that repeated out her window fifteen times a day. A contrail from bottom-left to top-center intersecting with bottom-right to top-left. All of them drifting up the window as they sailed toward the Pacific. What was everyone's hurry? This was also CWC's Eats Week on Uber Eats, and Winnie took advantage by ordering in lunch on her aunt's card. She kept getting sushi from New York. When the Wwlliamses returned in the evening, Winnie played up her ailments, as if they might suspect her of malingering.

She avoided being alone with Carsie for fear that her aunt would press her into talking about what happened. When Carsie brought her breakfast in the morning, she tensed up. But the questions never surpassed "How are you feeling?", "Need more pillows?", "Are you okay for lunch?" It actually was getting strange.

After three weeks, evidence against the TV boyfriend was becoming incontrovertible. Winnie, now mostly healed, sat on the couch watching while Carsie and her husband Mark made dinner in the kitchen. Juju was out. Carsie was venting, she sounded tired, and Winnie turned the volume down to hear.

"I get that," Mark was saying.

"Maybe if I were a better sister or something."

"It's because you were such a good sister that this is triggering for you. You're the good person here. You didn't ask to take her in."

"Fine."

"Don't get mad at me. If you think you could do more, then do more."

"She doesn't even want my help."

Winnie turned the volume up again almost to the point that she couldn't hear them. On TV the cops were taking the creepy neighbor down. Everyone was cheering. She'd lost track of why.

"You want to know what I think?" Mark said. "I think you're tempted again to take on all this responsibility to be the savior, and just like last time, it's out of your control."

"I'm not trying to be a savior."

"I know, I'm just saying, you're doing the right amount."

"It's fine, Mark."

"What's the problem?"

"I'm sorry, you're just—could you just tell her that dinner is ready?"

Winnie turned the volume up too fast. An elderly woman was dancing from the screen through aisles and aisles of JCPenney clearance. Mark appeared in the threshold. He looked at the screen, then at Winnie.

"How you feeling?" he asked.

"Fine."

He waited for her to say more, and when she didn't, he nodded slowly. "Dinner," he said and turned back into the kitchen.

It smelled like garlic. Carsie was already seated, using her phone to turn down the fan.

"I'm actually going to go out for dinner," Winnie said.

"Oh." Carsie's eyebrows raised behind her cat-eye glasses. "Do you need money?"

"I'm alright."

"Okay then," Carsie said, looking at Mark. "Have fun."

In a Gore-Tex raincoat to hide the probe entry scars along her wrists, she walked to the beach. The evening clouds were French vanilla sliding on steel, and the smell of the ocean waxed and waned. She made a pact with herself to stay out until at least sundown. At the beach, people stumbled out of pods wearing bikinis, carrying wine canisters. Boys played music and skateboarded along the promenade. The water thrashed erratically. The horizon sat flat and dizzyingly high. She sat on a bench and thought about opening her phone but couldn't think of anything on it that might interest her, which was weird and slightly scary.

She sat for forty minutes, looking at the blinding water, but then a man was staring at her, so she left. She walked around her neighborhood. It was full of restaurants that she'd never been to. Trucks passed, carrying smaller vehicles on their backs. She ended up reaching her street and just going into Subway. Inside, two women were speaking quietly, and on the television the president laid out his plan for clock holidays to accommodate day contraction.

She approached the counter and ordered a six-inch Cold Cut Combo. The server halved a loaf of Italian Herb & Cheese bread, which Winnie had once heard was made of shoe rubber, and began laying down uniform slices of pink mystery meat.

"Which cold cut is that?" Winnie asked.

"It's the combo."

She ate it as slowly as humanly possible, wanting to stay out long enough that her aunt and uncle would be in their room when she got home and she wouldn't need to see them. The women at the next table were talking about their kids. "Jeremy is having a really hard time with these active shooter drills," one of them complained. "They're making him not want to go to school." Eventually Winnie grew tired of the sandwich and came home, said a quick hello to her aunt and uncle and went straight to her room, the sun still well above the water.

Next night, she tried again.

This time, she went up Irving Street, its back broken by hills. She had in the past always avoided Irving on weekends, for she had once chaperoned Juju to the Irving and Helson Kung Fu Tea and had needed to hide from a group of her classmates sitting in one another's laps at the counter. Today, however, she forced herself to walk up the street at a regulated pace. The options were overwhelming. There were taquerias, al fresco cafés, fluorescent Korean BBQ chains. Dive bars amassed crowds of smokers on the sidewalk, men with long flossy hair and tight-skinned women with sunken eyes. How many worlds could there be on this planet, for it seemed that Irving Street and Twenty-Fourth held an entire world on its own, maybe two. The buildings along the retail strip were capped at five stories, each dotted with balconies where people drank wine and watched life and were life, and Saturday night was in their voices and in their dresses and on the air. They remarked at how San Francisco had changed. Winnie felt small but not small enough, making her way through the crowds on the sidewalk, reading Yelp reviews on her yellow plastic 670p. The wind carried a pleasant smokiness, which was San Francisco's only reminder of the ongoing, historic wildfire ravaging Sonoma County, for the smoke was mostly kept at bay—or as California's governor promised, "off bay"—by the Berkeley fanwall, a literal mile-long wall of fans (which of course made the fires much, much worse). Winnie breathed in through her nose and out through her mouth and tugged her raincoat sleeves into her palms. In a dim bar, three teenage girls danced around an old flatscreen jukebox.

She went into Lululemon. The people working there looked like they were dressed to chase her down. She browsed the Sarandex, and a song came on that she knew, but then the sales rep asked if she needed help finding something, so she left.

Outside, a tall, cute boy asked if she had a minute. She looked around.

"I don't mean to bother you, Miss," he said. "How's your day going?"

"Good," she said.

"Long, would you say? Have you heard of the IERS?"

She hadn't. He explained that the IERS was the international body, established A.H. 395,184 (FKA 1988 AD), responsible for maintaining global time and reference frame standards. But now, he said, the organization was slowing down the clocks. "Secretly and surreptitiously. You may have noticed that the angel Gabriel's star no longer returns to the same place in the night sky every twenty-four hours by the clock. At the height of Isha, the clocks may read A.H. 980,000:00, but the next night, they'll read 980,023:54. That's because the clocks have been compromised."

Winnie looked at the time on her phone.

"The IERS is in your phone," he said, extending his petition.

She said she was pretty sure the clocks weren't wrong; it was day contraction. By this point, she had read enough about day contraction to understand that it was happening, even if she wasn't sure about its seriousness or its causes. Startlingly, the boy laid a hand on her shoulder.

"You need to read," he said. "Don't let them think for you. What's your name?"

"Winnie."

"Do you know what metronomic music is really about, Winnie?"

"What it's about?" she repeated, trying not to betray her fear as strangers passed them.

"Spiritual death." His voice was rigid. "At least old-fashioned EDM kept a finger on life- and God-affirming themes like communal transcendence and procreation."

"Sorry—I have to go."

She turned around and walked quickly up the road to eat a six-inch Cold Cut Combo at Subway. After that, she didn't leave the apartment for four days.

But when Thursday came back around, she had a plan: a popular Mexican bar and grill, at Irving Street's nearest end. Her table for one was reserved online (if she'd had to talk to a host over the phone, she would have chickened out). She showed up on time in a turquoise sweater and was given a wobbly two-top under a technicolor Madonna in the corner. She ordered the chile relleno. The place had a cozy smell, like fresh chips. As she ate, she watched the bartender smile at patrons and skin limes. At a certain point, she looked around the restaurant at others eating just like her—she wasn't even the only one eating alone—and it occurred to her that *she was doing it.*

When the rowdy, just-drinks crowd grew from the bar and encroached on Winnie's table, she stayed put. She feared the waiter would force a check on her since they were beginning to scan IDs for new entrants, but instead he called her "señorita" and asked if she wanted dessert. She ordered the forty-minute flan. And though she was not one to believe in a socially aware mind-body connection, when she handed the waiter her pink debit card and he thanked her for coming, a chill ran down her spine. She walked home with her hands pulled snugly into her sleeves, smelling the mint and berry vapes of other pedestrians and feeling accomplished just to be alive, which (she realized that night) if you're really truly alive, is enough.

The summer passed. Her summer school classes were easy since most of the material was repeated, and she even got a B+ in physics, the best she'd ever done in science, placing herself out of the remedial track for the upcoming year. Upon rereading, she started to understand *The Great Gatsby*, moved by the ornate descriptions of Gatsby's longing for his first love, his belief that he could reinvent himself, and his publicity stunts for Daisy's affection. Her final paper was about how the green light was like a circuit vessel. She discovered Mia Farrow and watched all of her films. Mia Farrow reminded Winnie of her mom, and she realized that her ability to make this identification was a marker of her own growth.

When school resumed in August, she resolved to join an extra-curricular. She considered Modern Dance, but you actually needed skill for Modern, not to mention a degree of comfort in sleeveless jerseys. Same with the girls' sports. And while the French Society seemed fun (eating madeleines, trading fashion magazines), she didn't speak French. On the second day of school, she got an email from Nat Agarwal.

ATTENTION MEMBERS OF THE FORMER FUTURE'S ADVOCATES— ATTAINMENT ACADEMY'S NEW **ROTARY CLUB** WILL BE HOSTING ITS FIRST MEETING . . .

Wednesday after school. *Well*, she thought, *why not try liking people who might possibly like me for a change*. When she arrived, holding her bookbag to her chest, there were almost ten students there. Nat in her cattle tag was dictating bullet points to appear on the wall behind her.

"Eight hundred to nine hundred dollars that National will pool with other donations going to Liberia." Nat turned. "Winnie! You're here! Sit down."

She sat in the front row beside Nat's friend Luna Tsiang, whose shirt today said SUCK MY DICK AND KISS MY ASS, FRANK SINATRA IS DEAD.

The meeting lasted an hour, including icebreakers (Nat's favorite movie was the new *Kite Runner: Legacy*; Luna's favorite band was something called Aphex Twin; Winnie, without thinking, said her favorite drink was water). At the end, when people started packing up, she realized she'd been kneading an eraser the whole time and her knee was dusted in pink shavings. She brushed them off as Nat approached to ask Luna how she thought the meeting went.

"Good!" Luna said. "What did you think, Winnie?"

Winnie, putting on her backpack, said she enjoyed it.

"People were certainly enthusiastic," said Luna. At one point a junior boy had said his favorite food was the tears of the patriarchy. "Does a person *eat* tears?" Luna wondered. She and Nat straightened desks.

Nat said to her, "At the moment, I could eat anything."

"Sweetgreen?"

"You're on."

Meanwhile Winnie left the classroom alone. She started down the hall. The other students were already going downstairs. She turned around and caught Nat and Luna in the doorway.

"Hey," she said. "Would you mind if I came?"

She'd never been to Sweetgreen. It was kind of disgusting. Luna must have noticed her examining the nozzle on the spinach dispenser because she said, "Yeah, I sometimes wonder, what is a *sweet* green?"

Nat talked about her aspirations for Rotary. She said she wanted to do "real activism." Luna laughed at her, and she huffed, "I just mean I don't want to spend all our time talking about fundraising."

Luna said, "You're the one who wanted a 'more legitimate' club than what we had with Future's Advocates last year."

"You couldn't do that club?" Winnie asked.

"The school wouldn't let us keep using a meeting room because we didn't have enough members, and without funding, like we get now from Rotary International, we couldn't afford to advertise," said Nat. "Even in the freaking school announcements."

"I thought it would be cool even without school support," said Luna with a shrug.

"Then it's not a club, Luna. It's just us hanging out in your room."

Winnie was sorry to hear that they couldn't get people to join. She explained that she'd been in the hospital.

"I noticed," Nat said, nodding to the stitches along Winnie's wrist.

"Oh," said Winnie, stretching her sleeves. "No, it's not like that."

"No worries," said Nat. "They match Luna's."

Luna kept her arms crossed.

Winnie would learn later that Nat and Luna had only become friends the prior winter, when Nat moved to SF from LA. Their friendship, too, was still tender. She would learn that neither Luna nor Nat had ever kept many friends before. Luna had always been fine that way. But Nat was one of those people who needed others to "engage her." One day she'd seen Luna in the cafeteria reading *Animal Liberation*; she'd invited herself to sit (she had a number of thoughts about the book's undercurrent of ableism), and she hadn't left Luna alone since.

"Nat has opinions about, like, everything," Luna liked to complain. "Exhausting to hang out with one-on-one. But she's a good friend."

A good friend, Winnie thought. Could Winnie be a good friend? Even after another week of Rotary and then sitting with Nat and Luna in the cafeteria, Winnie struggled to feel at ease socializing. She said nothing without saying it in her head before and after. This was, she understood, what people called self-consciousness, though it felt to her like just the opposite, other-consciousness, since she had nothing herself to say but what she thought would come off well to Nat and Luna. That first afternoon, when they were in the Uber going to Sweetgreen, Luna breezily wondered, "How come every stop sign is the same shade of red? Like, who makes that paint?" and in the silence that followed, Winnie nearly choked on air, she was so unsure if she was supposed to answer, or if the question was rhetorical, or if it was a joke to be repaid in kind.

Or: There was her first time at Luna's, a garden-level apartment off Noriega Street. She met Luna's hairless cat, whom Luna introduced as Bella. Winnie said that that was a cute name since she couldn't say as much about any other aspect of the creature, and Luna and Nat burst out laughing. They pointed at the folds of skin on her head. "It's short for Cerebellum!" they said. Winnie laughed too, terrified that they might realize she didn't get it.

But as the months passed, without much change in Winnie's behavior, she started thinking less. As if some shell between her "true self" and her social self gradually thinned and disappeared, the things she said and did on the outside turned out to be who she was, and she was happy with that.

Nat, Luna, and Winnie liked to: make collaborative Spotify playlists and then skip all of Luna's songs; change one another's phone backgrounds to photos of weird boys from their school; present one another with gift-wrapped impedimenta (desk chair covers, wall-mounted pencil sharpeners, kitchen-size trash bins) found on clearance, no gift receipts; brainstorm meme ideas; talk about their families.

"My uncle's a moron," Winnie said, "but my aunt Carsie is fine. I mean, she tries."

"I respect Carsie," said Nat. "As a woman."

It was true. She supported the family, plus Winnie, while Mark Wwlliams—a "professional" house flipper—sunk their savings in ill-advised renovation projects. He was always blaming his contractors, the tax assessors, the buyers. You wondered where were these 40 percent of Californians who still didn't believe in day contraction, and then you remembered Mark Wwlliams, watching football in his brown toupee and baseball cap that said ARUBA.

"They're both kind of disappointing, though," said Winnie.

Luna said, "Most people are."

They knew about Winnie's mom too and asked about her dad. "You know as much as I do," said Winnie. Her mom had never wanted to discuss the man who proposed to her when she was twenty-four, got her pregnant within a year, and then left her with nothing but his wooden name. It was an understanding that Winnie believed she and her mom shared. The understanding of not talking about him.

Nat fanned herself with her newsboy cap. "Both my parents suck," she said. Winnie knew Nat and her dad fought—that was why they didn't hang out at Nat's house. Nat said he constantly pushed her to perform in school. Winnie had asked what Nat's parents did for work, and all Nat said was that her mom volunteered with the local arts board.

Luna's parents were Chinese immigrants working for a funeral home. They often popped into Luna's room to bring the girls micro-wavable potstickers and spicy strips. The first time Winnie came over, Luna's mom hugged her and spoke eager Mandarin for nearly two minutes. When she looked to her daughter to translate, Luna said only, "Mom says it's nice to meet you." Her mom teased her. Winnie could sense between Luna and her parents a tremendous love.

To keep up with her friends in conversation, Winnie started watch-ing the news. She read social justice basics before bed—pocket editions of Butler and Baldwin. One Wednesday after Rotary, she namedropped some of the titles to Nat. In return, a shake of the head. "That stuff's important," Nat said, "but outdated." She lent a copy of *Activism for the Circuit Age*, in which Winnie read about neo-doomer fashion and learned to use words like "eschatologico-feminism."

One day, as the school year neared its close, Nat asked if they had heard of Victor Bickle.

They were in Winnie's room. All the nightstands and chairs were stacked atop one another to make space for the hardwood waxer, who was supposed to come an hour ago. Winnie and Luna sat on beanbags on top of the rug on top of the bed. They were ostensibly studying for final exams, but they all felt well enough prepared. Nat and Luna had been a scholarly influence on Winnie, and she expected to finish sophomore year with straight As and A-minuses (Nat had made her calculate what she would need on each final to pull this off). Nat lay prostrate on the floor with her cattle tag dangling out of her messy hair. Its swing was mirrored in her tablet.

"No," said Winnie. "Who's that?"

"He's like this internet scientist," said Nat. "He has a show, but he's also in CWC commercials. And his show, like, is a CWC commercial."

"CWC is the worst," said Luna. She made small, seated bounces on the beanbags, trying to knock Winnie off balance.

"Oh my god, could you stop?" Winnie said, and Luna laughed.

"Right. So check this out," said Nat, brandishing her tablet.

It showed California senator (and CWC donee) Marnie Applebaum sleeping in a velvet-lined private circuit vessel cabin, with the caption: CWC CARGO

Luna and Winnie squealed. "What are you going to do with that?"

"Post it in Human Dignity Memes for Dignified Internet Queens," said Nat, "and email it to CWC management. I want to find this Bickle guy's email address."

Winnie said there was no way that CWC people would actually see it.

"They do!" said Nat. "I attach read-receipt triggers. I know they look. You can do it too."

"God damn," said Luna. "CWC's firewall is holeyer than Nat is holier than thou."

Nat rolled onto her back and checked her meme for errors. Winnie opened a window. The block always smelled like Subway. She thought about her friends and her life now, and it still made her sad to think there was a time when she didn't have any of this, when she fell asleep lonely and woke with stress cramps for no reason but that she was scared to live.

The hardwood guy came. Luna flirted with him but was too shy to get his Scroller handle. The girls hung out in Winnie's room for another few hours, then realized they all craved Subway, after which they said goodnight. Winnie returned home to find Juju in the kitchen.

"Want some?" Winnie said, pouring herself a glass of soymilk.

Juju said, "How do they make that stuff, by like, milking a tofu?"

Winnie pulled a chair off the table and sat beside her. Together they watched viral streams: a UVA girl complained about dormitory AC . . . a lip-sync of the vice president's latest gaffe . . . the Greatest BunnyWars Deathstreak of All Time . . . Coat Compactor vs. Spring

From A Real Pod Platform. Juju's posture was impeccable, and she breathed with her mouth open. Her avatar was a bedroom selfie that showed the straps of her training bra.

Winnie asked how she felt about finishing fifth grade.

"Well, everyone in my grade is pathetic," said Juju, still glued to the holograms. "So I don't really feel one way or another."

"Why are they pathetic?"

"They're very uncool," said Juju. "They're losers. None of them are on-point."

An octopus trapped in a fishbowl spastically changed colors as people dazed it with tinted lights. Winnie suggested that Juju join a club in middle school.

"Like what?"

"I really like my Rotary club. Maybe there's a middle school version."

Juju groaned. "That group of kids is one of the least on-point."

It wasn't just about popularity, Winnie said. "It's about joining people who make you feel good about yourself. A group that does good work and makes you feel like you're doing good work. So when you walk through the city and see all the vibrance of life, you can say, I'm a meaningful participant in all this."

"When I walk through the city and see all the vibrance of life?" Juju said. "When the freak do I do that? You know what makes me feel good about myself? Knowing I'm the most on-point fifth-grader." She tossed her empty can into the trash.

Winnie first visited Nat's house at the end of the school year. The girls had aced their finals and wanted to do something special before Nat left on vacation. So following the Rotary club year-end party (where they collected T-shirt sale proceeds), Nat and Luna surprised Winnie with a gift: a Claire's piercing gun.

"You said you wanted a nose stud, right?" said Nat. "It's gonna look so good!"

Winnie examined the box. The long needle. The smiling girl.

"We just can't do it at my place," said Luna. Her mom would make a stink. She didn't even approve of ear piercings.

They couldn't go to Winnie's either. The evening before, another freak storm had flooded the Wwlliamses' apartment, so the hardwood needed emergency desiccation.

"No problem," Nat said. Her parents were out of town. She called an Uber.

It brought them to a sleek double-townhouse overlooking Dolores Park. Winnie had been to the park before and wondered who lived in such huge homes. Nat unlocked the gate. Even with the park right there, she had a yard with its own rose garden and bubbling fountain.

"Your parents got a pod platform," Luna noticed. It was next to the driveway. There was a private pod with its name stenciled in green. MAIDEN INDIA.

"What? Oh, yeah," Nat said. "A couple months ago. It links up with the flight my dad takes when he goes to Mumbai on business."

Inside they spiraled quickly up to Nat's room, so Winnie barely glimpsed the hallways adorned with cricket memorabilia or the double loggia that encircled a courtyard at the house's center. Nat's room was messy. She had an entertainment wall across from her unmade California king and bookshelves organized by color. Winnie scanned the titles. All the red ACT prep books on top, followed by blue Advanced Placement manuals, *Between the World and Me*, *Youth to Power*, *Life and Times of Hillary Clinton*, *The Fountainhead*.

"I've heard of this one," said Winnie.

"Oh yeah, Ayn Rand," said Nat. "She's really important to me. She made me realize that I struggle to not get burned out by feelings of social obligation, so I'm working on self-advocating more."

Winnie had never imagined Nat as someone who needed to work on herself.

"Alright, let's do this," said Luna on the carpet, surrounded by needles and studs.

A drizzle pattered against the window. Winnie went to the bathroom and wiped her nose with rubbing alcohol, following the instructions. On her return, she had trouble finding Nat's room. She must have taken a wrong turn at the start, because she made a full circle through the house, around the central courtyard. She kept looking through windows and seeing the window she'd just passed across the way. Across the mist. The clouds were full of moonlight. In the courtyard's center was a long-necked bird of brass with its feet facing forward but its head turned backward, spitting water into the rain.

When she found Nat's room again, soft music was playing and Nat and Luna were on the bed together. They'd assembled the gun. Winnie sat between them. The gun was white and bigger than she had expected.

Nat's breath was warm over Winnie's ear as she positioned the gun. "I think I squeeze this," she said, "on the count of three."

Winnie told her to wait. She felt the needle against her nostril. "I can't see," she said.

"What do you mean?"

"Your hand is in my face."

"Is that a problem?"

"It's too close," said Winnie. She didn't like it. She pushed the gun away.

Luna laughed at her.

"Sorry," she said. "I just need to catch my breath."

The music was repetitive, and the rain fell forever. Luna said she wished she could get a piercing but her mom would kill her. "She even used to have earrings herself, but she's weird about me. She probably thinks I'll wear something tasteless like you, Nat."

Nat objected.

"You turned me vegan. My mom's never forgiven you for that."

"Your parents love me."

"How do you know?"

"They're always like, '*Oooh, Nat, Oo do-do-do.*'"

"Oh my god," said Luna, falling back on the bed. "That's, like, fucking racist."

Listening to them, Winnie still felt the heavy air of alcohol spilling from her sinuses. They talked about giving Luna a piercing somewhere her parents wouldn't see. The kit came with a nipple-piercing attachment. Nat egged her on. They looked at pictures online to see if a crimped barbell would be visible under clothes.

Nat asked Winnie, "If Luna gets one of these, will you go through with the nose stud?"

Winnie said she would do it either way, the angle just hadn't felt right.

"Fuck it," said Luna. "Should I?"

She went into the bathroom. Winnie couldn't think of anything to talk about with Nat, and it seemed like a long time before Luna returned, wearing just a green Calvin Klein bra, her chest ribbed like an adolescent boy's. Winnie noticed for the first time the pale scars on Luna's forearm. Luna asked if Nat had read the instructions. "Should I stand?" She apologized for her body, she was nervous, while Nat lined up the gun. The gray freckles on her nose were twitching. Winnie couldn't stop staring at her scars.

"Ouch!"

The sound, like a hole puncher, made Winnie shudder. Luna ran to the mirror.

"I think it's good!" she said.

Winnie asked if it hurt.

Luna only said, "No backing out now."

They disinfected the needle and tried again with Winnie. The butt of the gun was still in her face. Nat counted down from five. But she squeezed the trigger at two, exactly when Winnie got scared and turned away. She felt her nostril tear.

"Oh my god," Nat said. "Why did you do that?" She brushed her fingers over Winnie's face and came away with blood.

Winnie touched her face. Her nose burned. However, the blood seemed to come from her eyebrow, where the butt of the gun had smashed her.

"Your eye is gnarly," said Luna. "But I think the piercing is okay."

Winnie went to the mirror and looked at the little starter stud in her nose. It was alien, lifeless, beautiful.

Her eye, though, still bled an hour later. She didn't want to return to the Wwlliamses holding a bloody paper towel to her face. Nat said they could sleep over. They ordered vegan sushi and watched a Pixar movie, which they all agreed wasn't as good as the ones from their childhoods. Every few minutes, Luna went to the bathroom to admire her nipple, and Winnie had to explain what she missed. Afterward, they snuck downstairs for ice cream (Nat's maple kitchen was as big as half the Wwlliamses' apartment), brushed their teeth, and got in bed.

As they lay in the dark talking about Nat's upcoming trip to Mumbai, Luna asked Winnie, "Do you ever feel like visiting where your mom grew up in Alaska?"

The rain had slowed. Winnie was trying not to get blood on Nat's pillowcase, even though Nat had said not to worry. The pillow smelled like cinnamon.

"I've been there," said Winnie. "I mean for one, I was born there, but then also my mom and I went back to Keber Creek a couple of summers ago. It was one of the last times I spent with her before she, you know, sent me to live with my cousins."

Luna asked what it was like.

"We were only there a day. You had to drive there, so we spent the night in Fairbanks, which I remember a lot better than Keber Creek. In Keber Creek there wasn't much to see. My mom didn't know anyone; her parents died when I was a baby. We visited the mine where her dad used to work, but they'd built these big walls around it. I think my mom was self-conscious about tiring me out and we gave up looking for an entrance sooner than she wanted. I remember telling her I thought the mine was really cool even if we could only see the walls from the outside, but she was annoyed. She didn't seem to recognize anything. We drove down the road she'd lived on. She said it used to have a lot of mobile homes where mining families lived together, but now it was just landfill."

Nat began to snore.

"That's weird," Luna said dreamily. "Did you feel, like, any connection at all?"

"I remember feeling really close with my mom, because she seemed upset. But I don't think we even stayed in Keber Creek two hours. I said we should stay longer, but she was ready to start the drive back to Fairbanks. We didn't talk much on the drive back. She used to get that way."

For a minute, the rain was all there was, and Winnie worried that Luna had dozed off too. Then Luna said, "Weird," and rolled onto her back. She asked if Winnie thought about visiting her mom.

"In the facility in Nevada?"

Luna might have nodded, but it was dark and Winnie was looking at the ceiling. She thought about it a few minutes. When she turned to answer, Luna was asleep.

Mark Wwlliams

Winnie's uncle, Mark Wwlliams, on his living room couch was watching "Loose Water in Zero-G: A Science Hour Analysis." He wore his Fuck OSU T-shirt, sweatpants resembling jeans, no socks.

"Watch this," said Victor Bickle in shallow hologram against Mark's entertainment wall. "There's no limit to how large a droplet of water can get if it's floating in the zero-gravity environment of a circuit vessel. Even a droplet this size can adhere to the circuit vessel's ceiling forever—but I wouldn't volunteer to stand under it . . ." A slimy body of CGIed water stretched down from the studio ceiling while Bickle gesticulated madly.

What a great weekend, Mark thought. A new episode of his favorite program; his floors freshly desiccated and smelling of warm laminate; and he was finally about to close on the Presidio Lot he had been pursuing for over a year. He ate a handful of low-cal peanuts, making a sucking noise as he brought them to his mouth. He belched. It felt good to be Mark Wwlliams.

Bickle discussed water pressure, shape, and surface tension. He dumped a gallon pail into the air, then scrambled with his bare hands to push the pieces of water into one another.

Mark was going to get that Presidio Lot; he could feel it. It'd been a hard six months (not his fault), but the Presidio Lot would put him back in black. And for the price! The seller was practically giving it away for fear that another once-in-a-lifetime rainy season would make the place a sinkhole, financial and otherwise. That's what made it once-in-a-lifetime, Mark thought. It's not gonna happen again!

Yeah, it'd been hard, but he'd withstood worse. He thought back on the worst week of his career. When he bought that disastrous advertising campaign. He had been twenty-three, back from Ann Arbor with his fit, whip-smart Alaskan girlfriend and a crisp bank loan. The market was hot. He wanted all the world, or at least the Bay Area, to know his name. Williams! Williams.

"The works," he had ordered from that budget marketing firm. They said within ten days of payment they could have him on billboards and Instagram ads (Oh, Instagram!). They'd even throw in business cards. THE REALEST NAME IN REAL ESTATE DEVELOPMENT: MARK WILLIAMS.

"It's gonna be incredible," he promised Carsie. She was starting her career at Wells Fargo and worked all the time; he was masturbating more than usual. "Thursday," he said, "when you commute to work, you'll find this sexy face on every other street corner, watching over you."

On Thursday he jumped out of bed like it was Christmas morning, rising almost as early as Carsie. She was applying her makeup; he dragged her downstairs. "Any packages for me?" he asked their doorman, whose name he never remembered. The box was full of business cards, so smooth, so strong. He slapped one in Carsie's hand. "Check it out."

As she read it, her beautiful face sank.

"What?" Mark asked, reading it himself. Oh no.

It did not say the realest name in real estate was Mark Williams.

He ran outside. Garbage trucks squealed. The homeless rattled past. His business cards slipped through his fingers—the fingers that had made the error that would define him evermore—and blew away as he looked up to see his face across the street like some gauche god, THE REALEST NAME IN REAL ESTATE DEVELOPMENT: MARK WWLLIAMS. He vomited.

So yeah. That had been kind of an identity crisis.

Bickle closed out his show on the topic of water cohesion. "The positive and negative charges of the hydrogen and oxygen atoms make water molecules clump together." He smiled at the great big blob twisting and flexing in midair before him. "So if someone spills on your next CWC flight, don't be alarmed. Just step around it. The spill will keep to itself," he said. "As long as *you* do, that is. But if you don't—" he smacked the water, sending silver droplets flying out toward the viewer "—I hope you've got a good jacket."

He shook the lapels of his famous anorak (which grew delightfully more baroque with every episode), and bits of water dispersed in a slow aquatic halo.

Mark sat through the credits (he liked the punk rock theme song), then went to the kitchen. The kids were sitting around the island. "Anyone order a sandwich for *me*?" he asked.

Juju said no. He chuckled and patted her on the shoulder.

Nat offered the other half of her sandwich. She sat with Winnie. Studying. Even though it was summer. There was something seriously wrong with those girls.

He asked if it was vegan.

"Yes, it's vegan," Winnie answered. "We're vegan."

"Yuck," he said. He plated leftover lasagna and two Pepto-Bismols. "Let me just say: I don't know what you girls have against my friend."

"What friend?"

Mark gave a provocateur's smile. "You know."

"He means Victor Bickle," said Winnie.

Juju said, "You don't know Victor Bickle."

"No," he said. "But we're kindred spirits. And he's from Mom's hometown. And Winnie's. Nat, did you know that?"

Nat said he might have mentioned it before.

"You mention it all the time," Winnie said, looking over her tablet. "CWC, by the way, is like the most evil company there is."

"Don't tell me you're becoming one of those day contraction loonies. Nat, are you to blame for this?" He asked Winnie what exactly was wrong with CWC.

"They're just really bad," Winnie said. "I can't explain all the ways. You need to read."

"You should watch *Science Hour*. Everyone's got their problems with the westward circuit, yet everyone's using it."

"I do watch *Science Hour*," said Nat. "I already saw the new episode."

"You did?"

"Yeah, and look what I made."

She put down her homework and pulled out her phone to show Mark a two-paneled holographic meme. The left panel showed Abubacar Bankole Momoh, the famous Sierra Leonean climate refugee who, shipwrecked and bereaved of his family, clung to a floating slab of carbon fiber siding for two weeks, surviving on granola bar crumbs from wrappers fished out of the North Atlantic Garbage Patch, until he washed up on the coast of Portugal, where for his tribulations and celebrity he was ceremoniously awarded honorary citizenship (which was similar to real citizenship except instead of conferring authorization to remain in the country, it conferred a nice copper medal with the word "Portugal"). The caption on Nat's image was Momoh's legendary line, which, with a look half dead, he had delivered to the crowd of reporters who met him at the beach, having anticipated him for several days after following his unlikely journey in news drones across the ocean, through tempests and soups of starless fog and turns of blazing sun, "Sierra Leone will not drown. Sierra Leone will fly!"

The hologram's right panel showed Victor Bickle. He stood in the aisle of a circuit vessel dumbly considering a floating mass of water. His caption read: "Why not both?"

"Oh my god," Mark started. "You girls have been completely brainwashed by Scroller and the *Washington Post* and—"

"Dad," said Juju, pulling out one earbud. "Stop shouting."

DAYS OF 23 HOURS
AND 45 MINUTES

I was reading the *Washington Post*, a mindless way to kill time, standing in the 118th floor's elevator lobby, when Miguel came up behind me. I turned to see him. It had been one year since the afternoon on the rooftop deck when I had asked if he and I might get a drink.

"What are you reading?" he asked.

"Nothing," I said.

He had changed out of his work clothes into a baby blue tee. He was smiling at me. He asked what was wrong.

"Nothing's wrong," I said.

He laughed. "You look like you're about to cry."

I put my phone away. "I'm just thinking about things."

"What are you thinking about?"

I was thinking about how much a year had changed. Facing him, I thought about that afternoon, a year ago, when we had gone together to a beer garden in Hackney Wick. We had talked about movies, split the bill. It had been easy. No one stared at us. It wasn't really a date, but it was fun. Afterward I texted him that I enjoyed it and asked would he want to do it again. The next time, we went to a dive near his apartment, and it was a date, and it was harder. He said it wasn't a gay bar, but there did seem to me to be a lot of gay people there. He asked me if I'd ever dated women, and I told him the truth, which was no, and then I gave a long explanation about how I had never been a person who felt very strong physical attractions, and he listened patiently as if I understood what I was talking about. Although maybe he believed what I was saying as much as I believed it myself. People *are* all different, and the best thing to do is usually just to accept their own self-representations, something more easily done when you're still the age that Miguel and I were then.

"So are you strictly gay, then?" he asked me. I told him I wasn't sure, but that that label seemed fine. He told me not to be so glum about it, and I laughed—an embarrassed laugh—and kept laughing to myself when I thought about that comment for the rest of the date.

When we left the bar it was incredibly foggy, and people around were all commenting on it; apparently it wasn't normal even for London, and Miguel said, "I can barely see the road," and I said, "I feel like I'm in heaven," and he said, "Because you're so happy to have gone on a date with me?" I said no, but blushed and couldn't think of much else to say as we waited for our rides. He felt bad, I think. After the date, while I sat around thinking about texting him, he texted me a funny fake of him putting his foot in his mouth. I did one of me gouging out my eyes.

In bed that night I cried to myself. Buried in my hotel pillows, I thought about my parents calling me on my first night in New York and about the fact that I could never go back to Alaska. I cried for the anger that I'd carried so long, whose vacated space inside my heart would now need to be filled with something new.

The next week Miguel and I went to the movies. It was one of those summer blockbusters about global calamity where the thrill is in seeing the shot of your own city destroyed. Throughout it, I noticed Miguel nodding along to the dialogue. That was just his way of engaging. I was nervous the whole time that I was supposed to put my hand on his, but before I figured out what the right moment would be, the movie ended. We went for another beer, and then he invited me to his place, a studio flat in Edmonton so small the fridge door hit the bed, and we kissed. Another beer and we kissed some more. After a while he asked to go down on me. I had never taken out my penis in another person's company before, and as soon as I showed it to him, I felt like my blood was being drained from every other inch of my body. He began without ceremony. It took me a minute just to overcome my shock at the fact that it was happening. I hunched over to massage his crotch above his corduroy pants, but it was awkward to reach, and he told me to please stop. I focused anxiously on the ceiling, and soon my erection was lost, though he kept trying for a while. The rest of the night was spent consoling him. The next morning, I awoke nervous but hard, and we succeeded.

When we'd been dating a month, Miguel asked me if I wanted to try fucking him. He was so tight I didn't think it would fit. I worried that our bodies just weren't compatible. "I don't think it will work," I said in the dark.

Miguel gave me conflicting instructions ("Just angle upward and aim lower"). He had a muscular, goose-pimpled body and a smaller penis. "It's okay," he pleaded. "Keep trying."

"No, no, it's not working," I said. But then it did. I came almost immediately from the stress, then fell back and let my gaze wash over a poster of a cat. INTERNET ES TU DIOS!

The first time Miguel put his finger in me, it was like surrendering all my bodily functions. The next day, I moved gingerly through the office, feeling as if my rectum were dangling down my pants. I liked carrying that secret. In the elevator, flexing and relaxing, I wondered what secrets my colleagues carried under their own business-casual costumes. Eventually, sex with Miguel became easier. I stopped taking fifteen minutes in the bathroom to furtively wash and get myself to semi before every time. Sometimes I came early. Sometimes Miguel said it hurt and we finished by hand. It was completely up to us.

Not everything in our first year together was perfect. Miguel drank too much, in my opinion. He spent too much. When we dined, he always wanted to hold on to my hand, leaving me only one free hand to trade between my fork and knife, which was nice but made it tough to actually eat. But, no, it was nice. I was his only support system, but he was happy. Deep down, he loved the world he lived in, and I had come to love that about him.

Our relationship gave Miguel extra confidence. He was promoted to Senior Department Coordinator. His emails became witty, often teasing Cromwell Grant, who called him his "loaf." The summer interns called him "Mom" and loitered around his desk while he was trying to work. When I showed up, they dispersed with deferential nods.

"Now, why do the interns like you so much more than me?" I asked.

"Because, *minou*, I'm uninhibited."

"And I'm inhibited?"

Miguel raised his eyebrows. He often took jabs like that at me. It actually cut me a little, but it wasn't a cut worth scratching in the week leading up to our anniversary. Private items added to my Outlook calendar daily reassured me of his love.

Monday: "Because you make my bed in the morning."

Tuesday: "Because you have the most adorable, terrible haircut."

Wednesday: "Nice belt/shoes match today!"

Thursday: "You must be the only person in the world who stirs your Pepsi."

Our anniversary was Friday, the start of a long weekend for the clock holiday, and we planned to go dancing, as on our first meeting, at Petra Dance Haus. I waited for him by the elevators, reading the news to kill time, and when he arrived, in his baby blue tee, I don't know, it just hit me. It happened like that now and then. A copy machine down the hall cleared its throat. I pushed for the elevator.

"No, I'm not thinking about anything serious," I told him. "I'm just happy to see you."

* * *

We ate a tipsy dinner at a small Deutsch-Westafrikanisch restaurant and talked about work. We'd only worked a half-day that day. Not until the past spring, when sunsets were supposed to come later yet had continued moving in the opposite direction, had it become clear that our work schedules were falling out of sync with the sun. Now 90 percent of British adults understood that day contraction was real (an overwhelming consensus for a place like the UK). The Ministry for National Labour Standards, following the American government's lead, guidelined a five-hour clock holiday for resynchronization, after which businesses could start scheduling their workdays at appropriate intervals (currently intervals of twenty-three hours and forty-five minutes) by referring to the IERS Clockulator app or the scheduling app of their choice.

"It's crazy how fast all those changes happened," I said.

"I know," Miguel agreed. We both felt the crisis of day contraction was being handled appropriately. We cheersed to one year. We were excited to dance.

Nothing had changed at good old Petra Dance Haus. They played the old kraut. I was as poor a dancer as ever. I pinballed off strangers while Miguel chased me, apologizing left and right.

"Ay, Dios, slow down, will you?"

I pulled him close. It was impossible to come to Petra and not feel the mangled train of nostalgia course through you, shrieking sidelong from the retrograde PAs, and the triggers were doubled by our own personal history, so when we kissed, I couldn't help but circle through memories: nights out with the 118th, peeling off early to watch reality shows in Miguel's bed, him falling asleep fifteen seconds in, rolling over only to mumble "descansa" (a ritual blessing I had at some point come to rely on), waking up and getting tacos delivered. I still held my room at the Hilton but basically used it as a $200-per-day gym membership expensed to the company. All my stuff was at Miguel's.

When my eyes opened, I caught him taking a photo of us. I snatched the phone. Then my own rang.

"Ah!" said Miguel, grabbing it. "The world-famous Professor Bickle."

"Miguel," said Bickle. "Where's Tanner? Has he heard from Grant this evening?"

I backed away from the camera, laughing. A green light swept over us every nine seconds and another every six. On intervals of eighteen, it blinded.

"Bickle, don't you ever take a holiday?" Miguel said.

"Holiday? What day is it?"

"The clock holiday and—more importantly—me and Tanner's anniversary."

"Oh, I'm sorry," said Bickle, suddenly self-conscious. He asked what the two of us were doing to celebrate and apologized again, and I reached over and hung up on him.

"Hey!" said Miguel. "That was unkind."

I smirked around my plastic straw. "Oopsies, perdóname."

We left the club just before dawn. Stepping out into the jarring calm of the empty industrial zone, our voices echoed off underpasses and unmarked façades. Miguel asked me to order more toothpaste to his flat. I stroked his back, tracing his shoulder blades, and tried to get myself excited mentally without inviting performance anxiety. I almost never thought of Alaska anymore. We walked along a stretch of preserved stone wall undergoing renovation.

"This the Berlin Wall?" Miguel asked.

"No," I said.

"Must be something, though. There's a big German flag on that crane there."

"There are always flags on cranes."

"Why?"

I looked up from my phone—there were at least six fully caffeinated sodas in me—and joked, "So other cranes don't mistake them for the enemy." Miguel threatened to google it. I told him I ordered the toothpaste. "It'll be there by the time we're home. But I got the kind I like. Crest 3D White."

He was reading a message on his phone.

"What?" I said. "Don't tell me I'm wrong about the cranes?"

He shook his head.

"What?"

He sighed. "Grant and Bickle want us in the office."

It was all triggered by *Science Hour*.

Science Hour was in production for its third season, and expectations were high. Bickle was a nervous wreck. Critics generally agreed that the first season was a classic in a league of its own, but season two's ratings had held up, with shining moments including Bickle's breakdown of mechanical versus magnetic springs for docking platforms (ep. 2), his stress test of contraccelerator safety (ep. 5), and his energetic discourse on the psychological science of a True Service Mentality (season finale). Midseason, he appeared as an industry expert on Fox News, which took a liking to him and invited him back. Three times he was called in to shoot the shit with the boys on *Fox & Friends*.

He explained to Mike Mordel, "People denigrate the westward circuit while their own lifestyles would collapse without it. I'm one of very few people with the integrity to come out here and acknowledge all of the incredible things the industry has accomplished . . ." At the bottom of the screen, sandibee10 from White Plains, NY, called #ProfessorBickle a piece of shit. The hosts booed her.

The flack certainly got under his skin. People on message boards calling him a corporate stooge and sharing deepfake videos of him performing fellatio on long steel circuit vessels. One particularly bad week, he told me he wanted to "find" the teenager who had posted that Professor Bickle was what happens "when an incel attains all the things he thought would get him laid and learns that the problem was his personality all along." I suggested he take some time off.

He said, "Oh, they'd love that."

"We could do something completely different for a while," I said. "Take a leave from CWC and have you talk about other things to buttress your brand."

"I don't even know what I would talk about."

"There are always stories of corrupt regulators that we can amplify. There was that toxic baby formula scandal with the Consumer Protection Office last week. I'm sure an outlet would have you on to talk about how formula gets processed, what arsenic does to the body, that sort of thing. People don't understand that stuff."

"Tanner," he said. "I'm not backing down."

So production ran on season three. The season of shipping: an episode on parcel sorting that took the viewer on a 3D roller-coaster ride of Europe's central freight conveyor belts; one on price-quote algorithms with insane Matrix-style graphics; one on delivery logistics in which viewers could bid in real-time to have giveaways delivered live to their doors.

All the while, Bickle forwarded me hate mail that he received—as if it vindicated him. The more I read, the more it left me confused. All these people, all angry. At us. It was during those months that I first sensed something nagging at me about my work, but I dismissed it as nothing more than generalized anxiety in an anxious time. I had entertainment and nights out with Miguel, Ambien to fall asleep and coffee to get working in the morning. I was productive. This is what it felt like to be successful, I told myself, as Miguel and I headed to the office on what was supposed to be our holiday and our anniversary.

"Docking-dammit." Cromwell Grant hammered his fist on his desktop, sending cracks fissuring outward. I flinched. The cracks preserved a satisfying symmetry and were accompanied by a Foley sound effect before dissolving away. "How was I not warned about this?"

Bickle said, "I've been talking about this for months."

"You told me people were angry, they're always angry," Grant said. "But *you*," addressing Noah, his pollster, "didn't tell me how many people would be receptive to *this* drivel."

Noah cleared his throat. "I don't think—"

"Shut up," said Grant.

Kiko Alexandra entered Grant's office and took a seat beside Fez. When the door opened, I heard people shouting in the hall. The sun was just rising out the window, and my thighs were itchy from dried sweat. Miguel was with the interns in a different meeting.

"This is a huge cock-up," said Grant. "Look at the Beeb!"

Research Triggers New Scrutiny of Westward Circuit's Role in Day Contraction

A.H. 987,084:23, BBC Studios, London – Released to coincide with the airing of the third season of the popular edutainment program, *Professor Bickle's Science Hour*, a new report published by the EurPSY lab, a joint project of six universities coordinated by the International Union of Geodesy and Geophysics, pins the blame for day contraction squarely on the westward circuit and forecasts that exponential growth rates in global commerce reliant on circuit aviation could lead to a day contraction factor of x2 within a decade. The three-hundred-page report and its accompanying video series simulate in graphic detail the implication of a significantly faster planet, looking beyond shortened days to the potential for a 'nightmare of centrifugal force'.

The report's authors predict tides shifting from polar to equatorial regions to form an oblate 'equatorial bulge'. They also warn of a more pronounced Coriolis Effect—by which weather systems along the equator are deflected, feeding cyclonic storm systems. This force, played out on aberrant quantities of water pooled at the equator, may explain recent upticks in hurricane incidence. Hurricanes are now expected to intensify further.

Already, the video series has received over three million views and led to calls for boycotts of relevant industries. EU Environmental commissioner Chin-Hwa Hatakruen responded on Scroller noncommittally, saying the claims connecting day contraction to westward circuit commerce need further evaluation.

The study's authors discussed the impact of their report with the BBC. Cao Chunlan of Fudan University said, 'the fact that our report is able to rival the industry's own messaging indicates a public appetite for conversations about issues that really matter.'

Serge Brazhensky of MIT commented, 'There's no question that all the discussion around *Science Hour* helped get our work trending. People are starting to recognize that *Science Hour* is just another industry disinformation and distraction campaign. Scientists agree that days are running fifteen minutes fast, and CWC wants us to admire the efficiency of their pricing algorithms? The first step is getting the truth out there, and that means, as far as I'm concerned, deplatforming denial artists like Victor Bickle. Then the hard work begins. Either we reform how the developed world does commerce, or we can expect rising sea levels and storms the likes of which you and I have never seen before.'

"'The likes of which,'" Kiko Alexandra scoffed. Grant flashed her a look.

"It's not all bad," said Fez. "There are lots of people making jokes about the report."

"Have you ever heard of a dog's breakfast?" Grant said, cracking his jaw. "The problem with a dog's breakfast isn't that the dog doesn't have enough bloody brekkie. It's that the dog is going to town on mountains of hard-shell tacos and spag bol on my white rug."

"It's *Science Hour* that provoked this," said Noah. "We're seeing a public sentiment backlash."

Bickle's ears went red. "It's this that's ruining *Science Hour*. I've been saying for months we need to combat these day contraction people head on. I'm getting killed out there." He picked at his mustache so hard it looked painful. There were too many chairs pulled into the office, and when anyone scooted, pamphlets crinkled beneath them. Fez and Kiko Alexandra talked over each other. I looked around. So much trash. Grant was listening to Kiko Alexandra. His pupils caught blue glare, intimating intraocular lens implants.

I said, "What if we let Victor take a little more balanced stance on CWC?"

Grant looked at me. "What do you mean?"

"I'm just thinking, maybe it would help to let people know their voices are heard. To indicate that CWC is open to dialogue. It would at least help you, Victor, with your own credibility—and I think your sanity too—but beyond that, it could be a good look for the company."

"Sure," Noah said. "Tell them we'll build that Eastward Circuit."

"Is that sarcastic?"

Grant said, "CWC's not building some widdershins new circuit incompatible with our existing infrastructure."

I said I wasn't suggesting that.

"They're the ones who aren't open to dialogue," said Bickle.

Grant ruled out anything at all that validated day contraction. Kiko Alexandra cursed the IERS for fucking with the clocks.

"I think I get what Tanner's saying," said Fez. "Maybe people just want to be heard. I mean, if we really have to give up the Bickle asset, we can—"

"What do you mean?" said Bickle.

Noah said, "They're calling for your cancellation."

"—But," said Fez, "we should first at least try to use Victor to defuse all this animosity. He doesn't even need to talk about day contraction if that's off-limits."

"Yes," I said, glad to accept her support. "There are tons of different issues upsetting people, and it's always put Victor in a tough spot to have to dismiss them all, like, categorically. I mean, look at these for example."

I pulled out my tablet and showed some messages criticizing the circuit for providing unequal access, a complaint that, in my opinion, had some merit (I myself knew what it was like to live cut off from the rest of the world). There was a reshared article about the capital of Liberia, so underserved that one's only chance of boarding a pod was to bribe your way in or risk assault sleeping in line. Several emails copy-pasted the story of a shopkeeper driven to suicide when the circuit line to his block got discontinued. A meme based on *Science Hour*'s "Loose Water" episode suggested that Bickle wanted a Sierra Leonean refugee—prohibited from flying—to drown.

"A lot of .edu email addresses," Kiko Alexandra noted.

Noah said, "These are just loud kids virtue-signaling. They're not looking for *dialogue* with *Bickle*." Growing frustrated I tried to explain the decency of a gesture, but Noah just trampled on. "This customer profile wants to keep ordering udon from Japan to their dorm rooms while they pretend to care about the less privileged. They'll criticize, but they'll never stop using the circuit. In fact, they criticize *instead* of acting. They don't threaten our business at all. You'll drive us crazy trying to appease them. I don't understand this idea."

E-cig rolling between forefinger and thumb, Grant was still reading the messages on my tablet. He hadn't yet opined. I looked to him for understanding.

He said, "They're just loud."

Noah said, "Exactly."

"They don't actually want anything," he said, but with less derision than curiosity.

Noah missed the distinction. "Nothing from us," he said. "They just want to shout."

"And there aren't many of them."

"They're not a big movement. We need to focus on real threats."

Grant looked up and said, "Or not."

"I'm sorry?"

"Why's a day contraction report a real threat?" Grant asked. "It's shite. It's made-up, isn't it? At least exaggerated." No one said anything. "Meanwhile, this other movement's not big, but why not? It could be a travesty, this issue of . . . Kiko, what would you name this issue that Tanner's love letters here are on about?"

He always called her just "Kiko" and she didn't correct him. Without missing a beat, she suggested the term "equity." She said it with a smile, in on some joke that still eluded me.

Grant laughed. "A lack of equity! Yes, we never talk about the fact that a near-monopoly like CWC can determine who has access to global markets and who hasn't. What if *that's* a travesty? Tanner?"

"Well, yeah," I said, still missing the point. "I'm not suggesting it's worse than day contraction, but that doesn't mean it's right to ignore it."

"They're not as big as the day contraction movement," Grant said. "But why not? Why not unleash them?"

Bickle and I looked at each other.

"Kids are louder than anyone," said Grant, his gears spinning, heavy and sharp, "and there's a trillion-dollar industry validating their concerns by putting out content they'll want to read. Whinge up a storm about inequity. It'll be all anyone can talk about."

Noah said, "Even if they were big, they still wouldn't be serious."

"Bang on. So they'll be big and loud and not serious, and we have nothing to fear."

"*I* have something to fear," said Bickle. "It's me they'll attack."

"Why would they attack you?" said Grant, looking not at Bickle but at me. "Why would they attack their advocate?"

I understood.

"We're not manufacturing an issue to distract people. Not at all," Grant said. "We're reinforcing Victor's credibility as a fair and independent voice with a new season three premiere, focused on the 'real issue' near and dear to the professor's far-flung Alaskan heart."

His eyes, full of blue light, darted around the office, looking more and more fiercely approving as he described his plan.

"If you're trying to make this go viral," Fez was telling Grant, "we can't promise to control it. You think there's nothing to fear, but you could be wrong. People could demand action."

"Action on inequity?" Grant said. "No, I don't think . . . Even comms can only move people so much." He had the look of a chess player who saw the endgame but didn't yet believe it, and as he brought his e-cig to his mouth, before the strawberry fog shrouded his face, I was sure I saw a flash of fire.

○

"Have you seen it yet?" Nat asked.

It was their first time hanging out since the release of the day contraction report. Winnie confessed she hadn't really been following the whole thing, though she had seen videos about day contraction trending on social media, generative renderings of storms and shifting tides that frightened her in a tingly, useless way.

"Yeah, the day contraction stuff too," said Nat. "But I'm talking about the new thing. Victor Bickle's special on circuit inequity."

She loaded it on Luna's tablet.

CIRCUITIZATION AND ITS DISCONTENTS: A SCIENCE HOUR ANALYSIS

It was only four minutes and got right to the point with footage bursting from the screen. Two barefoot, pot-bellied kids puddle-hopped in the shadow of an eclipsing circuit vessel. Victor Bickle walked through a bizarrely photogenic sub-Saharan slum.

"Though the westward circuit famously promised to connect everyone to a world of goods and services," he said, "the reality for many is that basic necessities remain out of reach. The circuit's visibility has only exacerbated many communities' feelings of being left behind."

Winnie stroked Bella the cat as she watched Bickle explain that circuit equity was the defining issue of their time. It was difficult, she found, to know how seriously to take what she was seeing. The night before, she had stayed up late, her circadian rhythm off, reading about the year's Nobel Prize in medicine, which had been awarded to the researchers who came up with a way to eat cyanide. All the articles she found left her with the same questions. They all contained the same sentences, as if copy-pasted. When she had stopped reading and turned out the lights, the sun was already rising.

"Winnie, this is the part!" Nat said.

". . . formerly thriving railroad hub," Victor Bickle was saying, "relegated to a food desert, and my own birthplace—"

Winnie perked up.

There it was: Keber Creek, Alaska. The camera traced an open effluent canal, rainbow slick. She tried to recognize the road he was on from her brief visit, but there were no distinguishing landmarks, just the mountains in the distance. There was something strange about the way Bickle moved through the landscape. The gravel didn't give under his feet. The dandelions didn't stir as he brushed past. Either he was a ghost, or the environment around him was.

"For some months now," Bickle said, "we've made sense of the modern world together. But the *Science Hour* team stands in solidarity too with those trapped in the past. With this special episode, we call on those with power to bring equity to the westward circuit."

In an insistent tone, Nat kept calling the report "explosive." When it was over, she said, "It's just crazy. First the day contraction pressure, and now this. Even CWC's advocates are turning against them. You gotta see what people are saying about it."

Luna joked that maybe Nat's memes had reached Bickle after all.

"The circuit is just another tool for the global rich to elevate themselves at real people's expense," Nat said. "There's gonna be a march tonight. SFPD is already planning to close the streets to contain it. We gotta go."

"Will it be safe?" Winnie asked.

Luna said, "Fuck it. I'm in."

"CWC's CEO is making a statement," Nat said. She sucked sour sugar off her fingers, then snatched one of Luna's tablets to open CNN Live.

"Look, I saw Professor Bickle's show at the same time that you all did." Short and weary, CWC CEO Trisha Pitafi swiveled her head as if keeping at bay a pack of invisible dogs. A news drone zipped past. "I know Victor, and I've always appreciated his work, so I'm not going to just dismiss it now. This company is committed to doing things right. I've authorized a review of CWC's policies, and you can expect to hear much more from us about circuit equity."

"Hear more? We want to *see* more," said Nat. "We want *action*."

At sundown they called an Uber to Union Square. Winnie sat in back, her window open to the warm breeze of ocean and urine. They'd read on Scroller to wear blue, so she wore a blue baseball cap taken from Luna's closet. Turning it backward, she appraised herself in the sideview mirror. She noticed a homeless boy feeding himself soup. Their eyes met, and he mouthed something about fucking. Startled, she turned to check if Nat or Luna had witnessed it, hoping they had and could validate. They hadn't. Winnie was relieved.

Out their own windows, they watched the crowds in awe.

Rather than sit through traffic, they got out early (without bothering to terminate their ride). There were many people now in blue, filming one another's cardboard signs and asking the way to Union Square. SFPD vehicles drove over sidewalk curbs; the motion was quietly shocking to Winnie, almost metaphysical. Cars clogged the intersection, laying on their horns.

In a mass of jaywalkers, someone said, "They can't hit all of us."

A Chinese couple asked Luna what the fuss was about, and while she explained, two boys in bandanas crashed a drone (trailing a banner, "ALL ABOARD MEANS *ALL* ABOARD") into a cop's windshield.

Nearing Union Square, foot traffic thickened. Growing tense, Winnie pulled Luna by the hand. The protest seemed to reverberate around the block, an atmosphere of zigzagging elements spun off from the center of gravity in search of food and bathrooms, while new bodies spiraled in. Things got so crowded they couldn't move. Kids ahead were talking about cutting through Macy's. The locked doors rattled. A middle-aged security guard inside, holding his camera up like a riot shield, shooed them, and they cut through the Dyson Experience instead. Nat took photos. "This is crazy." The store was mobbed, and employees tried to push people back into the street. A boy in front of Winnie snuck some handheld fans into his shirt.

Union Square, when they made it, was unrecognizable but for the palm trees dangling over the sea of heads, sloped northward like a wave poised to roll Winnie over. There was at least one person speaking through a megaphone deep in the square, but he couldn't be made out. Most people didn't seem to be there in protest at all. They just showed up because they heard it'd be a scene. Of those who held signs, a few decried day contraction, but they were outnumbered by those plastered with the catchy new slogans protesting inequity, and these were clearly favored by the news drones, which skimmed like blowflies, swarming around the most creative and expensive signs, grateful for fresh meat. The sun was gone now, and all the lights seemed huge.

Winnie tried to calm her mind, to just be there in solidarity, but looking at people's banners around her, she couldn't help noticing typos. There were *a lot* of typos. It shouldn't have mattered. This wasn't a literary festival. Why, in the company of so many people doing the right thing, were typos on her mind? She recalled a book from Nat, *Collective Action: The Power of Real People*: "The Devil has enough advocates." And yet, even while she knew enough to be ashamed of her inclination to critique the people around her, she couldn't shake the sense that she wasn't quite like them. That even if she was present with them in the only way that could possibly matter—that is, in body—she still didn't really belong.

Luna squeezed her hand. She shouted, "We should get closer."

"Closer to what?"

But Nat wanted to maneuver to the side. She seemed annoyed with Winnie and Luna for not keeping up. They followed her around the crowd's edge. Everyone was chanting, "All aboard means *all* aboard," but when Winnie tried, the words felt awkward in her mouth, and she believed everyone was listening to her. A streak of pot smoke, like a ghost seeking a vessel, passed through her. In the center of the plaza, a winged woman perched on an underlit pillar—lifting a trident and lowering a wreath, oxidized to the ferric bone. To be all bone and no flesh, Winnie meditated. Pure contact. The smell of drugs. The rattle and hiss of words sprayed through the air. Pure contact. So high and so alone.

This wasn't time to meditate. Nat finally stopped alongside a police barricade, where the air opened to three idling SUVs.

People were chanting "*ALL* aboard" but none of them nearby. Nearby, kids were heckling the police.

"Move your cars, they're in everyone's fucking way," said one girl. A policewoman three feet from her stared at the middle distance. Winnie traced the haphazard creases on the policewoman's face. She imagined with fear and envy how much it might hurt to make yourself so numb, until the officer turned to her and said, "What the fuck are you looking at?"

Someone lobbed an open red Gatorade bottle into the police ring. Winnie jumped, but her Nikes got sprayed. The cops moved toward their cars. People in the center of the plaza were starting to boo. Winnie couldn't tell if the panic she felt was just the vibe. The news drones understood first. They vaulted above the palm trees. Luna asked what was going on.

Dispersal orders from the mayor. The police were telling organizers to send everyone home. A knot in Winnie's stomach started to relax.

Luna joined the collective booing. The SUV grilles huffed hot air.

"Let's go," said Winnie, linking fingers with Luna.

"You want to leave?" Nat said.

They all jumped at the siren. But no one seemed to be leaving. More and more items were being launched at the state. Water bottles; crumpled signs; branded silicone phone wallets that a Samsung booth had been giving away to demonstrators before the crowd got too crazy. Someone tossed coins. Winnie didn't notice the cops leaving their cars and ducking under the barricade, breaching the crowd in teams of two, until the teenage boy to her left yelped and was seized. People shouted, "What the fuck are you doing?" Kids pulled out their cameras. They were being cuffed and dragged into custody. Winnie was struck by the profound realization something was happening that wasn't supposed to happen.

Luna asked Nat what to do. Nat said they weren't doing anything wrong.

Two officers wrestled a girl down behind her. People yelled and filmed.

Backpedaling, Winnie said, "I'm not a part of this," to no one. And when the cop pulled Luna's fingers out of hers, she flew.

The Leadership
of CWC

By the next afternoon, it was clear to CWC CEO Trisha Pitafi that Cromwell Grant's strategy had worked way too well.

"Trisha, this is outta control," said board chair John Sugar Jr. in his phlegmy Alabaman twang over a private company holocall. "Did you see the damage to Times Square?"

"I did four appearances today. I'm on top of it."

She was dressed up in modest LED earrings and an understated pink cape, riding alone in a stretch SUV to a gala in Ketton for the European Heart Association, whose board she joined after a heart attack took her husband. That was many years ago.

"Not appearances—action. They've got a hashtag: #AllAboard."

"I know that. Cromwell's people made the hashtag."

"Look at Scroller. Look at NewsStream. They're even taking over MateMe! Eighteen-year-old girls describing themselves as Fun, Frisky, Free-spirited and Circuits Should Be Accessible to All. Cromwell promised us this market will keep flying no matter how much they complain. That it'd just be a useful distraction. But they're boosting our competitors. Look . . ." A *Wall Street Journal* article appeared over his shoulder.

Pitafi gazed out the window. The English countryside was full of birds.

He said, "Leuxtrak and WDYGO Airlines are seeing share prices *rise*. Doesn't matter that they're only six or seven cities apiece. Talk about equity in access. Well, this plan is failing."

At that last sentence, offhand and under his breath, Pitafi tensed. Every corporate board has a culture, and CWC's was one of circumlocution. "Failing" was not said between board members. "Facing headwinds" maybe. "Proving more complex than anticipated" or even "underperforming" but not "failing." The last time a CWC operation was identified by the board as a "mistake" was the last day Pitafi's predecessor reported to work.

"I'll take care of it, okay?" Pitafi said. "But it's not going to happen overnight. We can't move as fast as the internet."

"CWC CEO asks for things to slow down . . ." said John Sugar Jr., shaking his head.

When Pitafi called Cromwell Grant, he was on his stationary bike in his little Peloton room—on every wall, a shallow holographic screen to make him feel like he was biking through the Alps. The room was a forty-fifth birthday gift to himself after his wife gave him a dumb relationship coupon book. First thing every morning, he biked a thirty-kilometer loop, zero radius, and on weekends, as long as work was proceeding smoothly, he hit the bike again in the afternoon.

"Your work is *not* proceeding smoothly," said Pitafi.

"Really?" Grant said between metered breaths. He looked sidelong at her while continuing to pedal. He had programmed his Peloton to project holocalls on the left wall, transplanting the caller's head onto the body of a cycling partner who would ride alongside him. He did this because it cracked him up. "I'm serious," said Pitafi with her head perched atop the aerodynamic body of a white, male Olympian. She pumped his thighs. Her head was rotated ninety degrees, like an owl's. It bounced up and down, but her LED earrings didn't swing. Grant found those earrings incredibly tacky.

"I hear you," he said. When he looked at her, she looked away. She had trouble with eye contact. This was—Grant noticed—a problem with many female executives. He and Pitafi biked around the outskirts of a small white and garnet village. Toward Albula Pass, where the old railway and telephone line cut through the mountain. The pines stirred. He took a deep breath. It smelled like his house.

Pitafi said, "Well, how do we undo this equity disaster?"

"Undo?" said Grant. "What in bloody hell are you talking about?"

"It's a catastrophe."

"Let's double down."

"Your brilliant strategy of deliberately burning ourselves has lit us on fire, and you want to double down?"

"Isn't it intuitive?"

"No."

"People are demanding action. So let's take action. Expand the circuit network. Give them their pod stations in Africa."

"Whom do you expect to pay for that?"

He said, "All and sundry."

"What do you mean, all and sundry?"

"The NGOs, the ministers of foreign aid. Isn't Lynn Mollenkompf a trustee at the European Development Fund? Make her earn her board fee. If we can get those quangocrats to cough up, we might even be quids in."

It took Pitafi a moment to understand. Grant toggled the settings on his handlebars, and her body changed to the callipygian jogging figure of Israeli actress Ayla Amsler in costume for some upcoming superhero flick Peloton was promoting. He slowed down to watch her run ahead of him. They came over the pass, elevation 2,312, and began to roll downhill. He sped up. So did she, pumping her arms and legs at inhuman speeds. Amsler's breasts bounced in Pitafi's face as they descended into quaint Bergün.

"I've been thinking about this," Grant said, breathing steady and strong. "Circuit inequity is a humanitarian issue, right? A crisis of international development? If CWC expands to regions that aren't immediately profitable, the deserts and jungles we've always neglected, then we should be eligible for humanitarian money. Political money."

Pitafi said, "Investors are going to balk at us expanding into the very regions we've identified as unprofitable."

"They won't be unprofitable if we're not paying. Tell customers to petition their MPs. Flood their offices with bumf for the international equity coalition, headed by us, funded by them. I mean, we'll chip in a tad, just for the optics."

"You're not talking about optics anymore. You're talking about redrawing the operational map."

She went on about provisioning, regulatory exposure, and geo-political risk, her head now flapping alongside him on the distended neck of a Swiss grebe. Cromwell Grant nodded. But he didn't need to listen. Communications, he understood, was no doddle. Communications was hell. He never forgot how vastly outnumbered he was against the hordes, never discounted the craftiness of their best or the cruel intransigence of their worst. They tried to slit his throat when they demanded CWC spend its money dismantling everything it had built. He spun around, let them cut him where *he* wanted, where he would scar and grow stronger. CWC would take a hit now (yes, his plan would cost the company money, he understood that), but by doing so it would keep growing bigger and harder. He pedaled up the switchbacks of Crasta Mora, hairpin after hairpin, jibe, tack, jibe, tack, back and forth, the only way to ascend. The sky was a cloudless blue on the ceiling overhead. Better than the real sky, frankly. On one wall, the mountain, the crumbling gneiss, the Pitafi-headed grebe; on the other, air. A thousand kilometers of Western Europe. Mountains like paintings. Villages like toys.

He wasn't nervous or ashamed by the way his plan was playing out, by his boss's anxieties or what the company's sinecural board might think. Instead, he was invigorated. Finally, the whole company would have to fall in line behind his department. No more comms on the outside, putting out the decision-makers' fires. Henceforth, let *them* coordinate responses. Let them figure out provisioning, pricing, operational cartography, as comms demanded! Those decision-makers, with their capex budgets and swot analyses, one day for this they would make him CEO. Who ever knew of a comms chief becoming CEO, but whoever did comms like Cromwell Grant? The battles ahead, whatever they were, would start and end with comms.

Filed A.H. 1,040,424:02   *GRA_00CWC109872*

CIRCUMGLOBAL WESTWARD CIRCUIT GROUP LIMITED
MEETING OF THE BOARD OF DIRECTORS
A.H. 987,504

A meeting of the Board of Directors was called to order on Monday, A.H. 987,504 at 612 Broadwick Street, London, UK. The following board members were present in person or by holographic videoconference:

 Trisha Pitafi

 John Sugar Jr.

 Stanley J. Gruthol

 Sanjay Friend

 K. Marjorie Gross-Withers

 Lynn Mollenkompf

 John Arthur Douglas Splud

being all of the directors and constituting a quorum of the Board.

Attending the meeting as guests of the Board were:

 Susana Feng (secretary)

 Cromwell Grant (present only for strategic discussion as noted
  below)

John Sugar Jr., Chair of the Board, acted as Chair of the meeting, and Susana Feng acted as Secretary for the meeting. The Chair announced that proper notice having been given and there being a quorum present, the meeting would proceed with the conduct of business. The minutes of the following meetings were submitted before the Board for examination:

Board of Directors Minutes:
A.H. 987,044

Compensation Committee:
A.H. 987,020

Nominating Committee:
A.H. 987,025

The Board approved the minutes as presented and ordered that they be placed in the Minute Book of the Company.

The Board discussed recent public perception negativity facing the Company. Trisha Pitafi suggested tabling this discussion until Cromwell Grant's arrival later in the meeting.

Trisha Pitafi, Chief Executive Officer of the Company, presented quarterly financial results.

The Board discussed significant accounts payable to vendors for infrastructure projects. These projects include the construction of docking pod lots and docking pod stations ("docking sites") as well as the construction of ground transportation systems to integrate new docking sites into existing roadways, per municipal leasing agreements. Ms. Pitafi discussed Management's progress on bringing construction capacity in house. The Board reviewed draft agreements for the Company to acquire Turner Construction and Hampshire Engineering Group.

The Board reviewed the combined portfolio of the Company's financial arms, CWC Capital and the Circuit Forwards Fund, as of A.H. 986,832. The Board also reviewed liquidity projections and covenant compliance.

Cromwell Grant joined the meeting as a guest of the Board to present a communications-driven strategic initiative. The Board discussed this initiative. Ms. Pitafi lent Management's support to the initiative. Discussion lasted approximately three hours. The Board thanked Mr. Grant, and he left the meeting.

Upon motion duly made and seconded, the Board approved the following resolution:

RESOLVED, that all actions taken by the officers, directors, and agents of the Company in furtherance of the operations of the Company as discussed in the meeting are approved.

There being no further business to come before the Board, the meeting was, upon the vote of the directors, adjourned.

_____

Susana Feng, Secretary

DAYS OF 22 HOURS

It was during the breakneck campaign in the months that followed—the "equity push," as it came to be known—that I first began to feel ambivalent about my job. I was tired all the time in those months. I got home from work after eleven-, twelve-, or even thirteen-hour workdays and checked my company clockulator app to see how many hours until I was expected at the office again. The time we lost as solar days fell to twenty-three hours and then rapidly to twenty-two came strictly out of our own evenings (the department promised we'd get extra PTO once the equity push succeeded). I took twice the recommended dosage of Ambien to make the most of the five or six hours I had left for sleep, but they didn't always work, sometimes leaving me exhausted but restless and confused, my brain spinning in the dark, too fast to touch. I'd stay over at Miguel's and lie awake, almost feverish, rubbing his shaved head. On Sunday nights, I usually tried to give my mind a break from sleeping pills. I took to bed early. I blared white noise to drown out my thoughts. My thoughts were always about work.

On the one hand, I knew that I was supposed to consider myself lucky to be working on something so impactful. And the truth is, I was just doing what people wanted. Support was pouring in for equity-minded government programs and charitable foundations (including CWC's own philanthropic "Forwards Foundation")—initiatives that contracted blue-chip circuit carriers like CWC to launch new vessels and construct new docking sites for long-underserved communities. I was working hard because people counted on me. But what if the cost of our work really was day contraction?

As Miguel slept, I would look out at all the new blue lights insurging on the winter stars. Wouldn't I have wanted a pod station in Keber Creek when I was growing up?

Miguel nudged me.

I turned down the white noise in my earbuds.

It was A.H. 990,582:10, eighty minutes till my alarm. The room was warm. Robins and sirens trilled outside. Circuit vessels popped. Miguel said I'd been rubbing my foot against his in the same spot for half an hour.

"Is that how long you've been up?"

"I couldn't sleep," he said.

I recalled my first time falling asleep beside him, how much I'd disliked surrendering control of my body in another's presence. "Me neither."

We went out for a walk. There was a grassy hillside near his flat that overlooked the William Girling Reservoir. We made a lap, then sat on the damp ground, facing east, toward sunrise.

"I'm so tired," I said. "I don't think I can go into the office."

Miguel gently shushed me, laying his head on my lap. I retracted my arms into my jacket and felt goosepimples down my ribs. Behind us, the highway rumbled. Contrails materialized in the twilight. In the coming year, CWC's capacity was projected to double. Out on the reservoir floated a solitary pontoon on which a Thames Water Utilities employee stood like a gondolier, trolling his long-handled net, fishing for cans and tablet bags. Eddies trailed. Across the reservoir a graffitied garage stood stiff and achy, its chimneys puffing white steam like a man working through the morning's first cigarette.

"Could you give me neck rubs, minou?" Miguel said, and I thumbed his nape, trying not to talk, to just enjoy the air, the water, the grass, the dew, our touch.

"Miguel," I said. "Do you think the westward circuit really is responsible for day contraction?"

He frowned. "Haven't we had this conversation already?"

"I guess," I said, wishing I could play my distress for some kind of joke. "But not really. Like, not directly."

Miguel thought. His nape was soft where he shaved it each night, smooth, dry, and cold in the autumn air.

"Yes, there is day contraction," he said. "I mean, everyone knows that. But is it caused by the circuit? No. I don't think so."

"How do you know?"

"Neither of us knows. That's why it's being studied. I don't think it's helpful to pretend that you know better."

"Why did CWC's leadership deny for so long that days were getting shorter?"

He shrugged and said, "In my opinion, some of them are liars. But they've stopped. And now they're funding research into day contraction's causes. I mean, you know that."

The reservoir gurgled for a moment, then settled.

"I guess," I said.

I thought about my nervous first day at CWC. I imagined Miguel's. He had told me he came to his interview from his parents' house, wearing his dad's old suit, looking like a fifty-year-old straight man. He told me how proud his parents were when he got the job, and when I thought about that, I felt inadequate as a boyfriend. He returned his head to my lap. The stratus clouds turned pinkish, drawing day from the depths, and the horizon seeped with red. It was a red purer than the petals of a red amaryllis or the juice of a raspberry or the plumage of a male cardinal. Prismatic-light-filtered-through-English-particulate red. R255, G and B zero.

"It's beautiful, no?" said Miguel.

Like a tear in the sky's curtain came the sun. Its warmth hit my cheeks and chest. *If you've seen a sunrise*, I thought, *how could you ever be depressed in this world?*

And then I thought, *How could you ever do anything to hurt it?*

The sun traveled with frightening haste. In moments, it was fully airborne and the smell of dewy grass had lost its mystery.

"Te amo, Miguel," I said.

"I love you too, minou."

○

Getting arrested shocked Nat and Luna, and it changed them. It altered them each in their own way and to a greater degree than Winnie, who had managed to escape the police, could fully understand, though she tried. She watched as her friends' impending court date sapped their enthusiasm for being the weirdo smart girls at their school, girls who'd always flaunted their contempt for cafeteria power structures because they'd soon be off to Stanford or Berkeley. Legal recriminations, groundings from their parents, and disapproval from teachers whom they'd planned to ask for college recs did not fit their self-image. They had always been good girls, and so they were humiliated. Nat especially.

"I just feel," Nat said, looking out over the cafeteria, "like there's been an injustice. Like it's not supposed to be us in this situation."

Luna quietly ate salad.

"It really sucks," said Winnie. "I know."

"And you're not the one with a court hearing coming up."

"I know. I got lucky," said Winnie. She felt stupid for saying anything at all. She had decided that she wished she'd been arrested with her friends, but such a decision was meaningless, and she knew not to mention it. In after-school hangouts she was relegated to the sidelines while her friends read legal advice columns. Everything Winnie looked up was, for one reason or another, wrong.

Nat said she'd try to get her family's lawyer to defend Luna too, since Luna's own parents were no help. Luna had initially tried not to tell them, which made things worse; they learned from a coworker at the funeral home who saw Luna's name in the police blotter alongside the obituaries. She said that when they found out, they cried. Her case was more precarious than Nat's because of her alleged altercation with an officer after Winnie fled. The affidavit of arrest said Luna had "physically swung a blunt object" (*her phone?* the girls wondered). So in addition to the rioting charge thrown categorically at everyone booked that evening, Luna was accused of "battery on a peace official," a misdemeanor in the blue but indebted state of California, carrying a maximum fine of $2,000 and requiring disclosure on all college applications.

As their court date approached, they withdrew from the activities that, as a group, they used to relish. They no longer wanted to film a morning announcement to advertise the Rotary club, even though all summer they had been excited about it (they had planned a dance to the tune of "Deadibodi" by Fat Rasher). And neither Nat nor Luna showed up to the Rotary club's sorbet sale, leaving Winnie to oversee three sophomores on her own. She wasn't supposed to let them serve their friends free, since that was essentially stealing from the food shelter, but saying this more than once made her feel bitchy. Afterward, she texted her friends. It was a longer message than she intended, one of those where you don't realize until you hit send and see it in the channel, and she was embarrassed later that night when her friends didn't respond.

A week before the hearing, Nat's family decided against paying their lawyer to defend Luna.

"She doesn't want her case tied to mine," Luna told Winnie.

It was the first time in a while that Luna had been allowed to come over after school, and they sat together on Winnie's bed. Their homework was on the floor. California's schools had been letting out an hour early every day in an effort to make the teachers budget stretch through all the new days in each school year. As days kept getting shorter, a fifteenth week had been tacked onto the fall semester.

Winnie recalled descriptions of circuit vessels as ants running around a floating log, spinning the log backward beneath them. It hadn't made sense until she pictured layers and layers of ants, millions of them, all running in the same direction.

"Nat doesn't want your case tied to hers?" Winnie said. "That doesn't sound like Nat."

"Or her parents don't, or their 'counsel'—what's the difference?"

"Maybe Nat can still talk to them," said Winnie. She knew that Nat didn't get along with her parents. She wanted to believe filial strain was something she and Nat had in common, though Nat always avoided going into detail.

Luna said, "We shouldn't have stood right next to the fucking cops."

Winnie agreed.

"I was trying to help *her*," said Luna. "I flailed when they grabbed her. I know it was stupid, but that was my instinct. I don't know *why* it was, but."

Winnie said she didn't do anything wrong.

"I won't make that mistake again."

They listened to an album of Luna's choice by Delia Derbyshire. Winnie found it pretty slow and unpleasant. Every third song was interrupted by an ad for plastic bins designed to stack extremely fast "so you can get on with your life." They talked about nothing for a bit—sparkling water brands and finals—and discussed reducing Rotary meetings to every other week. Winnie added sticks of Juicy Fruit to the tough, briny wad in her mouth. Luna picked up the pack, considered it, then put it down.

"You heard there's a hurricane coming?" Luna said.

"Here?" asked Winnie.

"Could hit here."

"Maybe it'll destroy the courthouse," Winnie joked, but Luna didn't laugh.

When the album ended, Luna went home to eat dinner with her parents. Not wanting to eat with the Wwlliamses, Winnie walked to a ramen shop on Irving. She took a seat at the window counter and ordered the spicy shroom, which she ate in shallow spoonfuls, letting the steam fog her glasses. She thought about texting her friends, but the last text in their group channel was still her own. The ramen shop played old pop songs. Winnie thumbed her nose piercing and tried to think, but no thoughts really came to mind. She feared that even when this hearing blew over, her friend group wouldn't be the same. Outside, the trees rustled and let go of their leaves, and delivery people swatted them away as they dashed up the hill on scooters. It was a beautiful night, and it took Winnie a long time to realize that the pain she would feel if her friend group fell apart was heartbreak.

SENT A.H. 990,598:31 Hey - Just wrapped up the sorbet sale. Made almost 70. I missed you guys there!! It's okay. I know this has been a difficult few weeks, so I just wanted to say. I love you. You two are my family and I literally don't know where I'd be without you. Whatever anyone says, you are the smartest, funniest, most compassionate women I know and you don't deserve any of this bull shit! This weekend let's watch a movie or something at my place. ♥♥♥ please don't let this bring you down. I love you both so much.

Nat

Nat didn't know how to respond to that. She too had never had real friends before. She was reminding herself of this now. Should everything fall apart, she could survive on her own.

Alone in her room, she dug a box of clothes out from beneath her bed. Clothes from her old school. No, she hadn't always worn a livestock tag. At Juleaut Prep, when she was friendless, she'd wear anything to fit in. Thin gold anklets. Tennis skirts. Golf gloves, though no one played golf anymore. It was that kind of private school, in those particular years, the A.H. 950,000s. She begged her parents to let her transfer, and all those appurtenances got packed up and stowed until now, five days before her hearing. On the advice of her family's lawyer, she was choosing something tasteful to wear to court.

She found a diamond stud earring and tried it on in the mirror. Unable to tell if it looked good, she took a picture with her phone and sat down on her unmade bed to examine it. Luna probably wouldn't wear anything nice to court. Nat was annoyed that Luna was so mad at her. Sometimes Nat felt that Luna just wanted to resent her in order to justify her envy. Nat's therapist said Nat was too afraid of other people's envy. She said "envy paranoia" handicapped Nat at her old school. She was an Indian therapist, chosen by Nat's parents, and she didn't seem to understand Nat very well. Take, for example, the time Nat tried to explain why she felt more at home at her friends' houses than her own. "It's because I grew up in my home," she said, "so I don't feel I did anything to deserve to be there." In return her therapist said imposter syndrome is something all teens struggle with. As if Nat were no different from other teens! Nat just smiled back. It was fucking awkward. She wasn't going to spell out to Dr. TJ Maxxinista what it was like to sit in freshman world history and know that you're a centimillionaire. Or at least Nat was pretty sure she was. She wasn't a *billionaire*. Her family wasn't ranked by Forbes, but Forbes wrote about her dad once. The journalist said her dad was known by the workers of his Indian factories as the Pigeon. "He flies in, shits on everyone, and flies away." Some weeks after she read that, her dad at dinner complained about the Congress Party's tariffs, which at twelve Nat didn't understand, and she replied, "Okay, Pigeon," just to see how it felt. It didn't feel good. Her mom sent her to her room.

For her mom, she had little respect. Nat didn't see how you could let yourself be married off at seventeen without claiming any say in the matter, then carried to the other side of the world and busied with housework and flutter philanthropy like a toddler given a tablet to stop crying at the dinner table. Nat was seventeen now herself, and she would never. Her mom embarrassed her. She ignored her mom, and her mom just took it, which made it even more pathetic. Once or twice a year, for the past few years, they had a blowup—her mom going berserk at Nat out of nowhere for backtalking or for the grave crime of leaving a dish in the sink; she'd cry and call Nat an ungrateful little bitch, and Nat's father would have to step in, exasperated, and tell Nat to apologize.

She didn't discuss this with her friends for fear they wouldn't understand. She knew things were different for her. Because of the money. Plus, when it came to Winnie, you know, at least Nat *had* parents.

But she wasn't a *billionaire*. Her parents worried about tariffs, whereas a billionaire must (Nat imagined) be limitless and walk the streets pondering how profoundly strange it is that all her transactions are pretend because everything a billionaire wants might as well be free. Nat's family was merely a sharp weight on the fabric of society, but a billionaire, she thought, a billionaire tears through.

She blamed her parents for her inability to fit in. For her being the sort of person who got scared at the protest for equity. She supported the cause, but then in that crowd, her throat had narrowed. She couldn't help thinking how easy it would be for someone to shoot the whole place up. Or grope her. She had grown annoyed with Winnie and Luna for dragging when she tried to lead them toward an opening where they could breathe, which, yes, she'd known was a fence-off by the police.

Her parents' lawyer said any reasonable judge would throw her case out, and he said the assigned judge seemed perfectly reasonable.

Did that mean he'd be reasonable with Luna, too?

Nat wanted to ask the lawyer what he thought would happen with Luna's case, but her parents were always around, and the lawyer's time had already cost more than the maximum fine anyway, so her dad was all annoyed. Nat imagined the bill ticking up. Ten dollars per minute. Twenty dollars every time her mom asked the lawyer to reassure her that "expungement" meant the incident wouldn't affect college apps. The whole ordeal was ridiculous. And now a hurricane was coming too, threatening to delay everything. Nat should have been focusing on school, not these distractions. In the mirror, she unlatched her earrings, hating how much they made her look like her mom, and laid them by her clothes for Friday, wondering what Luna would say when she saw Nat dressed up, and hearing her mother, when the lawyer advised them against taking on Luna's case, warning Nat in a frail voice to beware bad influences.

DAYS OF 20 HOURS

The hurricane was now pummeling San Francisco. We watched the TV in horror, me and the Fighting 118th, in a tiki bar on the other side of the Pacific Ocean. Eventually I had to look away. Enough of a tempest swirled in my own head. Though I hadn't heard about the hurricane until a couple of hours earlier, this end to the night seemed inevitable, almost satisfying in its aptness. It was the kind of night that could only end in tragedy.

The plan had been a good old-fashioned 118th progressive bacchanalia. A Let-One-Thing-Lead-To-Another. A world crawl. It had been a while since Miguel and I had hung out with Kiko Alexandra, Fez, Noah, and Imani. I never believed the 118th was the healthiest support group. But lately Miguel had begun saying how much he missed their wild nights outs, nights that ended in vomit and confusion. At one point he remarked cuttingly that it'd been a long time since he and I had had a night of "just fun."

So that Thursday evening we all met by the elevators. Most of us had the next day off (we'd been pulling ten-plus-hour workdays with only ten hours' rest in between, so we were starting to get some extra three-day weekends). Waiting for Miguel, I made small talk with Imani, the oldest and sloppiest member of the gang, but also, it did seem to me, the most well-meaning. We talked about her transfer to a position with CWC's Forwards Foundation. Every time one of us stepped too close to the office door, the lock clicked, and the little gulping noise made me think of the urethral latch (if latch was the right word) that switches you from peeing to cumming. The wall across from the elevator used to say "CWC: MOVING THE WORLD!" but it had been painted over for obvious reasons.

Finally Miguel arrived. Everyone acted very excited that he was joining. He looked good. He stood by me, affectionately rubbing my back. No—he was smoothing my shirt.

Imani called across the circuit vessel aisle, "Where we starting?"

Kiko Alexandra and Fez owned the itinerary. The whole night would be an exploratory expedition for their new travel & lifestyle brand, one of a thousand online ventures popping up adjacent to the circuit's equity expansion. *Roads Less Travelled* published Scroller videos about hidden gems the two of them discovered in unspoiled corners of the world newly connected to the westward circuit.

"Plintontown, Missouri, USA!" said Kiko Alexandra. She pulled teeny jean skirts out of her Hermès bag and tossed them across the aisle, where they drifted until snatched by Fez and Imani. She had a devious look in her bright brown eyes. "We're going to a barn dance!"

Fields Barn was picture perfect. Red with white trim, gambrel roof, Xs on the doors. Cars lined the access road. The whole community was there, an all-out hoedown. We arrived as the sunset we'd chased from Europe sunk into the hills, releasing a cool breeze of gravel, tractor, rawhide, dried-up leaves, and hints of honey. It turned the clouds pink and moved along. The sun had places to be. It'd come back around and set again in twenty hours.

While the three women changed into their jean skirts (which Kiko Alexandra insisted on calling their "jirts"), Noah, Miguel, and I made nice with the widowed volunteers at the hooch table. They had a big groaning contraption that took white powder and spat out a cocktail

redder than the Solo cup it was served in. Noah took a sip and coughed.
The widows slapped their knees.

"That's strong," Miguel said, eyes watering, "but good."

"All yours, babe," I said.

A new song started to much jubilation, some electric fingerpicking
throwback I had never heard before. People jumped up from their pic-
nic benches, dropped corndogs still rotating on motorized sticks, and
rushed the dance floor in a river of plaid. They formed a big circle of
couples—couples of all ages: kids interlocking arms with their school
crushes, grandfathers dragged out by little girls. Miguel knocked back
both our drinks and grabbed me. We joined the circle as if stepping
onto a moving carousel.

To this day, I have not seen a cultural spectacle like the ordered
disorder of that round-dance. A leading couple claimed the center to
perform the most rhythmless, unpredictable, downright inimitable
routine they could improvise, and everyone else tried to follow, all
while running in a big circle—or jumping out of the way lest they
get mowed over like October corn. Helpless partners were swung
'round and 'round, and 'round again for good measure. Hats flew off.
Boots flew off and pants ripped. I tried following Miguel's lead, but
after those widows' brews, Miguel was wanting for balance himself.
The first song gave way to a second, even faster and more vicious,
like a player piano stuffed with electric banjos. By the third song, the
cascade of notes was sheer chaos. I would have suspected that the
music file was corrupted were it not for the regular *woos* belted by
the crowd in perfect unison at some imperceptible cue. A pigtailed
girl collapsed, but I swung by too fast to help. I stepped on a motorized corndog wheeling itself in circles. The Missourians whooped.
I shouted to Miguel.

"Wha?"

"Fresh air," I said, and he let me go.

Alone outside I felt better. The moon was three-quarters full above
the fields, and the stars were brighter than any I'd seen in a long time.

They reminded me of home. I looked up at the sky, feeling so close yet infinitely far below. *Tired.* The music faded into the sounds of sprinklers and wind and all the county's crickets having one big conversation across manmade miles of monocropped corn.

I'm working seventy-hour weeks, and the weeks keep getting shorter. I looked back at the barn, and I wondered (a question that had been troubling me more and more lately) was this really the work I should be doing? Almost every night before bed I was seeing posts about the cost of day contraction adaptations, about erratic weather, crossfires of political finger-pointing and record bonuses. *What if all my work was just causing harm?* I understood that the question of day contraction's causes was still being studied, but the evidence I saw made me terrified.

Earlier in the week, alone in Miguel's bathroom, I had tried to pray, like I used to when I was little, just to see if it would still feel like anything. I asked for clarity of purpose. But when I heard my prayer aloud, I felt embarrassed, as if I were merely talking to myself.

Imani laughed. I turned to see her tugging at her skirt. "I can't believe I'm wearing this."

She was a head shorter than me, even with her hair up, pulled so tight that it was as if she were trying to stretch the creases from her brow. That tension seemed to strain through her whole form, her upright back, her heavy hips, the way she tensed her wrist so that her bracelets wouldn't clink. The tension of her life and her age pulling apart.

"You and Miguel are the cutest," she said. "I get so happy watching the two of you."

Soon enough, the rest of the 118th rollicked out. Miguel came over and kissed me with such abruptness that I flinched. He put a cowboy hat on my head. "I was in the middle," he said.

"Hey," said Kiko Alexandra. She'd wandered a few yards off. "Look at these animals."

Some twenty creatures, shin-high, chattered in the middle of the gravel road. They looked like rodents in the dark, standing bipedally but hunched, with long tails.

Imani asked what they were.

"They're birds," said a voice. A coach light switched on, illuminating the birds' brilliant green plumage. "Resplendent quetzals, they call 'em." The speaker came up alongside us. She had boots, belly, belt buckle, and a big white hat.

"They're beautiful," said Kiko Alexandra.

"No, they ain't," said the woman. One came strutting toward her, and she kicked at it. It squawked, extending its majestic wings. The other birds mulled around in the gravel, stepping on one another's tails. "These quetzals are a goddamn infestation."

I sensed Miguel breathing close to me.

"They look tropical," said Kiko Alexandra, filming for *Roads Less Travelled*.

"They oughta be in Central America. But they migrate along magnetic waves, and the Earth's magnet-sphere being strung out to all hell by this all 'day contraction,' they showed up here one week, what unshapely beasts. They swarm above the farm, shitting on trucks and driving the horses skittish, and then they gather here lookin' for scraps."

"They don't know where they are?" Miguel asked.

"Nah, they don't know diddly shit, just another animal that can't keep its head. Like them turtles they say follow the magnet-sphere too far south and starve, or them arctic lemmings you see on Scroller, going mad in the snow."

She kicked at the birds, and they dispersed only briefly, flying a few feet off the ground before settling, like the dirt, back into their bevy.

"What happens," asked Noah, "when a circuit vessel crosses a hurricane?"

"It just deflects its orbit, a little jet to the side, and then back. Why?"

He flung his phone across the aisle. Behind him, the vessel's windowvision screen said WRITE YOUR REPRESENTATIVE—TELL 'EM WE WANT EQUITY NOW.

"This looks like it's going to be bad," said Imani, reading the weather reports from California.

Miguel leaned over to me. He whispered, "Why aren't you having fun?"

Fez and Kiko Alexandra had refused sockets, preferring instead to "surf" the aisle. They flipped upside down, legs flutter-kicking to the ceiling in their skirts. Their matching ponytails explored the space with wills of their own. I tried to ignore them.

"What do you mean?" I said.

Miguel said, "You seem irritated."

"I'm just tired."

"Phones away," said Kiko Alexandra, making one last somersault. "This is us."

We landed in the mountains and stepped out of our pod into a blaze of sunlight.

"Kuzu zangpo," Kiko Alexandra said with arms outstretched. "Welcome to Bhutan."

It was midafternoon. Local people ambled up and down the village streets carrying briefcases or resting their hands in the folds of long work robes. A few played on antique-looking tablets. Little pharmacies and royal government depots were open, with tattered Buddhist flags strung up over doorways, and an obsolete clocktower at the center of town chimed pleasantly through the valley. A terraced hillside sparkled with sporadic lights—the sun glinting off solar-paneled hats worn by paddy farmers who used the energy to power their portable rototillers. It was a breezy twelve degrees Celsius, monks lazed about the village square, and the nation's children were tucked away in school. Kiko Alexandra bounded past a community bank, running her hand across a row of prayer wheels in a niche along the wall, drawing a wake of disinterested glances.

I squinted at the sun, overcome with the urge to go to bed. My eyes were adjusting as we approached a whitewashed brick home where Kiko Alexandra promised "the best fucking *ema datshi* you ever tasted."

Courtesy of Roads Less Travelled:
Ema datshi, or 'chili cheese,' may sound folksy—a simple stew of chili peppers and local yak's milk curd—but like the Bhutanese Buddhists who eat it, its charm belies a violence within. Really good ema datshi is a civil war of flavor, waged between the repressive fat of the cheese and the insurgent fire of the chilis, much like the bloody civil wars fought between rival Buddhist factions pre-A.H. that devastated Bhutan and left the region's economy crippled to this day.

I find that the best ema datshi is at Wangmo's house on Zheki Lam. Wangmo is the most hospitable little woman east of the Wang Chhu (beware her inspiring lectures on the meaning of life and reincarnation!), and her kids are adorable. Her daughter Dorji's bedroom is the most authentic place for selfies. It's a cute pink nook lined with paper dolls, and the way the sunlight pours into the valley through the thin Himalayan air creates these golden prisms from every window that come out stunning with almost no filter.

Wangmo was outside when we arrived, hanging laundry over a slumping telephone line, but she dropped everything and welcomed us in. Her house was cluttered with cultural paraphernalia—lotus flowers painted on the walls, endless knots woven into cupboard screen doors, curtain-skirts on the doorways, and glossy images of the sixth *Druk Gyalpo* king pinned to every wooden pillar. Weeds shot up through cracks in the concrete floor and were left undisturbed out of either reverence or neglect.

The 118th immediately began to drain her alcohol. "Please, please," she encouraged, filling our ceramic cups with hot liquid from the kettle. It looked like water, but when she passed over the line with a Zippo lighter, it caught fire like gasoline. Each flame got smothered under a ladleful of scrambled eggs. *Ara*, she called it. I had a sip. It was poison.

"This is really authentic," said Kiko Alexandra. She gestured and asked, "What kind of eggs?" and was pleased when our host pointed out a chicken dashing across the kitchen floor.

(Though later, when everyone else was drinking, I saw her push a carton of Egg Beaters behind her spice pot. She gave me a conspiratorial smile, her teeth red from chewing betel nut.)

Wangmo actually spoke fluent English, though it took a few rounds of *ara* to loosen her tongue. She didn't get really chatty until round four. That's when she began her unsolicited lecture on Buddhist rebirth.

"You," she said, "are in cycle of un-aimful drifting, wandering, or very plain things. You do not know how your paths bend in the wheel of samsara or dharmachakra. These are the wheels turned by the Buddha in the turning of the wheels whereby he escaped the cycle of plain things." Her own prayer wheel spun hypnotically while she refilled my companions' cups. "Outside the cycle of rebirth and re-death lies great beauty, whereas the cycle keeps you like all plain things, portly and lame."

She went on in this manner, denouncing plainness, exalting god knows what, until her wasted guests sat on the verge of a metempsychotic breakdown, and then Kiko Alexandra implored as politely as possible, "Wangmo, how about that chili and cheese?"

"No more," Wangmo announced, giving her prayer wheel a hearty spin.

Kiko Alexandra asked what she meant.

She said, "You people keep coming here asking for the chili and cheese. We not had chilis for many, many weeks. Bad year for chilis. Too humid in the mountains. Isn't that funny? The valley is very dry this year, and the mountain very wet. We say 'chap phar kah chap jil pa chu kha ray,' the rain falls yonder, but the drops strike here."

"You must have some chilis, Wangmo," said Kiko Alexandra.

"Nope."

"No backup chilis? No dried chilis for winter?"

"No, Miss Kiko. This winter with our yak milk, we just gonna eat Honey Nut Cheerios."

Staggering back to the pod, Miguel held my hand. Fez was walking in front, trying to console Kiko Alexandra. Construction workers shouted across the skeleton of a temple.

"Slow down," Miguel said. "Why're you pulling away from me?"

In the pod—Welcome to CWC, Welcome to the world—everyone seemed a bit strung out. The windowvisions showed the mountains collapsing beneath us, and the Footsie was down 5 percent: the markets' first bad week since the circuit protests. In the circuit vessel's docking cabin, Miguel tugged my arm. He gestured toward a young man going the other way from us, into first class.

"That guy is really famous," he said.

I nodded. A woman's bag hit me in the shoulder.

"I want to show you." Miguel took out his phone. He was drunk. "Come on."

"I'm coming. Why are you yanking me?"

I tried to coax him to where the rest of the 118th sat, but he grabbed an earlier socket.

"Don't yank me."

"I'm sorry," I said, floating in the aisle.

The floor a yard below my feet flashed that all pods to the Californian seaboard were currently suspended.

Miguel said, "I don't get why you are so angry with me."

"I'm not," I said. "I just don't want to be here anymore. I'm tired."

"You can go home."

"It's fine," I said, dropping into my seat.

The cabin was filling up. I thought I smelled burgers, and I felt nauseous. The windowvisions said CWC was committed to your future. "It just seems like hypocrisy," I said, staring at the curved bright wall. "It's beyond hypocrisy. Hypocrisy says but then doesn't do, whereas this is projection—they don't do, so instead they say and say."

"I don't know what you're talking about," said Miguel.

I closed my eyes. "Just thinking about work," I said.

We didn't talk any more until we reached the tiki bar at the peak of Mount Pinault, a conical volcanic island jutting out of the Pacific Ocean. Sea levels had risen so much from the centrifugal effects of day contraction that at high tide, the bar, with its rooftop platform, was pretty much the only thing peeking out of the water. Already by this time, certain corners of the internet were abuzz with discourse on how to address rising tides, with approaches ranging from hardline abolition (grounding the westward circuit to see if that would help) to pragmatic reform (economic adaptation; migrant management) to industrious geoengineering (humidity trapping; water redistribution through transoceanic pipes or deep-sea fans; large-scale atmospheric controls; full-blown terraforming).

Each light in the bar was a different color, and you could smell Elmer's glue between the bamboo planes. Miguel and I sat at the end, half-watching Noah and Imani play *Big Buck Hunter*. "Fuck you, fuck you, fuck you," said Noah on a hair-trigger. The holographic fifteen-pointer leapt out, and Imani turned away with a little scream.

Miguel said, "I was so excited for tonight."

I turned to him. "Should we just go home?"

"I don't know," he said, cockling his water bottle.

Fez and Kiko Alexandra put "Cowgirl Play" on the music video wall, and a party of bridesmaids cheered.

"You keep getting into these moods," Miguel said.

I nodded.

"You get depressed and you need me to feel as bad as you do."

I didn't know what to say to that. My gaze rested on a heap of fish sticks in the trash.

"It's not right. It's really not right of you." He stood. "I'm gonna go up for fresh air."

"Should I come?"

"No."

I considered following but decided to go to the bathroom instead. As I crossed the bar, the bridesmaids spilled a pitcher, and the barman looked like he would cry.

At the urinal, I opened Scroller. I was the first in the bar to realize that something serious was happening in San Francisco. I read to myself for a minute, then flushed and hurried back out to turn on the bar TV. Within minutes, all eyes were glued to the screen.

It was utter destruction. It really seemed that San Francisco would be wiped away. CNN's drones kept getting knocked out, and they had to jump to other feeds.

"Oh my god," said Fez.

"Cowgirl Play" ended and "Huge Me Like U Do" came on. The barman turned it down. In the bathroom hallway, the bridesmaids made anxious phone calls. CNN's anchors kept saying, "If you're just joining us . . ." and a truck slid into the Bank of California building.

I took the stairs up to the roof, bracing for wind but there was none. It was night again, thank God, nothing for miles but a dark, fishy desert, shimmering with stars and satellites, the three-quarters moon, and a thousand sapphires popping in a steady crackle. How seamlessly the sky became its watery opposite.

Miguel sat on the edge, watching an oil rig breach the surface. I sat beside him.

"This hurricane seems really horrible," I said.

Miguel said, "Don't change the subject."

○

All week, Pacific Hurricane Sigma had been breaking news throughout San Francisco. It's not as if it came out of nowhere. On Monday, it had made its way up the Baja California Peninsula. Tuesday, still a hundred miles from the coast, it was categorized. A three. On Wednesday morning, more than twenty-four hours before landfall, there was a citywide evacuation order.

The girls, though, consumed in the preparations for their court date, were slow to react.

"This is so annoying," Luna said on Wednesday afternoon, watching the hurricane's path on TV. "Why does my life always have to have ten different things going wrong at once . . ."

Winnie was over. School canceled. The hurricane was expected on Thursday. Their hearing was set for the morning after that. Luna got up to call her parents. They were on a weeklong trip to China, taking advantage of the running CWC "Equity Weeks" deal to visit Luna's yeye in Henan.

"*Friday*," Winnie heard her saying into the phone. "I need to be at court first thing in the morning." . . . "Today is Wednesday here." . . . "No, Mom, it will be too crowded." She switched to Mandarin.

CNN went to commercial. A guy in a sombrero ate Willards Big Korn Bites and said, "Beeg, very beeg."

Luna returned.

"I'm not evacuating," she told Winnie.

She said she was too worried she wouldn't get back in time for her hearing. Everyone who left would be trying to come back Friday morning, the pods to northern California would be full, and the circuit was surge-charging for single-use passes. "You haven't looked," Luna said. "They cost a fortune. It's a stupid time to buy passes."

"But this is the time we need them."

"I'm not paying three hundred dollars for a single-ride. The media always hypes up these Pacific hurricanes, and they don't hit, and I'll be stranded God knows where on my court date."

"What's Nat doing?"

Luna said she didn't know.

"Maybe the two of you could use her family's pod."

"I'm not asking Nat," said Luna. "I'll be fine staying here. I have Bella to protect me." She picked up the cat. "What about Carsie and Mark?"

"They're all staying with Mark's brother."

Luna said Winnie should go with them.

"I won't leave you here alone in a hurricane."

"Don't be annoying."

"If you're staying, we'll stay together."

They argued, but Winnie insisted. They made a plan to stay at Luna's. It made Winnie nervous, but she was glad they'd be together. CNN came back on, and she was perversely heartened to see a report (however reproachful) from San Francisco's Tenderloin district about the homeless who weren't evacuating either. Well, plenty of people weren't evacuating quite yet. Everyone was used to the idea that they could be ten thousand miles away in an hour, and the hurricane wasn't expected until tomorrow morning.

While Luna went to the store to get supplies, Winnie went home for her things. On the way, she texted Nat. For some reason, doing so in Luna's company had seemed improper.

She wrote, "Hey. I'm going to spend the weekend at Luna's. WBU? You good?"

"You're staying in SF tomorrow?"

"Ya."

The streets had a strange, wiry energy, as if a population of ghosts had been stirred up and were corresponding just beyond the sensory limits of the living. Nothing was quite normal—there were, for example, too many working-age men going in and out of their homes in the middle of the day, and some stores were already closed—but no one seemed panicked. The sky was pretty clear. When Winnie was nearly home, Nat called her.

"You can't stay," Nat said. "It won't be safe, Winnie."

"It's fine." She hurried down Irving Street, past the Velvet Tap and Hardee's. Some people were outside drinking beers, but not as many as usual.

"No, it's not fine," said Nat. "It's just classic Luna being selfish."

Winnie explained Luna's stress about getting back in time for court.

Nat said, "Our hearing is canceled, obviously."

"It is?"

"My lawyer talked to the judge."

"But it's not officially canceled yet?"

"I mean, it's like almost certain."

Winnie considered telling Nat to talk to Luna. She didn't like being caught in the middle. But she understood that for the time being, her placement between them might be the only thing holding them together. Nat calling Luna—condescending her, telling her to trust her family's lawyer—was no good. "Luna doesn't want to risk it," Winnie said.

"Fine," said Nat. "We'll go with my family in our pod."

"We don't need to."

"Yes, we do. It's fine. All three of us can."

"Okay," Winnie said. "I'll tell Luna."

"My parents are leaving in two hours. Will you be ready?"

"Ah, so you girls are too good to evacuate among the riffraff," said Carsie.

The family's weekend luggage was already piled by the door.

"She's not coming with us?" said Mark from the hallway, heaving Juju's duffle, which, though filled with the smallest clothes, was larger than the other three combined. Three. Mark had already collected Winnie's stuff in a striped carpet bag. Inside, everything was crumpled, her shirts twisted, her toothbrush buried in the cup of her bra.

"She's going with the *Agarwals*," Carsie said.

Juju on the stairs was playing a stream of a half-naked woman getting pelted by paintballs. She watched with her mouth open, sickly fascinated.

"You sure you'll be safe?" Carsie said.

"Thank you, I'll be fine," said Winnie, hoisting her bag over her shoulder. She had enough to worry about without taking responsibility for her aunt and uncle's feelings. She said she'd see them on the other side of the weekend.

She beat Luna back to the apartment and sat in the kitchen, watching the clock. A.H. 990,738:40. Forty minutes since Nat said two hours. She fiddled with her nose stud. Bella hopped into her lap.

"It's fucking weird out there," said Luna when she finally arrived. She kicked the door closed behind her and dropped the groceries. It was now half past A.H. 990,739.

"Why did you get so many Lean Cuisines?" Winnie asked.

"They're delicious. And they last forever."

"Only if your freezer doesn't lose power." She handed Bella over. "Look, did you see my text? Nat said we should take her pod."

For some reason, Winnie had stood up with her bag, ready to leave as soon as Luna got home, as if this wouldn't be an argument.

"I saw," Luna said. "But I'm staying here."

"No, we're not."

"You can do what you want."

Bella darted down the hall.

"We're going. Get Bella in her crate."

Luna turned away, throwing her arms in the air. "She doesn't like the crate, I'm not relying on Nat, I'm not going. I'm not going."

Winnie grabbed her shoulders and spun her around. "Please."

Luna hesitated, then shrugged Winnie's hand off and wiped her bangs out of her face. She was smaller than Winnie. "No, I won't," she said. "I thought we were gonna hunker down."

"Listen," Winnie said. "I told Nat we'd be there at forty and now it's '39:30. We need to go."

"I thought you and I were gonna hunker down . . ."

They weren't out the door until a quarter till. Their Uber promised an arrival at A.H. 990,740:02, two minutes late.

Winnie texted Nat: "We are coming. What time exactly are you leaving?"

They hit traffic by the Outer Sunset pod station. In a closed-off street, municipal workers instructed a crowd of people to wait. Winnie stuck her head through the sunroof to see what was going on. The first drops of rain fell on her head and on the hood.

There were several hundred people being herded around, trying to board the public shuttle pod out of San Francisco. They had full suitcases, clearly unsure when they'd be able to return. They weren't staying in line very well, and workers in neon vests kept reprimanding them. One of the neon-vesters was giving instructions. Winnie couldn't make out his words, but she watched him pantomime holding some sort of railing. He performed the gesture of an arm being chopped off, then pressed a finger into the opposite palm, apparently to underscore that this was important, or that hands were important. His assistants distributed barf bags and flashlights.

He pointed, and that's when Winnie first noticed the pod docked on the corner. It wasn't a passenger pod. It was an oversized freight pod, the kind that shuttled shipping containers to and from circuit vessels' cargo holds—the basements of the sky, where there were no contraccelerator plates, no lights, no heat. She'd once seen Victor Bickle fly in the hold as a publicity stunt. He had ridden in a cushioned container, wearing a hardhat.

In groups of twenty, the evacuees climbed onto a conveyor belt and were transmitted into the freight pod's damp maw.

Nat stood barefoot in her garden, wearing a green shift speckled by rain. "They left," she said. "Now they have to send the *Maiden* back for us."

She explained that the *Maiden India* connected to a chartered line with only one vessel, which meant that when the pod ("she," as Nat referred to it) landed in about half an hour, it'd need to wait an hour and nineteen minutes before it could launch again, then fifty minutes inflight before it would return to the Agarwals' house. Then they had to wait for the vessel again before taking off, another hour nineteen.

"Hour twenty," Luna corrected. Everyone knew that a circuit vessel at thirty thousand feet took an hour and twenty minutes to orbit Earth. It was one of those universal constants you learned in primary school, like pi or the number of states in the union.

"No. An hour nineteen," said Nat. "I see the timetables every day."

"Your vessel is faster than others?" asked Luna, but as soon as she did, Winnie realized it wasn't the vessel that made up the extra minute, but the planet—faster than when they were in primary school—spinning against it.

In any case, they had almost four hours to kill. They sat in the kitchen, as the windows grew darker and darker. Raindrops were now splashing water out of the courtyard fountain. It was the fountain Winnie had seen through the window the night she got her piercing. The brass bird with its feet facing forward but its head twisted back. Nat, filling a bowl with pretzel thins, said the design was called a *sankofa*. The symbol meant "Go back for what you've forgotten."

"It means that to who?" said Luna.

Nat closed the pantry and studied her. "To me. For one."

"Can I put on some music?" Luna said.

"Go ahead."

She put on Moby, which she knew Winnie liked. The glass door to the courtyard was now slick with a constant stream of rain. Nat read the news on her watch. Luna kept refreshing the court docket to see if their hearing was officially postponed, but no changes appeared. No one was at the clerk's office when she called. Winnie ate pretzels one by one, drying out her lips. When they were so dry that the salt stung and Bella was asleep and Moby, turned way down, was stranded somewhere in his own B-sides, Luna left to use the bathroom.

"This is so like her," Nat said to Winnie. "Putting us through this."

Winnie broke a pretzel in her teeth and put the other half down on the counter. "It's okay," she said. "It's my fault we were late."

Trees scratched against the windows.

"She wants to punish me is it," Nat said. "She thinks my parents should be paying for her legal defense. I'm in my own trouble and she wants me to fight my parents for her. I'm not saying it's fair she's in trouble, but you can't expect other people to make everything fair for you in a situation that's fundamentally unfair."

"Stop," said Winnie.

"What?"

"I don't want to hear this."

A toilet flushed: the sound of water jetting through metered arteries.

"The *Maiden* should be landing, finally," Nat said. Bella woke up and mewed from her crate. Outside was starting to look a little scary.

Luna came in. "Shouldn't it be here now?" she asked.

"Yeah."

"Well, it's not."

They went to the front window.

"She must be there," said Nat, checking the time.

Winnie couldn't see anything beyond her own reflection. She straightened her posture.

Nat opened the door and stepped out. The wind whistled. Through rain falling on the park, Winnie saw in the distance a public pod ascend. But Luna was right. The *Maiden India* hadn't come for them.

"My parents said she took off at '01."

"Why don't we just get a regular flight?" said Winnie.

Luna said, "You want us to buy tickets right now?"

Winnie didn't think they should wait any longer. She suggested that they could still fly home on Nat's pod to make sure they were back in time on Friday morning.

"No, we need to be along the chartered line," Nat said, annoyed. "It's not—the lines don't connect. We're on a chartered line, you understand?"

Luna said they'd just have to wait until it came around again.

"Another hour and twenty minutes?" said Winnie, stepping back inside. She wiped her glasses on her sleeve, but her sleeve was wet too.

"Hour and nineteen," said Luna.

"Hour and sixteen by now," said Nat.

A faraway pod rocketed straight into a storm cloud. They closed the door.

Winnie went to the laundry room to dry her sweatshirt. While the dryer ran, she examined her scars. It was something she did almost any time she was in a bathroom alone. They were less elegant than Luna's, which she often noted on her friend's left wrist, shiny and pale as if the skin had been smoothed over in Photoshop. Her own were splotchy, a terrain of burns and surgical entry wounds up to her armpits. She ran her fingers over them and felt nothing. The dryer spun on high. She was nervous about leaving Nat and Luna alone while she waited for the dryer to finish, but she tried never to expose her scars in their company, so to do so now (she thought) amidst so much tension, would feel charged, as if she were trying to force some kind of grotesque intimacy.

When her sweatshirt was dry enough to wear, she returned to the kitchen to find that her friends stood on opposite sides. The wind was audible now, and leaves swirled around the courtyard. Nat was saying that she could usually track the *Maiden India*'s location.

"Do you often need to keep track of it to know where it is?" asked Luna.

"No," said Nat. "She's usually on schedule."

"*She*, sorry."

"No. 'It,' I mean. It doesn't matter."

Luna said she was sure that the *Maiden* was really reliable. "Except, of course, the moment you're in trouble and you need her. Then all promises are off."

Nat looked up from her phone—a "buffering" circle spun above the screen. "I'm here, aren't I?" she said. "I waited for you to get here."

"I didn't ask you to wait. Winnie did."

Thunder cracked.

"It's not Winnie's fault you came late."

"I didn't want to come."

"I'm sorry," Winnie said. "I thought it was the right thing."

Her phone sounded. Then the others' phones and the kitchen monitor. On Nat's watch she saw the yellow emergency alert. The storm surge had hit early. All pods were grounded. San Francisco was officially cut off.

The first time the power went out, it only lasted a minute before Nat's generator kicked in. The second time, it was for good.

They argued about boarding up the windows but couldn't find any wood. It wasn't clear to them whether they should camp on a high floor or in the basement. They were afraid the basement would flood. On the other hand, its walls seemed the most solid. If a tree fell on the roof and it collapsed, would they be safer if they were farther down, away from it? Or would that just trap them beneath more levels of rubble? They kept disagreeing, even while swapping positions. At almost every suggestion, Nat said she'd already thought of that. Their devices displayed four bars, but when they tried googling, it went nowhere. The sky was evacuating its depths, the heaving of an indisposed God. They went to Nat's mom's office to get nearer the router. The air was putrid. Lightning flashed, and the thunder followed almost instantaneously, like something inside their house blowing up. A framed photo fell to the floor. It was of twelve-year-old Nat and her mom drinking piña coladas.

On the other side of the desk, Luna jumped. Winnie heard the squelch of the carpet before she saw the flooding herself. Water was seeping in from the powder room.

"Did one of you leave a window open?" Nat said.

No. The toilet was backing up. Nat threw a white Triplo Bourdon bath towel on the floor, and they went downstairs. The flooding there was even higher. The worst thing about it was the color—jaundiced, leaving residue on the walls. They could feel a draft. Closed doors were rattling, and they realized a window must be open. They split up to find it.

Winnie took the east wing. Her arms swung as she dragged her feet through ankle-high leakage. She felt so stupid. Outside, a vacant police vehicle sloshed through red lights, lurching floodwater down the street, commanding in a robotic voice that everyone keep calm. A cactus cartwheeled by. Sparks jumped from wet wires. She heard mewing. *Bella.* They'd forgotten about her. She ran back up the stairs, two at a time. The roof creaked, as if a giant's hand were trying to lift it. Raindrops pelted like stones. Bella was on the floor of the office, her crate half full of water. The computer above her had finally loaded a webpage about storm safety, but the article was blocked by a five-minute ad, which said that instead of restocking sodas, your own online "vending machine" could generate five to ten thousand dollars of passive income every month selling customers to local businesses.

Winnie took off her sweatshirt and bundled Bella inside. They both shivered.

"It's okay," she heard herself saying. "It's alright, sweetheart."

The wind howled. No—that was the sound of Nat screaming.

Winnie hurried downstairs, holding Bella to her chest. Nat and Luna were in a guest bedroom Winnie hadn't seen before. They'd found the breach, an open glass patio door, but they couldn't pull it closed. Wind blew in every direction. The sankofa fountain had gotten uprooted. It clanged around the courtyard, flipping like a docked fish, smashing the tilework. Water spurted up. Winnie was afraid that the sculpture would roll into them.

"I can't get it," Nat shouted. She let the door go, and it flung back 180 degrees with a slam against the exterior wall.

Luna took hold. She managed to pull it halfway closed, so that it was perpendicular to the house, a sail in the wind. Winnie heard her groan. The door wanted to tear off, and when Luna wouldn't let it, its hinges shrieked. It seemed like the glass would burst. She screamed into the storm—not words in any language, and the sound was swept up over all the houses and the fences and decapitated peonies. She gave one last heave, and the door crashed shut.

Suddenly, the sky was blue. They caught their breaths. Winnie sat Bella on the tousled bed.

"Is it over?" Nat asked.

Tentatively, she reopened the door. The courtyard barely held a breeze. She stepped out. They could see the storm behind them, a rigid wall of white clouds. Winnie came out with her arms crossed over her belly. The air was shockingly cold. She approached the sankofa, no longer animated, beside its gushing pedestal. Its head was twisted upward; its toes contorted down.

"The eyewall passed over," Winnie said. "We're in the eye now. We should stay inside."

"It's circling us," said Luna.

"It doesn't feel like anything," said Nat. "It just feels normal."

"Just damp and cold," said Luna. She smiled at Nat. "What does it remind you of?"

"Fucking Whole Foods."

"Come on," said Winnie.

"Yeah, let's go in," Luna agreed.

Nat nodded at her. "Alright."

They stood inside behind the closed door, Luna saying how strange it was that right in the middle of it, you wouldn't know anything was wrong. Nat, studying the sky, said that *she* would know. Luna and Winnie laughed.

Rain started to speckle the glass. The next eyewall loomed. Wind picked up. Winnie's fear returned. She suggested they move away from the door, but there was no time to talk. As suddenly as it had granted reprieve, the storm was back. Nothing had changed.

It was as if Winnie had been picked up, brought to a place that made no sense, and returned to a life she still didn't understand. The sankofa, undead, body-rolled around the courtyard. It was getting closer to the walls. It took out a tree. For some reason they stayed there, watching it. Not for long. Only thirty seconds or so. But they didn't back away from the window when Winnie said they should. And when the wind switched and the hulking brass bird started to move on them, she was paralyzed by the shock of her fear coming true.

It rushed in their direction—smashed the glass and flew into the room.

And then, of three, only two still stood.

Part II

My Family

42,000 HOURS
(OR FIVE YEARS) LATER

The entertainment annex attached to my old church was in shambles. Its scripture-themed video games were being desecrated before my mother's eyes. Had God wrought this? she asked herself. Had she?

Her nightmare: The arcade floor was suddenly making money.

There were players at every station and others crowded around watching. Customers tripped over power strips. They swamped the snack bar. My sister Ashtyn (now fourteen) and her friends, enlisted to help manage the pandemonium, couldn't make enough frozen pizzas if they tried, and every time my mother looked over she saw them leaning across the counter, flirting. The brutalizers had shown up that morning out of nowhere. Out of the clear October sky. It'd been three years since Keber Creek's multi-pod station had opened as part of the Equity Push. The gold mine had been the reason the town made the cut, and before long the circuit brought enough investment and new technology to whittle the mine's payroll down to zero. Since the mine went fully automatic, the town's population had fallen to under fifty, most of whom had taken up radical survivalism like my father, staying to live off the land and the scant welfare checks. Their loose community had attained minor celebrity status on doomforums.net and r/whenshtf, which held up Keber Creek as a spiritual pillar in such decadent times, an off-the-grid Zion, where a cult-like community of a dozen families were all prepping for the End in complete independence, together. A strange turn for the little town.

My family had begun their day as usual. They woke rested on five hours' sleep, let the dogs out, fed the pigs. They walked a mile to the church for morning services, sat in the front pew and nodded while Louis Tornkin prayed for a mild winter. My father grunted that only idiots prayed for God to go easy on them, and my mother ignored him. Then they heard voices and stepped outside to share in the shock of their fellow congregants at seeing that while they prayed for precipitative temperance, a shower of tourists had landed in Keber Creek and were letting themselves into the annex.

My mother and some of the other women rushed to dispel them. They'd gotten about five of the twenty visitors back out into the parking lot (while ten more showed up), when old Gerald Tumesky instructed them to stop. They asked him why.

The tourists were paying.

It was the first time in a year that outside money had come to my parents' people. *Ark Tycoon* was literally backed up with quarters. Tumesky ordered that frozen pizzas be brought up from the cellar, the quarter dispensers refilled, the girls put behind the counter. They had to receive this plague of patronage.

While Tumesky and my father argued, my mother pushed past a group of teenagers. They swiped at the curls twisting out from the screen of *Delilah: Hair Ninja*, having piled their coats in the doorway to liberate indecent crop tops and cellophane leggings; some of the girls wore nothing above the waist but their brassieres and the boys wore disgusting padded bulges sewn into the crotches of their pants. And the phones, she thought. All of them on their phones, recording themselves constantly. Filming every corner of the arcade like Big Tech's surveillance team.

She knelt down to fix a power strip, and someone walked into her. "Oh, fuck, I'm really sorry," said the girl. "I was looking at my—"
"Your phone! I know!"

A boy playing the *Tower of Babel* Tetris game shouted, "Can I just get one square block for Christ's sake?"

She yanked him from the booth. "Out," she cried.

The boy stammered. He had slick hair and shiny eyes and overall gave off the impression of great interior wetness.

"Out, out." She drove him toward the exit. His friends followed with their cameras.

"What'd I do?"

"You took the Lord's name in vain. You've broken the rules," she said and pointed to the ANNEX RULES sign by the bathroom, on which God's ten commandments were printed.

He said, "I thought that was a joke. 'Thou shalt not murder'?"

"That won't be a joke if you're still here in five seconds." When she shoved him through the door, a new podful of customers took his place.

She fought her way to the snack bar, where Ashtyn was making googly eyes at some lanky, half-dressed geek. My mother instructed her to fix her shirt.

From the other end of the bar limped her friend Gail Myrtle. She said, "What's going on here? Who are these people? They said Keber Creek was posted on 'Roads Untraveled.' What the hell is Roads Untraveled?"

Other Keber Creekers stood in the doorway, bickering. The naked trees threw their arms open in jubilant surrender.

"That little fucking louse," shouted my father. "He's behind this."

Ashtyn mumbled, "You can't blame everything on him, Dad."

But when my mother first saw the crowds, she too thought of me. And she must have known with dread that the reminder would bring out her husband's worst. It had been seven years since I'd left, seven years without contact, and while I had all but forgotten about my parents, my father cursed me weekly. In the spring, he had turned sixty-eight, and my mother, still shy of fifty, came to realize with some shock that her husband had passed the apex of his life. He was no longer aging up, but down; getting shorter; losing muscle, hair, and teeth; dispensing memories faster than they could be acquired and systematically unplugging neural connections as if preparing to leave home for a long trip. My mother was my father's second wife, married to him at twenty-two. She'd seen in him a strong father figure. Now, she took care of him, and her son was gone.

He came to the counter, shouting, "These people need to leave." Ashtyn told him to go home; they could handle it.

But he pushed around her. "Enough," he said. "Enough."

"Randall, don't you touch that rifle," said my mother.

Teenagers at the nearby machines turned as my father came up with an M16. People screamed. The games whirred. He fired his round into the ceiling, raining plaster on the counter. Skin pressed to skin, everyone rushed for the exit. Ashtyn covered her ears. The sun was already setting, stretching shadows across the parking lot.

"I've stood up to you people my whole life," he shouted as all the visitors fled back to the pod station.

DAYS OF 12 HOURS

I was now twenty-seven years old. I hurried down West Third Street. It was a brisk autumn day in Manhattan, workmen were dressing the trees in their seasonal red-and-orange synthetic foliage, and the Shell was high. Clocks blinked A.H. 1,033,368:03. I didn't need the clocks to tell me I was running late. These days, I was always late.

Yet I couldn't avoid the clocks (atop sidewalk kiosks, alongside buses, below the map I studied on my phone), omnipresent like an occupying force conscripted to police time amidst the past years' turbulent day contractions. A.H. 1,033,368:03, and the sun was falling and I'd just woken up. I was supposed to meet Bickle on the hour, but I'd overslept, having absentmindedly taken a full six-hour dose of Ambien+ instead of a half-dose. I couldn't sleep at all without Ambien. I never was a good sleeper, and the sun these days had me all crossed up. The days were half as long as they used to be, and I had twice as much to do. Everything was rushed.

I rounded the corner at MacDougal and saw Bickle tilting back in a metal café chair.

"It's not like I was given all this on a silver spoon, you know," he was saying as I approached. "All my life people have gone after me, denying me the recognition I've worked for, but I just stay, you know, right on it." He picked at his mustache, which he continued to dye dark brown, even as his stubble went gray. The stubble never showed on camera. "And when people tell me I'm not good enough for this or that, I just keep pushing."

"I see," replied his assigned profiler from *Feed*. The profiler hadn't started recording yet. In fact, I hadn't really missed anything. All the profiler had done so far was meet Bickle outside the café and ask, "How's it going?"

Someone was drilling in the Shell above. I tuned out the noise.

The profiler, an ungainly college grad, explained that his piece would reflect on Bickle's personal experience of celebrity, with a focus on his increased visibility in the past five years. I had arranged the profile after Bickle complained that he should be getting more sympathetic media attention. It had been six months since his last "pains of being famous" piece in *The New York Times Magazine*, and he worried that people might stop caring about his struggle.

"So to start," said the profiler. "You've been in the public eye for almost a decade now, going back to—"

"The Queensboro Bridge thing, yeah."

"Right, which is when I first heard of you. But it wasn't until you began representing CWC—"

"*Communicating* about the Westward Circuit, I'd say."

"That you became practically a household name. Especially in the A.H. 980,000s when you championed the Westward Circuit's Equity Push."

"Ah, the Equity Push," Bickle said. "The good old days."

The profiler turned on his dragonfly drone and released it into the air. It immediately got in my face. I saw myself in the little monitor, my golden-red stubble and hair gelled into a tower as I had taken to wearing it. Bickle accepted a large to-go coffee from our waitress, and we proceeded down West Third for some city shots with the dragonfly reversing ahead of us, first at eye level, then from our feet, looking up. In the background, a cascade of circuit vessels rained like a daytime meteor shower, *pop pop pop pop*. Percussion to sirens unseen. Over the clang of footfall on iron hatchways, Bickle reminisced about that time when the expansion of intercontinental commerce seemed like manifest destiny.

"People didn't realize how good they had it back then, when circuit equity was booming. It was incredible. Suddenly you could get anything. I mean for pennies on the dollar, people were buying pounds of saffron, mint and paints and branded jeans and knockoff gaming consoles, furniture and microchips and that amazing Tupperware they had back then." He listed startups that had found their markets in those couple of years. There were many. In time, visas for passenger travel tightened (after the East African migrant crisis following Hurricane Lance, the volcanic arc refugee incident, and the Great Fog Flee), but even then, commerce from the circuit reached anyone with a tablet or with access to an internet kiosk of the sort that sprung up next to docking sites operated by e-sellers, NGOs, local warlords. "I remember mountain ranges of industrial recyclables . . ." The Equity Push was a windfall to small business owners, it was a windfall to middle-class consumers, and it was a windfall to the rich international capital and commodity exchanges through which everyone else's windfalls flowed . . . that is, until the circuits vessels flew too many too quickly and in the fall of A.H. 1m, the crash.

The market crash. Giving rise to the Shell. I looked up.

"The crash hurt a lot of ordinary people," said Bickle.

I stepped over a Nando's wrapper. We walked around the subway entrance, temporarily closed for suicide cleanup. A vendor sold foam miniatures of the Statue of Liberty, hoisting her sword.

It's difficult to trace my thoughts on the crash from then to now, with all that's changed. For one, it feels to me now, despite hindsight's weakness for teleology, *less* inevitable than I recall it feeling at the time, for at the time of the crash, people were strikingly unsurprised by the sudden loss of trillions of dollars in market value. They were angry, of course. Many people online were outraged. But surprised? Not really. At least not convincingly. Before the crash, analysts had been saying that the market, which had boomed for two whole years, was due for a correction. Even I, who knew little about inverted yield curves or the all-telling second derivative of the Cass Freight Index, had been aware of the economic paranoia proliferating through Aviation Tower and the studios of CNBC as Bickle toured in promotion of Equity Week deals at the dawn of the megahoram, the millionth modern hour. People didn't know when the crash would come, but they said growth couldn't last forever. And a consensus formed around what would break it. At the megahoram festivities, while fireworks detonated over Buckingham Palace, days stood at 18 hours, and the tidal shifts from poles to tropics were starting to register on economic yardsticks. The shoreline crept ten meters inland in equatorial port cities like Jakarta, Bangkok, and Lagos; that July, the Amazon Basin flooded, spoiling a millennium's worth of biodiversity and an entire year's export of copper and charcoal; even highland coastal cities like Accra saw grim ocean waves scaling their bluffs. The markets chugged along through frothing seas while talk of vesicular finances swelled, until suddenly on a foggy Thursday in New York, upon no particular occasion and seemingly without warning, the bubble burst. Apparently the bankers determined it was time. Or close enough, anyway, and as CWC's CFO said, it was better to sell off a month early than an hour late. By such logic, I thought, it was a miracle that the world experienced any growth at all.

We cut through Minetta Green, which Google Maps labeled a "natural haven." Pods spurted from the head of the World Trade Center. An old man, prostrate on the sidewalk, wore a sandwich board that said FIGHT STRESS.

What was growth? I wondered. Suppose I and a friend had one hundred dollars and our fists, and we took turns exchanging the hundred (as fair a price as any) to get to punch each other in the gut. Could we report at year's end that we sold ten thousand units of service, made a million dollars each (spending it therapeutically), and contributed two million to GDP? It seemed an exhausting way to end up with one hundred dollars and abdominal bleeding.

Of course, I also wasn't so sure I had a friend.

"When you joined CWC," the profiler asked, "did you expect that your career would reach the heights it has?"

"If by heights you mean I'm spending all my time either talking to people like you or getting faced by online trolls, then no, I never imagined these soaring heights."

I opened my mouth to interject, but not before Bickle said, "I'm joking. But for all it's become, I really am tragically underpaid. That is no joke. That's dead serious."

"For all that what has become?"

"My career. My life."

"Would you say there's tension in your relationship with CWC these days?"

"That's putting it mildly. Cromwell Grant thinks he can do everything himself and fails to appreciate what anyone else brings to the table. CWC needs to learn to treat its people right. Who was it who pulled us out of the recession? I wasn't just the leading advocate for the Equity Push. I was also, later, a leading public advocate for the solution that got everyone out of the market crash."

"The Shell, you mean."

"The Shell."

Above the arms of plastic trees thrown open in jubilant surrender, the dragonfly whizzed around for establishing shots.

Bickle said, "The Shell gave cities like New York their vibrance back."

I looked up, then back down at the city. That much, at least, was true. There was no sign of recession anymore, at least not financial. After witnessing the sinusoidal nosedive of that rollercoaster that was the stock market—that strange weighted poll of the pecuniary, political, and personal sentiments of a few wealthy individuals and their few million emulators—I recall having my second formative experience with market psychology: watching the world react.

The reactionary word in the seats of power had been "stimulus." I remember scrolling Apple News one spring day while I updated

Bickle's socials and noticing that every headline suddenly mentioned it. To attack our ecological issues as industriously as possible, taking all contractionary reforms off the table. "Why aren't *we* talking about stimulus at CWC?" Bickle said, and soon after, stimulus was expounded in ad campaigns and inauguration speeches. It was pursued by central banks, which honored the monetarist's triple mandate (to combat unemployment, stabilize inflation, and boost stock markets) through the purchase of trillions in corporate bonds. And it was discussed at summits between nations newly intertwined by circuit commerce, where ideas that only months earlier would have seemed outlandish suddenly found new exigency. Most of my CWC colleagues wanted submarine piping to redistribute water. This solution to day contraction's most disruptive issues was cheap and relatively noninvasive. "Idiots," I once heard Noah saying by the coffee machine. "It won't disperse storms." He favored ducts in the sky—a sort of global climate control.

So did Miguel. For a time, he got crazy about it. He posted multiple times per day about the wonders of sky terraforming, sharing links from sources I had never heard of. The debates everyone was getting into confused me, and I avoided them, but it wasn't that I didn't care. When I was in primary school, we used to play a game. Ms. Barrel gave us prompts, like "Should computers replace teachers," and for pro and con, the students would run to different sides of the room. "You have to pick," she'd tell me, gesturing with approval to the little mob picketing for her own termination, and when I couldn't choose (until that year, I'd never had a computer *or* a teacher), she told my mother I was slow. I recalled this game the spring after the crash, and it seemed a good way to raise little monsters. That spring I got extremely tired. I avoided work. For a week, I didn't respond to Bickle's messages. I was lucky not to be fired.

Soon enough, scientists determined that the oceans hadn't just shifted toward the equator. They had swelled. Sea level gains of five meters in the tropics were offset by declines of only four and a half meters at the poles. This was apparently very bad. The Earth was spinning so fast that not only had water been pulled toward the center of the ball, but gravity's squeeze on water there and everywhere had relaxed: The oceans had lost pressure. And that meant air pressure was threatened too. To reassure markets on a planet spinning faster and faster, policymakers needed to move water, stop storms, and hold air. They needed to dominate their realm without compromise, while couching any proposal not as mere backtracking but rather as an inspiring step ahead to an unprecedented future.

I can't remember when I first heard about the Shell. I know I heard about it as "the Shell" before policymakers came up with its more technical name, the International Climate Retention Facility. I probably laughed it off. It was one of those things that no one was taking seriously until all of a sudden everyone was.

The Shell grew from a confluence of fertile conditions: a large idle workforce; a spirit of, if not collaboration, at least mutual entanglement by global governments; an activist class loathe to let a good environmental crisis go to waste; dovish central banks; well-capitalized multinational corporations sitting on trillions in dry powder.

As one of the largest of those corporations was CWC, whose beefed-up construction subsidiaries were looking for new life after the Equity Push, Bickle was out there every day sowing seeds.

Of course, now that the Shell was old news, people who had endorsed it were once again criticizing the government contractors bringing it into messy reality. Criticizing CWC. And Bickle.

I thought about whether the Shell was inevitable and about what "inevitable" possibly meant. I remembered my first days in New York, how the sun used to stay down for twelve hours or more, and the Chase building lit the whole sky violet over Downtown Brooklyn. I couldn't have imagined then that day contraction would cut those nights in half, and that even now with everyone in agreement (even online provocateurs, even congresspeople) that day contraction was entirely due to circuit commerce, no one wanted to slow things down. In fact, people relied on the circuit's speed all the more. Everyone expected days to contract further, and that was fine, given that the Shell was going to smooth out commerce's unintended hiccups.

"You walk around, and you see humans' capacity to reinvent themselves," Bickle riffed as we walked through Washington Square Park. Riders on one-wheels (and the new fad, No-Wheels, which were just one-wheels where the wheel was a little smaller) did fifty-fifties in the empty fountain. Bickle said, "Amidst everything that's going on in the world, we keep moving forward. And that's what my own life is about. You know where the word 'evolution' comes from?" He waited for the profiler to say no. Then he said, "From Latin, for unrolling a scroll."

The sun was setting again. Shop lights switched on: the color scheme of the city flipping into negatives. It would make good footage. We stood in the glow of a mobile kitchen emanating chicken and charcoal. A student in line rubbed her temples and said, "I feel like I'm at war with the world around me, and every day I lose a little bit of ground." Her friend looked sympathetic. I put my hands in my pockets. Under a statue of Sacagawea, several men, shirtless to the cold, whipped themselves with shoelaces; this had nothing to do with the Shell or day contraction. It was just New York.

"Hey, Professor!" someone said. They snapped a picture. Behind them, the graffitied leg of the Washington Square Arch said BILLY WAS HERE and LOOK UP.

I looked up past the streetlamps, past the canopies of plastic trees, rooftop water towers and chimneys, news drones, helicopters, the wisps of cirrus clouds, and crisscrossing contrails. At twice the altitude of the circuit vessels, far above the clouds, the Shell was half-constructed over New York. Eventually, it would enclose the planet, an airtight, all-encompassing climate control powered by external solar panels, with plumbing to convey water and rain it down where it was needed, containment for atmospheric pressure, fans to disperse storms, plus timed lighting (and more importantly, timed darkness) to synchronize days and nights everywhere as people dashed around the world. It promised all the comforts of life indoors, globalized.

For now, a work-in-progress, it extended as a finished gray ceiling from the southwestern horizon before the tiling stopped, and from it continued skeletal beams of russet scaffolding, like fingers from a hand reaching across the sky.

Back at the Oxford Street Hilton, I lay on my bed. It was my seventh year living at the Hilton, though I'd relocated to a larger suite a couple of years ago when Miguel moved in. We decided to keep the hotel rather than his flat because as long as I left my permanent address as Alaska, CWC let me expense the hotel fees. Anyway, it was nice not to be tied down by a lease. The suite had a king-size bed and a view of the London Eye. A pod up from the roof could get us to the circuit, and an elevator down could take us to the bar, the indoor pool, or Marks & Spencer. There was supposed to be a gym too, but it was closed for renovations, so while I lay, Miguel lifted weights with his shirt off, facing the closet mirror. Forty-pound bicep curls. At first blush, he didn't look like he'd be capable, but when he picked up the weights, muscles materialized. I watched his pecs flare. His collarbone was slightly off-center, like a rotated necklace.

Finishing a set, Miguel cursed and dropped his dumbbells on the bed, where they sank into each other with a *tink*.

He said, "They should give us a rent concession if they don't open the gym. Or people are going to move out."

I laughed. "It's a hotel," I said.

He had earbuds in. "There is no space in here," he shouted. He did high-knees in place. I watched his penis flop around in his shorts.

He too was feeling overworked, entrusted with Cromwell Grant's fractaling hourly calendar, his external correspondences, his daily paperwork, and a litany of personal favors (including, last month, fabricating travel expense reports to conceal an affair from Grant's wife). Grant was an executive director of CWC now. As his star rose,

Miguel, his "loaf," swept up the meteoric dust. But unlike me, Miguel never wanted to talk about work stress. He just believed he needed to work harder the next day. The next "day."

There was no clear workday anymore, just an endless stream of five-hour shifts, which we took on and off sporadically in an attempt to keep up with our stream of tasks, scattered appointments, the sun going round and round. When Miguel and I were free to relax at the same time, I felt almost okay. We still watched reality TV together and laughed at how bad it was. Miguel did impressions of the characters, deepening his voice in mock stupidity. He rested his head on my chest. I teased him for checking ten times whether his five different alarms were set before bed ("snooze-proof," he said), and once it was time to turn out the lights, we wrestled over who should get out of bed to do it, and we kissed. I asked if he was in the mood for sex about once a week (a "week" being 100 hours, per CWC's clockulator, completely divorced from the motions of the sun and defined by the fact that it was the frequency of our twenty-hour-long full-company "weekends," which Miguel and I routinely worked through). He'd say yes, but all too often we'd end up working too late or needing to wake up too soon, or our bed schedules didn't end up overlapping at all. It was especially on those occasions when I would leave work alone (switching my work profile to AWAY, popping an Ambien and drawing the blackout curtains, and trying hurriedly to catch some sleep before I'd have to log back on) that in my solitude, my anxieties struck.

The feeling that all my hard work (and everyone's around me) was to no end but a hastening of the world's decay had now sat with me for so long that its sentiment had leaked out, had diffused through me and come to color in dim shades of senselessness almost everything I saw. Not just my work, but the dirty streets of London, the entertainment all around, the clothes in my closet, and my love with Miguel. On my worst days, it was a slow crisis everywhere I looked, and one I trusted myself all the less to understand.

At this point, I had been working for CWC for seven years.

In my despairing moments, I wished Miguel and I would both just quit our jobs and do something earnest that we could feel good about. Something we could be proud of. But what was this "earnest" alternative? The naïve on fictional shows fantasized about moving to farms in the heart of the country. Big factory farms were all I could imagine, Monsanto towns—the whole thing was a joke. I had *escaped* Keber Creek.

One night when Miguel was stressed by work, I floated the idea of us quitting. I wanted him to discuss it with me as a real possibility. Instead he flashed me a look befitting a petulant child, a boy refusing to wear a jacket. He had asked me before what work I'd rather do. I'd said, "janitor," and proceeded to fume at him for not taking me seriously. I'd *been* a janitor, I could do it. Why wasn't that serious? It was insulting to people—to me—that he found janitorial work so unconscionable. And yet, without knowing why, I too believed that such a life was no longer an option.

If he would have admitted that CWC bothered him too, we could have talked it out, but he thought I simply couldn't take the workload. He said that if my job wasn't satisfying me, I should quit, but that Grant trusted him and he appreciated how hard Grant pushed him. The implication was clearly that I wasn't attaining as much success as he was. The way he talked about it, the pressure of a boss's reliance became a sort of currency, and in that respect, he suggested, I was comparatively dispossessed. Was there truth to this? Bickle still trusted me with administrative tasks but solicited my input less and less. Over the years, he'd grown less trusting of everyone, embittered by critics and (increasingly) by CWC, the latter of which wasn't possibly paying him enough, he felt, to put up with the former. I suspected Bickle was seeing someone romantically, for I had noticed email drafts, minimized on his tablet, with subject lines like "Hi" and "Thought you'd find this funny" and one, "Missing you." Was it the competing demands of his personal life that made him less satisfied with his treatment at

CWC? (Or less satisfied with me as a confidant?) I was embarrassed to say that I didn't know.

I reflected on this as Miguel finished high-knees and started his crouching routine ("*squats*," he always corrected me). He was listening to the *Roads Less Travelled* podcast. I went to the bathroom. My spray had lately gotten more erratic. It made me feel like an old man. As a kid, I'd feared that I would spray if I "loosened" myself by jerking off. I washed my hands for a long time, counting the seconds. When I looked up, the mirror was open, and I saw shelves of hotel-sized Le Labo shampoo-to-go, Advil, Ambien, caffeine pills, a rubber-tipped gum stimulator that Miguel used religiously, a rolled-up tube of Crest 3D White and a glob of toothpaste turned crusty, shaving cream, rosewater aftershave, Glide, and soap scum where I had expected to see myself.

I came out of the bathroom and said, "Want to go for a walk?"

"¿Pa' dónde?"

"Doesn't matter."

We walked alongside the Thames, downstream. The river was crawling with silver carp and sitting low, waiting for the Shell to reach this far north so the pipes that ran through it would bring back some of the water that was pooling in the mid-Atlantic. Miguel and I climbed down from the concrete promenade to the silty bank the river had relinquished. Bottles jutted out of the hard sand. Clumps of plastic twine. As we crossed beneath the undergirding of the Hungerford Bridge, a train went over, prompting a wave of those invasive carp to leap into the air. Out the other end, I looked at the sky. It was the violet hour, or the violet half hour anyway, and the heavy blanket of night softened modernity's edges, leaving only the substructures that underlay the noise, the dark shapes of buildings from low angles, the city with which I had once fallen in love. Yellow streetlights shimmered in the river's remains like long candles, and I imagined the city as it had been when I walked to work in my first weeks, twenty years old and eager to see the boy with whom I had spent a night behind the Petra Dance Haus coat compactor. (The mere thought of coat compactors made me a little bit sick with nostalgia.) I remembered taking photos of Big Ben. How many rounds had Big Ben made since? Maybe not so many in the grand scheme. To a symphony that had been playing since the reign of Victoria, 60,000-odd hours were just a few trailing notes. We walked below a wooden pier. A Schweppes can bobbed past. The London Eye served booth after booth up to the gloaming, and across from it, that other circle, the old clock-tower, held its ground, calling either four minutes to midnight or four minutes to noon.

"Qué impresionante," said Miguel and pointed straight ahead. In the cup of sky between the buildings, the unfinished Shell peeked out on London. He was one of those people who drew inspiration from the majesty of the Shell. "It puts things in perspective," he said.

I nodded, even though to me, staring at something so big had the opposite effect: It yanked everything so far from perspective as to cause vertigo. I took his hand. I said, "Yeah," and I remembered how we used to watch the sunrise.

I'd poured so much into my relationship with Miguel, devoted so much of my life to him, it was scary to be reminded that the relationship hinged on the strengths and flaws of another. Sometimes, I realized that Miguel was totally contained within a body, and I was startled. I couldn't believe that in spite of the boundlessness of my devotion, Miguel was just a single person. A fixed volume. One shirt size and not the others. He wasn't everything. He was just the one I had.

Big Ben knelled uselessly. Miguel looked at his phone. I inspected something on the ground and determined it was a seagull carcass, and we kept walking.

"What are you reading?"

He said he was RSVP'ing for the winter gala in Beijing. We were both supposed to go. It'd be full of Shell people. CWC folks and celebrities.

"Is Grant's wife coming?" I asked, simultaneously aware and not aware that what I meant was *Will you be free to spend time with me?*

"No," said Miguel. "Bickle isn't bringing a plus-one, is he?"

"Not that I know of."

"Should be another exhausting evening."

Without responding, I watched him type. I knew that if an outsider listened to our fights, it would be my side (my quitter's attitude, my constant need for consolation) that would be considered immature. In my head a song echoed, "Don't let the sun catch you crying." I wished that knowing a song like that would give me power over my life. Lovers had written on the wall, which was rough and wet to the touch. K+R 4EVER . . . SALLY♥RACHEL FOREVER . . . TIG&SAM . . . on and on, cleaving the city like time. I took Miguel's hand. He could type one-handed. I thought about us behind the coat compactor, him telling me not to cry. I considered how it felt to be alive back then, and how it felt to be alive right now.

○

Winnie waded into her garden, soaking her socks in dew. She didn't own the garden, it belonged to her apartment complex, but she was the only tenant who ever used it, so she saw it as hers, her peonies and her jacaranda tree. Her hammock hung inverted, filled with rainwater in which the withered skins of fallen flowers spun. Safe haven for mosquitos. She shook it out. In a big sweatshirt and little shorts, she lay down and waited for the swinging to stop completely, more than it ever could. The muggy fabric itched the back of her knees. That was fine with her. She was trying to distract herself from bad thoughts. Randomly, she was humming "Deadibodi" by Fat Rasher, which she hadn't heard in years. A gecko scampered up the garden wall, juking over shards of glass. The wall had been one of Luna's conditions. When Winnie and Luna visited apartments a few months earlier, their listing agent waxed about the myriad ways emerald and ruby glass shone atop the many walls that cut up SF2 (mounted with screens showing ads like SLEEP AT LAST and LUXURY—YOUR WAY, covered in graffiti). Every apartment complex in the Castro neighborhood was parceled within such walls. Never, it seemed to Winnie, had the world been more interdependent and simultaneously more splintered, everyone believing themselves more than ever to be different from one another, but in reality . . . well, this was a thought on the way to the bad ones. She closed her eyes. Twenty-two years old, she was healthy, college-educated, still had practically her whole life ahead of her.

Indigo light shone through the jacaranda petals. Her little canopy, her shelter from the sky. In SF2, Shell piping stretched from horizon to horizon, a chain-link fence against heaven. Each week, a few more of its honeycomb gaps got filled with smooth tiling. The Shell's most basic features were operational already. Its overflow drain chambers pumped away oceanwater and stabilized sea levels; its pipes conveyed this water as far north as they reached (now almost to Washington) and rained it down when rain was needed; its thousand air-conditioning vents steadily dispelled fog and did a reliable job of routing major storms. But not until it was fully filled in, encasing the whole planet, would it be able to contain air pressure, or restore twenty-four-hour circadian lighting, or—crucially—generate revenue to pay back its funders. She heard the welter of all that celestial construction, like stage thunder. Suspended workers negotiating cables the width of their thighs. When she focused, she could hear the low undertone of the machinery running too, although that was hard to separate from the ambient noise of a city at work, building itself deeper into something strange that no one had planned. In the wake of Hurricane Sigma, the westward circuit had not restored San Francisco. Instead, SF2 was born. The past five years' commerce had made rich cities richer, but it merely made the ruin of San Francisco into more of itself. Where the hurricane had left a bridge only half-standing, there were now two bridges half-standing.

Potholed two-lane roads were expanded to potholed four-lane high-ways. Outside Winnie's building, addicts lay across the gum-pocked sidewalk claiming they wanted to bring back God.

The flowers above Winnie's hammock hung like tiny trumpets. When she reached up to pluck one, it fell right off the bone and wilted at her touch. Luna would be home from work soon, unless she was out on another date. She was these days always conjuring boys from MateMe—meek, vacuous romantics who worked in tech and crypto and sought a headstrong girl to tell them what to do with their lives. She would boss them around for a month or two, then quit the relationship at the first sign of revolt and find another subject before she might have to address the murkier realm of her own life choices. This was her way of coping. They both had them. Winnie couldn't believe it'd been five years since Nat had died. (She dropped the flower and placed her hand on her face.) It didn't feel so long. The end of her teens, over like that. Her friend's life leaking into a wet Persian carpet. Trying to pull the bad thoughts from her mind. Hammers ringing, repairing the clouds. The sankofa with its broken neck, and the Wwlliamses with their pride in Winnie for getting a job at a startup that she didn't understand, making rent for an apartment in a city disintegrating, as if everything were alright.

"It is alright," she said. Her mindless fingers opened the weather. TODAY'S WILDFIRE RISK: LOW :) She put her phone back down. "It's alright," she said again, closing her eyes.

"Have you and that tree started talking to each other?"

It was Luna calling out from the window six stories up. AC vents drooling.

"Come inside," she called. "I rolled a J, and I can't smoke alone right now."

Their apartment smelled of fresh ground bud. Winnie left the lights off. Luna asked if she was going to work soon.

"Pretty soon."

"A quick smoke then?" said Luna.

It was clear she needed it, and Winnie obliged. She peeled off her socks and sat in the living room, amidst the dirty laundry. "I'm only taking like one hit." She lit their candle ("Saint Emily Dickinson") with a match, then brought the wick to the end of Luna's joint, letting Luna do the honors. They had a whole drawer of electric vapes but got high this way, the "acoustic vape," as if that were some kind of protest. Luna had shed her bra, and the bump of her barbell showed through her brown Forest Service polo. She handed Winnie the joint, then put on an album, *World of Echo*, then slumped down on the floor.

"I decided to end things," she said.

"Oh."

"He was never going to change. I didn't want him to leave his job for *me*. He's the one who complained about it and said it was against his values and all that bullshit I told you about."

"Right," Winnie said, but she didn't remember. She hadn't taken this one seriously at the start, hadn't paid attention to the stories of their early dates and so had spent the month that followed, or had it been two, avoiding any conversations that might expose her (and fill her in). She opened her phone. Drought was displacing five thousand children per week in Mongolia; people were donating to have more rain sent through the Shell. She closed her phone and took a hit. The joint was small, and sucking it made her feel like a child.

"All his bitching was just a performance to make him feel okay about changing nothing."

"Mm," said Winnie.

"People in that sort of job do that."

"Are you okay?"

"Yeah. I've something to ask you." Luna took another hit. Neither said anything for a while. Saint Emily flickered, a little jewel of beautiful rage.

They'd moved in together when Winnie graduated college. Luna had been working a couple of years already at the Forest Service, recruited among a thousand do-gooders and washouts who needed work during the recession and found it in soil erosion. Funded publicly (and barely), the Service's unofficial slogan was "Low pay, hard work, and more!" Luna bounced between conservation camps. She was a senior corps member now, currently stationed at Brasher Falls, upstate New York, leading a team in digging rock dams to mitigate landslide risk, which was elevated across the country though no one really knew why. She hadn't finished college. Winnie sometimes suggested night classes, but she seemed to be the only one who still saw in Luna the straitlaced Rotary club vice president anticipating matriculation at UC Berkeley. Luna didn't appreciate those reminders of her old self, her in her ignorance before her misdemeanor conviction put Berkeley all but out of reach and the hurricane killed her reaching spirit. For her, the end of high school was a flirtation between commiserable despair and repellent acts of self-sabotage designed to convince everyone that the just desserts she'd been served were lip-smackingly to her taste, acts like showing up half an hour late to the ACT, or cussing out her A.P. Chinese Lit teacher so instead of a college rec she got a GPA plumb bob. She arrived at SUNY Albany, which took her parents' 529 plan, and pledged the hardest-hazing sorority, saying that she was game for whatever and then some. She fit right in and dropped right out the bottom. That's when Winnie caught her. Luna went to rehab, got off the wrong drugs and on to the "right" ones. It was just the two of them now.

They only talked about Nat when they were high. Sometimes they laughed over funny memories. Other times they criticized. Luna wanted to believe that they'd already grown apart from Nat before the hurricane. She compared the unspoken end of their friendship to a gradual elastic deformation—hard to notice but also the hardest kind of rupture to mend. "Maybe," Winnie said. In high school Winnie had missed things. She had, for example, underestimated the role of money, underestimated it routinely and deliberately because if she had acknowledged incompatibilities between herself and Nat and attributed them to money, then logically the problem would have to be

Winnie's lack. *She* would be (in her own mind) the one unqualified for Nat's friendship. In that way, among others, Winnie now understood, incompatibility charged the attraction. Still, she missed Nat.

"You've never accepted Nat's death," Luna said once at the end of a long, stoned night.

But then, how could Winnie accept it, since she'd seen it herself. Since she'd had to stand on the couch holding Nat's surprisingly heavy body for three hours while the water surged up to her knees, stumbling and dropping her—far too physical an object to have anything to do with their friend, their friend who was so much a disembodied concept to Winnie that even in life Winnie couldn't picture what she looked like. How did Luna accept that Nat was that rag doll body, which Winnie now pictured every day because she had seen it with her own eyes.

"She's just dead, she's just dead." Luna honestly couldn't say it any more than she already did. It is a material world, she liked to say. That's the material nature of things. Nat, who lived for her grades and for making memes, who was well-behaved, if a bit insensitive, sometimes she would piss off her best friends but she expected you never to stay mad at her, she got split open one day and there's no fixing that. "That's things." Like Winnie's mom. Like everyone, running circles around the abyss. Across her mind the bad thoughts drifted like plastic bags in water. She sank her face into her hands.

"What's wrong?" Luna asked. Arthur Russell was mumbling and tapping his microphone.

"Nothing," said Winnie.

"So, it's not till December. But I already RSVP'd since I thought Fier would come with me. I don't want to go alone. It's a huge gala. Lots of Shell people and celebrities."

"For sure, I'll come," said Winnie absentmindedly and asked for the details. The sun was already coming down. Deliquescent Saint Emily partook of sea salt and sage.

The gala was going to be in Beijing. Black tie. Luna talked for a while about what she could wear. She said what Winnie should wear (famous dresses Winnie hadn't taken out in years). She wondered who they might meet.

Winnie asked how Luna had gotten an invitation.

"The Forest Service bought some invites to lottery off to corps members as a holiday prize. Just for people on at least their fifth rotation."

"That's amazing you won."

"More or less." Luna pulled her knobby knees into her chest. "Sofia from my team, you remember her? She won an invite."

Winnie studied her. "I hope you're not saying what I think you're saying."

A fly buzzed. Luna gave a twisted smirk, her first expression of joy all evening. "I've never had luck, but I have karmic credits to trade in."

"Are you serious?" Winnie stood, lightheaded.

Luna followed her into her room. "What?" she said. "What?"

"Your prescription is for *you*. If you keep trading your pills away to corps members for shit like gala tickets, then you're not taking your pills, and whose problem is that going to become?"

"Other corps members have trauma too," said Luna. "Sofia wanted them."

"Then she should get her own prescription." Winnie turned on her bedroom lights, breaking the spell. There were soiled coffee mugs puzzled together on her nightstand.

"Okay, big pharma."

"And what are you?"

Luna said, "A woman-owned business."

"I need to get ready for work."

"Sure."

While Winnie dressed, Luna watched Streamscape on the floor. She never liked to be alone. Winnie paid her glances through the mirror and felt bad.

"I only act this way because I'm seriously worried about you getting yourself in trouble," she said.

Luna nodded, keeping her eyes on the screen. They tried to take care of each other, but it was hard. Once while high, Luna had said that there was no redemption in life except the redemption of blood equity. For the rest of that night, Winnie hadn't said a word. Sometimes they got high and just ate ice cream in silence.

Another thing about living with Luna: She kept an Emergency Supplies cabinet above the microwave stocked with granola bars and canned lentil soup, but then when an emergency actually occurred (such as the shooting on their block a month ago, when the police wouldn't let anyone out of the building for over six hours and Winnie was starving), she said Winnie couldn't eat that stuff because it was "for emergencies."

After the paramedics had taken Nat's body away, Luna had paced up and down the street. "What are we supposed to do now?" she said when the ambulance was out of view. "Should we lock up the house or something? I don't know. I seriously don't know."

Winnie said they didn't need to do anything, but Luna just kept shaking her head and saying she didn't know.

For a long time, Winnie had tried to move past what happened to them. She went to UCLA for computer science and threw herself into her studies, avoiding parties, preferring to spend her Californian evenings in the library, embedding for-loops in for-loops to frightening depths. No one tried to pull her out. Her randomly assigned freshman suitemate, a depressed Peruvian who studied film and lived on Cary Grant romcoms, was the only girl with whom Winnie interacted, and then only to discuss cleaning schedules. After living together for almost a full year, she asked if Winnie had any sophomore housing plans, and when Winnie said no, she said, "Would you like to find a place together? You seem like you could make a good roommate." Luna found that story hilarious. Sophomore year, the girl fell ill and

went back to Lima, but her parents kept paying her room and board—
a sort of prayer-in-cash that their daughter would recover. The next
year, Winnie got a studio off campus.

She had a couple of experiments with romance. The first was finals
week of her freshman year. She was in the library late one night (this
was back when nights were still long enough for it to get late; that
subversive feeling of "lateness," of reaching night's penetralium, was
one she already associated with bygone youth). A senior whom she'd
often seen across the lab came over to ask if she'd eaten. He must have
noticed her stealing glances. He wasn't particularly handsome—his
neck seemed never to have swallowed its baby fat—but he had a seriousness to the way he worked, which she liked, and she'd once seen
him holding hands with her machine learning TA, a frail junior girl
whom Winnie admired if only for lack of female CS role models. The
dining hall was closed, so they went back to his apartment, and he was
gentle, but it still hurt. He kept asking if it was okay, and she gave shallow nods, hoping he wouldn't notice that she was there. Afterward, he
put on jazz and talked about how sad he was to be graduating. When
Winnie left, she called Luna.

The second was soon before Winnie's own graduation. She had to
graduate early, at the end of her junior year. She was one of a whole
cohort of scholarship students who were given early diplomas when
the market crash wiped out the UC endowment fund. As a result, she
found herself graduating in the middle of a recession, and the stress
of job searching woke her in a panic almost every day that spring. She
went to career fairs and bounced between recruiters for Walt Disney
and Lockheed Martin. It felt like she was applying for everything.
One week, after a series of video interviews, she believed that she was
going to be a concierge at a hotel in Japan. Picturing a life of wake-up
calls and sake service, she tried to fold what she knew about herself
into this new self-conception. Another week, when she didn't get that
job, she convinced herself that she wanted to go into finance. Not
for years had her sense of identity been so unmoored. It was strange

and painful, trying to prove to the world that she could be valuable to it and having the world tell her no. During this period of confusion, she met the only boy she'd ever date, and only for a short time at that, one from the apps, an aspiring comedian named James. His MateMe profile had him at 5'9" and "wise," but he was more like 5'8" and clever. He worked birthday parties for rich families in Malibu, then did the open-mic circuit during off hours. Winnie hated attending his mics. Several times, she was the only audience member who wasn't there to perform, and every comic directed their new jokes at her, scrutinizing her for laughs. They all made the same riffs on day contraction ("Thank you, you've been here all week."). A surprising, but soon tedious, number used their five minutes to "open up" about how they'd thought of killing themselves.

James was desperate for affection, and that's why she put up with him. She needed his need. He made her feel like a hero just because she had the power to give (likely carnassial) blowjobs, and she availed him of this power often. Aware that she was filling her sudden and daunting need for career validation with the orgasms of a twenty-year-old boy, she nonetheless preferred acting out her debasement rather than bearing it quietly in respectable solitude. People all around seemed to be performing their misery in public; it was something to do in your twenties so you'd have something to tell of your suffering later.

But what came of that relationship was her introduction to James's uncle, Chip Knoepffler of BodyThink. At a Memorial Day barbecue in a muddy San Jose park, Uncle Chip threw a vegan burg'r on the grill for Winnie but made her stay and watch it cook because he didn't believe it would "work" the same as a regular burger and he refused to assume responsibility for any product that might besmirch his record as grillmaster. James was hardly talking to her that day (he was still upset with her for confessing the previous night that she didn't see the point of comedy), so she had nothing to do but listen to Chip Knoepffler talk about his business. His splotchy head was topped by a slick of yellowing white hair, courtesy of laser therapy.

Pushing sixty with all his might, he wore what was clearly his "fun tie": little pictures of the late Elon Musk in sunglasses. Without ever really explaining what his tech startup BodyThink did, he boasted to Winnie that they had the "cream of the crème" with respect to strategy analysts. Three MBAs; two early promotes poached from Goldman Sachs; and Chip himself had been a VP of brand strategy back at Scroller. The team was churning out decks and decks celebrating everything their flagship app would accomplish. Now, they just needed someone to make the app.

"Honestly," he told her, "it shouldn't be so hard to find a programmer. We've got funding enough for the crème." Moisture gathered in the folds of his forehead. His fun tie seemed to be strangling him. James, across the park, chugged a Blue Moon to the chanting of his cousins, unaware that they were making fun of him. "But it's got to be a fit, you get it?" Chip said. "Not someone who'll try to steal the show."

Gray sweater over her sundress, Winnie said, "I can code."

Within a month, she had dumped James, walked at graduation, and reported for her first day at BodyThink.

Since then, times had changed. The sun rose through the Shell patchwork every fourteen hours, then every thirteen hours, and now every twelve. She worked five hours on, ten hours off, and spent her time off napping or smoking alongside Luna without any real routine. She saw no problem in being high or exhausted; she was holding down her job, so she was doing what she was supposed to. It was just hard, and getting harder, to ward off the bad thoughts.

"Luna," she said, "will you be here when I get back?"

"Yeah."

Leaning against the windowsill to pull on her flats, Winnie looked out. The morning sun illuminated a bright vertical line in the distant northeast: the nearest Shell support column. Entwined with piping and elevators, it rose up from the ground to the altitude of circuit vessel, thirty thousand feet, and then higher, twice that high, to sixty thousand feet, where it held up the weight of the Shell.

Winnie pushed her fingers through Luna's pixie cut and saw the news on Luna's phone. Earnings reports were in. Stock markets were up. Across the world, people were getting paid to do absolutely nothing.

All you had to do was get through the day.

Cromwell Grant

Late morning, fresh off his Peloton, Cromwell Grant, Executive Vice President – Communications and newly appointed executive director to the CWC Group (at fifty-one, the youngest director on the board), sat at the end of his bed with feet in loose black socks planted on the egg-shaped rug that tied the room together without distracting from the magnificent vista of the limestone driveway turnaround that his wife, a forty-seven-year-old former model now pursuing a cross-cultural studies Ph.D., had littered with "crafty" paper lanterns and other handmade Autumn Mooncake Festival geegaws, which (because the driveway fully insulated the house from the road) only Grant ever saw and which irritated him to no end. Work gave him reason enough to feel tense, and it didn't help that he had recently broken off his affair with a perky Swiss flight attendant (his "route rat"). He pressed a button to drop the blackout curtains. In the tepid lamplight and the smell of his body post-workout, damp buttocks on the throw quilt and one of many nameless Roombas crawling by, Grant scrolled through hard-core teen options on his 16090p. Each holographic pair copulated in his lap for no more than fifteen seconds before transfiguring into new lovers with an impatient flick of his nondominant hand. After six and a half minutes, he shot airplanes.

He soaped himself in his steam room and donned his terrycloth robe. His sons, twelve and thirteen, were in the game room studying. He popped in.

"Anyone fancy a FIFA break?"

"We're with our tutor."

"Ah," said Grant. "Chinese homework, eh?" He bent down to say hello to the tutor, a bubbly college girl on their tablet screen. "I'm glad they have you to help them with this, Suzie. This stuff is like Chinese to me."

"We're having fun with it, aren't we boys?"

"Fun! I reckon you're up to no good," said Grant. "Well, fine, you're allowed to smoke dope and drink beers with them as long as they pass their placement tests."

She laughed. "Okay, Mr. Grant."

He tried to kill time answering emails, but time proved hardier than he hoped. His inbox these days was inexhaustible. Shell construction in seventeen Contract Districts was behind schedule, and in the other C.D.s it was coming in over budget. The construction subsidiaries that CWC had developed to build infrastructure during the Equity Push were now fully adapted to the business of Shell construction, making CWC the eighth-largest Shell contractor in Europe and twelfth-largest in the world. But holding that market share was a constant ball ache, and regulators at the Santiago Commission hadn't been making things any easier. This month a freeze was put on CWC's North American construction by the Commission's engineering compliance officer, the maladroit son of a Korean chaebol whose appointment CWC Comms had backed as a favor to his father, to get him out of the family business. Now, he was alleging control deficiencies in coil suspension components. As if he knew the first thing about coil suspension components. (Not that Grant did.)

But he wasn't even the worst CWC beneficiary lately turning on Grant. The worst was Bickle, constantly whinging about his job and demanding "credit" for his hard work (i.e., more money). Grant's prize hog had been given the finest Dolce lipstick for seven years, but he wanted more; he expected a turn with the farmer's daughter. Another

$500k when Comms was already overbudget from fielding all the scrutiny visited upon the company in the years since the market crash. Bickle had no shame. Celebrity had gone to his head in the worst way. He sent Grant emails on a weekly basis, venting about the shit *he* had to eat, saying the company was devaluing *his* image.

Well, this would be all fun and games, typical talent care, except that Bickle had no legal instincts. He wrote things that shouldn't appear in writing under any circumstances, wildly embellishing CWC's shortcomings in order to exaggerate the company's dependence on him. In company emails, he claimed he was covering up criminal wrongdoing for Grant. Suppose those messages were ever for any reason subpoenaed: didn't he see how incriminating they were? It'd be "insiders openly discuss gross abuse!" and they might well both end up serving at Her Majesty's pleasure. Grant couldn't decide if he should reply telling Bickle to cut it out or leave the messages unread, to preserve some thin pretense of never having seen them. He probably ought to notify the Icelanders. Those were Bickle's lawyers. Icelanders! The man wouldn't shell out for reputable counsel. He seemed to want lawyers whose advice he could justify ignoring.

"FIFA time, FIFA time," said Grant's younger son, Careca-airplaning into the kitchen. His brother whispered in Grant's ear from behind, "EA Sports: It's in the game."

"You two against me," Grant said. That way he could beat them both. He would be thinking about Victor Bickle and playing dirty.

Filed A.H. 1,040,508:02 GRA_00CWC109884

To: Cromwell Grant
FROM: Victor Bickle
SENT: A.H. 1,030,663:45
SUBJECT: F&F

Cromwell,

If you saw yesterday's Fox & Friends you'll know that the nitro-glycerine investigation came up and, like you instructed, I said more research is still needed into demo site leaching. What do you think was the response I got? What did I say it would be? Streamscape fucking slaughtered me.

Once again, I'm out there wiping your ass, and without any new consideration being given to my pay in over three years. You're really going to tell me we don't have "the budget" for my raise?

All rights expressly reserved,

Victor Bickle

Filed A.H. 1,040,508:02 GRA_00CWC109885

To: Cromwell Grant
FROM: Victor Bickle
SENT: A.H. 1,031,261:23
SUBJECT: Sailing

It's about proper appreciation! Maybe someone might dig into your little budget and see if a hole could be plugged up somewhere, perhaps in the vicinity of Brazil, perhaps in the vicinity of the presidente's new Ilhabela retreat. Just saying what I'm hearing. Waiting for the day when

THAT one hits the press. And who do you expect to take that heat?
You might look and find me gone. Gone sailing in Ilhabela!

All rights expressly reserved,

Victor Bickle

Filed A.H. 1,040,508:02   *GRA_00CWC109886*

To: Cromwell Grant
FROM: Victor Bickle
SENT: A.H. 1,034,128:58
SUBJECT:

This quarter I'm keeping a list of all the backlash CWC has courted that's
fallen to me to clean up. So far it includes: price signaling, illegal dumping, blind eye to human traffic, lack of internal controls (many), inhu-
mane treatment of stowaways, overaccruing docking site royalty reserves
(improperly carried at quarter end), discriminatory hiring, faulty coil
suspension components, undisclosed vendor relationships, Shell screen
installation behind schedule, Shell construction harnesses (infertility concern), pod cancellations, Shell Switch-On Day keeps getting delayed.

I know my value to this company. I am not just protecting you for my
health. I'm the face of this company, and I expect to be paid like it!

Filed A.H. 1,040,508:02   *GRA_00CWC109887*

Ex. 301

END OF EXHIBIT

SELECTED EMAILS OF DEFENDANT VICTOR BICKLE
A.H. 1,030K – 1,035K
SUBMITTED TO THE COURT A.H. 1,040,508

DAYS OF 9 HOURS

Bickle stepped off the pod at Piccadilly Circus to the sated chirps of sparrows shaking their wings in plastic plane trees, the trusty chime of an old library clock, and the sour, honking moloch of a dog-eyed people who hadn't slept well in years.

"Wanker," spat a middle-aged mother, slapping a car that lurched into the slushy intersection. A crowd of tourists before the Streamscape-famous Piccadilly Lights all struck the same poses beneath a sky crawling with circuit vessels and rumbling with construction. Bickle appeared briefly disoriented before seeing me and hurrying my way.

I was there to escort him to Aviation Tower for his meeting with Cromwell Grant and CEO Trisha Pitafi. Awaiting his arrival, I had his lawyer on the phone.

I pulled out one earbud and said, "Magnús wants a word with you." Bickle shook his head.

"Magnús—I'm sorry," I said. "He's not—"

Bickle took my earbud and hung up the call.

I said, "Your lawyers believe this stance with Grant is ill-advised."

We pushed through the crowds. Tourists who had been taking selfies in front of the Lights' ad for GAP Tween Underwear were starting to notice Bickle and take selfies with him in the background. Some shouted his name, trying to get him to look. Pretending not to hear them, he checked his hair, then strode across the six-way intersection, narrowly avoiding death.

Bickle visited London every couple of workweeks but usually flew straight to the pod platform on the roof of Aviation Tower. I knew he liked to minimize time spent in London's labyrinthine streets, which he found tortuous compared to the orderly grid of Manhattan, his adoptive home. But Aviation Tower's pod platform was closed today. All across London, as in New York and elsewhere, CWC pod platforms were undergoing renovations. Many if not all of them were growing old and beginning to tilt. They tilted only a degree or two. An almost imperceptible amount, but significant when scaled up by the number of pods that had to burn energy adjusting their trajectories midair because their launches were off. The platform atop Aviation Tower was one of the original spring-loaded models, long overdue for replacement anyway, and CWC was happy to donate it to the National Museum of Science and Industry. Still, it was curious that every one of the tilted platforms in London and New York, no matter what kind of ground it sat in or which way it opened, tilted precisely south.

"Magnús wants to remind you that your pay was just renegotiated last year. He feels it's inappropriate to ask for a renegotiation now," I said.

Bickle said he didn't intend to ask.

"He said there's no basis for it in your contract."

We turned right onto Brewer Street, with its car dealerships and smears of dogshit. Luffing banners read IT's ALL ON BREWER!

Bickle said, "Grant thinks you can just bind people up in contracts. I want a world where we're not signing 'contracts' but 'expands.' How about that?"

"What?"

Too much noise. Beyond the powder blue atmosphere, the Shell, half-solid, half-scaffolding like the semidome of an amphitheater or the partially cracked roof of a jalopy convertible, whined at the commencement of a thousand power drills.

"It's like living inside a factory," he said.

I said, "Could you stop a second?"

He did. Over his shoulder, the setting sun was a cold pinpoint between steel beams. A new machine sputtered overhead, like a lawnmower kicking to life, and Londoners up and down the street ignored it.

"With all due respect," I said. "If it's appreciation you want, are you sure a raise in pay is going to make you feel that?"

His gaze wandered as he considered this. I traced it up to the North, which was still open to the sky. Or not the sky, per se, since the sky was contained within the Shell, in the sense that the Shell was enclosing plenty of atmosphere. More than enough atmosphere to say that even to the South, where the Shell was fully constructed, the sky was still there (if it could be said that the sky "was" anywhere). So then what did the North open up to if not the sky? What did Bickle see gazing as far as he could? Nothing, I supposed. An infinity of nothing and the waning moon.

"I don't know," he answered. He looked back down and kept walking. "But it's better than not a raise."

I left him outside Grant's office suite with a final word of warning. "Don't push things too hard."

Annoyed, he drew his bottom teeth over his mustache. "I don't agree," he said. He knocked on Grant's door and let himself in without awaiting a reply.

I went to find Miguel. The office was at half capacity, CWC's midweek hump shift, A.H. '40 to '45. Shell construction pealed outside with the wearying insistence of a phone ringing in someone else's office, noises like cricket chirps that come to signify quiet.

Miguel sat at his desk with two cups of coffee, stirrers still spinning. He said, "I can't believe he's picking fights with Grant again."

"It's not my choice," I said.

He handed me my coffee. Sugar, no cream. "I'm not saying it is."

"He just freaks out sometimes. I can't control it. Grant will deal with it."

I took an absentminded gulp and got burned.

He leaned across his desk to take my hand. "I'm proud of you for working so hard."

I said nothing. The coffee machine left a certain plasticity that brought me back to when Miguel and I would linger by his desk, drinking cup after cup, trying to suppress our nerves after everyone else went home for the night.

He stroked my arm where my sleeve was rolled up. I angled away.

"Minou," he said.

"What?"

"Je suis excité."

"What?" I faced him. He was stretched over his desk, looking up.

"En serio."

"Here?" I said.

"The IT closet?"

I thought about it. I wanted it badly.

"Or wherever."

"Why don't we go home?" I said.

"There's an electricity in the IT closet. You'll feel it as soon as I unzip you. You'll feel my mouth when I'm still a centimeter away."

While I thought, he fit two fingers into my eight o'clock belt loop.

"I want to," I said.

"Come."

A few copyeditors were in the kitchen, whooping whenever they got something in their crossword puzzle. The sun was setting, closing the office into its own little world.

"Let's go home."

He was flat across his desk now, creasing papers, pinning his rolling chair with his toes.

"What's wrong with us?" I asked.

He said yo no sé.

The elevator dinged.

"You know I want to," I said. "I keep asking you before bed."

Someone entered the office. Miguel let go. I lurched forward a step.

"Tanner!"

It was Imani. She was up from the building's lower floors, where for the past three years she had directed the Forwards Foundation. I'd barely seen her in that time. Muddy snow boots freighted her waddle and completed her pantsuit in an affluent-functional anti-chic sort of way. She asked Miguel why he was on his desk.

"Trying to reach that," he said and pointed to a pen on the ground. It was closest to her, but I bent for it, perhaps out of an instinct to shrink. Coming up, I realized that Imani, who hadn't made even a gestural offer to pick up the pen, was pregnant. It was strange to see. I hadn't thought her one to ever settle down. She asked what brought me to the office, and I answered, not knowing if I should comment on her apparent pregnancy (realizing that of course I shouldn't, but feeling how odd that was when staring at a friend, if estranged, who was so obviously pregnant). I looked at Miguel.

Miguel looked pleadingly, fuckingly, at me.

I looked back at Imani. "How have you been?" I managed.

"Can't complain!" said Imani. "How about you guys?"

"You are going to decide how this meeting goes," Grant told Bickle. "Whether we leave here as friends depends entirely on your actions."

His seat was raised so he could hulk over his desk, which made him look equal parts menacing and tired. Enthroned emperor to an office overrun by trash—classic westward circuit ads now catacombed beneath Shell screen catalogs and construction timetables. Bickle eyed a bowl of red apples on the desk, trying to determine if they were plastic. He wasn't going to embarrass himself by taking one.

Outside the window a flurry of snowflakes rode updrafts in a scramble to prolong life above wet city streets. They were lit by the

Shell's provisional lanterns, which shone through thin patches in the clouds. In the distance, a column of light extended to the Shell from the ground: it was the nearest Shell support pillar, way out in Mitcham.

Bickle said, "I want Pitafi here."

"She's coming."

"I assume you've told her about my demand for a raise."

"No," said Grant. "For your sake, I did not."

"What do you mean for my sake? You know, Cromwell, I'm the face of this organization. They're writing profiles on Victor Bickle while you sit behind a desk, fucking things up. If I'm going to continue to yoke my career to this stumbling, ten-headed beast, I demand appreciation."

"What career?"

"I'm sick of this disrespect."

Grant interlaced his fingers. His office reeked of strawberry vape; his recycling bin overflowed with crushed coffee cans; his wife, on her Islam rotation, had prayer alarms going off throughout their house five times per day. Practically every hour.

"Yeah," he said, "this is gonna fly like silver carp. I'll be full of beans as King Hal and tell you, Bickle, that you need CWC far more than it needs you. What do you say to that?"

A spider outside the window clung to a web arching in snowy gusts. Spiders often got to the 118th floor and then couldn't find flies. They froze dangling from Grant's head jamb.

Bickle said, "I'm not wasting more breath until Pitafi's here."

"Horses for courses! Horses for courses!" said Grant. "You know, if you weren't making such a Peter O' of yourself, I'd accuse you of breaching your contract and claw back everything we've paid you already. As it is, you ought to be grateful that I've kept your incessant badgering from Pitafi, because frankly she's the only one saving you from the sack. She thinks you've done a good enough job helping this company through some stormy waters in the past, and sacking you will be a whole thing that she doesn't need right now, especially with the board all nervy about bad press in the month to come. But Pitafi doesn't have to work with you every day like I do. She doesn't know the full extent of what an immature arse you can be, so if you know what's good for you, you'll drop this rubbish when she gets here."

Bickle asked why the board expected bad press in the month to come, and Grant sat back in his chair. He rolled his head around on his meaty neck.

"Next week," he said, "a team of researchers for the Santiago Commission will be publishing a memo. We know the subject: 'Super-Climatic Effects of Day Contraction.' The old john dory is that the memo's going to ring alarm bells about centrifugal effects that go beyond changes in weather and sea level. Effects even the Shell can't correct."

"Like what?"

"Perceptible losses in gravity."

Bickle picked his mustache. "Weren't people talking about this years ago? Back in *Science Hour*, like, season four. You said gravity loss wasn't real science. 'Not in this epoch,' you said."

"What time of day did you ask me?"

"Ha."

"Have an apple."

Bickle reached out tentatively. The apple was real. He said, "When do you think we'll start feeling centrifugal effects then, if you're the scientist?" He ate his apple by taking only shallow bites first, until all of the skin was gone except small red islands around the stamen and stem. It was how he'd always done it growing up in Keber Creek.

Grant said, "If I were an expert, I think I'd be investigating why every pod platform in the Northern Hemisphere has started tilting south, and every one down South has started tilting north. I'm telling you this before it goes public so you understand that this isn't the time to play reputational brinksmanship."

"Because if I'm not around to be the friendly face of industry, CWC will get its comeuppance."

"No," said Grant. "Because if you're not with CWC, I will make sure that every ecological oversight this company has made in the past seven years gets pinned to you like you're a Hungerford gum drop on Hock Tuesday. You're playing chicken in the battery cages of a slaughterhouse, my friend."

Bickle threw his fleshy white apple at Grant's head.

Grant ducked. Then stared in disbelief at Bickle, whose anger now shone unbridled as the door opened and Trisha Pitafi entered.

Imani's husband Henry arrived at Miguel's desk. Wearing both his backpack and his wife's gaping leather purse, he seemed tense from a long day not yet over, emails still outstanding, anticipating Lernaean replies. He didn't seem to notice how preoccupied Miguel and I were. Imani kept asking questions about how my work schedule was adjusting to these shortened days (the funnel down which all idle chatter eventually fell) and lateraling my answers to Henry. "You've been napping a lot too, babe, right?" *Everyone is napping a lot*, I thought. Imani complained about all the pod platform renovations forcing her to walk so much. "At the worst possible time," she said, giving me a chance to ask about the pregnancy, but I missed it, distracted by Miguel, who had turned morose. He said, "Something is wrong with us," quietly to himself. That was when Noah appeared.

"Oh my god," said Imani. "It's like a Fighting 118th reunion!"

Noah had been taken off Grant's team after the Equity Push and moved upstairs to lobbying, where the overbearing sycophancy he'd first directed entirely at Grant could be distributed across a multitude of playmakers, convincing each that he was their man and no one else's. He kept his hair out of his face by gluing it to the side of his head and wore one of those suits that was all one piece—jacket and shirt and tie conveniently stitched together so everything stayed perfectly in place. Suits for idiots, I thought.

"I like your suit," I told him.

"Thanks. It's what all the MPs wear."

I smelled his sugary gum, which he said was the new Juicy Fruit energy gum, and he passed around the packaging the way some people circulate pictures of their kids.

Miguel stood beside me. I rested a hand on the small of his back, to say *I'm here*.

Noah asked how everyone's work schedules were adjusting to these shortened days.

The Forwards Foundation was trying to fund Shell programming that would have a positive social impact. Imani said, "We're donating to charities that want to buy Shellspace rights for awareness campaigns. PSAs and 'The More You Know,' that sort of thing."

Everyone said that was great.

"If only Kiko Alexandra and Fez were still here," she said, marking that moment when an office conversation burns through the present company's outermost recitals and, for fear of making anyone feel heat, turns its focus upon those who have left, always with a mix of bemused scorn and envy. Kiko Alexandra and Fez left CWC early in the recession, when circuit shares plummeted and CWC cut everyone's pay. They started their own media company.

"I myself was just happy to not be laid off," Imani said.

"I considered leaving," said Noah to me.

Miguel mumbled, "Why didn't you?"

I flashed him a look.

"But see what they're doing now?" said Imani. And everyone nodded because everyone did. We saw Kiko Alexandra and Fez even when we weren't looking—on Streamscape, in posts shared by distant relatives, and on a big screen outside the Harold Pinter Theatre. Last time I checked, the *Roads Less Travelled* podcast had eleven million subscribers. There was something irresistible in the way they bantered on the podcast, even to me, who used to speak to them regularly in real life. The way they laughed in headphones was different. More intimate.

"I tried," Miguel whispered to me.

Noah said the full idiom is *The more you know, the less you understand.*
"It's from the Tao Te Ding."

Henry kept checking his email, like a junkie scouring the same
spent baggies, while Imani talked about the Beijing gala in two weeks.
She said Kiko Alexandra and Fez would be there. No one asked what
the hell was the "Tao Te Ding."

"What do you mean you tried?" I whispered back.

"I offered. But you never meet me halfway."

I looked at Miguel, but couldn't find his eyes. He had fleshy little
ears, which I used to fit entirely in my mouth. For the first time, I
let myself imagine life without him. And though I didn't long for it,
simply imagining it as a real possibility, one that I could survive, with
some advantages even, scared me. I searched inside my chest for the
kernel of love I'd tried for so long to take such good care of.

Finally Imani said, "Sorry, but are you two okay?"

I looked at the ground.

Miguel said, "Things have been not great for some time."

Everyone looked at him, hoping for a punchline. None came.

There was silence for a moment, only a moment, and then Noah
asked Imani when the baby was due.

"What is going on here?" said Trisha Pitafi.

"I'm not being appreciated," Bickle announced. "I want a raise."

Pitafi said, "Let's take a step back."

Bickle righted his chair and everyone sat. Pitafi wore no jewelry
except the wedding ring she'd held on to through widowhood. The
prior week she had become CWC's longest-serving CEO, with a tenure
entering its ninth year. A celebration was held at the American Club.
She'd spent the whole evening entertaining large accounts.

Grant said, "I've told him that his contract—"

"Suddenly Cromwell is the paragon of contractual fidelity," Bickle
said. "Give me a break."

Pitafi asked what the hell he was talking about.

Bickle said, "This company is a disgrace. I want my raise."

"He's off his trolley," said Grant.

"I'm keeping the trolley on the tracks. And given the roadblocks you just told me CWC is headed for, I have half a mind to up my demands."

Pitafi said, "Why do you think you deserve a raise?"

"I assume Cromwell has forwarded you my emails."

She looked across the desk to Grant.

Grant said, "Over the past several months, he's sent me an accelerating bumf roll of compromising emails, defaming the company in a brash attempt to neg us into paying him more, correspondences which out of legalistic concern, I did not expose you to."

Bickle threw his hands up.

Pitafi asked to see the messages, and Grant passed her a tablet. Projected from the screen was a stack of emails five centimeters high. She read the first in silence. Outside, the Shell's work-lights were dim in night mode. The building's blue beacons underlit flurrying snow-flakes. Grant and Bickle watched Pitafi read as frenzy sobered into guardedness, which was the sign of real, lethal hostility. She swiped through, scanning every second or third correspondence, until she'd seen enough, at which point she jotted a note with her index finger and slid the tablet back to Grant. Bickle watched her expectantly.

She stood. "I'm sorry," she said. "I need to excuse myself."

She had no possessions to gather. She pushed her chair back a step, even though it wasn't under the desk. And with all the abruptness of time-honored protocol, she took her leave.

The door closed behind her.

Grant read her note. His eyebrows lifted. "You're surfed, Bickle."

"What?"

"You're axed," he said. "Redundant. Contract terminated. Ta for your service. You have twenty-four hours to surrender any confidential CWC work-product in your possession, and if you ever disclose to anyone any confidential information acquired during your time here, we'll take you for every farthing you're worth."

"Excuse me?"

"Yes, you've been excused," said Grant, a smile creeping across his face. A sticker on his desk flashed: I Donated to Water Mongolia—It's Up to Each of Us.

"I am the face of this company."

Grant laughed. "Save it and scram."

"Where'd Trisha go?"

"Get the shite-out-of out of here," said Grant. "And know one last thing. Because sometimes when these sorts of relationships end, people in your position get ideas, they think of turning their platform against CWC, and that's something our comms department has learned it's best to nip in the bud . . . So. If ever, out there, you speak ill of CWC, I promise you this: that I will see to it personally the world finds out about the daughter you abandoned."

"What are you talking about?"

"Very good. You can keep that up, pretend she doesn't exist. Just know that I know."

Bickle said, "I don't have a daughter."

"I put a team out to find her," said Grant. "Back when we first met. You think I would have hired you after your disreputable little departure from Columbia without making sure I knew every single side to the story? I know your story better than you do."

"You said when I came here that I didn't need to worry about Columbia."

"And now you're leaving. Welcome to worryland, Bickle. That is, if you cross CWC. Or you can keep your head down, enjoy retirement, and your fans never need to know about how you cruelly forsook your Alaskan love and her little girl."

Bickle was standing. His feet slid on discarded brochures. He shook like he would bash Grant's head in, but instead, he grabbed a tablet and flung it at the window.

"You're lying," he said.

But Grant just laughed, while the tablet fountained holographic documents into the air, fritzing out, prismatic and crepitant.

○

The first argument Luna posited against having kids was that in this society, a child could never grow up to do enough good to outweigh all the bad demanded merely for the preservation of her life. You couldn't possibly expect the child you created to come close to net positive, someone to be proud of. Not that there should be no humans at all, just that a person born on today's margin, a margin extended by industrial food, a labor market of annular exploitation, a social imaginary whose entry fee was not only truth but reason . . . At best, if you were lucky, you might raise a child possessed of the strength to feel sad when looking upon sunlit fields of trash. And who would be to blame?

BodyThink shared an office space with four other impact-driven start-ups, and Winnie liked to situate herself in the interzone, a stranger to all. She'd only recently come into full knowledge of what her company did, and she wasn't particularly motivated to help. Standing at one of four chest-high counters that all bore identical woodgrain patterns, she pressed her hands to her ears to tune out the steady drizzle of typing, the muted duotone footfall of leather shoes on antistatic pile carpet, the chime of a backspace attempted where none was allowed, and she browsed Reddit. (r/BadCode: *If programmers weren't God's laziest children, why would there be 3.2k posts here devoted to '**unexpected {**' memes while no attempt has been made to figure out why my headphones keep connecting to my neighbor's vibrator . . .*) Twin smokestacks outside punctured the marine layer. Rainclouds hung heavy but hung on. Someone said Winnie's name. She turned.

There were only a dozen other employees at BodyThink. Six were "Strategy Analysts," and this was one. They were all guys between twenty-two and thirty, and they called themselves the "analists" because they were all about fucking the incumbent competitor up the ass. Winnie turned her phone over and crossed her arms. She kept a crewneck sweatshirt at the office because even in November the office ran AC. Maybe it was supposed to keep people awake. Winnie still felt tired most of the time, just tired with a feverish chill. The same temperature outside would rattle teeth, but something about knowing the cold was intentional apparently made it less bothersome to Winnie's coworkers, and Winnie was one of the only women in the office who treated herself to more than a light blouse. Her sweatshirt said, "ALL YOU NEED IS LOVE. AND COFFEE." It was the kind of sweatshirt you were left with when all of Target's best minds really had run out of ideas.

The analyst asked if she'd have the KPIs by EOD; she just said yes and yes until he returned to his buddies at their usual desk, talking their usual shit about BodyThink's CEO Chip Knoepffler. Secretly, they all wished they'd been hired by one of the incumbent competitors. BodyThink was a startup thirty years too late with a CEO thirty years too old who founded it essentially as a grudge-play after being laid off from Scroller when that company restructured to form Streamscape. He wanted to prove that he could start his own Silicon Valley unicorn, but this was A.H. 1,034k. All the new, "disruptive" tech firms, like Streamscape, had ownership tracing back to Facebook, Google, Amazon, or the Chinese government. BodyThink would have needed hundreds more programmers to compete, and honestly they could have done without Winnie, even she would admit.

She hadn't done any honest work all shift. The strategy analysts thought she was performing a major update for the beta, but really she was just shuffling the layout, which she did every month to stay ahead of them. She had to claim ground where she could. For the longest time, even the basics of the company's strategy eluded her—it all seemed needlessly complex, especially since BodyThink's app, if it ever left development, would not make money by costing customers money, nor would it even go for free, but rather it would undercut the competition by listing on app stores for as low as negative 2.99.

"This is basic stuff. What do you think everyone else is doing?" said Chip Knoepffler. "What's the difference between our plan and Printing Presto offering ten-dollar credits to first-time users? Or Cell-Cell buying 15,000 users from winfox.com, which Winfox provides by raffling off gift cards to account holders who download Cell-Cell? Cell-Cell still sold-sold to investors for five bil. And what makes Cell-Cell any better than the BodyThink PocketPuncher?"

The BodyThink PocketPuncher. That was their flagship app. When installed, it tracked its user's location, motion, lighting, temperature, online activity, speaking rate, and other data to produce a copyrighted chime when its algorithm detected unhealthy behavior. Unhealthy Behaviors of particular concern to the user could be selected in the app's settings, and the app was preloaded with several common UBs.

For instance, if the app identified your location to be McDonald's, you might get a push notification:

"POCKETPUNCH! INSTEAD OF MCDONALD'S, CONSIDER A HEALTHY ALTERNATIVE AT: SUBWAY. FIFTEEN SUBWAY LOCATIONS NEAR YOU. SUBWAY—EAT FRESH."

Or, if it detected you washing your hands for fewer than twenty seconds, you might get a:

"POCKETPUNCH! SKIP SCRUBBING WITH PURELL ADVANCED HAND SANITIZER. SWIPE TO ORDER AN 8 FL OZ TWIN-PACK TO 'HOME' FOR 15% OFF WITH PROMO CODE PNCHED." Which, when swiped, would be followed by "POCKETPUNCH! PURELL ADVANCED SCREEN WIPES FOR THE NEXT TIME YOU TOUCH YOUR PHONE ON YOUR WAY OUT OF THE BATHROOM."

If your screen time exceeded three hours in a single (nine-hour) day, you might get a Punch to "CONSIDER A GLOBIMED VIRTUAL THERAPIST

TO RECONNECT WITH YOUR LIFE." Unless, of course, you spent those
hours on the BodyThink PocketPuncher, in which case you were fine.

The second reason, Luna said, was that to make someone go through
this is a very serious thing, and you need to be damn near certain
they're going to enjoy it.

While walking home from work, a strange thing happened. Winnie
thought she saw her mom. It happened on her way out of FiDi, its
mirrored towers multiplying circuit vessel paths, as Shell construction did its violence on the night. A hawker begged tourists to buy
handbags. Winnie was weaving around the homeless, thinking about
the triumph of deregulation, of app-based transport, app-based food,
and app-based health that made everything just cheap enough to keep
a billion underpaid workers alive, this world where the value of everything was driven down, when she turned on Post Street and found
herself in Union Square.

   She hadn't been there since she was a teenager at the equity protest.
She looked at her phone. Her map labeled Union Square a "Famed
hub for retail, dining, and nightlife." That winged statue in the center
still stood high and pure on its pedestal, almost regal were it not over-
shadowed by an inflatable Christmas tree. Two cops leaned against a
trash bin, eyeing the homeless, who in turn lay under the tree, watching
it ripple. Like dry water. No-wheelers kicked up silver dust and sent
geckos scrambling.

   The woman who reminded Winnie of her mom took shuffly,
zombie-like steps. Her head lolled. Winnie came up behind her on
the moonish, Shell-lit sidewalk and saw that she was hunched over
a little girl. At first Winnie thought that mother and daughter were
playing a sort of walk-on-my-feet game. The mother held the girl's
arms while the girl, in polka-dot tights, dragged her legs inward and
out. Every few steps, she landed on her toes and her foot collapsed,

laces down. The mother lifted her, saying try it again. Winnie realized that the girl had some kind of nerve damage. For a while, she walked behind them, almost with them, very close to the mother. She couldn't help hoping to witness some improvement. Then they reached a crosswalk, the mother lifted the girl, and Winnie took her opportunity to pass.

The rest of her walk was uneventful, and she was sleepy when she reached the walled, residential streets of the Castro. She was looking forward to taking a nap before she and Luna headed to Beijing. It would be fun, the gala (she told herself). She could use a night of fun.

Kiko Alexandra
and Fez

"Welcome back to the *Roads Less Travelled* podcast! I'm Kiko Alexandra." "And I'm Fez." "Coming to you live from our studio in snowy Brooklyn! So. We've got to talk about all this hullabaloo—" "This brouhaha." "—over gravity."

"Right, K.A. For those listeners who have been living under rocks for the past half-month—" "Where we might all be living soon." "—basically, the Santiago Commission put out this report saying that the effects of the planet spinning faster—" "Which everyone now agrees is caused by the westward circuit." "Not everyone." "God Bless Florida." "—those same effects that pulled tides toward the equator are starting to be noticed elsewhere, more powerfully." "Okay. Buildings are starting to tilt toward the equator." "They say Europe on average is finding itself on a one-and-a-half-degree slope. That's one point five." "And countries at the equator?" "They don't slope, right? But gravity there only exerts so much centripetal—" "Word of the month. Google Trends like a pod launching." "—force to combat the spinning, and the spinning is starting to register. So it'll feel exactly like gravity is weaker." "And what are we talking, Fez, like moon gravity?" "Nowhere near that extreme. The moon's gravity is about 17 percent of Earth's. The worst places in the world right now, according to the Commission, have gravity that's about 95 percent normal. You're not gonna feel the difference." "And of course, the circuit industry denies all this." "Right, and we'll get into that."

"@sarahriot in Chicago is writing us that she thinks the slope in her apartment is *more* than the Commission says." "Ha!" "Trust your gut, girl." "Call your landlord." "Let's not forget, though, Fez, the Commission's studies are from late November. The planet was rotating back then in, how long?" "Nine hours, at least." "And now we're below eight. So in theory, the report's already outdated."

"I tried measuring for myself. I used a level app on the sidewalk outside my apartment." "Your apartment's on a hill, Fez." "It said I'm on an eighteen-degree slope." "You know how you're supposed to perform that measurement, right?" "Oh god, I have a bad feeling I'm about to actually learn something." "Draw yourself a warm bath. Then take your clothes off." "Is that a necessary step or do you just like to get me naked?" "Both. Light some candles. Add your salts, your lavender oils, your bubbles." "Glass of rosé." "No, that'll make you dizzy, screw up the measurement." "Okay." "Then get into the bath with your best friend." "My imaginary boyfriend." "Your phone. With the level app." "Ha!" "What kind of phone do you have?" "K.A., you don't know what kind of phone I have?" "I just forget. Does it float? If not, you'll need to put it on a wooden board or something. But the slope of the surface of the water will tell you what you want to know." "What I want to know is when we're going to get *Science Hour with Kiko Alexandra*. Although, I think if you're trying to distinguish between gravity and rotational acceleration, you might have slept through a lesson on the Equivalence Principle." "Are you saying my experiment is wrong?" "And yet it feels so right. Let's just move on."

"Well, Fez, that mention of Science Hour—" "A throwback." "Yes, ten points for throwback. Brings us to the saga's next episode, which is the response to the report from industry leaders like CWC." "Our own work–alma mater." "You can just imagine Cromwell Grant—" "Communications chief at CWC. Our old boss." "Flipping out about this report." "Perhaps even breaching his standards of English etiquette."

"English! For our listeners, that's an inside joke." "Ten points for inside joke." "Our goal is just to have more fun than the listeners, isn't it?"

"Anyways. Lesser reported, K.A., but you and I having worked there, we know what a big deal it is—" "The response we're not going to hear." "CWC has terminated its relationship with television scientist Victor Bickle." "What is Bickle's Ph.D. in, I've always wondered." "He's a spin doctor, K.A., in every sense." "Terminated after seven years as CWC's tireless spokesperson." "A rocky seven years." "And by all accounts, the separation was true to form." "Bickle's been tight lipped about it. We know how that company writes nondisclosure agreements." "We do know, but legally we cannot say."

"What will be interesting, I think, will be to see if people keep using the circuit. You could even imagine these gravity shocks prompting an *increase* in business and human migration. And it's obvious long-haul shipping has benefited from the demands of I.C.R.F.—" "Shell" "—construction; however, in the past two weeks, CWC's shares have lost a third of their value." "Huge hemorrhaging. Almost as bad as during the recession, when CWC last came under fire." "They were able to turn that crisis into an opportunity by positioning themselves as part of the solution, developing their contractor arm and offering it in service of the Shell." "But that's always been a more competitive market, and CWC's management must envy those competitors right now who aren't plagued by lawsuits and brand erosion." "For those of you following market movements." "Not us."

"Meanwhile, the Shell construction continues with more urgency than ever, ringing like Christmas bells over here, as we are six months from the scheduled global Switch-On." "Fez, does the Shell scaffolding ever remind you of long fingers reaching across the sky?" "You know, no. No, it doesn't." "I wonder if the world will ever see Professor Bickle again." "K.A., I think you and I might see him tonight." "Why's that?" "He's still on the guestlist for tonight's Chairman's Gala in Beijing." "No kidding." "Never do." "Well, if he shows up, we'll let you all know what he's wearing."

DAYS OF 7 HOURS

The National International Exhibition Center outside Beijing was tilted much more than a degree and a half.

The building was a tan eight-acre block with high windows and a concave roof, topped with flags that flapped in the sleety winter wind. It was a proud venue, dominant over its municipal subdistrict. To the Southeast was a view of downtown Beijing's skyline, to the West, the mountains of the Lingxi Scenic Area, and above, the sleepy work-lights of the Shell, flickering behind melodramatic clouds.

Inside the exhibition center, several hundred employees—one and a half for each of the night's anticipated guests—were assuming their places: within coat check booths; beneath animated maps of nearby circuit lines; five paces from each revolving door, holding umbrella bags and trays of champagne. They were stationed between portraits of Communist party leaders and behind cocktail bars in each of the half dozen rooms—the ballroom, the piano room, the east and west buffet rooms, and so on, partitioned by retractable, rolling walls that extended to the high ceiling. They were in red vests, checking that every wheel was locked; they were in outstanding toques, ducking under charms that hung diagonally from overhead range hoods. They bumped into chairs bolted in place as they hurried down the floor, carrying heavy crates of ice. Outside restrooms, they waited with mandarin-scented towels. Outside photobooths, they waited with sign-up forms. Their styluses were attached to their tablets by light chains because a loose stylus was liable to roll quite a ways before lodging itself under one of the tables, on which long, red tablecloths descended at striking slants.

A busboy, taking his last break, slid around on the sweaty seat of an askew toilet. He flushed while still seated (a courtesy flush, they called it in his rural hometown) and felt water run up the side of the bowl.

In the exhibition hall, employees were counting down from *sān* and powering on the floor-to-ceiling screens. The screens communicated across the length of the room, casting far-flung holograms: a man from the east wall meeting a woman from the west, taking her hand in an act of perfect synchronicity and twirling her. The space between their hands was almost invisible. She stumbled downhill, it was that steep, but landed weightless in his arms.

This first dance was silent to the security agents in the basement, who watched on CCTV screens. Such screens were stacked a dozen high on the south end of the wall and only one screen high on the north end due to the angle of the basement's ceiling, more like that of a typical attic, like the attics of the agents' childhood homes. And in this way, the entire National International Exhibition Center rested upon a nostalgic conflation of up and down.

An agent gestured with his QX semiautomatic pistol at the CCTV screen wedged into the vertex of the room. In it, a revolving door caught the light of a limousine pulling around. The night's first guests had arrived.

Doorway attendants were trained to take coats from below, so as not to obstruct the view, which every new entrant absorbed with the same expression, half panic, half stupor. First instincts were animalistic fears that the exhibition center's interior was collapsing on them. The attendants were trained to take coats from slack, surrendered arms.

An attendant passed a coat to a checker, who put it on a metal hanger and let go. *Sheeeen*, like a zipline, it slid down the long, steel pole.

"O casaco do senhor, por favor," to the elderly deputy I.C.R.F. commissioner, who managed, barely, to ask on just how much of a slope this exhibition center was built.

"Vinte e cinco."

Miguel and I arrived in a cab from the Jingzang 42a pod lot, didn't notice the building's architecture, and didn't stop fighting as we came through the revolving door. I had finally gotten my wish: I no longer worked for CWC. The day Bickle and I were let go, all the stresses I had taken for granted—projects on my work calendar, professional relationships to tend—disappeared. That was two what-would-have-been-workweeks before the gala. I spent the first sitting around London, watching TV, waiting for Miguel to come home. It made me feel like his pet. The second, I started asking him if he wanted to quit too. And when he said no, I asked why. And when he said he liked his work, I said he just didn't know anything else, that neither of us did, but that we could figure it out together. Right before the gala, he worked fifteen hours straight, a triple shift, not coming home when he was supposed to, and I thought he was doing it to spite me. He may have done it to avoid me. As a result, I'd spent our commute to Beijing going through all of the talking points that for fifteen hours I'd tested in my head. I said that he was staying in the job for fear of the unknown, that didn't he see all the negative reporting about CWC in the news, that Cromwell Grant was making a tool of him . . . These talking points worked even less well in person.

"I didn't judge you when you lost your job," he said as I came out of the revolving door.

"What does that have to do with what I've been saying?"

"It's not fair for you to take it out on me."

"You think that's what I'm doing?" I said. We turned away from each other so two attendants could remove our coats. "This isn't because I lost my job. I've been saying for a long time I want us to be together more. I hardly see you, and when we are together, you're obsessed with work. We, as a team, have no sense anymore of what's really meaningful."

I took both of our coat check tags and chased Miguel up the foyer to the exhibition hall, where attendees were starting to congregate.

The revolving door spat up influencers and tastemakers. There was a loud, bald advertising exec in purple lipstick and the gaudily tattooed, jet-setting heir to an app dynasty with a lover under each arm. There were stars in feather boas. There were athletes in gold chains. But for every one of these flashy figures there was a whole social circle of plain-featured powerbrokers who naturally cherished the outlandish company out of a deep need to feel down-to-earth if only by comparison (which was the only yardstick they knew). These were CEOs and fund managers with goofy smiles and clips of daughters on their phones. Mosquito-legged women who lamented all the fanfare as they took the slope in heels and good husbands in admittedly silly but convenient one-piece tuxedos who were pretty healthy, pretty charitable, and by all accounts pretty nice outside of work. Lastly, there were the jittery, done-up twenty-two- and twenty-three-year-olds at the launching points of promising careers assuming they could keep their button noses to the grindstone—except tonight, their bosses told them, let loose, enjoy the ballyhoo while you're still young enough to bring loss to an open bar. They had been looking forward to tonight for months. It was these gala-goers whose tight, sheepish cliques I found most distasteful.

On an English-language panel in the exhibition hall, the facility's twenty-five-degree tilt northward (contrary to the landscape's slight southward trend) was hailed as the prototype for a high-gradient future.

"As the world turns on its head, the National International Exhibition Center will become only more comfortable. Expeditiously constructed in preparation for a burgeoning southward slope, the new design epitomizes the five-year plan's strategy of 'forward development.'"

An employee distributed frictiony stickers for phone backs, branded with the logo of a Chinese state-owned construction contractor, one of the gala's sponsors.

Miguel and I, accusing each other of not listening, hiked through the middle of a holographic dragon dance.

Winnie arrived before Luna, who would be coming straight from work. She got stopped just inside the revolving door by an attendant who said the venue's facial recognition software failed to match her to the guestlist. She often had trouble with facial recognition software. "I guess I just have one of those faces," she said, tugging on her skirt. She tried to hold on to her excitement as other guests streamed in around her.

A group of yuppies entered, saying, "Where'd you come in from?" "Chile. You?" "Budapest. You?" "Cameroon. You?" Incoming guests avoided acknowledging Winnie until they were out of earshot, at which point they commented on the impressive security. Outside, the sleet was mounting.

Cromwell Grant strode in, sans wife, accompanied by CWC chairperson John Sugar Jr., twenty years Grant's senior, also sans wife, both with bags under their eyes deeper than their pockets, coming off a second consecutive week from corporate management hell, feeling alive.

"There's a reason God gave us two legs and only one brain," said John Sugar Jr.

They found the piano room full of familiar faces and ordered two Black-and-Tans.

The piano played Tchaikovsky's "Romeo and Juliet," which was one of the songs it came with.

There was a bang. Grant and John Sugar Jr. turned. Across the room, the Santiago Commission's seventy-five-year-old deputy Shell commissioner had knocked over a tray of steaming red bean buns. They watched with delight as the hapless old man—saying, "Oh oh oh"—attempted to stop buns rolling downhill.

"How come these Commission jerks show up at every party we go to?" asked John Sugar Jr. in his corncracker twang. Sugar Jr. was a crapulent grandfather of nine with his face shrink-wrapped around his skull who had made a career of predicting the worst in every situation, whereby he was usually proven right. A hero of industry, he professed an abiding devotion to the advancement of humanity, despite his contempt for just about everyone in it. Cromwell Grant was one of the few he liked.

Grant said, "Try cheaper parties."

The deputy commissioner pleaded for help kicking buns uphill, hoping an attendant would notice.

By that point the men verifying Winnie's identity had multiplied. They were passing tablets crisscross, looking from Winnie to the images on their screens, when they received a call for cleanup assistance from the piano room. They asked Winnie to wait a moment, and all twelve of them walked off.

Winnie stayed by the doorway. She took out her phone to check for messages from Luna and to appear occupied. Earlier that afternoon, she had spent five minutes looking in the mirror after her makeup was finished, thinking about how this night would be fun and promising herself she would try to enjoy it. She kept refreshing her messages, until a notification appeared: "PocketPunch! Make connections and start conversations with real people on MateMe." She lowered her phone.

Just in time to see the revolving door churn out two familiar faces.

"Hey," she said. "You're *Roads Less Travelled*, right?"

Kiko Alexandra and Fez, in papery mini dresses with triangle cutouts, said, "We are," and strutted past.

A coin rolled down the carpet from the exhibition hall and struck Winnie's foot. She bent to pick it up.

"Yo," said Luna. "Sorry I'm late."

Winnie looked up.

Beneath the heating vent that blasted the revolving door, Luna's black hair fluttered. Its ends tickled her shoulders, which sat above the surface of her strapless black-cherry dress like a column of ghostly lipstick peeking from its tube. She'd painted her nails white and powdered her cheeks magenta. Winnie had never seen her so done up. She looked years older.

"Were you waiting for me?"

"They told me—" Winnie began, but the guards were gone.

"Come on." Luna took her arm.

Miguel and I made our way to the west buffet room and took dumplings. I didn't want dumplings. I *know* he didn't like dumplings. The less dipping sauce they absorbed, the more he drowned them.

He said, "For the time we have together right now, you could try to enjoy it, no?"

"What do you mean for the time we have?" I said. "Is this more time than you want to be spending with me?"

"What?" he said, about to set his plate down on a tilted high-top table when a server materialized to slide a frictiony coaster underneath. He said, "In what world is that what that means? I feel like I have the crazies."

"Don't you think CWC has distracted us from the really important things in our lives?" I said. "We've been together seven years and we're still not engaged. We're not settled. We live in a hotel."

"You are the one who wanted to stay in the hotel."

"Years ago."

"Now that you can't expense the room to CWC, you want to change everything—"

"That is not why."

"It is."

"Maybe now that I'm not at CWC I have the distance to consider that a real home we actually take care of might be better than a hotel room optimized for its commute to work—"

"I don't know why you are putting all this on me right now."

I said, "I feel like I'm not even allowed to discuss what kind of life we want to create together."

"I had thought we were creating it already," said Miguel, as his dipping sauce ran off the edge of his plate.

* * *

Winnie and Luna walked through the ballroom, where a hologram of the late Faye Wong had taken the stage and begun performing a medley of remixed Inner Mongolian folk-punk songs to an empty dance floor. They entered the east buffet room and got in line at the bar. To look out the vast windows was like gazing at a dark, nautical horizon from a careening ship. Sleet ran sideways across the panes. Inside, the chandeliers hung at a stunning angle, forming beautiful, tangled clumps of electric light, and long formal gowns trailed cooperatively across the checkered floor even while their models stood still. Ahead in line, two couples talked about their favorite ski resorts. They alternated naming resorts and agreeing that those were good ones. "Darling is the slowest skier on the mountain," one of the wives said. She did an impression of her husband's wedged turns while the husband laughed magnanimously. "I made him a shirt: Thirty minutes or your pizza delivery is free."

"What are you going to get?" Luna asked Winnie.

"I don't know. What are you getting?"

Luna ordered a scotch and soda. Winnie got one of the specialty drinks, a Ginger Twist.

They stood at a table without much to say, but it was nice not needing to talk. Looking around, Luna chuckled. Winnie did too; it was quite a scene. At a lower table, someone fell out of his tilted seat. It was still early enough in the night that nearby people noticed and pretended to care, but the truth was that everyone's footwork was getting sloppier. Guests dodging down the room's slope were entering that stage of drunkenness where one leans into his momentum, relaxing the reins a bit to prove the reins are still in hand.

"See anyone hot?" said Luna.

Winnie looked at her and nodded.

At the top of the piano room, Cromwell Grant and John Sugar Jr. had amassed a small audience. In addition to a disgraced former mayor of New York, who was steadily supplying them with bourbon, having brought his own fifth of quality stuff from a Hudson Valley distillery, there was a financial advisor John Sugar Jr. knew from one of his other ventures, the advisor's two junior associates, Noah (whom Grant could never shake at these functions), and the young Emirati nephew of the CEO of Dubai Ports World, a client.

Grant and John Sugar Jr. leaned against the wall.

"Look at this swaying meadow of gray roots and bald spots," said John Sugar Jr. He nodded at the roomful of people downhill. He had a way of nodding downward even while flicking his head up; it was something about the shape of his neck.

"How tabbies love to toad," said Grant.

"You know the one thing I like about this party, though?" said John Sugar Jr., holding out his plastic cup for more bourbon. "Social climbers are forced to get their exercise."

The audience laughed—Noah with a particularly fawning woof that hurt Grant's ears. Grant finished his own bourbon, somewhat painstakingly, and took a refill. He always got drunk when he was with John Sugar Jr. The scrawny old man was built like a ShamWow. And once drunk, the blood sport began. At least that was how Grant saw their exchanges. Contests in cynicism. To be caught emitting even a whiff of naïve hope around John Sugar Jr. was to be dead in the water. So if he said that everyone in the room was ugly, you attacked their integrity too. Pretty soon, it became a competition in black levels. Whose worldview could render greater depths of dark. Banter with him was no-holds-barred, nihilistic escalation. And that was what the audience liked.

"How long do you give it," said John Sugar Jr., raising the ante, apropos of nothing, "until everyone in this room is dead?"

Grant looked around the room for the youngest person, but this meant he was taking the question too earnestly, and John Sugar Jr. pounced. "Whatcha looking around for?"

"Young people."

"Cradle robber," said John Sugar Jr. The audience laughed. "He is," John Sugar Jr. said. "Don't say I said it."

Grant said, "Could be hours. All and sundry wiped out in a tragic accident."

"A building collapse, maybe," said John Sugar Jr. "Killed by the Chinese state. House of Usher–style."

Grant, not keen to be baited into a game of criticizing the surveilling government, said, "That or they all crash on their flights home. Probably CWC flights, the way the past two weeks have gone."

Even prodding this personal sore spot didn't faze John Sugar Jr. "Oh, that'll just prove the company's out to kill everyone, won't it? Who knows," he said. There was something tickling his face. He flared his nostrils. "Maybe CWC really is gonna kill everyone. It'd be news to me. People say CWC controls everything, as if we're some kind of plutocratic masterminds. It always feels to me like we ain't got no control over anything!"

"I wouldn't get your knickers in a bunch," said Grant. "I'm sure whatever problems the company's creating, our Risk Analytics department is keeping very good tabs on them."

This got a cackle from John Sugar Jr. "You know the one about the risk analyst who wants to see if his new pod can fly?"

Grant shook his head. The room was beginning to spin.

"Risk analyst goes to the roof of Aviation Tower, gets in his pod, and tentatively rolls it off the edge. As he plummets past each floor, the people inside hear him saying, 'So far, so good.' 'So far, so good.'" John Sugar Jr. slapped his knee. Noah ribbed one of the financial advisors. The piano started playing the "Thieving Magpie" overture.

All the rooms were beginning to spin, Winnie felt, and she and Luna got another round. They were talking about the drainage issue in their shower when a wiry, middle-aged man interrupted.

"Luna Tsiang, one of our lottery winners," he said. "Are we having a good time?"

It was Luna's regional director. His face had the radiant shine people got from anti-inflammatory creams indicated for rashes caused by dermal fillers used to treat facial "hollow-out"—the common side effect of weight-loss pills. His wife stood behind him with two bottles of beer and a bored expression. Luna began to introduce Winnie, but Winnie stepped in for herself.

"This is a wonderful party," she said. "Thank you for making the invitations available to us."

He asked, "Do you work for me, too?"

When she said she didn't, he shrugged as if to say, *easy come, easy go*.

He and Luna spoke for a few minutes about how much funding he was going to attract tonight for his region. Winnie knew that Luna didn't like the culture he set in his conservation camps—he kept productivity leaderboards, pitting squad against squad—and so she was surprised by the deference Luna showed him. Luna kept nervously pushing her hair behind her ears. He left eventually, spotting a government contact across the room whose arm he intended to pump, and his wife followed. Her look conveyed utter despair at having gotten all dressed up to watch her husband degrade his employees and pump men's arms. Luna dug around her purse for her pill bottle, took two, and followed them with a gulp of Riesling.

"What an asshole," she said.

I had a beer, only because I didn't know what else to do with my mouth. It tasted foul. Miguel made us leave the buffet room since, he said, I was about to cry, even though I wasn't. We walked to the end of the hall, where we could be alone. In a private corner, we stood at a distance from each other, crooking our necks against the inward-leaning wall. I could tell he was furious with me, but I didn't deserve it. He said he was tired of being abused.

"We don't understand what's happening in our own lives," I said, my head spiraling in repetition. Couldn't he grasp that I was doing this because I cared about us? About him? Because I was one of the only people who really did care?

He rubbed his eyes, and I could see there'd been a shift in him.

"That's right," he said. "You don't understand what's happening in your life, Tanner. And you've got to figure it out. Conmigo o sin mí, and it'll be without me if you ruin what we have by making our relationship a dumping ground for your self-loathing. I didn't force you into anything."

"I'm not saying you did," I tried, but he kept going.

"This is my life you forced yourself into, and I like my life. I liked it before you came. I'm not apologizing for it now, not to you or anyone. Okay, Tanner? Take it out on someone else. Go back to Alaska and shoot fake queers with plastic guns in your little arcade. I'm done."

I didn't know what to say to that. I tried to catch my breath.

He said, "You were running away when you crashed into me that night, and nothing's changed."

I said, "I just love our relationship so much."

He stopped talking and looked at me.

I didn't know where those words had come from. They had ridden up my throat between convulsions and sounded pathetic. I took a deep breath. "I don't even want to think about the start of our relationship," I said.

"Fine."

"It makes me too sad."

I had barely gotten the words out when I broke down, my sorrow compounded by the sight of itself. I dropped my bottle. It rolled down the length of the carpeted hallway, spurting beer.

"Tanner," said Miguel, exasperated.

How was I in this impossible situation? I stood with him in the empty hallway, feeling the foundations of my life shifting underfoot, but still thinking maybe the discussion we were having was productive. Still hoping I might make him see things the way I had come to see them. Certain fights are healthy, I thought. Certain breakups are healthy, teleologically. The word breakup made me gag. We had fought before. A good fight goes down before coming back up. A couple rips through the canopy, grounds itself, and bounces. Was it normal

to feel like the ground was dipping away from us, like we might just
keep falling and falling through the outlines of ourselves? Miguel said
our issues had been going on for far too long. I couldn't bring myself
to say more (every time I opened my mouth, a sob bubbled up), so I
wiped my eyes. We started walking. I took his hand, and he let me.

In the east buffet room, unbeknownst to me, we walked within one
table of Winnie and Luna. Winnie felt sad to see lovers quarrelling,
and she looked away.

"You hungry?" Luna asked her.

In the buffet line, some teenagers were drinking Dream Cream.
Winnie took a plastic plate and served herself a ladleful of pork-free
mapo bean curd with a side of cucumber and wood fungus in a clear
sauce. One of the teenagers uncovered a platter for her.

"You should try the roast duck," he said. "You will love it, especially
with mustard."

"No, sorry," said Winnie. "I don't eat that."

The boy took no offense. He said, "You should eat mustard."

"Not mustard," Winnie tried to explain.

"Everything is better with mustard. The only thing I do not like
better with mustard is my women."

One of his female friends punched him in the arm.

As Winnie kept moving down the buffet, she noticed, behind her,
Luna chatting with a tall, drunk man. The buffet was beginning to get
traffic from the ballroom, a new kind of traffic, sweaty and disoriented.
Some spun-off dancers seemed genuinely confused to be filing past
steaming trays of Peking duck in what they thought was a conga line.

In the ballroom, Faye was rewriting pop history as a throat-
singing metalhead. She was making noises very much of the flesh.
The screen behind her invited all those who "feel so INCLINED" to
remove their shoes and slide down the dance floor. Women who had
been hiking up and down the slope in heels didn't need to be asked

twice. In black stockings, young salesgirls suddenly became experts at the moonwalk.

Men were drenched in sweat, but when encouraged to remove the jackets of their tuxedos, they blushed and swore they weren't too hot.

The agents directly beneath the ballroom were no longer able to mistake their basement for an attic.

"This is Ming," Luna said to Winnie, bringing the man back to their table. Winnie watched him shovel duck into his mouth.

"I used to be vegan," Ming said. "But at a certain point, there was just nothing to gain. Hey, look, that's *Roads Less Travelled*."

Across the room, Kiko Alexandra and Fez walked from the bar with a group of well-known stage actors. They'd removed their heels and were so focused on avoiding streams of sweet and sour soup that they didn't notice Miguel and me until they'd nearly walked into our table.

It was an awkward encounter. We remained seated. They introduced their friends, who pretended not to notice that I'd been crying (they were actors, thankfully). Miguel asked them if they had tried the duck, and they said no, not yet, and they were about to extricate themselves when Fez had the mind to ask me if Bickle was coming.

"I don't think so," I said. I admitted that I actually hadn't heard from him in the days since we were let go from CWC, so I wasn't really sure what was going on.

They left, and as they did, I imagined how they must have seen me. I imagined them thinking that I never did know how to make it in this world.

In the piano room, the ex-mayor had unstoppered another fifth. The audience was getting too drunk to follow the banter. Grant was pretty sure the piano was starting "Romeo and Juliet" again. He excused himself to the loo, leaving John Sugar Jr. to monologue about the pleasures of being alive to witness the sixth mass extinction event.

("Planet's been around forty-five million centuries, and yet our parents left us the rare privilege . . .")

Grant pumped his brakes all the way down the piano room and down the hallway, and managed to traverse the restroom without breaking his neck. A puddle had amassed along the restroom's downhill edge, lily-padded with floating business cards.

He couldn't stand up straight at the urinal, the dividers being arranged like a series of escalating backslashes, so he leaned into the divider beneath him and fired at the urinal cake like the scene in *Elastic Girl IV: Twist Flip* where Ayla Amsler shoots Bruce Jorgen in the face while sliding down a melting glacier. He was shaking out the drops when someone tapped his shoulder.

"You and that old guy you were drinking with, you work for CWC, don't you?"

The speaker was a heavyset American man, possibly a Jew, around Grant's age.

"Yes," Grant said.

"You fucker," said the man. "I'm a shareholder. My retirement relies on CWC stock. I lost thirty thousand dollars because of you this month."

Grant stepped up to the man's level. He examined his tuxedo. Ordinarily, he might have taken the precaution of striking such a man with overwhelming force. But he felt unthreatened. Perhaps he liked the way the man choked on choler at the sight of him. Or perhaps he was secretly at ease under the protection of a totalitarian state.

"I suppose then that you are poorer than you were last month," he said, and he folded his penis back into his fly.

Winnie watched Luna's new friend Ming peel ribbons of crispy skin off of a roast duck. His fingers were red with *tianmian* sauce. And maybe it was the spins pushing things to extremes, but she set down her drink and said abruptly, "I think I'll go dance."

"Right now?" said Luna.

Winnie felt irritated. It came from nowhere. From inside her. She couldn't explain it, but suddenly she was remembering her first solo date on Irving Street, and she wanted to be alone. "You finish eating," she said. "I'm just gonna go. You'll find me."

She walked away rather quickly (blame it on the slope) while in the vast windows behind her, the sun, for the fourth time in twenty-four hours, burst over the horizon.

At least three people in different conversations commented that "it always happens so fast."

More people poured into the gala. They came from work and from other holiday parties and from their beds. Word was spreading that Beijing was the place to be. Some had invitations they'd planned to blow off; some weren't invited at all. The entryway attendants scrambled to remove the latter and remove coats from the former.

Amid this rush entered Victor Bickle. He wore a late-995ks shawl lapel. His mustache was soaked with rain. No one took his coat.

He sent me a message saying he'd arrived. Then he wandered into the exhibition hall.

Grant headed back for the piano room but made a wrong turn and found himself somewhere else. He queued at the bar for a cup of water. The woman in front of him was alone. He liked the slight bend in her uphill knee and her little black purse, from which she extracted a pill bottle and tapped out two white tablets.

"Too much fun?" he asked.

She turned. There was a moment then in which he detected the real her (startled and maybe a year or two younger than she first appeared) before she composed herself, made herself his equal, and said, "It depends?"

"I don't think you understood the question," he said.

He read the drug label: RAPID SEROTONERGIC STIMULANT—INDICATED FOR ACUTE ANXIETY; DO NOT TAKE MORE THAN TWO TABLETS . . . She tapped four out and handed them to him. Maybe she did understand after all, in a backward way. For too much fun, take two. For mere fun, the sky was the limit.

They washed down their pills with a glass of Riesling and a bourbon neat.

"Intended and conscious management of the country is key to the five-year plan's strategy of 'Forward Development,'" boasted the looped presentation playing in the exhibition hall. "Through thoughtful conduct of the socialist mechanism, the Chinese economy continues to adapt and advance."

Bickle watched from the bottom of the room the great screens rising above him. He hadn't left his Manhattan apartment in two weeks. With his blackout curtains drawn and the screens on his walls set to images of windows at night, he kept thinking about what Cromwell Grant had told him. He didn't know if it was true. The better part of him believed it wasn't. Could he possibly have a daughter, the daughter he'd searched for those years ago and never found? He tossed and turned; he wrote maternity wards up and down New York, requesting records; he sought old Alaskan contacts, friends of his late father, siblings of his childhood friends, but when they responded with their bumpkin delight at being graced by a message from the "famous Professor Bickle," he ghosted them without disclosing the reason for his initial overture. He grew exhausted.

I didn't know about any of this. His message to me upon arriving at the gala was our first communication since the firing, and even that I didn't notice immediately. Miguel and I were sitting at a table in the east buffet room, trying not to argue, talking about the food and sartorial mundanities. The conversation was, frankly, horrible. It was the sort of small talk colleagues make when they've already said goodbye before realizing they're parked in the same direction. And yet it was pleasant too, built on more rapport than we could possibly shed. We could easily chat forever, and that, to me, was the most horrible part.

Nothing lasts forever. I was complaining about my shoelaces when Miguel's gaze wandered across the floor and landed on Grant.

"I don't know why I'm telling you about my shoelaces," I said.

"I can't bear this anymore," said Miguel. I watched him get up and walk toward Grant's table.

Grant was feeling much better. Better than ever. The pills made him feel young. They also stimulated his appetite, so he and Luna shared a plate of soup dumplings. Her seat was tilted down, and she had to sit at its edge as if preparing to pounce across the table at him. He liked that she hadn't commented on his wedding ring. Some women try to bring that into it when all you're doing is sharing dumplings. Their conversation shifted from gala fashion to the venue, and Luna said, "I think it's tragic that we've gotten to the point of preparing for tilted buildings."

"Why is preparedness tragic?" Grant asked.

"I just mean the necessity of it."

"If you were queen of the world," Grant said. "Queen—"

"Luna."

"Queen Luna, what would you fancy?"

"Hmm." She pushed her hair behind her ears. "I think I'd stop the westward circuit."

Grant laughed in spite of himself. He hadn't mentioned his work. He leaned forward, which was difficult since his chair tilted back. It made him conscious of his gut. But in a good way. Everything physical was good. "See you on the guillotine," he said. "How many people's livelihoods do you think rely on the circuit?"

"I don't know."

"What do you do, Luna?"

"I work for the anti-erosion corps in the States," she said, with haughtiness at first, before seeing his point. "But it's not like I'm

glad that shifts in gravity are causing landslides and forcing us to
dig dams."

"Forgive me if this is a dumb question, but what would happen to
those precisely calibrated dams if the circuit suddenly stopped? That
couldn't possibly be good for landslides."

A little stumped, she laughed bitterly. "Look, I'm not, like, making
geological calculations as a corps member. I'm just getting up early
and shoveling. For me, it's about being a part of something bigger."

"Sounds rewarding."

She sucked her teeth. "It's really tough," she said. The way she was
leaning made her hair keep falling across her face.

Grant smiled.

She seemed like she might up and leave, but she didn't. She just
recrossed her legs. "Well, what would you do? If you were king?"

He liked the hint of challenge in her voice. He said, "I'm no king.
Really, if I were king we would all have been royally goosed a long
time ago."

They were interrupted by Miguel. He came over seemingly just
to tell Grant that he had forwarded some meeting requests at the
day's end.

"Okay . . ." said Grant, looking at Luna and smirking. "Thank you,
Miguel. Is that all?"

After a moment, Miguel said yes and left.

Grant said to Luna, "Some people are obsessed with work."

As the ballroom shook from head to toe and everyone was singing
though no one knew the words, Winnie danced alone. Others paid her
no mind as she closed her eyes and moved her arms. Why did she worry
so much about fitting into a world where men in sweatshop-sewn
suits devoured dead animals and bureaucrats starved themselves to
get into magazines. Where even her best friend, whom she loved, was
in so many ways fucked up—reliant on pills, boy-crazy, emotionally

constipated. She spun herself. She deserved to be happy, if only for an hour, if only by herself.

If only she had gotten that hour.

I, abandoned midsentence, checked my phone and saw Bickle's message. I hurried toward the exhibition hall, and found him standing in the corner, enveloped by the screens. He was watching footage of tilted cities being raised from the dust, so effortless in time-lapse.

"Victor," I said. "You're here."

He turned.

"I haven't heard from you in two weeks. How are you?"

"Been better, Tanner. Been better."

He handed me a limp frictiony sticker and drifted toward the next room. The sun was behind the dark, tiled portion of the Shell, and the artificial line separating night from day split the mountains in half. I heard a man in the restroom line recounting some business conquest. "I always say," he said, "that one contract alone put my kids through college."

Another man added, "And your therapist's kids!"

"Can I get you anything to drink?" I asked.

"Sure," said Bickle. "Whisky would be nice."

"How long was I gone?" Grant asked John Sugar Jr., which you can get away with when everyone's drunk enough. He introduced Luna to the group—the ex-mayor, Noah, and the Emiratis. Plus, they'd picked up a famous TV horse whisperer.

John Sugar Jr. said to Grant, "Guess who's here."

"Dame Vera Lynn," Grant said.

"Bickle."

"You having a laugh?"

"I'm serious."

"Victor Bickle?" Luna said. "You know him?"

"The gentleman scientist himself," said John Sugar Jr.

"The walking, talking gentleman's sausage," said Grant. "And you don't want to know how that sausage got made." He drank.

Luna watched him drink, and when he noticed her cup was low, he filled it. She was starting to get a bad feeling about him. Perhaps it was the ages of his friends, or the knowing smiles they directed at her when she arrived with him.

"You like Victor Bickle, sweetheart?" the horse whisperer asked her.

"No," she said.

John Sugar Jr. leveled a bloodshot eye her way.

She looked around. She wanted to go find Winnie now.

Grant leaned into her ear, said he'd fancy another Qfizoft. While she fished out her pill bottle, she sensed him looking through her purse. He took it dry. She took one too; she was feeling incredibly tense. "I'm gonna go," she said.

He asked where.

She said she had a friend on the dance floor.

He said he'd like to dance.

They walked together. His gang of friends and acolytes followed, laughing at nothing.

"You and I ought to get to know each other better," he said as they entered the ballroom. She looked for Winnie. "Give me your number."

She said no.

He said why not.

"What do you mean, why not?"

"One reason why not."

She said curtly, "I don't have a phone."

"That's all?" he said. "We mustn't let that stop us." He held out a phone. "Keep it," he said. "It's one of the new ones. I get them sent to me. This one I use just for flings. I've hundreds more at my office. And here I already have the number."

"You're drunk," she said.

"You drugged me," he replied.

He startled her by trying to jab the phone down her dress. She snatched it from him. He laughed. It was a great belly laugh. She hurried away, but he caught her at the dance floor's edge.

"What are you doing to make the world a better place then?" he said.

"Get away from me."

"Do you find the question vulgar?"

He got in front of her. She retreated, bumping into people as they claimed spots in the ballroom for the evening's final exhibit.

"Thank you for the drugs," he said, no longer pursuing. When she'd created enough space, she turned and ran. He shouted after her, "This night has opened my eyes!" Laughing, he stumbled into the mob.

Faye's musical climax was set against rising synths. The outro repeated an anthem refrain, "*Saihan mongol mori min,*" but people chanted along with their own interpretations, until she exploded in a firework of pig squeals. The lights dimmed. Winnie pushed her way out of the crowd for cooler air while the final exhibit started onstage.

It was essentially a repackaging of what had played in the exhibition room all night. A holographic bureaucrat stood in a high-def rendering of the very building they were already actually in, with subtitles like, "The National International Exhibition Center—finally, the future is now. But first, what is this future, by the numbers?" The graphics were pretty arresting.

Standing against a wall, Winnie texted Luna. Sweat drenched her back. Everyone around watched the presentation. She figured she ought to plan how to get home, and she opened a map on her phone but then lowered it just to take a breath and think for a moment *I had fun.*

I do like being alive.

Bickle and I entered the ballroom from the west and saw the field of upward-tilted faces flickering green and blue under the stage. We took an open space along the wall. The presentation showed summer lovers lying supine on gently sloped roofs. They gazed upon constellations that claimed to be even more abundant than those that came before light pollution and smog, even clearer than the heavens had ever been before—an entire universe of stars and comets, which would be visible above all of China's cities upon the completion of the Shell. It was a vision of the future, but beneath it, Bickle laid eyes on the opposite.

He saw Winnie.

"I'm going crazy," he whispered.

I didn't know who he was looking at. There were a dozen or so people between him and her, swaying in the room's aquatic hues. For him, though, it only took a glimpse to recognize her, even bathed as she was in lilac, highlights glinting off her glasses and off the sweat that rolled down her temple as she retied her hair. She clutched her phone beneath her armpit, smooshing her chubby bicep against it, and raised her other arm over her head.

"She looks exactly the same," he said.

"What are you talking about?"

He pushed his way toward her. The lights went pink and yellow and teal in the sweaty air. Her eyes were closed, consumed in concentration; she pulled her hair through a loop and let it fall over her shoulder.

"Excuse me," he said. "Is it possible? Are you—"

There was an explosion.

Still standing where Bickle had left me, I jerked toward the stage. For a split second, everyone froze. Mic feedback rang out in empty alarm. And then someone screamed, and it was real, and like a livestream catching up with itself, the entire room went into a frenzy. Bickle was shoved against a wall. People fell to the ground almost immediately, and all efforts to avoid a downhill stampede were abandoned: On the stage, there was a man of flesh and bones towering amidst the holographic city, throwing plastic yellow grenades into the crowd.

Noah, hesitating at the bottom of the room, slipped and was crushed beneath actors and younger lobbyists. Grant and John Sugar

Jr. survived, running off in different directions. On the other side of the room, a falling woman grabbed Fez's hair and almost took her down, but Kiko Alexandra caught her and they made their escape. My first thought was for Miguel, but I didn't know where he was. I dodged up the room for Bickle but couldn't overcome the avalanche of bodies. I felt the heat of an explosion, and a man driving me downhill collapsed into my arms. Before I could drop him, I felt his back wet with blood.

The attacker was underlit pink and green. "*Revolution,*" he shouted again and again. "*Revolution!*"

Luna made it out.

Someone tried to climb onstage, but the attacker kicked him down. I made it out.

Bickle was still standing, smashed up against the wall, but Winnie was on the floor. Her glasses were askew. Her phone was shattered, and she clutched her wrist.

"Get up, you have to get up," Bickle said to her.

He bent down to grab her but got a weak grip: one hand on her shoulder and one beneath her ribs. Someone kneed her in passing, and she rolled into Bickle's shins. She was trying to curl up for cover.

"*Revolution! Revolution!*"

"You have to stand, Claira, we have to get out," he said.

"*Revoluu—*" There was a crack of gunfire, and a string of blood exited the attacker's neck. He tumbled through a spinning hologram of the night sky. The stage was rushed by security agents.

Bickle wrapped his arms around Winnie, thinking of Claira outside the gold mine when he was seventeen. He pulled her up into him. He was downhill and almost fell backward.

She landed on her feet and ran away.

The Department of Health and Human Services

Like a sleepwalker, he thought. Another walk to work. Job within a mile of his mom's house to stay off the circuit. The West Texas soil cracked under his boots. In the ruins of society certain animals emerge—winged cockroaches erupting from drain holes, cormorants huddled in shade eating cigarettes, a shared nature impressed upon animals who thrive in this sort of environment. People mowed them down in souped-up Toyotas bought for fear of grav loss that they couldn't explain because grav loss was a hoax, like voodoo and vaccines, spread to keep people living in fear. Open your fucking eyes. Arriving at work with a perverse grin to match the photograph on his government ID, he found the public complaint line switchbacked to the door. People sweating. He imagined them trying to run from his grenades and he laughed.

How many views would his videos have tomorrow? He wouldn't be around to see. After Beijing, he would be an idea, a brand. His mom would be crying tomorrow. That's for treating him like a retard. Six more hours and then never again. Fuck the doctors and their drugs, fuck the preachers and their lies, he'd be remembered as a mother-fucker who came here and didn't take shit. Fuck you, God.

A beaner girl pushed a reimbursement form for cholecalciferol deficiency through the cashier's slot shrieking a hangnail staple across the hot steel tray. She was taking vitamin D for bone pain, muscle weakness, and asthma. She didn't think the UV panels in the Shell were working right. Take some vitamin F-yourself and go back to your own country then. He laughed. Like a sleepwalker.

"You're not even answering the questionnaire."

Enough planning. He just needed to do it. They would claim that everything in his life led up to this, and they would be right. Nothing was going to stop the revolution of bodies.

DAYS OF 5 HOURS

I made it out of the gala and got broken up with.

Apparently Miguel had gone home without me. He didn't know about the attack until I texted from outside the exhibition center. In the drizzling rain, gala attendees stood jacketless and trembling as ambulances and paramilitary vans blocked their cars from getting in. I walked through them, past the flags, up the road. The Shell blotted out the sun. More ambulances sped by, turret-lights spinning.

Miguel wasn't in our suite when I got back. His suitcase was gone. He'd left his razor and what laundry of his happened to be in the hamper, and his phone charger, and a note handwritten on Hilton stationery. I flipped it over.

Minou,
I do not feel good when I am with you. You do not make me feel good about myself. I love you, but enough is enough. It's not like we didn't try. I'm staying with my parents. I would prefer if we didn't talk for a while.
Writing that was the hardest thing I have ever done.

Lo siento.

I sat against the windowsill. For a minute or two, my most pronounced emotion was embarrassment. I drafted a message to Miguel saying that I got his note, but instead of sending it right away, I scrolled up—backward—through our texts.

Don't read it tonight. Call as soon as you get home.

                                                    I need to process.

Did you see my note yet?

                                                    Leaving . . .

Where are you?

Oh no.

What?

                        There was an attack. I think people died.

Physically or emotionally?

                                                    Are you safe?

Hey

                                                    Hello?

I read and reread my draft text, pressure mounting in my chest, and then before I realized it, I was looking at the suggested tips in my ride-hailing app. I shook my head, returned to Messages, and pressed send.

                        No need to call. I understand.

I expected him to call anyway. Deep down, I anticipated breakfast with him in the morning. We hadn't truly ended a conversation in seven years.

But Miguel responded *Okay* and all our conversations were over without even a period, like turning a page and hitting the back cover.

Some days later, I visited Bickle in Manhattan. In fact, it was A.H. 1,034,952, officially Christmas Day. Five sun cycles of festive joy. Pods were crowded. I was glad to have someone to see. The Village bore no snow, but the air was cold and construction robust, and already my memory of the gala's nightmarish end was blurring with the real nightmares of the intervening nights and with "eyewitness accounts" I'd read in the news from gala attendees lucky enough to have seen less than I did. The news was reporting eighteen dead and over seventy injured. I didn't grasp what a big deal the attack was until I saw it on the homepage of the *Washington Post*, which I'd always read specifically for the perspective it lent by being so far removed from my own personal life in London. And then it dropped out of the headlines, replaced by the story of a collapsed housing project. I checked the *New York Times*, *BBC*, *CNN*, needing to dig further and further down to find their coverage of the gala attack. By Christmas, it was old news. I didn't feel entirely bad about this, though it did seem a little fast for the world to move on.

I walked from Waverly to West Tenth. There seemed to be a slight acclivity to the street, maybe a couple of degrees uphill whereas I remembered it having sloped faintly downward. Any slope I felt was probably just my imagination, but I was having trouble sorting fantasy from fact. People lumbered with toys and groceries. Plastic tree tips glowed.

The thing that really bothered me was that since waking up that morning, I hadn't been able to picture Miguel's face. I looked at a photo and thought, *Right—of course*, but then minutes later I was drawing blanks again. It was the same as trying to picture the face of the gala attacker, or my own face, or the Shell. They refused to fit in my mind. Since waking up, I couldn't remember what anything big or important in my life looked like.

In the mirrored elevator, I faced myself. *This is what I look like*, I thought. Everything I wore—my green cords, my heated vest, my hair gelled in a neat tower—looked like a costume.

Bickle welcomed me inside his penthouse. The blinds were drawn, and there were empty bento boxes (and worse, half-empty ones) littering surfaces as far from the kitchen as Bickle's king-size bed, which was unmade with the bedroom door obstructed by a heap of laundry.

He wore a button-down shirt and fuzzy pajama pants. He must have been in meetings.

"Just talking to Magnús," he said. "We're trying to finalize the severance, but CWC's lawyers won't make time. They're juggling investigations. The whole company is struggling and looking for scapegoats. Magnús thinks upper management is about to get shuffled."

"Yeah," I said, not really able to focus. "I saw their stock fell another 5 percent." I sat down on the horseshoe sofa.

"Might have been for the best that we got out when we did," Bickle said. "Anyway, it's good to see you. Really."

"You too."

We talked a little more about CWC-in-the-news, avoiding discussion of the gala, but it found us eventually.

"I'm still quite shaken up," I said. "In many ways, my life right now feels like a nightmare."

The sofa was plush. Bickle took off his glasses.

"I don't mean to be hyperbolic. Just that certain qualities of the experience . . . I can't think of any way to describe them but a bad dream. Like the 'how did I get here' feeling of it all." I groped for words. The ceiling fan spun so quickly it seemed to move in reverse.

Bickle told me he understood. We talked about the news coverage. He said he had avoided it. I told him that was probably wise.

"I just feel completely confused," I said.

"Mm."

"After the attack, Miguel and I broke up."

Bickle said, "Oh." I looked at the floor. "I'm sorry, Tanner." I nodded, knowing this conversation was something I had to get through.

He asked if I wanted to talk about it.

"No. I'm just tired of the whole thing. I don't know. I've been thinking of going back to Alaska."

"Really?"

"I might not stay long," I said. "I just find myself wanting some tradition, a connection to the past. Like, maybe even going to church. If I can manage to buy into all that again. I don't know." I shook my head at my own words. *Buy into that.* "I don't know how my parents will react."

"They'll be happy to see you."

"Maybe."

"Believe me," said Bickle. "They're your parents. It'll be messy, but it's worth a try."

"Yeah."

"Funny, there was actually something *I* needed in Keber Creek, as it happens."

"Oh?" I asked.

"Yeah," he said, picking his mustache. "Just a question answered. Maybe you could help me out when you're there." He said there was a woman whom he'd been trying to get in touch with. He was hoping I might go through the marriage records in Keber Creek and see if he had the wrong name.

"A woman you . . . you and her . . . ?"

"No," he said. "She doesn't know me, but I knew her mother. She's not around anymore."

I waited, giving Bickle a chance to continue.

He said, "I only recently learned that the daughter existed. I had thought—well, I was misinformed. When I learned, I wanted to reach out to her, but now I think her name isn't the same as her mother's."

"You want me to find her father's name?"

He winced at the question and avoided my gaze but nodded.

I said it'd be no problem.

We walked out of the apartment and said goodbye at the elevator. He surprised me by putting a hand on my shoulder. "Thank you," he said. "For everything. We'll get through this."

"I'll call you from Keber Creek."

The elevator arrived. I entered. And as I did, I was overcome by a feeling of having reached the line's end.

The thing about the line's end, though, is that it's always the worst place to stop.

Next morning, I came down from my hotel suite, suitcases in tow, and queued, behind families ending pleasant holidays, to check out of the Oxford Street Hilton.

At the counter, the receptionist asked me if I had enjoyed my visit.

How to answer that? Packing up, I had found one of Miguel's socks under the bed. I don't know how long it'd been there. I left it. I almost cried rolling my suitcases into the hall, hearing the latch close *ch-chk* behind me.

The receptionist said, "Well, if you wouldn't mind leaving a review, you'll be automatically entered into our weekly drawing for a free night's stay."

"Okay." My keycard was still in my pocket. I'd been planning to hold on to it as a memento, but now I didn't know why. I handed it over.

"Ah, thanks," the receptionist said and dropped it in a bin.

I walked across the lobby like I had a thousand times before. The elderly doorman smiled.

"Goodbye, Maxwell," I said.

He said, "Safe travels, sir."

The pod that would take me up to CWC vessel 311 with service to Keber Creek's Jefferson Station was two blocks away, past restaurants, chalkboards touting full English breakfasts, places that I had never tried but which I now felt I would have loved to go to with Miguel. I walked slowly, holding on to feelings I didn't understand, and when I arrived at the platform, the pod was there. I scanned my phone to board. The turnstile, however, didn't budge.

"Come on, bruv," said someone behind me.

I tried scanning again. Nothing. I squinted at the screen.

CWC ACCOUNT LOCKED.

I had been banned from CWC's circuit.

I scanned again even though there were people waiting. I kept trying to scan until the turnstile locked and the pod took off. I kicked the platform. I think someone called me a shithead.

I looked up other ways to get home and ended up buying a one-day pass on the budget circuit, WDYGO Airlines, which offered a route with an obscene number of transfers, taking me around the world three times before delivering me to Keber Creek. The planes were dirty. Each time I boarded a new connecting flight, I was welcomed by an identical holographic stewardess who said, "Welcome to Where Do You Get Off Airlines, where do you get off?" I answered and was directed to the appropriate cabin. There were no seats; everyone just floated in zero-g, holding grab-straps on the floor or the ceiling while the windowvisions played an epileptic montage of soft drink ads. It was supposed to be edgy or hip, but it just seemed dangerous.

It was night when I reached Keber Creek: windless, quiet, and well below freezing. All I wore was a peacoat over a heated vest. I stepped out of the pod into the open-air station and a flurry of snowflakes washed across the floor. Outside was Main Street. I expected Christmas lights under the eaves, but the street was desolate. It took me a moment to realize that it was not just night; it was true night. There were no work-lights in their gridded constellations; there were stars. The Shell didn't yet extend this far north.

I crossed the station lawn, crunching through snow up to my knees, carrying my suitcases. I walked along the gold mine wall, behind which labored no living souls, just machines, big and small, performing their tireless rituals. At a certain point, I began to notice the number of buildings that had fallen into disrepair. My old school had its windows shattered. Gus's hardware store was empty. The only edifice that wasn't dilapidated was the church. That, at least, looked pretty much how I'd remembered it, although the belfry, which I recalled towering over the street, now seemed quaint to me. I kept walking, noting all the abandoned homes.

It was a long walk, and I began to fear there'd be no one on the other end. I passed a vehicle hollowed out by the elements. I dragged my suitcases along a stream, ice creeping in from its banks. Around a stretch of woods in which I used to take the dogs to play. I used to watch videos on my phone while they gamboled about, looking for those little birds. The snow lay now, immaculate, between thin, naked trees.

Snow fell softly, fulfilling nature's promise, on the street where I grew up. There was a row of vacant houses, then the Tumeskys', whose horse stood stock-still in a trapezoid of light cast, to my relief, from a kitchen window. At least some people did still live in Keber Creek. Then there was a stretch of darkness. And then my home. A light was on. The big tree in the yard was buried up to its armpits. I dropped my suitcases on the front steps. Then picked them up and set them down gently. Then knocked.

In her blue pajamas, my mom opened the door.

"Hello?" she said. She looked confused. I remembered those pajamas.

"Hi, Mom." Our breaths hung weightless beneath the stars.

"What?" she said.

I just stood there, not knowing what to do.

"No," she said. "No. Is it really?"

Ashtyn appeared. Fifteen years old.

"Where's Dad?" I asked, my heart racing. Ashtyn shook her head.

My mom said, "This is real." She made space. I came in.

○

Winnie and Luna took a workweek off to get over what had happened at the gala. They spent the first fifty hours reliving the trauma through every account the internet had to offer. They spent the next ten high, but after a panic attack, Winnie declared herself unfit for weed. (Even less fit, that is, than she was for sobriety.) They didn't go out. They ate soup from the emergency cabinet. Winnie took long showers, kicking the water toward the drain (they kept calling their super; he said it was happening to everyone). One hundred hours deep, in the light of St. Emily, they played buckhorn in the kitchen.

"Have you felt," Winnie asked, "like the attack had a kind of inevitable quality?" She watched the buckhorn spin. Luna won again. "Like this tide of evil had been drawing nearer and nearer for a while, and we shouldn't have been surprised that it found us?"

"Or came close at least," said Luna, not quite engaging. "It could have been worse."

"It still could get worse."

"Did you feel that way after the hurricane?" Luna asked.

Winnie looked out through the blinds, bars against the provisional sky. "I'm not sure," she said. "I think then I was more inclined to look for things that I could have done differently."

"Do you blame yourself for the gala attack?"

"A little bit maybe."

Luna grew stern. "You know, Winnie, it's not right for you to put that on yourself."

"I know. I'm sorry," said Winnie, looking at her hands.

"Or on me."

"Forget I said anything."

"I don't want my life to be in the news ever again," Luna said. She said she wanted to live outside of current events, to be permitted to just pass ahistorical time. Without speaking they played five more rounds, and the spinner landed on Luna for four. An ant crawled up Winnie's arm. She thought it felt nice before registering what it was, then she cried out, ran to the window, and flicked it. Down below, some drivers did donuts, backing up traffic for blocks. It was Christmas day. When she returned, she suggested they rotate the board. They did. The spinner still landed on Luna.

"Do you think that's because of . . ."

"Probably just the table's uneven," said Winnie and tried spinning again.

*   *   *

When it was time for her to return to work, she was almost relieved. Though that didn't last. The BodyThink PocketPuncher had finally attracted the attention of a major pharmaceutical company, opening doors for new Unhealthy Behavior programs, which Winnie's coworkers believed would revolutionize healthcare. The app now targeted depression, attention disorders, and generalized anxiety.

"Caught early enough," Winnie heard her boss, Chip, telling a potential investor, "these vicious diseases can be punched right out of the system."

BodyThink stood to get 10 percent from pharma for every referral. As long as the app proved effective, that is, so they were testing like mad. Chip made all employees keep the beta active on their own devices around the clock. He said it was time everyone in the BodyThink gang got serious about the mission or else handed him their letter of resignation.

Winnie spent hours in her hammock, moving too slowly, listing too far, not sure anymore what was her imagination. She pinched the naked buds of her jacaranda tree. She was, in part, avoiding Luna, whose company lately felt like a betrayal of Winnie's loneliness. Luna skulked around with a new phone that she said she'd gotten from a guy at the gala. She said this with flippant indifference, which Winnie took to be her way of bragging—it was a really expensive phone.

"I guess he enjoyed his time with you."

"He was just a drunk asshole. We didn't even do anything."

"You're keeping his phone, though."

"My phone. I put my SIM in."

"He probably wanted you to see his dick pics first."

"I'm telling you, he was drunk. The next day he texted me. Fucking asshole. He said whoever had his phone was committing theft against the CWC Group, which is where he worked so you know he's a prick. He's probably fired now. I read they're having massive layoffs and old employees keep leaking stuff to the press."

She showed Winnie the "CWC" embossment on the back.

"Did you give him Qfizs?"

"No," said Luna, but Winnie knew she was lying.

Still, they ate together when they were home together, and sometimes when Winnie fell asleep under her jacaranda tree, she woke up to find that Luna had come down and covered her over with a blanket.

Enthusiastic about research showing a national rise in mental illness, Chip gave back-to-back office tours to potential investors. He had too many showings to keep straight. He wore his fun tie every day, hoping it would become iconic.

"In such a topsy-turvy world," he said, "demand is only going to grow for services like ours that return power to the individual to seize control over their own well-being."

Around the trunk of Winnie's tree, little latex construction flags appeared, blue with white print, JUST GET IT DONE. She pulled them out with the weeds. Her hammock smelled starchy from rain. Every time a circuit vessel *popped*, her stomach leapt. She couldn't stop seeing the gala attacker. Pulling a tuft of grass, weighing it in her hand, she tried to think about things that made her happy. All those things—the trees, the sky, human communication and trust, genuine health, diversity and creativity of thought—seemed to be the very things people around her were sweating and slaving to subdue. Why? Why did she have to live in a civilization that conspired to destroy the elements that made people's lives worth living? Just so "well-being" companies like hers could "return power to the individual" by selling them short-lived substitutes? Was that even a conspiracy? Where was the master plan?

Between work shifts, she had enough time to sleep five hours, sometimes six, after which she woke up to the artificial night and the dark or the light or the violent gloom of the sun being sealed out, and she had the startled thought, *what am I doing here?* And maybe she just needed a new job, but some despair roots itself so deep as to crowd out even a memory of joy or a belief in its possibility, and given that, how could you make a change? All directions turned inward. Were there other people who felt that way, she wondered. Did everyone?

Beyond the garden wall, other people were laughing. She had nightmares of the entire world enclosed in the Shell, locked in a room with itself. Winnie once watched a cooking show where the host said, "Inside the chic restaurant is a kitchen like a scene from hell." That was how she saw the world. It was also how she saw herself. In that sense, maybe she did fit in, whether she wanted to or not. Maybe she was made for this place.

Her beta of the BodyThink PocketPuncher chimed. It informed her that spending hours alone moving back and forth outside her own building indicated that she might be suffering from Developmental Topographical Disorientation, and it suggested she download Google Maps.

She swiped the notification away. But the next day, she did search for directions. To find out where to go to find out where she came from, and vice versa. She had to know how she ended up in a world that was like this. She decided to visit her mom.

The circuit got her as far as Dry Basin, Nevada, and from there, she took a car. Its driving computer sat on the front seat, connected to the dashboard by loose wires. She drove thirty minutes, escorted by a decommissioned phone line from one desert horizon to the other, the pale landscape lighting up each time the sun appeared behind the crumbly Shell patchwork. In these glimpses, you could see just how fast the sun was falling. Migratory circuit vessels and resplendent quetzals stormed the cloudless sky. Up from the mirage wriggled her mother's facility.

The car eased to a stop and was overtaken by a dust wave that broke against the windowless façade. Dust already piled up the sides of the building, as if pulling the building down into the desert floor.

She stepped into the heat. The Shell was making noises she'd never heard in the city. Guttural throbbing. A saguaro lay dead with one arm rotting and one arm still held up, waiting for someone to return its high five. The car drove away.

A rush of cool air met her in the facility's entrance. It had the sepulchral smell of damp stone. There was nothing inside but a gallery of beds encased in glass, each with a holographic number suspended above it, and a reception desk where a pimpled orderly sat. He was at least thirty but had a boy scout's smile, which he flashed over a video game on his desktop.

"Hola," he said in the lilt of someone who spoke absolutely no Spanish. His character took a shot in the chest and died with an apathetic grunt.

"I'm here to visit my mom," said Winnie.

The orderly had her sign in. "Do you know the patient's capsule ID?"

Winnie shook her head.

"What's her name?"

"Claira Lynx."

"Of course," he said, recognizing her face. "Forty-six." He pointed to the middle of the gallery.

Winnie wove through the beds. She heard the orderly resume his game. The air conditioners keened, recirculating an unnatural chill.

46. The number didn't blink. Winnie looked down and saw the mound of her mother's feet beneath a blue blanket. She walked around the bed. The blanket swelled and sank over her mother's chest.

When Winnie had last seen her mom, at the Wwlliamses' apartment, she had looked worse, gaunt from the pills they put her on after her first attempt. She had come over to take Winnie for a walk but ended up yelling at Carsie for colluding with the doctors who wanted to track her diet. Winnie spent the hour in the kitchen watching them fight, and at the end when she walked her mom out of the building, her mom had said she wished Carsie were dead.

Her cheeks were fuller now. A small, pale, serene face nested in hair so blond you could almost see through it. Her eyes were closed, but Winnie couldn't shake the sense that behind her crusted eyelids her gaze was darting frantically, looking for a way out.

Winnie put a hand on the glass.

"Hi, Mom," she said. Her own voice scared her.

There was a small touchscreen at the head of the chamber. It flashed: LEAVE A MESSAGE; OR SEND LOVE FROM YOUR OWN DEVICE TO ALAMO.PAT46@COMANICATEBYPATIENTLINK.COM.

The screen was damp. She wiped it, thought for a long time, and wrote:

Mom,

I thought I could make a life without you. But you're the one who made my life in a literal sense that I'm finding less and less trivial, and I'm not really sure why you did. I don't like it here very much. Is it unfair for us to expect that our parents bring us into a world they haven't already given up on? If I could accept not being here, this would be easy, but I'm not like you I'm not. I maybe almost died recently, and I realized my desire to live is so arduous that it probably doesn't even justify itself, but there it is. Mass catastrophe feels in some way right. A great, climactic conclusion to all of this. Like the society would get what it deserves, not that I'd wish that upon anyone in particular. I'm thinking of Carsie, my coworkers, Luna, etc. Remember when we used to sit on the beach, looking at the horizon? You always told me I was just too close to see how the horizon curved. How the world really was a circle. But the farther I recede, the more unbearable it seems to me that the world could go on and on, over and over, a circle in any sense. That no matter how far I trace it, I will never get to the

MAXIMUM CHARACTERS USED

She moved "Mom," from the address to the subject line so she could finish the sentence.

THANK YOU FOR USING COMANICATE BY PATIENTLINK!

The 46 atop her mom's bed sprouted ephemeral roses. Her mom didn't stir. On the other side of the room, the orderly died again.

YOUR MESSAGE HAS JOINED **162** OTHER WELL-WISHES.

This surprised her. She didn't know anyone else who would be writing to her mom.

She opened the Well-Wishers Log. Her own message was listed on top. Only her name, the subject, and the timestamp showed. The next message was anonymous with subject: OUR DAUGHTER. It was barely a week old. There were messages going back for years, all anonymous, going back to the night Winnie's mom entered her coma, the night Winnie cried looking at the horizon from Ocean Beach. A.H. 975,946. Submitter: ANONYMOUS. Subject: BEING TOGETHER.

She approached the orderly.

"Excuse me," she said. "I have a question about the patient messaging service."

The orderly paused his game, suspending his avatar mid-leap.

"My mom has gotten a lot of messages that I don't think she'll ever read, and I'm wondering if I could read them?"

Knitting his eyebrows in a gesture of understanding that blanched his forehead pimples, the orderly told her not to lose faith.

"Okay," said Winnie. "Sure. The thing is, the messages are about me."

He asked how she knew.

"I think they're from my dad," said Winnie.

"Can you ask him?"

"He left us before I was born. I've never met him."

The orderly blushed. He closed the game on his desktop. Patientlink had a process for granting authorization to next of kin, he said. "But, I've never pursued it before." He seemed to be grasping for words, trying to sound professional. He said if she wanted, he could "instigate" a claim. She asked how long it would take.

On behalf of Patientlink he promised she'd have her answer by the end of March. He'd simply need her to affirm her identity.

Imani Handal

It should have been a festive occasion. But at the Forwards Foundation's 50,000-hour Anniversary Banquet, there was no raucous laughter. Hushed rumors passed between the two hundred attendees. Most were CWC employees, and they greeted not with back slaps and feigned delight, but rather with genuine relief at the sight of one another, for they didn't know who was still with CWC and who had been purged.

Word was that the purges weren't over, so even their relief tonight was tenuous. The axe had been whittling its way through Aviation Tower since the holidays—since, that is, the media and its politicians had seized on public panic over grav loss, and six states' attorneys general had joined California's public trust claim against the company. The highly publicized investigations had driven CWC's stock price to its lowest point in years. Then came the leaks. Thousands of internal documents started finding their way to the press, to competitors, and eventually to offshore databases, searchable to the public. The exact source, or sources, of these leaks weren't known, but the leaks' causes were clear enough. CWC's data integrity had always been slipshod (its cybersecurity team never having quite mastered even simple email scanning), and with so many investigative journalists prodding so many laid-off employees, with so many hacktivists homing in on such a decapitalized infrastructure, it wasn't surprising that the company started cracking up. Some of the spurts that came out were ugly and intimate—internal emails documenting racist jokes and office affairs.

Numerous employees had come to the banquet tonight without their spouses. CWC officially found itself in a downward spiral.

Already half of the company's C-suite had grasped the golden handshake, and lower-level managers were being P45ed en masse. New management was trying anything to signal a fresh start. When the re-org began, the outgoing managers made martyrial attempts to push the ship in the right direction as they jumped off, nominating their own replacements and reassuring their deputies, in somber communions crammed into boxed-up corner offices, that business would go on. When the replacements and deputies started getting let go, the assurances quieted.

Imani, the Forwards Foundation's executive director, had planned the banquet months ago and was just glad anyone had turned up. They'd had to change venues last minute. It was supposed to be at the Commons Lounge next to Aviation Tower, but street protests there threatened safety and traffic flow, so they moved to the only event space they could book on such short notice. The basement level of the London Eataly.

She walked through Ravioli Et Al.—cautiously, to keep her balance—toward a sit-down nook called La Pizza & La Pasta. Her child had been born four months earlier, a healthy boy. He was home with his father.

At the bottom of a half-flight of stairs, she found her assistant conversing with Miguel. They held on to opposite handrails. Gravity in London was 93 percent and slanted five degrees.

"Having fun?" she asked, catching her descent with a hand on her assistant's shoulder. "I know there's a weird vibe."

Her assistant tried to reassure her.

She asked how Miguel was. Miguel shrugged.

"I heard that Grant refused to tender his resignation," Imani said.

Miguel spoke so softly she had to lean in to hear. He said Grant was on paid leave.

She nodded. "It seems like your whole department's in limbo—and just when the company needs you."

Miguel was put on leave too. He didn't know why. Imani suggested that the firm must be looking for a better job to assign him, in case Comms got shuffled.

"These men in Legal keep calling me," he said, "asking me questions: Have I seen such and such document. I don't even know what they're investigating."

"No one really knows what's going on," said Imani. Her assistant excused herself.

Stuck with Miguel, Imani tried to strike up conversation about the upcoming Shell Switch-On, but he expressed indifference on that subject. He was, further, indifferent to the protests, the Foundation's banquet, her life—his indifference was indiscriminate.

"Man," he said. "I just don't want to lose my job. No me chingues, that would just be more than I could handle."

"Mm."

He drank his beer. She watched a guest behind him stumble into a chair.

Thankfully, she was pulled away by a CWC VP named Mario Crespi. A short, dark-eyed quinquagenarian whose bald head was shaped in such a way as to make observers automatically imagine his belly, Crespi had bounced through just about every department at CWC over the course of his career. Imani knew him mostly by reputation. "How are you, Ms. Handal?" he asked. She couldn't tell if the formality was supposed to be ironic. He swirled red wine in so wide a circle that he nearly punched someone passing by. If there were betting pools for who would be fired from CWC next (and surely, somewhere, there were), Imani would have gone all in on Mario Crespi.

She said that all things considered, she was happy with how the banquet turned out.

"I'm glad to hear you're enjoying it," he said, "since it will be your last as director of the Forwards Foundation."

"What do you mean?"

Crespi chuckled benevolently. "It's nothing personal," he said. "CWC is pulling the foundation's financial support. It has been judged an extravagance, under the circumstances. But I have good news for you. Cromwell Grant has been let go, and you are to be tapped to replace him as CWC's chief of communications."

Imani didn't know what to say.

"You needn't say a thing," said Crespi. Indeed, he didn't give her the chance. He gestured at the shelves of Nutella. "Are these included? As part of the banquet catering, I mean."

She shook her head.

Crespi shrugged and put two jars into his briefcase. "I love Nutella," he said. "Reminds me of home."

"No." She was so confused. "That's stealing."

He laughed and slapped her arm gently and said, as if she were being adorably naïve, "I *understand* that, Ms. Handal."

He zipped his briefcase.

"Well, you'll have to excuse me," he said. "I've another banquet in Budapest, but I hope you'll consider the position. If you accept, you'll be reporting straight to me." He poked his own chest with his thumb. "I'm CWC's new CEO."

DAYS OF 3 HOURS

In Alaska, so far from the equator and its grav drain, it was almost like nothing had changed. That first night, I took my father's old couch. Wind whistled against the windows. The cushions kept shifting under my weight. Too tired to unpack, I fell asleep in a chalky old parka that I used to wear when I was fifteen. I slept twelve hours. It felt good. I awoke with the sun's rise, but the sun didn't get very high and set again twenty minutes later. Changing, I found in a pocket of the parka a mini-bottle of Listerine, a matchbook, and a pack of American Spirits. I pulled the cellophane, tapped one out, and sniffed. It'd been years. *Natural tastes better.* It was stale, but I didn't care.

I trekked out to the woods and smoked it in the dark. The tobacco tasted to me like pine trees. I thought about London and tried not to think about Miguel. Instead I scrolled Streamscape food channels till the cigarette was done.

When I returned home, the lights were on. My mom and Ashtyn were in the kitchen. I smelled scrambled eggs and toast and something else. Coffee.

"You drink coffee now?" I said.

"Oh, don't give me that look," said my mom over a camping stove that said First i drink the coffee, then i do the thing.

Ashtyn (the same girl who used to sing that coffee was the Devil's diuretic) said that the Church had reinterpreted the Word of Wisdom years ago. "Without coffee, how could Church leaders possibly per-form their duties in these days of contraction?"

I shook my head. And poured myself a cup.

Of all things, what my mom asked about London, what she said she had always wondered, was whether it was true that the city streets suffered from weekly sinkholes.

"Sinkholes?" I said, sitting down. "I guess. You learn to ignore them."

My mom said, "A real city ought to take care of its roads."

I asked what had happened to our town. "All the stores looked shuttered."

She told me about the mine's automation and the gradual exodus from Keber Creek. "The first year was hard on the community. But your father was prepared for it. Others, who stayed, took after him. It's good people left here, a little extreme like your father was, but God-fearing people."

I learned how they'd been living, on jimmied solar panels and duct-tape and supplies bought once a month, weather permitting, from North Slope. Who'd have predicted that my father's radical way would be the way of the future—at least the future of his little world. I asked, "How long has it been?"

"Since?"

I nodded.

"Not long," said my mom. "At the end, I heard him pray you would come home, and here you are. I guess yesterday was seven weeks."

Only seven weeks. The news caught me off guard.

"You okay?" Ashtyn asked.

I asked how it happened.

"He was so bullheaded," said my mom, managing to roll her eyes. "He'd never had his shots of course, and after he got bitten, he refused to be taken to a hospital. He said he felt fine." She twisted her hand to show me. "Right here. I didn't even see the mark; I just thought he chased it out of the house. To the end, he was fighting me off, afraid

I would subject him to socialist medicine. It wasn't only the lemming that killed him."

"I think he was just ready to go," said Ashtyn.

"I don't know about *that*. But he was going to do things his way to the end."

I pieced the story together from fragments. I think it took me so long to understand in part because it seemed so pre-modern, to die of rabies. So distant from what I had, in the preceding years, learned the world to be. To die because of an animal. I could understand dying at the hands of another man, but an animal . . . And then, it was hard to understand too because it was my own dad. A quote from Streamscape came to me. EVERY MAN IS BORN AS MANY MEN AND DIES A SINGLE ONE. I imagined my dad seizing at the sound of water. It shouldn't have mattered—he'd already been out of my life for years—but it was hard to grasp that he was gone forever.

A week went by. Then a month. I helped my mother. I would enter rooms to find her shaking her phone, and then (following a video on my own phone) I unscrewed the back and saw that my father had removed her battery. He'd put in a smaller cell and stuffed the gap with tinfoil. I drove to North Slope and bought her a new one, for which she never quite forgave me. Cleaning, I discovered a bin of my old crayons and wondered if she'd kept them out of nostalgia. She laughed at that suggestion. "Your father collected those. They'll burn if you're out of candles." I brought them—along with a broken television, a bag of duct-tape rinds, and several jars of expired mayonnaise—to the trash dump behind the mine.

Alaska's annual polar night came and went. The total darkness used to last four days; now the Earth had learned to cram in eight times as many flips. I watched the stars twirl. I put off Bickle's favor. To be honest, I was experimenting with forgetting about Bickle, with putting that whole life behind me. As foreign as my family's lifestyle had become, there was something nourishing about the Alaskan air and the quiet of the trees. The freedom to sleep until I felt rested. The power to look up and see the sky. When Ashtyn had time (outside housekeeping and tending to the dogs and pigs), she and I ventured through the ghost town to the church, where we hung out in the entertainment annex, eating pizza and watching movies.

I enjoyed telling her about my time in the big cities. She listened to my accounts of German nightlife and absorbed secondhand the layout of London—what neighborhoods were on the rise and which were best for which cuisine. One afternoon, she asked me about foreign men.

"You got a thing for foreign men?" I teased.

A blush crept up from her turtleneck sweater. She said she was watching a drama about Interpol detectives, and the lead was South African. "I like his accent," she said.

"You should go somewhere," I replied. "Anywhere. Get outside of here. There's a whole world out there, and it's so much easier to see now than it was when I was your age. You have to."

Ashtyn said she liked Keber Creek.

"This place is backward. Now more than ever. You don't know what you're missing."

"I don't feel like I'm missing anything."

"You are, though. Trust me. It's not healthy for you to stay here your whole life. You have to get out and see how the world really is."

"What about Mom?"

"Take Mom with you."

"I've thought about it," she said. "It's something I thought I'd do once Dad was gone."

"Why wouldn't you?" I asked. "You'd have to be crazy not to."

She twisted her stringy red hair. "It's just that you left," she said, "and you don't seem much happier."

"Well, no." I thought about that. "I was happy. I am." I said things were a little confusing for me at the moment, but those were my own problems. Not problems with the whole world.

"When you were gone," Ashtyn said, "Mom said harsh things about you. She was shown the pictures of you and your boyfriend on Scroller by other people in town. It was hard on her, but I want you to know, I didn't agree with her. And I don't. I think eventually the Church is going to change in certain ways, and people like you will be welcomed back. I just prayed that you were happy."

I mumbled thanks, and she hugged me, and I felt sick in a dizzy way, like the pull of a drawstring on a windup doll. It was homesickness, I realized, but for what, I didn't know. It can be horrible to come home, to wonder if you really did change like you'd hoped to when you left. I blinked. The game machines were pushed into a corner, collecting dust. I thought about my childhood in Keber Creek, all my old anger, and my anger now.

After the gala, I had watched a video of the attacker, before Streamscape took him down. He was in his mom's bathroom, talking about how he would "break through," and though I wouldn't admit this to anyone, the video was, for me, heartening, for I had feared, imagining that disaffected young man, that when I saw his videos I might—not sympathize—but maybe . . . identify. I didn't though. I watched the video and thought with relief, *I've never become that.*

I rested my chin on Ashtyn's shoulder and breathed.

I sat on my dad's couch, my couch, and watched the news. CWC continued to downplay their circuit's damage to the environment and claim everything would be corrected—more than corrected, improved—by the Shell they so selflessly rushed to complete, but meanwhile headlines were dominated by reports of gravity loss entering exponential territory. Estimates for the cost of building reconstruction and bridge closures ranged from many billions to over a trillion dollars worldwide, and if day contraction continued at its current rate, major cities would become uninhabitable. The US was already seeing an uptick in unemployment claims from workers furloughed by the physical loss of their workplaces. LA was using reconstruction as a chance to double homeless shelter capacity. With nuance that only confused people, the Santiago Commission demanded that governments pledge to keep day contraction within a limit of two and a half hours while Commission scientists admitted it might already be too late.

By March, days fell to two hours and fifty minutes.

Alaska's days grew longer in March, but its nights shorter, and snow dried out along the road to form black-winged crystals of ice. I read about the shifts going on in the rest of the world but couldn't feel them. I got the sense that people everywhere were talking about the shifts without really feeling. Or maybe we all felt it, felt it at a spiritual level even, and were just responding in our own ways. On the news, Choneros rebels in Ecuador were hijacking cargo pods. The US government had committed to keeping the circuit lines open, and I watched their soldiers—our soldiers—move through Quito, a city at the leading edge of gravity's attrition. The equator, where the circle of the Earth's rotation was the widest, was spinning people the fastest, and the centrifugal effects, rather than pulling north or south as they pulled other cities toward the equator, pulled straight up. I noticed the length of the soldiers' jogging strides while the men fleeing them stumbled down dilapidated stairs.

Meanwhile, across Europe buildings were being buttressed. The Oxford Street Hilton, I read, was getting reset on a graded foundation. I brought it up with Ashtyn. It wasn't something we usually talked about, and she admitted that she had started praying to God a reform would be made to stop things getting any worse.

Coming out of the shower one morning, I checked my phone and saw that I'd gotten a message from Bickle.

Hey, Tanner, it said. *Just checking in. How are things back home?*

In spite of myself, I was grateful to hear from him. I wrote back promptly, sharing the news about my dad, and a bit about my mom and sister, telling him that he'd been right when he said they would welcome me. He asked about Keber Creek. *Same old*, I wrote. *Well, I guess some things have changed.* He was sorry to hear about the mine's automation. His responses were caring, and maybe it was me still processing my own dad's absence, but they struck me as gently paternal. Once we had exchanged several messages, he asked if I'd had a chance yet to look up the name he'd told me about. I promised him I would do it the next day.

The only organization in Keber Creek that salvaged marriage records was the church, so the next morning as the sun was setting I dressed to walk over there, hoping I could get in through the back door (or else jimmy one of the windows, which I still knew well enough from years of custodial work). On my way out of the house, I ran into my mom and Ashtyn and asked where they were headed.

"Church," Ashtyn said.

My mother's gaze met mine. I could see the hope buried there. She'd been asking me to join them at church since I first showed up.

Well, I thought, it appeared I'd be doing good by some more people that morning.

The three of us walked briskly beneath the northern lights. They blazed brighter than ever, agitated by the magnetic effects of the planet's spinning. When we reached the lamplit chapel, a dozen other families were there, pretty much the whole town. We sat in the middle. A few old acquaintances filed past, taking my mother's hand, calling her sister and eyeing me with distrust. Several of them wore guns at their hips. The grocer's son, who in middle school gave me a black eye for a stray changing-room glance, sat beside Ashtyn, teasing her over the return of her freckles. I was glad when the service started.

The forty or so congregants sang the sacrament hymn while Bob Yost uncovered consecrated elements—sliced Wonder Bread and water in Dixie cups. Like the body, the bread was broken, into bite-sized pieces. The only ornamental décor was a warped photograph of Christ above the water fountain. A musty smell drizzled from the rafters. I sat and listened and tried not to think about Miguel.

The sermon was delivered by old Gerald Tumesky. He lived down the street from us and was one of the men my dad had most respected. I recalled those two chauvinists whipping themselves into an eschatological frenzy. Passing a double-action revolver back and forth, condemning cans in the yard. I remembered the smell of the gunpowder.

"Lamentations today," he said without making any eye contact. A long, pale scar wormed its way over the folds of his neck.

Haltingly, he read Lamentations 1:8, of the sins of Jerusalem and the punishments visited upon its later generations, "forced to buy the water from their own creeks. Their land, and they're paying for the wood . . ." As he spoke, Ashtyn and my mother murmured amens. He read the plea of the people of Jerusalem, Lamentations 1:21, that the Lord bring the day He had announced. "Not a day of relent," he said, growing louder, pushing through a frog in his throat. "A day of retribution. A day when the . . . the castigation that had restored their own faith would be finally unleashed on the world at large."

"I look out at all of you," he said, "who know that Jesus Christ won't be waylaid by these monstrosities, on the land and now the sky, and I see it. Let Jerusalem crumble at His feet. It's crumbling now. These are the people who tried to touch heaven . . . Instead of stones they used brick, and now instead of bricks we have . . . someone help me, what is that shit called?"

Bob Yost whispered to him.

"That's right," Tumesky said, nodding. "If you don't think we're living at the end, look around . . . The Feds are already in Fairbanks." He brought his hand down on the podium. "The Devil doesn't go down without a fight. The book said this would happen. Next he'll be in North Slope and Cold Foot and the one after, but when he gets here, he's in for a holy, holy, holy . . . Ha! I'll fight like hell . . . leave it all out on the field, and it'll all be over soon. You have got to carve yourself out a space in the world to come, because no one is going to make space for you. That is something my uncle Byron used to say . . . Bootheel Byron . . .

He belonged to a congregation down in Texas, and he wore long, red, you know . . . That was best in those days for restitching boots."

Faltering, he looked around as if he'd suddenly forgotten where he was. Then his gaze landed on his wife in the pews. He said, "There you are."

His son-in-law helped him down and walked him to the water fountain, beneath the photograph of Christ, which he tenderly touched, while members stood. Ashtyn and my mother joined in the leftover bread. I squeezed my way through the crowd and quietly entered the church's back office.

I found the town's marriage certificates in a wooden crate, sorted chronologically. The earliest dated back to the A.H. 700,000s. Ancient history already. Thirty years ago. Looking for the record Bickle had asked about, I flipped through names I vaguely recognized, former colleagues of my father. I pictured the brides and grooms dressed in the old styles and wondered when they'd been laid off and where they'd gone. Were they still married, I wondered. What did they think of each other now?

When I fell in love with Miguel, at Petra Dance Haus, it was the way he asserted himself, his drunken abandon. It was a courtship shaped by chance encounters, by passing needs and thoughtless gestures, but then it was also something more. Love is deeper than the times. It transforms interactions into something timeless. Miguel's desperation, for our nights of blithe dancing and laughter about nothing, taught twenty-year-old me that I wasn't alone, there was another person here, if only one. Someone else who was insecure about his body and his reputation and who wanted help forgetting about everything that was wrong. Ultimately, it was toxic, our love, as true love must be. It was love for Miguel's shortcomings, and this, too, was love's power to transfigure: that true love is convincing oneself that something bad is good.

There weren't so many marriages each year, and the names grew more familiar as I kept flipping through certificates, growing afraid I'd missed it. *L*, I repeated. *Lynx*. Finally it was there. CLAIRA LYNX . . . MARRIAGE MAY BE CELEBRATED . . . LELAND PINES. *Pines*. I took a photograph, checked it for legibility, and headed out into the sun.

"Tanner Kelly."

Old Gerald Tumesky was standing in the church parking lot, waiting while his son-in-law loaded his truck.

"Randall's boy," he said to me. "Coming to pray. You got a lot to pray, pray, pray about. Randall dies and you return from Lord knows where. First the feds install themselves in Fairbanks, then you appear . . . The Book says when the prodigal son returns to beg forgiveness it's not him but the father who falls to his knees. A fall for an old man isn't like a fall for a young man. The young are built to take it. The old go down, it's cracked femurs . . ."

He kept on like this as I walked across the parking lot, the sun at my back.

"First you're here," said Tumesky. "Next it's the feds . . ."

○

As Winnie's heart grew heavier, her body grew lighter. She had felt it as early as February.

"I'm starting to feel it," she said to Luna. "The effects they talk about in the news. This nauseating lightness, like I can't quite command my momentum."

She wasn't the only one. That month, a union organizer dumped a truckload of cauliflower onto the governor's lawn. His video manifesto floated around Streamscape, claiming the state's annual subsidies, based on yield weight, weren't adjusting for grav loss. The governor's

electoral strategy had always been to attack the opposition for letting day contraction mount, but it was unclear what either party was
doing to abate it. Their accusations appropriated rhetoric from old
campaigns: the party of the worker, the party of government largesse,
the party for farmers, the party for affordable food.

Luna instructed Winnie to stop watching the news.

"It's a curation," Luna said.

Winnie said so what.

"So, curations are distortions."

She sat with Winnie in her hammock, their toes brushing the grass.
Enough of the sky was now covered that the Shell was able to keep
SF2 lit even when the sun went down, and Winnie found discomfiting
the comfort she took in the vanquishment of nighttime.

"The mind is a curation," Winnie said.

"So direct it at something different," said Luna. She pointed out
the blossoms on the jacaranda tree. She nodded at its roots, the soil,
a bird, the bugs, a gecko. "Imagine what it's like to be him," she said
of the latter. "His whole day is basking."

"The geckos are an infestation. Our culling efforts kill them by
the thousands, but we're too incompetent to do them the courtesy of
killing them before they lay more eggs."

Luna kept swinging the hammock. Winnie tried to ignore the
irritating motion: too slow, like a pendulum moving through water.

Eventually, Luna said, "I don't know, man."

Winnie took the victory bitterly, as a child who suspects an adult
letting them win. She looked up at heaven or the Shell. "I still haven't
heard back about my mom's messages."

"How long has it been?"

"Almost a month."

"So they said it might be a half month more," said Luna. "Don't
worry." She gave Winnie a light shoulder check. "I'm really proud of
you for learning more about your parents—"

"I haven't learned anything."

"But you will," Luna said. "I mean, I don't think you need to, but since you feel you owe it to yourself, I support you. It's not easy what you're doing. I'm proud to be friends with the sort of person who takes an obligation to herself seriously. No matter what you learn, I'm proud of you."

"Thanks."

She hadn't dared explain to Luna what it was she wanted to learn. But by now Winnie knew with total clarity the question driving her to her mom. She needed to learn what string of fate had pulled her into this particular world, and if it could still bind her here.

Half a month passed, and all Winnie received from Patientlink were junk emails.

COMING SOON: YOUR PERFECT MEDICINE MATCH – The suspense is mounting. Maintaining momentum for better medicine Let's get to it. Hi Winnie Pines click below for your trial . . .

She called the facility, and the orderly on duty said that due to the ongoing gravitational crisis, response times may be delayed. On her walk to work, she saw more and more billboards for Shell Switch-On Day parties. The Switch-On had been postponed again after flooding in Indonesia exposed more design flaws—tons of seawater leaked back into the equatorial Pacific, reminiscent of pre-Shell tide displacement; three hundred people had died while the Santiago Commission and contractors bickered over repairs. Nonetheless, experts believed this postponement would be the last. It would be a summer Switch-On. The market was up. The clubs in Las Vegas were already selling tickets four months in advance. NO WORRIES! they said. PREPARE AHEAD AND CELEBRATE VEGAS STYLE WHEN THE I.C.R.F. CREATES HISTORY.

The advertisements made no mention of the new crisis consuming headlines—the crisis of gravity, which the Shell, beyond stabilizing sea levels, had never been designed to address. Policymakers who had championed the Shell didn't acknowledge it. Perhaps they themselves had gotten so used to the idea that the Shell would help things—it would fix the weather, the tides, the lights—that this new crisis felt unfair, a shifting of the goalposts when they were finally getting close, which couldn't possibly be their fault. Even Winnie caught herself indulging this fantasy, that what mattered for now was that the Shell was almost done, not the fact that gravity was slipping away under her own feet. The Shell screens were being installed overhead, a testament to everything still going as planned, and it was possible, in fragmented moments, to believe.

The moments of life seemed increasingly fragmented to Winnie, moments of hope having completely lost touch with those of panic. The mood on Streamscape seemed to flip day-to-day without any change in the underlying situation, and Winnie felt herself cycling through worldviews, frenetically, because each and every perspective she adopted was untenable. No lens on what was happening around her—not obsession with the news, not trust in one party or another, not fury, not nihilism, not radical compassion—failed to give way, sooner or later, to a world that was cognitively uninhabitable. There wasn't a worldview that could make sense of the tragedy she saw unfolding in her lifetime. No ideology could resolve the fact that in this modern place, a new sky was being constructed on the backs of living men. That while the poor played music on stoops because their hard work entitled them to some respite and the rich ordered cocktails on patios because their hard work entitled them to some respite, governments and NGOs were paying contractors to obliterate the world before it could reach their children. And yet to live as if you really understood this brought you nothing. Worse, it made you a depressive, counter-productive pariah to be ridiculed by strangers and suffered by friends. God's honest truth was that Winnie's obsessive thoughts, and her corresponding pain, were not useful to anyone at all.

In the kitchen doing dishes, she placed a mug on its shelf only for it to slide right off and shatter in the sink. It was her UCLA class mug. She had noted the downward slope of the shelves on that side of the room and already warned herself not to stock dishes there, so as she collected the pieces of her mug, her frustration was directed inward. According to her phone, their apartment now sloped five degrees.

The next day, the entire shelf slid off its pegs.

She and Luna hammered it back in, ordered a dozen no-slip pads online, and went through the whole apartment, sticking two-dollar leveling shims under the legs of each chair and table. It took longer to do than they expected, and then they hurried back out to work.

One warm day in mid-March—while Winnie weeded her garden beneath the Shell's daylights, wearing headphones to tune out the construction around her and above—everything abruptly went dark. She first assumed a power outage, but streetlamps were still lit; it was only the Shell that had blacked out. Her tablet buzzed, an emergency alert:

SF2 CITYWIDE CURFEW IN IMMEDIATE EFFECT.

She called Luna at work. No answer. She went upstairs (nearly tripping on the tilted steps) and ran her fingers through Streamscape, trying to figure out what was happening. Everything felt so urgent that she didn't have time to read more than a sentence of any one article. Fox News called the curfew "martial night." Luna came home thirty minutes later, locked the door, and asked what was going on.

Winnie told her that farmers from the Tulare Basin were skirmishing with police.

"Skirmishing?"

"I don't know," Winnie said. "All the headlines use that word, I don't know. They're like, smashing windows outside the Moscone Center."

"What do they want?" said Luna, sitting down in her tight Forest Service green jeans.

Winnie kept reading. "Tax cuts." A police drone flew by, lighting the blinds cherry red.

Luna asked, "What do tax cuts have to do with anything?" She pulled out her CWC phone (as if a nicer phone than Winnie's would make the news make sense).

"I don't know."

The curfew lasted seventeen hours. When it ended, San Franciscans were greeted by National Guardsmen at every corner.

Winnie went out less. Each time she walked to work, the young soldier on her block eyed her. Soon the broken glass left by the riots had mostly washed away to wherever that sort of thing goes with time, and what remained was just common litter to be stepped around. Depending on their work schedules, people drank coffee or vaped or took nightcaps on the stairs at Castro and Market, and those who had no work schedules anymore nested around the entry to the Castro Theatre, which was being converted into a shelter. The soldiers made themselves useful protecting these groups from one another. The days were humid and had no beginning or end.

In April, gravity in SF2 was at 88 percent with a seven-degree slope, and contraccelerator plates, like those in the floors and ceilings of circuit vessel sockets, were installed in Winnie's apartment building. They made a chilling hum and seemed to get stronger at odd hours, and they had a startling effect on the stomach whenever you stepped into their range from the hallway, as if you had suddenly stepped off an escalator you'd been on all your life. But overall, they functioned well enough to make gravity inside the apartment straight and sound. The plates became ubiquitous in stores and offices, basically anywhere with walls close enough for the synthetic graviton field to span. Bosch and LG came out with consumer models, and people argued over which was better. Some Streamscapers Winnie followed, whose sardonic wit managed to merge all the anxiety of pessimism with optimism's idleness, said they didn't want plates in their homes, that they liked low gravity, they'd shed fifteen pounds in four months. The global weight loss plan. Winnie tried to laugh, even though grav loss felt nothing like weight loss. Rather, it felt like having those pounds still inside you, rebelling against your sense of balance. She stumbled when carrying her bags out of the grocery store and felt nauseous when she stood up from tying her shoes, and when she was in her hammock she tried her best to stay perfectly still. *Pop.*

Riots flared again before Easter, but the curfew was imposed quickly. Winnie and Luna were less scared this time. They lit candles, made emergency soup, watched movies.

At work, Chip buttered up investors, clapping their backs while the contraccelerator plates hummed, boasting that he enjoyed curfew nights. "I actually think it's healthy to get time at home," he said, putting on the airs of a thought leader.

By late April, things once again quieted down. This seemed to be the new rhythm: ever louder outbursts and ever eerier lulls. The vacant homes of the emigrated wealthy went up for sale along Dolores Park, and beaming middle-class families moved in, chasing their own personal dreams, which already felt dated. Most significantly, the tempest of construction that had been raging above the sky (which in hindsight people acknowledged as a possible source of some irritability) died down as the hardware of the Shell was finally completed, screens and all, a month shy of the scheduled global Switch-On.

On the eve of Easter, which Winnie was to observe at brunch with the Wwlliamses, she walked home from work. The pods rose and fell around her, the lungs of civilization. It had been raining earlier, and she knew her garden would smell of mulch and wet concrete. She felt small beneath the country's neatly gridded ceiling, within the peace of a day that was precisely engineered to last for as many hours as you wanted—even if this was an illusion of day, in turn only an illusion of peace. Even if beyond humanity's immense alloy shield, the Sun was now coming around every two hours and forty minutes.

When she reached her building, she found a municipal van parked outside. Her front gate hung open, and she followed the sound of men's voices to her garden. Three government men in reflective vests and hardhats stood around a squat machine. Winnie asked what they were doing.

They addressed her as if she were the intruder. The foreman, cradling a tablet, spoke through a bushy beard, "We need to trim this tree."

Under her jacaranda tree, one of the workmen positioned the machine, a sensor-laden hydraulic scissor crane, folded down into a mobile dolly.

"You can't," Winnie said.

"No can't," said the foreman. "A new power line's going here. You want electricity?"

The third man wandered off a few steps, vaping stimulants with his eyes closed.

"Please," said Winnie. "It's going to bloom again this month. It's a jacaranda."

The foreman's eyes met hers. For a moment she thought he understood. But then he tapped his tablet. "It will still be a jacaranda," he said. "We just need to cut here." He gestured across a swath of branches.

The machinist coaxed the saw-head up, its blade sliding with a hiss of metal on metal.

"Please," Winnie addressed him. "I look up at those flowers when I sit in my hammock. It's my life. It's practically all I do anymore."

"Sounds nice," the machinist replied, wiping sweat from his brow.

The third man emptied a cartridge from his vape and flicked it over the garden wall, but he misjudged the height or the gravity and it bounced back off the neighbor's satellite dish.

"Don't cut too much. Tell me where you're cutting," she said. "Or, wait. Maybe you can come back tomorrow." She looked up at her window, hoping Luna might see what was happening and know what to do. The building leaned away from her, its AC units dribbling used water down the wall. The foreman shook his head. He said he was sorry, and maybe he meant it, but when she continued entreating, he had the machinist throttle the saws to tune her out. She didn't know what to say. She feared that to perform her outrage would seem like a cheap attempt to manipulate him, so she tried to maintain a reasonable tone but heard her voice cracking. "You can't do this," she said, "with everything going on."

The foreman faced the rising machine.

"Look around," she said. "San Francisco is gone."

He turned, exasperated. "Lady," he said. "Could you please let us do our job?"

After the hurricane, the Wwlliamses had lost their old place near the coast and bought a new apartment with the insurance payout, which was disappointingly small. Winnie commuted there for Easter brunch by foot. It was at an intersection that was lively—with a HomeGoods and an arepa stand and a permanent residency of seagulls—but not very pretty. When Winnie arrived, Carsie opened the apartment door and gave her a hug.

"Watch the step," she said giddily. "New floors."

Winnie felt the lurch from the contraccelerators as she entered.

Juju, now a curvy high school junior, stood by the kitchen island looking at her phone. She didn't acknowledge Winnie.

"Hi, Juju," Winnie said. "What are you watching?"

"I don't know," said Juju.

Brunch began with the same lack of coordination that characterized every event at the Wwlliams home. Carsie played a recording of her favorite Easter benediction, while Mark served his "world famous" mushroom tart. He no longer wore his greasy brown toupee. Growing up, Winnie had hardly ever seen him without it—only when she walked in on him watching TV with Juju, and then he'd quickly go put it on. The resurrection, Carsie said, more than any other scriptural element, illuminated God's glory. "These onions are good," said Mark. "They're strong."

They talked about the Shell and about the Switch-On. The state owned the rights to the Shellspace over California, and involvement in the Switch-On was being overregulated, Mark argued, to confine access to "the people in power." He said, "They claim they're weeding out foreign influence, but it's all political crap. They hate businesses, the people in power hate us having power of our own."

Juju begged him to drop the conspiracy theories.

"I'm not a conspiracy theorist," said Mark. "It's the governor who claims some foreign boogieman is using the Shell to infiltrate society. I'm calling out conspiracy theories. I'm a conspiracy theory theorist. These whackos' theories that corporations and the westward circuit and Streamscape and the Shell are all part of some international plot against them, that's what's making life impossible for us rational people who want to accomplish something productive." He said the conspiracy theories all represented the same disintegration in public trust—there were videos about this. "I'm telling you," he said. "The theories are all connected."

Carsie ignored him. She was examining her daughter's legwear.

"What are those?" she asked.

"These?" Juju touched her jeans. One leg was long, the other short. "Semis," she said.

"Semis?"

"Like the song. 'Shoot up a Walgreens, fuck life in my semi jeans . . .'"

"Oh yeah," Mark confirmed. "I saw a video about that. It's a look."

When they finished eating, they carried their dishes to the sink, stepping over contraccelerator cords as if they'd always lived that way. Winnie pulled Carsie away from the dishwasher.

"Can we talk?" she said.

"Yes," said Carsie. "Of course."

They went to the master bedroom, where the apartment's musk was strongest. Seeing their unmade bed, Winnie imagined her aunt and uncle cozying up together during police curfews. Carsie sat on the bed, imitating openness, her Easter necklace, a glass orchid, hanging from her neck. Winnie remembered how Carsie had not been there for her after her electrocution. She wondered if Carsie thought that was nothing. She wondered if her aunt, in choosing to sit, feared some sort of denunciation, and she wondered if people ever feared consequences they didn't already believe they deserved. A siren passed outside. Winnie shut the bedroom door behind her.

She said, "I visited my mom."

Carsie said oh.

Winnie nodded.

"Are you okay?"

"Don't." Winnie put up a hand. "I don't need comforting. I didn't visit her for attention. I didn't even want to tell you."

"Okay."

"It was scary, seeing her."

Carsie, after much consideration, said, "We don't need to be scared."

"Not 'we,'" said Winnie quietly. "This isn't about you."

"Okay."

Winnie faced herself in the mirror. She wore her green nose stud. Sometimes the piercing surprised her. Looking away from herself, she said, "Do you know how to contact my father?"

"Your father? Pines?"

Winnie nodded. The request hadn't felt as large in her heart as it did coming up her throat. Carsie asked if this was "for blame."

Winnie said no.

"I haven't heard anything about him since you were born," said Carsie. "I'm sure he doesn't even know what happened to your mom."

"I don't blame him for what happened to my mom. I just want to talk to him."

Carsie sank into thought. "I don't know how to put this," she said. "I mean, I don't really know much about him. And of course, you're welcome to contact him. You should. But I should just warn you that you might not like him."

"It's not about that."

"*I* blame him for what happened to your mom."

"I'm not asking him about my mom," said Winnie. "I need to ask him about me."

Carsie looked confused. Winnie tried not to feel small, like someone needing permission, as Carsie studied her, waiting for her to explain.

Finally she said, "I'm going to ask him why I'm here."

There was a period of quiet.

"Here like . . . ?"

Winnie bit her lip.

"I would say," Carsie said, "that's something you need to answer for yourself."

"No," said Winnie. "No, I don't agree."

"I don't think, sweetheart, that it's a matter of opinion," she said and touched Winnie's arm.

She saw immediately that this overture was a mistake, and Winnie, her heart racing, her eyes boring into her aunt's, was glad, because her aunt was wrong and ought to know it. Every child asks their parents why they're here, she thought, whether they ask or not. And whether they answer or not, parents answer. She was owed an answer.

She got the phone number. But that didn't mean on her walk home she wasn't still annoyed with her aunt, and she was arguing with Carsie in her head when abruptly the Shell went dark. She looked around—thinking it must be an emergency curfew, but even then the Shell never went this dark—until she remembered: This wasn't a curfew but rather the final maintenance test of the screens before the Switch-On.

By the light of lampposts, she took long strides downhill in the attenuated gravity, while circuit vessels drifted against the unlit clouds.

Groggy soldiers slumped against blue post office boxes, hugging their rifles. They jolted up now and then at a *pop*.

When she got home, Luna was sleeping in her hammock. Luna had been having nightmares lately; Winnie often heard her moaning across the hall. She slept tightly curled, her thin arms folded across her chest. Without disturbing her, Winnie peeled off her own socks, lay her sweater on the grass, and climbed into the hammock behind her.

Her dismembered jacaranda tree creaked inward, arching over them. It wouldn't blossom again. Along its severed limbs strips of bark folded in on one another. Bats flew familiar loops. Winnie heard them chirping. She could smell her friend's hair, a smell that Luna might have been embarrassed by, like baby powder, and she held her close, afraid to shift her weight. She feared the tree might break, that they might fall, but they didn't. At an angle, the world spinning, they floated.

○

With just weeks until the Switch-On, Shell construction finally washed over springtime Alaska. It was noisy and bright at all hours, but we expected this. My mom and sister went to church with bags under their eyes and coffee in their flasks and complained about how little sleep they got. Ashtyn kept asking why the Shell was even still being built and what it was meant to accomplish. Our last glimpse of open sky, through a narrowing gap in the Shell, was of the aurora borealis flashing like crazy. By late May, the construction continued north, the clamor faded, and by the start of June, the sky everywhere was sealed.

Luna

In her nightmares, she traced a wall in the dark, groping for an exit, but the wall just kept curving, left, left, left, and the scraping grew louder behind her. She couldn't remember who was chasing her until she woke. Then she looked out the window to see if the man was still there.

You never know quite how long someone's been stalking you. When Luna first took note of the man parked outside their apartment, was it because she was seeing him for the second time, or more like the third or fourth? He always sat in different cars in sunglasses and rumpled hats pulled low. Peeking through her blinds, she considered all the debts this man might possibly have come to reap—app dates rebuffed, coworkers sold a couple fewer pills than promised on a bet they wouldn't count, the cokehead barista at the skater café whom Luna never tipped. One night she convinced herself that he was DEA staking her out, that Winnie was right about the seriousness of selling her meds, and yes, her panic wasn't helped by the weed, but just because you're paranoid doesn't mean they're not after you—who said that? What she really feared, and so naturally fixated on, was the possibility that he was the man from the gala, the CWC guy, whose name she didn't know, only that he was aggressive, and rejected by Luna, and (in his mind) robbed. She snapped the blinds shut.

She was afraid to bring the stalker to Winnie's attention. She thought Winnie would blame her, regardless of who he turned out to be. Winnie would tell her to throw away the CWC phone to be safe and stop selling her pills and keep her paranoia in check. They didn't even know the man was after Luna and not some other resident of their building. But Luna just had a feeling.

Which was confirmed on the morning of the Switch-On, when he was there while she and Winnie left for work. For the first time since Luna had noticed him, he got out of his car. It was clear he was getting out to approach them. Winnie was tying her sneaker, thanking Luna for agreeing to spend Switch-On Night at home, saying she knew the police said they had everything under control, but there would be so many people out in the streets tonight that it just seemed safer . . . Luna watched him. He didn't look like the man from the gala, but his height appeared similar at a distance and his figure was obscured by his large, shapeless anorak. She told Winnie to hurry. Winnie asked how long until Luna's pod, and he descended the hill toward them, but hesitantly, as if he didn't quite know what he'd do if he caught them. He didn't catch them. Once across the street, Luna looked over her shoulder and saw him backstepping to his car.

The anti-erosion corps only worked a half shift that day, Luna's squad accomplishing little at that. A senior corps member, she tried to keep her juniors on task, but everyone just wanted to chat about their Switch-On plans. Their dam was months behind schedule anyway. Developers, stalled in their wake, kept filing complaints with the State of New York. It was hot. Everyone itched. She leaned on her jackhammer and looked through the bright green trees as a circuit vessel split the burning sky. Gnats shoaled around a fallen maple, and the ravine air collected mud and smoke. Along a sewage pipe marked with orange paint, which ran from the houses above, some of her juniors crushed Adderall pills to stay awake. She sat with them, taking bumps at her turn and reading about how crowded the pods would be tonight, WORST TRAVEL DAY OF THE YEAR. She tried to use her phone, with its CWC embossment, without panicking that the man might still be waiting at her home.

On the trenchwalker back to camp, one of the rookies grabbed a seat beside her. "You okay?" he asked. He was a nice guy—not her type, but she didn't mind his timid advances.

"I'm fine," she said.

The trenchwalker bounced side to side down the hill in the low grav. He asked what she was planning for the Switch-On. She said she and her best friend Winnie were just going to watch from their garden.

"Makes sense," he said. "I don't really see much to celebrate. People still talk like the I.C.R.F. will fix everything, but if you ask me, it was made to move a little water and a lot of advertising." He was trying too hard. She looked out the porthole window at the approaching pod platforms, while he kept on. "If you do decide, though, you want to get out of the house tonight, text me and maybe we could meet up. We could ignore the Switch-On together."

"Sure," said Luna, as her pod came down.

Vessel WDYGO 5206 was so packed she almost didn't make it on. She squeezed past people, pulling herself up and down the cabin, high and searching for a spot. Everyone was trying to get home or away from home in time for the Switch-On, and the windowvisions said WDYGO is committed to your freedom.

She worked her way back to the docking cabin as they neared SF2, but when the threshold opened, no one made space for her inside the pod. She'd never seen a pod so crowded. She nearly got caught in the turnstile. The inner door closed, leaving her on the same side where she'd started, and she had to go all the way around the world again, which (thanks to the ground below spinning eastward) no longer took the hour and twenty that it used to, but rather took only fifty-eight minutes, the circuit more efficient than ever.

When she finally landed, SF2 was dark. She exited the pod, and to her surprise, no one new got in. She watched the pod return empty to the altitude of the glowing circuit vessels, halfway to the Shell, which was flickering, absorbing power for the life it was soon to begin. There was less than an hour until the Switch-On. No one was in the street; even the homeless had disappeared. She hurried home, unsure what was happening. An ambulance sped by, screeching as it negotiated a steep hairpin turn in 85 percent grav. She spotted a crowd drinking in Rikki Streicher Field beneath the floodlights, black and white. A bottle shattered, galvanizing them to cheers. She turned uphill to avoid them and heard a gunshot and started to jog. Winnie called.

"I'm almost home, just missed my stop . . . what's going on?" Luna glanced over her shoulder. "I mean I missed it the first time. I'm almost home now." A helicopter shook the sky, its garbled megaphone saying all cars were offline and everyone should return inside. There was a horrible smell, like trash burning. "No? I never got a curfew alert," she said. "Okay, see you in a minute." She hung up and struggled with the key to their gate. Wind rustled government flyers feathering their apartment complex wall. The gate opened.

A man grabbed her wrist. She screamed.

"Please," he said. "Let me in."

It was him. And now she recognized who he was. She knew him from TV.

"What the fuck," she said, slamming the gate shut. "What do you want?"

"Please let's go inside and we'll talk."

"I didn't do anything wrong," she said. She was too high. Way too high. A not-so-distant gunshot made Victor Bickle jump. His car was nowhere to be seen.

"I'll explain," he said. "Please just open the door."

"You're stalking me."

"I'm not. Look, open the door. I didn't come here for you." Something blew up on the next street, cloaking a helicopter in an ascendant parachute of smoke. This had to be a drug dream, Luna thought. Bickle turned, and she took off.

* * *

Her feet flew downhill in the low gravity, bounding off the asphalt. She neared a crowd engaged in chaotic physical repartee with a fleet of blaring National Guard vans. Market Street had been cleared of protesters. She turned onto it, swinging around a lamppost to control her momentum. He followed. Smoke hung silver in the air. Through the fog, her mind tried to make sense of the pursuing apparition of Victor Bickle, a hologram incarnate. So it *was* CWC coming after her? Winnie texted again—*Where are you?*

She removed her SIM, turned around, and threw the phone. "Just take it!"

It went into the grass. Bickle, winded, stopped to see what it was.

She didn't wait. Forward again, she met a gust of heat: a retail bank ablaze. The low gravity made the bustling Riot Control seem to prance as they yelled at one another, unable to juggle the simultaneous demands of putting out the fire and seizing the perpetrators. *I need to get clean*, she thought and wanted to cry. She had no clue what was happening anymore. Two officers turned and commanded her to halt, startled to find her behind their line. She ducked into a deserted construction lot.

Cool shipping containers cast long, overlapping shadows. She leaned against one to catch her breath. Bickle was gone.

The shipping container said EVERGREEN and below that, someone had scratched a message into the corrugated metal: KATIE JUMPED OFF THE ROOF KATIE JUMPED OFF THE ROOF KATIE JUMPED OFF THE . . .

"Look at you."

She turned. Between her and the fence were two shirtless men, their sweat pearling in the dark.

"Give us your money," one of them said. "And your phone and your jewelry."

Luna dug through her pockets for her wallet. She flung it a few feet away and tried to run, but he caught her and with surprising force threw her downhill into the container's wall, which clanged like construction or war.

"Let's load her," said the smaller man.

The other said, "Shut up."

The sky behind them belched green smoke. Flares showered from helicopters. Luna said she didn't have anything else. The small man, getting agitated, waved a knife.

"Give us your phone," the larger man said.

"I don't have one."

He grabbed her shoulders. She kneed him in the groin and tried to run, but the smaller man dove and caught her leg. She stomped on his hand. Suddenly she was blinded by a spotlight.

"You are under arrest for breaking curfew," said the unmanned National Guard drone. "Freeze for identification."

The men fled.

She ran the other way, losing the drone amidst the maze of shipping containers. There were gravel shingles stuck to her cheek. She gasped for air, vaulting up the teetered sidewalk.

She reached her building, went through the back gate, and collapsed in the yard, still high out of her mind, completely confused, thanking God she was alive. That was when she noticed that all the sirens and barks were fading, being drowned out by the rumble of a numinous music, a cloudy monotone thrum, like a thousand orchestras tuning to concert pitch. Her ears popped. *Am* I alive? She looked around, but everywhere was black, and then, the sky seemed to open up—the Shell was gone. Heaven was crowded with constellations that she remembered from before memory, the ancient arms of the Milky Way. And the fullest moon she ever saw in her life beamed down on her from directly overhead.

PERFECT DAYS
The Switch-On

That morning, the morning of the Switch-On, my mother poached eggs in her little kitchen in Keber Creek. She squabbled with Ashtyn over saving coffee for the night's festivities ("We can just brew more later," Ashtyn tried), and I let out the dogs. It was bright and mild outside, and little wildflowers were blooming under the house. The dogs tackled each other. As I watched them, I was thinking about how I was no longer able to keep promises to myself.

I decided I wouldn't stay up for the Switch-On. I didn't want to go with my sister and mother to watch from the church parking lot, where the men would be cursing and the young women praying and my mother saying wrong thing after wrong thing about how the Shell worked. I took walks through town now and then, but generally avoided other Keber Creekers. When I walked to town, I went to the pod station and watched the pods fall. The station had been first built by CWC, but the pods that now fell each hour bore the names of younger, more agile airlines that had bought CWC's routes at fire-sale prices. The pods never brought anyone to Keber Creek (they only served to collect gold from the mine), so I didn't see why the pod station bothered my neighbors so much, and I was surprised at summer's start when old Gerald Tumesky's son-in-law led three men with sledgehammers to smash the station's platforms. They got through two before state troopers landed on the third and arrested them for vandalism. The platforms were promptly repaired. All summer the vandals had been held in nearby Pine Cross, and Tumesky had been preaching war.

Who needs the trouble, I thought, lying on the couch watching CNN's coverage of Switch-On Night around the world as Ashtyn and my mother made one last appeal for my company. As they left the house, the dogs howled. I drew a cup of water from the tap.

"Wen and wia pipo go fit view di Shell Lagos style . . ." "Crown Prince's address to appear on the first broadcasts over the Arabian . . ." "More unrest in SF2 . . ." Everywhere CNN showed, it was night. I lay back. I hadn't exercised in months, and my body felt soft. Now that I was alone, staying home felt pointless—a boycott that no one minded. This had become a typical feeling for me, this pointlessness, without Miguel around. The night before, I had dreamt, as still happened now and then, that Miguel was having sex with me, and as I muted CNN and closed my eyes, considering the possibility of a repeat performance, I permitted myself a ripple of pathetic excitement.

I cleared my head, wishing that when I woke up again, I would be someone different.

There was a knock at the door. The dogs yelped. I peered out the window, slightly ashamed to be caught in untimely repose. A young man stood outside, holding a padded envelope.

It was a delivery boy, who was pretty cute. He greeted me with a smile. His motorbike lay in the wet grass.

"We don't order deliveries," I said.

"Sure," he replied and asked in a Brooklyn accent whether I was Mr. Kelly. Thinking of my father, I replied that I was Tanner.

He handed me the envelope. "This package contains legal documents," he said. "You have one hundred hours to answer the complaint that accompanies this summons."

I opened it while the delivery boy—the process server, as it turned out—leaned in to read.

"Wow," he said before I understood what I was seeing. "You used to work for CWC? And now you live out here?"

UNITED STATES DISTRICT COURT
SOUTHERN DISTRICT OF NEW YORK

CWC GROUP LIMITED,
Plaintiff,
vs.
VICTOR BICKLE, TANNER KELLY,
MIGUEL ORIOL,
Defendants

Civil Action No. 78:C-cv-9836.27921

Jury Trial Demanded

COMPLAINT

1. This is an action for money damages brought under the Computer Fraud and Abuse Act, 18 U.S.C. § 1030, by CWC Group Limited ("Plaintiff") against Victor Bickle, Tanner Kelly, and Miguel Oriol (collectively, "Defendants").

2. Plaintiff alleges that from A.H. 974,000 to at least A.H. 1,034,448, and possibly on a presently ongoing basis, Defendants stole physical property as well as confidential, proprietary, and trade secret information and disseminated the purloined information, including personally sensitive data, to media outlets for profit and-or to harm Plaintiff.

3. Company information leaked by defendants has been subsequently republished and read by millions of internet users, threatening the solvency of Plaintiff's core business.

4. Victor Bickle is a discredited former professor of engineering with a history of mishandling confidential information, who was employed by Plaintiff during the relevant period.

5. Tanner Kelly is a longtime associate of Victor Bickle and a janitor by training, employed by Plaintiff during the relevant period.

6. Miguel Oriol was employed by Plaintiff throughout the relevant period. He is an intimate personal affiliate of Kelly. Oriol furnished

information that Kelly and Bickle could not have accessed otherwise. Given the close relationship between Oriol and Kelly, Oriol knew or should have known about the full extent of Bickle and Kelly's actions.

Request for Relief

7. The theft of physical assets imposed replacement costs on Plaintiff. Plaintiff demands that Defendants pay compensatory damages of at least $50,000.

8. The distribution of purloined information to media outlets harmed Plaintiff's competitive standing, brand reputation, and ability to procure investment; it obstructed ongoing regulatory proceedings; it also inflicted reputational injury and emotional distress on Plaintiff's employees, which continues to harm productivity. Plaintiff demands that Defendants pay compensatory damages of at least $125 million.

I read and reread the strange document on the stoop, beneath the paper moths, the process server gone, everybody gone, the Shell lights flicking out one by one as the Switch-On neared. My breath quickened, my neck constricting. Bickle didn't answer the phone. I tried him again. Then, not knowing what else to do, I called Miguel.

"¿Qué onda?" he said. He sounded drunk.

"Miguel?"

"Wait, who is this?"

I almost cried at the sound of his voice. "It's me," I said.

There was ruffling on the other end; the background noise got quieter. He asked why I was calling him.

"Where are you?" I said.

He said he was in New York, Washington Square Park, watching the Switch-On.

"We're being sued," I said.

"I'm sorry to hear that."

"You are too."

"What do you mean?"

"I just got served a complaint. They think we leaked data from CWC."

"What the fuck?"

"You, me, and Bickle."

"You and Bickle maybe."

"We didn't do anything, I swear. They're pinning all these data leaks on us. I thought maybe you'd know something about it."

"I don't know what you're talking about, Tanner," he said, and tried to hang up but I told him to wait. "What," he said.

Neither of us said anything.

He hung up.

I called again, but he didn't answer. I breathed in the scent of pines and septic shedding. It was ninety minutes until the Switch-On, and I suddenly felt with clarity that I did not belong in Keber Creek. Returning to Alaska in the first place had been a delusion. A dream of unattainable futures or irretrievable pasts. I couldn't live through this (this world, this life) out here alone.

It was twenty minutes until Switch-On by the time I reached New York. A dangerously crowded pod dumped me downhill at Broadway-Lafayette; the street was mobbed. Spectators lobbied for access to fenced-off patios. The rooftops all full, bouncers drew money from the queues and young men climbed atop trashcans. I texted Miguel. The lights of Manhattan dizzied me after five months in Alaska. I saw shoulders, thighs, and midriffs naked to the fecal summer air. Police abounded. I remembered arriving in New York at twenty years old, how it'd felt like stepping into a dream.

"Miguel!" I called, but it seemed impossible that I would find him.

The endless throngs were punctuated by billboards, storefronts, flashing logos on stalled cars: advertisements all, amidst breathing bodies dressed for display. The whole city might as well have been a live staging of a social media feed. Racing upstream to Washington Square Park, I suddenly understood how my life had become a thing so worthy of enmity. Questions that had tortured me for years were thrown into relief by the neon all around, and whereas for so long my inability to answer these questions made me doubt their premise, suddenly, as I ran through the Switch-On crowds searching for Miguel, it was obvious. It was the color of a screen under a rural boy's bedsheets and the taste of the air in a place like New York City. All around, I saw the conflation of virtue and accomplishment being fused like a plate installed in the brain, the computationally complex question of how to live being substituted for the heuristic of social validation. How could I—as a twenty-year-old innocently wishing for significance—have stood a chance at cosmic dignity in such a place, a place where any patient meditation was beset on all sides by a thousand screens diverting attention's reverence to those who expropriated and despoiled? It had felt so good to believe that if I worked hard in the service of those around me and they were rewarding me for it, then I must be a good person, but now I knew that such logic had ruined me, and at twenty-seven I felt the terror of a recovering alcoholic in the world's unending crapulence, fighting my way uphill through the burning promise of another new New York.

New trees in the park were broken in half. New Sin-é, smothered in PAs, inflicted 808 rhythms upon the street while people tried to get inside. Circuit vessels strafed the city with languid bombs of commerce.

I thought of Miguel and everything wasted in our relationship because of our inability to understand what the world was doing to us. I thought of my father, who quite literally died for what he believed in—far from the only person I knew to do such a thing. Would we meet the same fate?

I asked myself if amidst it all, I could still love Miguel.

And my answer was yes.

If I could hold on to this understanding, then (I believed) I could love us both enough for us to be worthy of each other. He and I could forgive each other and together make our own meaning of the world we shared.

"Miguel!"

There he was, in a white tracksuit, trying to balance an empty bottle of Absolut on an overfull recycling bin. He turned to see me and started walking quickly away.

I called for him to wait.

"Leave me alone."

We squeezed through a ring of college kids chanting "I-C-R-F." I grabbed his wrist. The air was thin, and I was out of breath.

"Hazte para allá. No quiero hablar contigo—" he said.

"—Please. I've been thinking about things."

He shook free. No-wheelers leapt over the fountain, over its stream spurting too high in the low gravity, splattering water onto the plaza. A man cried out he'd won the lottery. Eight minutes until Switch-On.

"Where are you going?"

Miguel weaved toward an open pod. Everyone was piling against the turnstile. He budged his way up to the front.

"Wait—" but he disappeared inside. I had to update my Sig Air payment method. A little arrow spun. People were spinning into the turnstile at the same time others were trying to spin out. Just before the gate locked, I made it in.

Gripping the center pole, a finger's width between my hand and his, I said, "I don't usually fly Sig Air."

"Well, I got banned from CWC," he said.

"The lawsuit must be a mistake. The company's collapsing and managers are feeding one another scapegoats."

"I don't even want to hear it."

Our feet levitated. We kept getting pushed into each other, and the dissonance between my memories of intimacy and the new, cold ordinance of estrangement so confused me that, barreling skyward at four hundred meters per second, I held my place in my own life story as if by only my fingertips. "I love you," I said. "And I think we shouldn't have broken up."

He swallowed. Passengers were angling to be first out of the pod, squeezing one another. They were watching the countdown on the walls and refreshing their ETAs in Google Maps.

"I love you, too," said Miguel. "But no."

And when the pod latched, he shoved his way into the vessel.

Someone shouted, "You think you're the only one in a rush?"

I dove through after him. The vessel was thick with bodies. "Excuse me," I said, but other people were saying *move*. They had to get off this flight: The Switch-On was in five minutes and it would never be repeated and not all of them were going to make it. I pushed my way around people, trying to keep a grip on the monkey bar system of grab-handles, but they shoved me back, against knapsacks, grunting and whining and churning, compressed into a microcosm of an already too compressed world. An old lady repelled me with a gift box, and I bowled into someone's kid. I lost Miguel. Faces turned on me, some upright, some horizontal, all stamped with the circuit traveler's hollow glare, each eye a fire gasping in a sealed glass chamber. People, I thought. All of them were people. I tried to pull myself upright, but my hand groped the sari of a young woman, who swung her purse (*ELEGANCE IS AN ATTITUDE – KARL LAGERFELD*) at me and missed, braining a trollish man in earbuds, whose tablet cracked, and someone shouted, "What's your fucking problem?" and suddenly everyone was defending themselves.

"Be civil!" someone said, managing to film the scuffle for a second before losing his phone. That video, *Ride Rage on Sig Air Insane*, would go minorly viral (2.6M views). I tore through the docking cabin, swinging my boots ahead of me, until I caught Miguel between my legs.

"Let me go!"

We tumbled into the next cabin, yanking at each other's shirts. A man kicked us away from his socket, and I, trying to protect Miguel's crown from striking an overhead stowage bin, stepped on the lap of a shrieking college student.

"You made me hate myself," Miguel said, landing blunt slaps on my back. "I was never good enough for you."

"You were," I said. Passengers were starting to fight their way into the docking cabin, only to find themselves feeding the fracas. The windowvisions depicted two geometric planes—the augmented navy of Lake Erie and a digital rendering of the Shell—pressing the wrinkles from the vanishing line of the horizon.

"Estás delirando."

"I know."

"Why didn't you support me?"

A man tackled both of us, hoping to arrest the spread of violence, and we sailed through the air, snowballing into more people trying to flee or fight.

"I understand now," I said, "that we were both just figuring out how to survive—" someone kicked my mouth, loosing strings of bloody sputum. Miguel's face smooshed against the windowvision, in which London, Canada, shot toward us.

Pressed up behind him, I said, "I take responsibility."

Two fathers were punching each other in the head, both shouting at their kids to stay away. One minute until Switch-On.

"Let me go," said Miguel. "I want to get off."

I coughed blood against his nape. I said I would keep chasing him around the world if that's what it would take.

"It's easy to chase someone around the world," he said. "Shit. What matters is staying put once you find them."

"I haven't been able to sleep."

"You couldn't sleep even when we were together, minou."

"I spent thousands of hours of my life hugging you while you slept like a baby."

"I know," said Miguel, wriggling free. Missing a shoe, his tracksuit torn, he called down the twisted aisle, "I was awake," just before being swallowed by the spate of passengers who would make it down with thirty seconds to spare.

○

She'd said she was right outside. Winnie paced. There were sirens nearby. She texted again.

Luna, answer. Please.

"Times Square, we have one more song till Switch-On. Playing the hit single off their new album *Speeding in the Cone Zone*, put your hands together for Cone Zone . . ." Winnie lowered the volume and turned down the burner on her stove. She'd planned to brew ginger tea (she and Luna liked tea even in the heat of summer, as they'd once read that hot drinks make you feel cooler, and they thought that was funny and decided to believe it). Water boiled so easily these days—the centrifugal effect on atmospheric pressure. Her ginger browned on the counter.

The text to Luna wasn't delivered.

She looked down at the street. There was a man in a big jacket jabbing at the intercom keypad, as if he expected a building like this to have working buzzers. A two-bit explosion resounded outside, setting off car alarms. Luna was nowhere to be seen. Winnie pulled the window closed.

Holograms of Times Square's holograms hurdled from her tablet behind the couch. She turned the tablet over, trapping them against the rug. The street outside began to thrum. She opened the rear window and looked up. For a moment, she thought the thrumming sound outside was some kind of orchestral music.

"Here in New York, the first deployment of the radial compression . . ."

The thrumming grew louder. Shell support pillars around the world were telescoping inward, hugging the atmosphere to the ground. Winnie's ears popped.

And then the Shell lights above her switched from dim to totally black, and all the streetlamps in SF2 cut out. She looked out the rear window, into the yard. Luna was there.

"Luna!"

She didn't respond. She was lying on her back.

Winnie rushed down to her, tripping on the contraccelerators' invisible step, and knelt beside her in the grass. She pushed Luna's hair out of her face.

"Oh my god, what happened to you?" she said.

Luna was panting, looking up at the sky. "Is the Shell gone?" she murmured.

Winnie looked up. It took her eyes a second to adjust to the new sky before she realized it was full of stars. As if the Shell had opened.

How long had it been since she'd seen stars? Their constellations twinkled in HD like rhinestones on a velvet dress. Circuit vessels showered through. The ambulances continued to wail. And rising over the west coast in a paper-perfect circle, the moon cut a blinding hole through the vault of night. It rose and rose, humongous and deaf—you could almost feel the Earth twisting beneath its weight—until it stopped. In San Jose, it must have halted in the northern sky; Santa Marians might have spotted it on the horizon, if they weren't distracted by another identical moon in the direction of LA. But in SF2, it positioned itself directly overhead.

"Am I in heaven?" asked Luna.

"No," said Winnie.

The moon spun around. Or more precisely, it flipped. For it was not spherical but flat as a coin, and on its other side, now visible, was a woman's face. The thrumming stopped. Winnie could hear her heart.

The woman in the sky blinked. She looked down upon Earth with eager eyes, as if she herself were perplexed and excited by what she saw. She began to smile. Her lips parted. And her celestial voice said: "Juicy Fruit!"

PART III

The Justice System

UNITED STATES DISTRICT COURT
SOUTHERN DISTRICT OF NEW YORK

CWC GROUP LIMITED,

    Plaintiff,

    vs.

VICTOR BICKLE, TANNER KELLY,
MIGUEL ORIOL,

    Defendants

Civil Action No. 78:C-cv-9836.27921

Videotaped Deposition of Victor Bickle

Taken: A.H. 1,041,269:00

Location: Bláber & Bláber LLP

              Suite 314, Skólagarður 15, 640

              Húsavík, Iceland

VIDEOGRAPHER: Good morning, or as we say here in Iceland, Góðan daginn. My name is Helga Helgisdóttir from the firm Big Ears Legal Transcription, located right here in Húsavík, and I am the videographer. I am not financially interested in the outcome of this action nor am I related to any party in this action with the exception of Magnús Bláber, counsel for the witness, who is my second cousin.

This fine fall day marks the first of two during which the deposition of this witness will be taken, and for the record's sake, by

"days" I refer of course to our wonderful Shell-Standardized days
and not two-and-a-half-hour solar days. At this time, will counsel
and all present please state their appearances and affiliations for the
record?

MR. BLÁBER: Thanks, Helga. And thanks all for doing this in our
offices here in Iceland. I am Magnús Bláber, Esq., of Bláber &
Bláber, counsel for the witness.

MS. RIVERHOUSE: Jane Riverhouse of Norton, Sweiss, Stills,
Kaufmann & Lasko, for plaintiff.

MR. UMBER: Antonio Umber of Norton, Sweiss, Stills, Kaufmann &
Lasko, for plaintiff.

MR. STITCH: Steve Stitch of Norton, Sweiss, Stills, Kaufmann &
Lasko, for plaintiff.

THE WITNESS: Victor Bickle.

VICTOR BICKLE, having been first duly sworn, testified as follows:
EXAMINATION

BY MS. RIVERHOUSE:

Q. Mr. Bickle, we're here to discuss your alleged involvement in the
sabotage of CWC through theft and leakage of valuable CWC data.
I'm going to start with some questions about your background, and
in the second session my colleagues will focus on your relationship
with CWC.
So to begin, could you give us a brief summary of your education?

A. What do you want to know?

Q. Please, Mr. Bickle. Where you trained, where you went to school—

A. I got my bachelor's at the University of Washington. I was there on
a scholarship sponsored by the mining company that my dad and

basically everyone in my hometown worked for, Anglo-Ontario Mining. I'd apprenticed in their mine as a teenager, and the scholarship allowed me to leave Alaska, so.

Q. Did your scholarship obligate you to return to work for Anglo-Ontario Mining?

A. Yes, it did.

Q. And did you indeed return?

MR. BLÁBER: Relevance.

MS. RIVERHOUSE: It's relevant because we're establishing his record of representations to employers—

A. For personal reasons, I didn't return to Keber Creek, no, but—

Q. Being?

A. I was—there was a woman I was with.

Q. Okay go on.

A. But I honored my employment contract by working at the firm's office in Seattle.

A. Got it. And after that?

A. I received my Ph.D. in mechanical engineering at NYU and then taught at Columbia.

Q. Where you remained until your dismissal?

MR. BLÁBER: Object to form.

A. [Inaudible]

Q. We need you to answer verbally; the recorder can't hear you shaking your head.

A. It's a false premise.

Q. I'm placing before you Exhibit 85. Could you give us a bit of color on this document?

A. At Columbia, faculty were protected from termination without cause by our union contract, so disciplinary action had to be initiated by notice from the Office of the Associate Provost, and that's what this is.

Q. This is a notice of disciplinary actions for what?

A. It's complicated.

Q. Could you please read the fifth line into the record?

A. "Use of professional authority to exploit others, in addition to the theft and misuse of university data. This process—"

Q. You can stop there. When you were hired by CWC, did you disclose that Columbia University was investigating you for an incident of data theft?

A. Cromwell Grant was aware.

Q. And was this raised as a concern?

A. No, he said he believed me that the accusations were baseless. He sympathized. And I just want to say, there's absolutely no resemblance between what happened to me at Columbia and what's alleged in this lawsuit.

MR. BLÁBER: Just answer the questions.

Q. Would you say that you have a history of stealing data from employers?

MR. BLÁBER: Object to form. Don't answer.

A. I resent that.

Q. Would you say that Exhibit 85 indicates such a history?

A. Is that what this is about? My experience at Columbia is the reason you chose me as a scapegoat for CWC's data leaks?

Q. Page 2 of Exhibit 85 refers to "the events of A.H. 962,784," yes?

A. If that's what they called it.

Q. I'm just asking if you see the line.

A. Yes.

Q. To your knowledge and recollection, what were the events of A.H. 962,784?

A. I asked two students doing clinical hours at Columbia Teaching Hospital to give me records.

Q. What kind of records?

A. Electronic health records.

Q. And these were confidential.

A. Barely.

Q. Then why did you need to coerce someone to retrieve these records for you?

A. I didn't coerce.

Q. Do you agree that the exhibit uses the word "coerced"?

A. The exhibit does.

Q. Why do you think it does?

A. The students said I offered to improve their grades.

Q. And you maintain that they were lying?

A. It's my right to improve their grades.

Q. And this is why you were formally disciplined at Columbia?

A. No.

Q. No?

A. No. The reason I was disciplined at Columbia has nothing to do with this. The real reason I was disciplined is that I was speaking out in the media about development projects around the city and getting a lot of attention, and colleagues who didn't like my politicization of the department went after me. They went after me, which is typical in academia, not unlike what's happening here I might add, and they did it this way, seizing on this thing with the so-called confidential records, to get around my having tenure.

Q. What were these confidential records?

A. I'm telling you it's not relevant. It's personal—

MR. BLÁBER: You don't need to answer.

MS. RIVERHOUSE: I'd like him to answer and then we can decide on relevance. He says he wasn't stealing his employer's data. If he doesn't want to explain what he was accused of stealing—

A. They were records about a patient I knew intimately. A friend from childhood. I heard she was unwell. If you have to know, she had attempted suicide, her first attempt, and I wanted to know where she was staying so I could get in touch with her. Okay?

Q. Is this by chance the woman you mentioned earlier?

MR. BLÁBER: Object to form.

Q. Fine. Let me ask again, if this woman was indeed a friend, then why did you need to coerce someone to find out where she was staying?

A. She and I weren't in touch—I mean. She had left me and stopped answering—You know, this is completely personal, actually—

MR. BLÁBER: Calm down, you still don't need to respond.

A. I was the victim in all this Columbia nonsense. And what I thought was understanding from Cromwell Grant I see now was his way of finding someone whose vulnerability could be held as a weapon—

MS. RIVERHOUSE: Will you please instruct the witness to sit back down.

MR. BLÁBER: We need to recess a couple of minutes.

THE VIDEOGRAPHER: Going off the record.

Big Ears Legal Transcription, Húsavík

The Elephant Never Forgets!

DAYS OF 2 HOURS
AND 30 MINUTES

Winnie arrived at 280 Wabansia Ave., Wicker Park, Chicago—a brick duplex across the street from a school playground. From the duplex's left-side door, 280A, a woman emerged with a Shiba. Winnie moved to the stoop's edge to let them pass as she approached 280B, where the mirrored mail slot was engraved with her own name. PINES. She rang the bell to meet her father. She was ten minutes early, or twenty-three years late.

It was afternoon in Chicago, as it had been in SF2, as it was everywhere now in the synchronized world under the Shell. The Shell whose screens switched between bright day-mode and dim night-mode on comfortable circadian intervals; the Shell whose plumbing, now perfectly fine-tuned, pumped water from where it pooled and rained it down where it was needed and whose vents blew storm systems right apart; the Shell that finally solved all the problems of five years ago and that was now, since the Switch-On, starting to make its money back.

A sitcom thundered in the sky. *"You're telling me!"* Cue laugh track. The Shiba tugged its leash, and its owner craned her neck to watch the sitcom, which was one of many programs playing in the media collage that stretched from horizon to horizon. Nasdaq tickers ran around the sitcom's borders, and in diamond screens recurring in a stripe from north to south, young women danced to some new song,

"Back, back that up," flaunting red backpacks. A single cloud coasted by, and above it, the Shell reported no chance of rain, light breeze (3.2 mph), solar day of 2 hours 36 minutes, solar energy excellent, temp: high of 72 Fahrenheit, grav: low of 82% g with a prevailing bank of 8 degrees. Across the street, schoolchildren playing soccer argued about switching sides after the uphill team scored again. CPD officers watched them. The door opened.

"You must be Winnie."

Winnie's father's wife cradled a baby in one arm and extended her other, winging her cashmere shawl, to draw Winnie into a hug. Winnie hesitated for fear of crushing the baby, but the hug wasn't so tight. Inside the threshold, the doormat said White Sox Family. In the foyer mirror, Winnie observed her own impatient wince, her hugging face, which doesn't expect to be seen. The baby cried anyway, for no reason.

"Leland will be out in a sec, dear. He's looking forward to meeting you. Would you like to come in?"

Winnie's hair, reflected, looked crazy, and she felt the sudden impulse to just give up and go home. At home Luna was waiting for her. It'd been three months since the Switch-On, and things had quieted down again in SF2. People were able to sleep. The government was figuring out what to do about gravity. Luna, after being mugged on Switch-On Night, refused to pity herself. She took on an extra shift at the Forest Service, saying they needed more hands and that the physical labor calmed her mind while she worked on getting sober. No such source of calm had found Winnie, though. She still lay in her hammock thinking about her mom, about the gala, about Nat. She felt more alone than ever. Her tree had died.

"I'll wait out here," she said, and Mrs. Pines didn't protest. The Shell screens said Lemon M&Ms were back. Then her husband appeared, zipping his coat.

The resemblance gave Winnie whiplash. He had her round jaw, almost invisible eyebrows, and half-lime eyes. Their hair was the same blond, though his was neatly combed forward and cut. They shook hands. His grip was large and warm. He wore jeans and a Nike Golf polo. His smile was just as sad as hers.

She couldn't get over their resemblance even as they walked away from the house and he explained that he wasn't her father. They descended Damen Street in small steps. A CTA bus climbed past, bouncing easily in the diminished grav ("WARNING: CANNOT MAKE SUDDEN STOPS"), and he directed her to jaywalk with him, leading them up to an inclined jogging path that the city had built along another decommissioned El track. Houses alongside the path were for sale, abandoned by families who'd moved farther north, while underfoot, the homeless slept in tents.

"Your mother and I weren't right for each other," said Leland Pines as scooters rushed by. Couples were out enjoying the weather. "She had particular needs, and God knows I wasn't mature enough to marry."

He was twenty-eight when he met Claira Lynx. She was tough, short-tempered, twenty-four. In a Greek diner in San Bruno, she served him a Mythos and a history of the Audi R8, seeing his parked outside. "She knew my car down to the screws in the carburetor," he told Winnie. "I didn't understand half of what she was talking about. It was one of those beautiful miscommunications that you wish would last forever." Claira rolled up her sleeve to let him feel the smooth space where months of serving saganaki had singed away her little blond arm hairs.

"I don't know why she wanted to marry me." He chuckled. "I think she was impressed by my apartment."

It became clear even before their courthouse wedding that Claira was in a bad way. "She refused to meet my parents. I had to dress her and drag her to the car. She used to scratch me. Things would get really physical between us." Reflecting on this, he gave his arm a nursing rub. His pale eyebrows dipped. "It only lasted a year before we split." Cue laugh track.

Their trail crossed beneath the doubly elevated Blue Line as forty tons of ungreased machinery made its clanging northerly ascent. Together, they watched the Shell awhile. A caveman (whom Leland

Pines knew from breakfast cereals and chewable vitamins before Winnie's time) delivered his renascent slogan, "Lemon-emon-ems!" On the other side of the world, Cromwell Grant (whom neither Leland nor Winnie would ever meet, though he had in his way changed their lives) heard the same ad broadcast over his driveway while his wife and two boys got into a cab without him.

Leland said, "She must have conceived you pretty soon after leaving me, because I heard you were born about nine months later. I heard she had been staying with an old childhood flame but then left him too. She was back in her hometown in Alaska then, and we were only in touch to execute the divorce. Your mom wasn't pregnant when she left me. I know that for sure."

Winnie asked why she left.

"Well, the relationship was never going to make it, that much was clear. But the night she left, I remember we'd had a big fight." His gaze caught on passing cars. He didn't seem like someone women would find attractive. "What I remember was she'd been ignoring me, keeping herself from me, well aware I couldn't handle that sort of withholding. I was young and needed her attention, and she knew that better than I did. So she was asking for it. But that night, I got carried away with her. I feel terrible, but you can understand, our whole relationship worked like that. I believed that was what she liked. These were different times, too. It was all very messed up. She forced me to act like Mr. Tough Guy when I was just a kid."

Winnie eyed his hands, gripping the railing.

"I was sorry when you informed me that she's not well," he said.

Winnie asked when they last spoke.

"Well, you said you're twenty-three, right?" he replied.

They returned to street level. Winnie began to feel dizzy, as if the slant were changing under her feet. The screen on a scooter station strobed.

"You wrote me that someone's been sending your mom messages," said Leland, leading Winnie toward a vending machine at the Six

Corners, where three officers were questioning a homeless man, telling him he could leave his blankets. Leland asked, "Have you still not
gotten access to those? I'm sorry to tell you they're not from me. Do
you want anything? I'm getting a Sprite. They did seem to be from
someone who loves your mom, or used to. Perhaps they are from your
father. Your real father."

"Do you know anything about him?" Winnie asked softly.

The vending machine accepted only the new-gen payment apps
that everyone was supposed to get but no one seemed able to work.
Leland tried to ping his, but it didn't take.

"Let me pay," said Winnie, reaching into her sweatpants pocket.
She didn't know why she was offering.

"I got it," said Leland.

"Really," she said. "I'm the one taking your time."

"Don't be silly."

"Please."

"Winnie," he said with force. "Stop it."

He paid and punched G-4 two times. Two plump Sprite bottles
dropped from the machine's eyes into its mouth. He wrenched them
out like teeth.

"Here," he said. "No, I don't know anything about your father."

They headed back to his house in silence, as the Shell screens to
the West began to tint amber, rolling the city gently into Friday night.
It was a very nice tint, a public courtesy, and people snapped photos.
Winnie noticed a girl studying the people studying the sky. The girl
was fourteen or fifteen with her hands pulled into her sleeves. A public bus bounced down the street between them, and Winnie couldn't
remember where she was. She nearly stepped in front of the bus when
Leland, like some faceless bumper, pulled her back. A circuit vessel
popped.

The Shell said, "Your generation values *new* experiences." Winnie
looked up. The little diamond screens blazed red for CWC. No—
CWC was blue. This was some new brand, reminiscent of CWC, but

maybe it'd be different. Leland Pines beside her smelled of aftershave. He had his own daughter, whom he tucked into a safe, simple crib at night.

"I do think," he said when they reached his stoop, "it would be best, Winnie, if you and I didn't keep in touch. I'm glad we met, but I have my own family. And for my wife's sake. You understand?"

He tarried for some reaction. She gave none. She needed to say no; no, she wouldn't let him get away, but her body was losing faith. She couldn't fight anymore. Her arms and legs consorted with the pavement, the Shell, the cops and kids, and the presence of her father who was not her father or he was. She trembled. She didn't understand anything. The whole world sat off-kilter, folding in on itself, and the sky cried for her attention, and her father nodded.

THE VIDEOGRAPHER: Góðan daginn. We are on the record at A.H. 1,041,293:03 to begin session two of the deposition of Victor Bickle.

EXAMINATION:

BY MR. UMBER:

Q. Hello, Mr. Bickle. In this session, I'd like to discuss your relationship with CWC, and let's try today to maintain decorum.

During your employment, were you from time to time trusted with information that CWC considered proprietary or confidential?

A. Yes.

Q. I'm placing before you Exhibits 297–301. Do you recognize these?

A. These are emails I sent to Cromwell Grant while he and I were negotiating my raise.

Q. Why did you feel entitled to a raise?

A. I'd been at the same pay level for three years.

Q. Did any agreement, written or otherwise, promise automatic increases in your compensation?

A. I feel like that's the natural expectation.

Q. What is?

A. That, you know, things will keep growing.

Q. In these emails you say you are keeping "a list of all the backlash CWC has courted," and you go on to make what amount to criminal allegations against your employer. Are you aware that documents which have been used to propagate all of these allegations were later obtained by media outlets, including illegal offshore websites?

A. Well, were they true?

Q. That's really not the matter at hand, now is it?

MR. BLÁBER: Object to form.

Q. Would you say that there was an implied threat in these emails? That you were demonstrating inside alleged knowledge of the company— price fixing, illegal dumping, and all the rest that's written here—as blackmail, so to speak, the implication being that if your raise were not approved, you might leak this information?

A. Are you joking?

MS. RIVERHOUSE: Mr. Bickle, please.

A. Cromwell Grant was the one who made threats. He threatened me.

BY MR. UMBER:

Q. In what way did Cromwell Grant threaten you?

A. He said he would tell the press I had abandoned a daughter with my ex-partner.

Q. And had you?

MR BLÁBER: Relevance, relevance.

A. No! I mean, I didn't know until just a few months ago. When she left me years ago, she told me she had miscarried, and then I wasn't in touch with her, like I said. I didn't know about any child. The fact that Cromwell Grant knew all along—

MR. BLÁBER: Relevance. Please.

MS. RIVERHOUSE: The witness is the one bringing this up.

BY MR. UMBER:

Q. Might you say your career as a public figure, insofar as it has been a quest for recognition and approval—

MR. BLÁBER: Object to form. Foundation. Badgering the witness. Relevance.

Q. —could be seen as an attempt to prove something after this personal rejection that seems to be so significant to you?

A. You're going to speak about the purpose of *my* career while you go to work every day initiating frivolous lawsuits—

MR. BLÁBER: Relevance!

BY MR. STITCH:

Q. Mr. Bickle, I'm Steven Stitch. Do you have in your possession a cellular device that is the stolen property of the CWC Group Limited?

A. What?

Q. Please mark this Bickle Exhibit 103. This is a record obtained this month from CWC's internet provider, and it documents the GPS location of one of the communication department's phones, which Cromwell Grant failed to turn over to the company upon his resignation. In our own inquiry, which is in the production, Grant reported the phone missing as of A.H. 1,034,808, when he was at a gala in Beijing. You, Mr. Kelly, and Mr. Oriol have all testified to having been in attendance at that gala.

Over the next several months, this device was pinged in California and your home state of New York, and then—following the night of the Switch-On—every ping on this device has come from this residential address—reflected on the map correspondent to column 1—in New York City.

Mr. Bickle, does this match your residence in New York?

A. You already know my address.

Q. Then I ask you again, do you have at your residence a phone that belongs to the CWC Group Limited?

A. This is bullshit. Someone gave me that phone during the Switch-On. Not Tanner or Miguel.

Q. I remind you, sir, that you have sworn to give truthful evidence, and that duty is impressed upon your conscience.

A. What's next, you're going to tie me to a missing office stapler? I've had enough of this.

Q. Excuse me? Are you threatening to contemn the court?

THE WITNESS: Turn off that camera.

MR. BLÁBER: Decorum and relevance, everyone!

THE WITNESS: "Relevance!" Relevance to what? This whole matter—

MR. STITCH: The witness's obstructionism will not stand, nor will it count against our time. I reserve the right to redepose.

MS. RIVERHOUSE: He's not allowed to leave.

MR. STITCH: We have a justice system in this world, sir, and it exists to mete out justice, keep the camera rolling!

THE WITNESS: This is so unhinged from everything—

MR. BLÁBER: Everyone, please—

MR. STITCH: Justice! An impression stamped upon human civilization by nature itself; a trace of its essence, an indication of its will, an announcement of its purpose, and a promise of its favor. And while it is clear to all who have lived in this sick world that justice between men remains a dream and distant comfort, it is our duty as world citizens to do whatever it takes to move our earthly dominion closer to Justice's blind bosom. That is the work we do here today, and we'll do it tomorrow, and we'll do it all year if we must. This isn't a matter of mere schoolyard arbitration; a sweeping injustice has been alleged in your own lifetime, Mr. Bickle, and the justice system will root it out. However long it might take, justice will be done upon you in re Circumglobal Westward Circuit Group's purloined data.

○

Walking off of Leland Pines's lawn, Winnie felt like she might choke. She blinked. The sky over Chicago darkened with storm clouds. Sudden hail. When it rains, IT POURS: MORTON SALT. Then Mindie Dillenberger was livestreaming from her fake bedroom. Winnie leaned against a parked truck, believing if she took one more step, she'd lose her mind. She clutched the bust of her sweater. She thought that she *should* lose her mind.

She didn't though. She couldn't. It seemed to her that going crazy was the only thing a rational person could do, and yet in the park children laughed and kicked the ball too high and she stood in the street another minute, then another—dressed, her rent paid, having just managed an entirely polite goodbye with the man who was probably her father and who only needed to ask to make her disappear—and still she felt lucid. Anger rose in her, making no contact with the walls. Why, she wanted to know, didn't something break for good? Either in the environment around her or else in her heart? How did everything just continue on and on?

Circuit vessels shone in every color now. *Oh, Mom*, she thought, sliding against the truck. She kept thinking about how her aunt had admonished her against contacting Leland Pines, had said that Winnie's question was one she had to answer for herself. She had known the answer herself already but wanted so badly to deny it. To deny that she was in this world deeply and truly without a reason—and could remain so for a lifetime, getting along just like anybody else.

She was in a circuit vessel then, spiraling north. She didn't remember where she'd boarded . . . it didn't matter. The windowvisions showed a homeless shelter in Miami that had collapsed, the death toll stood at seventy, but Winnie saw nothing. She couldn't say where her eyes rested—maybe she stared unnervingly at other passengers, maybe she focused on the smudged lenses of her glasses. It was as if her eyes themselves were pixelated screens too close to see. She willed the vessel to fly faster.

WELCOME TO THE FEDERAL SERVICE AND RELIEF CENTER AT KEBER CREEK read the sign when she landed. No one was around. It wasn't how she remembered it from her visit with her mom. The air smelled more of gasoline than gravel. The Shell was quiet. She stepped out of the pod station and looked up at a huge, blue Arctic sky full of birds and misty little watermarks that said YOUR AD HERE. She stumbled onto Main Street, lined with orange cones. The trees were real—a cool

September zephyr blew crushed leaves across the road. Atop the station, a barn owl tried to sleep. Not a single shop was open.

She walked toward a tower in the distance, the belfry of the church. She hadn't felt so heavy in months (gravity in Keber Creek was still over 90 percent). It wasn't altogether pleasant. The church parking lot hosted a large white bus with SERVING YOU across the windows. She was so tired.

Unbeknownst to her, one week earlier the U.S. Federal Emergency Management Agency had designated Keber Creek an official disaster relief zone, transporting emergency supplies into our little town from Fairbanks, where their multimillion-dollar resettlement facility was already at capacity. Americans eligible for resettlement fell into two rough categories: those whose homes were compromised by grav loss, leaving them at the mercy of insurance claim backlogs; and those whose workplaces closed, leaving them unable to make rent. In interviews, members of each group seemed to consider their own circumstance more transient than the other's. Camps were constructed for them in Cold Foot, North Slope, even Abenaki Run, before reaching us, and I read in an article later that our town had been one of FEMA's easier developments, being almost empty already. The article described a "small, radical community" more or less squatting in houses on which they owed years of back taxes, several of whose leaders "pushed back" against the first FEMA surveyors. These violent elements were quickly arrested or shot and the others stayed in their homes, allowing the Federal operation to proceed. In the town center a mile from my house, the operation was underway when Winnie arrived.

The church was unlocked, and she walked in. There was one man inside, mumbling and swaying. She was afraid to draw his attention. She didn't think she could muster the charisma—the hackery—requisite for verbal intercourse, not until she slept.

It was old Gerald Tumesky, the last of his kind, and he stood. He was accustomed to the church's darkness and didn't notice her as he

made his way to the water fountain, where hung the warped photo
of Christ. His movements were weary as he tugged the photo. Christ
didn't yield, and when he finally got purchase, it tore. He cursed. On its
descent, a shred of glossy paper caught light from the open back door.

"What are you doing here?" he asked, suddenly noticing Winnie.
"You came with the rest of them, didn't you?"

"I was born here," Winnie replied.

"It's over," he said. "We lost. This place belongs to Satan and the
government now." He turned and stumbled out into the woods. She
watched him grow distant in the rectangle of light from the threshold, white from all the shiny leaves. Lacking energy to make sense,
she sat down on the floor. *It's over*, she repeated, running her fingers
between the planks. *And if it's over, then what next?* She watched Gerald
Tumesky shrink into everything out there, everything left; and that
was (she knew now, beyond equivocation, beyond rational thought)
absolutely nothing. That was the sky may as well be a ceiling. That
was the sun may as well be 60 watts. That was her retinas may as well
be screens because even communication between real people was just
secondhand theater in this world. She came from nowhere and had
nothing to hold on to here. Not *why*, she thought. *Why not*. Why not
let go of your mom and your body and Ocean Beach in the sum-
mertime and the feeling of a community marching for a future that
will always remain in the future, let go of your friends, let go of the
teenage anxieties that kept you awake, and take life in thirty-second
slots. Hit refresh and watch it all turn over. Your eyes beat faster. Your
world is perennially new.

The Patientlink Emails

When the packet Winnie had requested months earlier from Patientlink finally arrived in the mail, she had been missing from her apartment for forty hours. Luna had tried calling Winnie's aunt Carsie, notifying the police, even messaging Winnie on Streamscape (which Winnie never checked anymore). The police suggested Luna phone prisons and jails nearby, but when Winnie last said goodbye to Luna, she was on her way to Chicago—she could be anywhere. Luna was worried about her. She hadn't looked sane on her way to meet her dad. Luna had feared that if the meeting didn't go well, Winnie might truly crack.

"Whatever happens," Luna had told her as they walked to their respective pods. "You have me."

Castro Street's rolling peaks were stacked atop one another to the North, each one higher than the last. Helicopters throbbed in and out, watching for riots, and the Shell listed 311 extensions for housing support.

"I know," said Winnie.

"And I have you," Luna said.

Winnie had nodded, looking up at the shuttered sky.

Luna walked along Ocean Beach, trying to think like Winnie, wondering where she could have gone. The shoreline's slope was steep enough that sand slid downhill as she walked, a sort of dune face that just kept going. The beach was littered with sea wrack, wrappers, and rotting fish pulled ashore by the current, which ran only gently south, hurdled as it was near the shore by a maze of breakwaters and bulkheads. The surface shimmered red, violet, and green. Magpies exhausted themselves flapping upward, mothing toward the screens. She looked at the horizon, thinking of something Winnie had told her: that when Winnie was little, she hadn't believed the world was round. Luna imagined her friend as a kid, perturbed by the horizon's apparent flatness. What would a kid like that think now, when they looked out at an aslant horizon that undulated in slow peaks and troughs over underwater drains? Or at turbines and jets affixed to an orchard of 60,000-foot pillars holding up the Shell?

Where—she asked herself—would the twenty-three-year-old version of that girl now go?

Luna returned home, out of ideas, hoping against hope that Winnie might miraculously be waiting for her there. She wasn't. But leaning against their door, the Patientlink envelope was.

She brought it into the dark apartment and tore it open. There were more than one hundred printed emails, well-wishes sent to Winnie's mom. Luna sat cross-legged, holding them in her lap, and read the sheet on top: the most recent message from Victor Bickle to the ghost of Claira Lynx.

SENT: 1,038,771:56
To: Alamo.Pat46@ComanicateByPatientlink.com
FROM: [BLOCK] Victor.Bickle@qmail.com
SUBJECT: Switch-On Night

Dear Claira, my love,

Today I was finally going to do it. I was going to do it yesterday as a matter of fact, so as not to subject myself to the carnival unpredictability of today's Switch-On, but she didn't leave home yesterday (or I didn't see her). And so I stood this morning outside her apartment, the streets wiry with excitement and forecasts of unrest, rehearsing in my head *I sent you a message in Streamscape, you didn't see it. I've been trying to reach you for . . .* But when I approached, she and her roommate hurried to distance themselves from me.

As if they knew who I was and were avoiding me. I was so surprised by this reaction that I let them go while I remained, planning to try her again when she returned. I watched the Shell and the clock until nightfall, and then before I could catch her again, everything went mad. I've told you about the neighborhood she lives in, but you wouldn't believe it. A lot of neighborhoods in this country have gone that way now, I suppose. In any case, I confronted her roommate, and she—the roommate—reacted with terror. I couldn't understand. Does Winnie know who I am? I thought I was the one stalking *her*, but her roommate, in flight, dropped a phone, and it's *my* phone (or one like it, a CWC comms phone like I used to have). How did they get my phone? What's their design? I was confused and, I must admit, fearful. I rang and rang her bell, but if she was home, she preferred to leave me to the streets than permit me even so close as her lobby. The possibility now occurs to me that she knows who I am—perhaps has known all along—and reserves a special place of spite for me inside her heart. Why shouldn't she? Why should I have thought she'd spend her life waiting for me to figure out I had a daughter and come make amends? You and I abandoned her. You did it knowingly, whereas I merely let myself believe you when you told me she didn't exist, but now the damage is done. Why should she ever forgive us?

Still, the sight of her . . . Well, it made me wish I had you. I spend so much time these days thinking about you that I forget how cruel we were to each other . . .

I'd pray for her forgiveness if I had anyone to pray to in this world. I would pray even that she haunt me, planning some kind of revenge. But I know that what I really deserve is to be alone.

> Let it be my punishment then to believe that she followed my public downfall, read my pathetic messages to her on Streamscape and saw my wretchedness collected at her doorstep, that she and her roommate went so far as to get their hands on the flotsam of my life just to know my character, and she locks her doors at the sight of me.
>
> Victor

Rain began to patter against Luna's window. The late-September clouds burped with orange thunder. She skimmed through the next pages. Every email was from him.

He described months of trying to get in touch with Winnie to no avail. He talked about finding her address and watching her from across the street. ("... She wore a jean jacket and a small stud in her nose. Did she buy it for herself ...") He reported spotting Winnie at the gala before the attack. (" ... all alone, tying her hair up the way you used to in the summer, the lights were strange so I mistook her for you. And drawing closer, compelled to know if you were okay, I realized she was smiling to herself, and I almost choked on a sudden and surprising heave of joy.")

He wrote about how confused he was over Claira's deceit, and then, days earlier (as Luna scrolled back further), how he was angry and would not be writing her anymore.

Did Winnie know about any of this? Luna hadn't told her about the run-in with Bickle on Switch-On Night. She'd been too embarrassed at having gotten herself in trouble by keeping that CWC phone, especially since Winnie had criticized her for taking it in the first place. So she'd told Winnie she lost the phone in the mugging. It had never occurred to her that Bickle had been pursuing not her but Winnie. It turned out Bickle was the person Winnie had been looking for too, and Luna had found him—but now she couldn't find Winnie.

She got to the one message in the PatientLink folder that wasn't from Bickle: the message that Winnie had left her mom when she visited the facility in Nevada. Luna read it several times before continuing on.

Once she had gone back ten months, Bickle's messages stopped being about Winnie (or even Claira). They were just therapeutic ramblings about Shell construction, and the market crash, and people with names like "John Sugar Jr." underappreciating him.

> . . . because he thinks I'm just
> Some TV clown. I have a degree, I have followers, I have connections . . . and every time—every single time—anyone has ever told me I'm nothing special, I've gone on to . . .

There were, Luna realized, years of entries. Victor Bickle sharing his entire life with someone who would never respond. The pages accumulated across her floor.

> . . . My roomba has taken to circling the rim of my bathtub at staggering speeds for no apparent object but its owner's amusement. And I am, in spite of myself, amused. Thank goodness for that, since it hasn't cleaned anything properly in ten years. I would feed it a treat if it weren't so sure to crush it and roll right over. I miss you . . .

She read for another three hours. Victor Bickle vented about "soft profiles" and hate mail; he gave sanguine updates on the Equity Push; he spitballed ideas for episodes of *Science Hour*. He wrote often about his assistant.

By the time she reached the final email, the first email, her heart was heavy, and she didn't know if it was with remorse or dread.

Sent: 977,376:32
To: Alamo.Pat46@ComanicateByPatientlink.com
From: [block] Victor.Bickle@qmail.com
Subject: CWC Clip

Dear Claira,

I write to you again. Or to this strange Patientlink inbox. I don't know why. I guess it felt good the last time. I might actually hit send this time, even if you never see this message (and likely wouldn't want it).

I know you wished to be left alone. Well, you've gotten your wish. Oh, Claira. I don't know if I should be glad I tracked you down when I heard about your first attempt—at least I got to see you those last times in New York and beg you not to do this, this rash thing that you've now done beyond undoing. But of course, now I'm back to square one trying to get over you, like an hourglass turned on my head. I suppose in fifteen years I hadn't made much progress getting over you anyway.

When you left me fifteen years ago, when we were twenty-six, I did not believe that it would be for good. Why would I? You had left me before. You'd been leaving me since we were teenagers in Keber Creek. I want you to know that I still see you that way, smoking in your father's truck behind the mine. I see your eyes close, telling me to get out, and I smell the cigarettes, the seat leather, the corn oil exhaust that made dogs go mad when you drove by, your dirty hair, the smell of a kid. I hear you snorting with laughter, sitting on my cot, reading leftwing Twitter while my dad was at work and snowmelt from the roof dripped down my bedroom window, and you never wore a shirt. I feel your long toes poking through wool socks. You had a rapid, know-it-all voice you used when you criticized your dad (for being a miner, like my dad, like everyone's), which I couldn't resist, and which, when turned on me, made me wimpy with rage. I still hear that voice, as well as the snotty, daughterly sobs you heaped onto my chest when you told me you were going to leave Keber Creek whether I was "man enough" to join you or not. You know, I actually *wanted* to work in the mine like my dad until you and I started hanging out after school and you showed me videos of that comedian you liked saying people like our dads didn't believe in science, that they were hicks, and I sat beside you, wanting to deserve you, ashamed to have been raised with no ambition.

When you left Alaska, it took me a year to catch up to you, being the nervous one even back then, afraid to leave before my scholarship came in. I didn't want to leave. My last night before flying out for UW orientation, my parents and I took a walk along the autumn creek, and they told me they were proud of me, and I cried. But I left nonetheless—to prove I could be the man you wanted. It was never enough. You stayed in my dorm room, but only when you weren't staying with that talent agent in LA, the one with the Porsche and the big camera that "loved you" (more than I ever could), or the sales manager at Amazon who must have been thirty-five years old. No matter what I did, I couldn't help representing something shameful to you. And then when I was starting my Ph.D. and trying to bring myself to date other people, longing to move forward with some traction for once in my life, you said you'd met someone, he worked in finance, and you were getting married.

If I had expected you to leave me for good, I would have expected it then. But no, a year later you were back, with bruises you refused to tell me about, clearly having just escaped something bad. I let you stay in my apartment on 146th Street while I went to classes. The child came so quickly. I didn't want a child either, Claira! It's not as if I was trying to rope you into something. But I was prepared to be there for you. I loved you. I loved that in May, just when the wheatears would have been returning in Keber Creek, you sat by my burglar-barred window and whistled

their song. And some days, you seemed to love me. But then you'd
carp that you didn't leave Keber Creek to live in a tenement with room-
mates and rats, that you couldn't possibly raise a child with a man who
was not only making no money at twenty-five but intended to live off
TA stipends for years to come. It became a nightmare. We shouted at
each other on the streets of Harlem while strangers jeered. We couldn't
afford the doctors in New York. When you walked out on me, my only
thought was *am I still responsible for this kid?* And when you called
me the next week to tell me of the miscarriage, my prevailing sentiment was relief.

I want you to understand this from my perspective. I want you to see
how long you kept me from moving forward in my life—and still do.
I've never gotten over you. I gave up trying.

I want so badly to tell you these things. But there's no way for me
to get what I want, because you're gone. Will there be another round?
A part of me wishes I could rule it out, that this twisted thread could be
over and cut, but even your abandonment refused to commit. No ends,
just this teetering in limbo. A coma! Do you find it as horrible as I do?

I'm attaching my new TV slot. You always liked men who were
on TV. Well, here you go. And isn't it ironic that your dream, in the
end, be trammeled by your faculty for comprehension, which always
seemed inexhaustible, at least next to my own.

Perhaps I'll write again. Otherwise, know I'm thinking of you.

In love and friendship, if not need,
Victor

ATTACHMENTS: WhereInTheWorldIsBickle-FINAL.mpz

Luna set the final page down on the rug, picked up her tablet,
and began to write Bickle a reply.

DAYS OF 2 HOURS AND 15 MINUTES

I didn't read Bickle's deposition when it was taken. Magnús Bláber encouraged me not to. He said it would needlessly disconcert me, for Bickle's manner had been predictably erratic, but (he assured me) overall our case was on track. Plaintiffs were grasping at straws and as long as Bickle kept his cool around the judge, the matter would soon be thrown out. "The suit is juridically apodal," Bláber had told me; he said, "Be on with your life."

So I was alarmed—upon waking at my mother's house some days after Bickle's depo—by the urgency with which my presence was suddenly requested in Húsavík. I pulled on a sweater and hurried off to the pod, passing the FEMA vans (to which those of us who remained in Keber Creek were slowly growing accustomed) and our gutted church, its façade hooded under a banner, FEDERAL/REPONDCO. SHELTER NO. 91. At the station, two newly arrived families asked where settlement vouchers were checked. I said I didn't know, and I boarded the pod to Iceland.

It was Miguel I worried about most as I hiked along the Húsavík retaining wall, the ocean thrashing on the side opposite, intent on moving south. Cold, fishy mist blew over. An Aalborg Aspdin crane spun like a weathercock, making no distinct shadow as the light hit it from all sides. In variegated Shell screens, Icelandic talking heads drizzled overlapping streams of political outrage on the wide coastal boulevard that I crossed looking both ways, which were somehow both in the direction of the wind. Of all that made no sense about the lawsuit—its frivolity, its calumny, its expense—what most upset me was Miguel's inclusion. My poor Miguel, who had never been anything but loyal to CWC. I thought of how he'd spent his twenty-fifth birthday chained to his work computer . . . and this was how they repaid him? It was one thing to go after Bickle (for offending the wrong people); maybe me too, for I had ridden Bickle's star and wouldn't pity myself now. But Miguel? Just because he knew us. Just because he'd been stupid enough to associate with me, who spoiled everything I touched.

Bláber's reception area was empty. I signed in. I flipped through complimentary English-language newspapers ("MARKETS WOBBLE"), inspected the *Life and Times of Jonsi*, and rested my head against a thirty-gallon aquarium in which, with every visit I made, new tropical fish appeared to have given up the ghost.

(What I didn't know was that while I'd been flying west over the Pacific, Miguel had been flying west over the Atlantic, and as I sat in Bláber's office, Miguel was stepping off a pod in Keber Creek.)

A junior associate came up the stairs, saw me, and stopped.

"Does Magnús know you're here?"

"I just signed in," I said, but she was already hurrying down the hall. I heard shouting as an office door opened and closed. Still another five minutes passed before Bláber appeared with his face flushed and his suit unzipped.

"Sorry for the wait. That was the other side on the phone," he said. "They've rejected our settlement offer."

"Oh," I said. "You tried to settle?"

"A Hail Mary." He beckoned me back to his office.

"But I thought the case was gonna be, like you said, dismissed—"

"Not anymore," said Bláber. "Miguel has done something very foolish." When he got to his desk, he rifled through papers. Out the window, Nordic children bounced on a parachute trampoline.

"Miguel?"

"He just cracked. His depo was practically over, he'd barely said anything—Miguel doesn't *know* anything, what could he possibly say—and then he broke down."

"What do you mean?"

"It was completely pathetic."

"Is he alright?"

"He said he was guilty! He started crying and said he couldn't handle any more shirking of responsibility."

I gripped a bookshelf. I was shaking.

"Miguel is the one who leaked CWC's data?" I said.

Bláber looked at me like I was dumb. "Of course not," he said. "He didn't have anything to do with CWC's data leaks. The kid has something else on his conscience. He deserves to be punished, he said; he wanted to be on the record stating that he understands why his career at CWC should end like this—that he deserves to lose it all. He's turned religious or something. I told him, *the courts do not work in mysterious ways, you dope*. If you've a penance to pay, go shovel shit in an erosion camp and let me handle the lawsuit."

"So he made a false confession?"

"Out of nowhere. And now our whole case is screwed up."

As I processed this, I realized it wasn't my hand that trembled; it was the bookshelf. I felt the wall. It was buckling.

Bláber's woolly ears were turning pink. "It's the lack of *order* that gets me," he said, pounding his feeble fist. "I thought *Bickle* was the loose cannon."

The windows rattled. The children outside were being ushered off the trampoline.

"Hey," I said. "What's going on with the building?"

"Why do I even try?" said Bláber.

There was a titanic boom. Shouting associates sprinted past. Fleeing into the hallway, I found the roof collapsed barely two doors uphill.

I followed the evacuees leaping down entire flights of stairs like hysterical silver carp, until we were safely across the street, standing in the park with all the kids. Sirens wailed.

The Shell said stay calm until the earthquake passed.

Bláber emerged gasping for breath.

"My practice!" he cried as the building slowly gave way.

Icelanders pulled out their phones to film. I stepped back. My own phone buzzed. An emergency alert. But there was also a text.

20 min ago: "Your friend is here to see you. I kept him from mom."

"I have to go," I said, pushing through the growing mass of evacuees. I caught a departing pod, which shook but achieved liftoff over the expanding ruin of Húsavík.

A family of five joined me on the pod down to Keber Creek, asking me all the way if I knew where settlement vouchers would be checked. The pod walls showed clips of a young woman who said she used to be sad. When we stepped out at Jefferson Station, a half dozen volunteers ambushed us with water bottles and blankets.

"I live here," I said, throwing them off and trudging out through the autumn foliage.

The Shell showed reruns of *Juneau Pediatric Triage* while FEMA teams cleared trees. I walked the half mile toward town until I reached the church, where I found people erecting porta potties. Others unloaded bedrolls from a truck. A hundred people waited to check in. They'd all arrived in the last two hours; I didn't know where from. Someone had run an extension cord out to the arcade machines and was lighting them up in the parking lot. I heard my sister yell from inside the entertainment annex.

"You can't rush it!"

The door was open, and two teenage boys swung brooms. A bird had gotten in. A wheatear. Despite her frustration, Ashtyn was laughing.

"These boys won't believe the bird's afraid of them," she said.

I asked who they were.

"He's Austin, and the tall one's James. They drove up from the Greenfoot camp. I came into town today for the camp opening, just to watch, but they clearly needed help, so."

"Where's Mom?"

"She couldn't bear to see all the people arriving. She's at the Kailins', reading bible." Ashtyn watched the FEMA men carrying coolers, then she looked back at me and blushed. "I figure, after all these years, at least the games are gonna get some use. Maybe these new folks will like them and learn something."

Refugees in line pointed out a brilliant yellow poplar to their kids, while volunteers chased a gust of fliers blowing into the woods. WELCOME TO THE FEDERAL SERVICE AND RELIEF CENTER AT KEBER CREEK. PLEASE BE READY WITH ID AND . . .

"You texted me about someone who came," I said. Gravel kicked up by the trucks was bitter on my tongue. Ashtyn nodded across the parking lot.

"He got here this morning," she said. "I intercepted him wandering toward our house. Recognized him from your posts."

Sitting against a chain-link fence, Miguel wore white jeans and a shearling coat. His stubble had grown out, mostly on his neck and cheeks. I walked halfway across the lot to him, past children gathered round a whirring machine. He noticed and moved, on reflex, to stand, before deciding it was too late or didn't matter.

I said hi.

Miguel said hi, and I sat.

The ground was littered with damp, beautiful leaves decomposing. Circuit vessels popped. Chairs were being dragged to a clearing so the elderly could watch the Shell.

"I just saw Bláber. He said our case won't be dismissed."

"Yeah," said Miguel. "I kind of freaked out. Then I felt like I had to come and see you, and Bláber told me you were here."

"Are you alright?"

"Been better."

"Me too."

I was cold and felt like my nose was dripping, but when I touched it, it was dry.

"So you made, like, a false confession?"

"I didn't say I stole CWC's data," said Miguel. "I just said that I had come to feel guilty for what I had done at CWC and if this was the universe's way of punishing me, I didn't care to fight it."

"When did you decide to do that?"

"I didn't know I had decided anything until I did it," he said. "I was sitting in my deposition, talking about my work this way and that, these rehearsed answers the lawyers had coached me on to make me seem like the most honest, honorable guy ever to grace the earth, and then something switched, and I simply couldn't do it. I guess the way I saw myself in relation to things has been changing without me realizing it for a couple of months, maybe since London started to tilt, maybe earlier. Just watching things happening in the world. When they asked me questions in that deposition about my career, and I was forced to review it all—the coordinating I did for Grant during the Equity Push and the market crash, and also correspondences between me and you from when we were falling in love—" (He pushed through the words, eyes fixed on the ground.) "You were right about some things. And I know you cared about me. And I miss you."

"I missed you too," I said. "And I also have regrets."

"I started feeling crazy during the lawsuit," Miguel said. "I got really scared in loops thinking about justice."

"You were afraid you'd be punished?"

"I was getting more afraid I wouldn't be."

"You didn't feel punished already?" I said.

"Tal vez sí. Maybe I did start to feel punished, and that's why I finally asked what I had done to deserve it. I guess that's something you only ask when you have to."

"So then why the false confession?"

"To draw enough punishment to make it end, maybe. I mean, I don't know what I deserve. I don't know what any of us deserve." He nodded to the line of people anxiously folding and unfolding their vouchers.

"So I guess we have to keep worrying about this lawsuit."

"There's always something." Miguel shrugged. He said, "There's always a million somethings. The key, I'm learning, is in discerning what's important."

I thought about this. "I don't think the lawsuit's very important."

"There have been a lot of things that weren't important."

Music was coming from one of the arcade machines. Smaller kids stood back at the margins. I watched the adults queuing to receive their bed assignments. They, unlike their children, didn't speak to one another. All they had in mind was to get their beds. Earlier that day, the *Anchorage Hourly*'s dueling op-eds had debated whether the FEMA camps were ghettos to enisle the homeless or vanguards for the next great American migration. I couldn't possibly know what the future would hold. I wanted to think that perhaps things always got better.

"For so much of the past seven years, I felt bad," I said. "About who I was and what I did to other people. But even then, I didn't feel bad enough. I'm sorry."

"Oh, minou," said Miguel. "You never felt as bad about yourself as you should have and you always felt worse about yourself than you should have. The right amount is a scarier thing. But I believe you really were trying your hardest to face it."

I thought about this. I wiped my nose. I looked at him. He was crying.

"It will be okay," I said.

"I don't know."

I held him, remembering just how small he was. Even though he was sobbing into my neck, he didn't stop scratching a mosquito bite on his ankle until I pulled his hand away. I brought his chest to mine and squeezed him as if afraid we'd be flung apart. Surprised, he parted his lips with a little *pah* in my ear. He squirmed. He made me feel too much, and I held us together, pouring myself from my heart back into his.

Over his shoulder, through my tears I saw people running in place. It was at first a strange silhouette—figures on a stage, moving their legs and getting nowhere—and then I realized they were dancing. Dancing like mad. I blinked and watched and thought that Miguel and I, hunkered together, might have been somewhere else. I thought of Petra Dance Haus. Then the glare cleaving the figures receded, and I saw that they were kids playing upon the *Dance Dance Revelation*.

I remembered the song, one I'd torrented into the machine myself. "Glory, glory . . . Gimme glory . . ." The logo spun: *DDR* with "*revolution!*" struck through. No revolution. Holographic John of Patmos, ghostly in the light of day, modeled the steps, crying, "Face the beast!" as cardinal arrows flowed up past scenes of demise: the seven bowls poured onto Earth, men scorched by fire from the sun, a city buoyant with frankincense in all manner vessels, and edifices of sin reaching unto heaven, now come to naught, while the kids moved for movement's sake.

Miguel sniffled. "What are you watching?"

"Just lights."

He turned to see the children jostling for space, then turned back and looked into my eyes. The northern wind blew by. Behind him, the Dance Gauge hit zero, the apocalypse stopped, and the screen said FAILED.

○

A week passed. Winnie remained in the church with a fever that flared, then broke, then flared again. She was dimly aware of having been moved to a cot in the corner, the church growing more crowded hourly with each shuttle's arrival. Her comprehension of the influx waxed and waned—for some time, she feared that she was in hell and that it would just keep filling up forever. She watched colors shift along the stained-glass window above her, filtering the already colored light of the Shell.

Unfortunately, even when her mind cooled down, it wasn't quite what it had been. She stayed in bed, sleeping as much as she could, taking little interest in her surroundings while awake. The woody smell of the church when she first arrived was becoming drowned out by the growing odor of bodies. When shuffling to and from the bathroom, she kept her eyes half closed. Opening them once to look out the doorway, she saw a humongous animatronic Jesus—ringed by children—demanding "your best shot." She got back in bed. At a certain point, you stop caring to know.

The next time she slept, she dreamt of her father, and when she awoke, I was setting a cup of coffee on her bedside table.

"Oh, hi," I said and apologized for waking her.

She considered whether to respond. She still felt strange.

I said I'd brought my coffee machine from home, and there was milk and sugar too. She watched me push my bangs out of my eyes, noting their asymmetry; she could tell they'd been cut so as to be worn gelled up, and they gave my face (in her estimation) a sort of aborted quality.

"How are you doing? People have been worried about you."

She asked who.

"The other volunteers and people. Those of us who have been helping out around here the past week."

She sat up and put on her glasses. "I'm not a refugee," she said.

"Okay. I'm not going to ask for your voucher."

"I'm from here."

"You are?"

"Está viva. How are you feeling?"

"I think she's still a bit out of it."

"Did you get her name?"

"It's Winnie," she said.

"I'm Miguel, and this is Tanner."

Miguel informed her that we'd been checking up on her all week. "Tanner took care of you when the medics went back to North Slope."

"Thanks."

"It's nothing," I said. "You were alone. I'm glad I was able to help."

She didn't want to converse and so was relieved when Miguel and I left to help the other volunteers lay out sandwiches. She waited until we were gone, then she got out of bed to use the showers while everyone else ate. The water was metallic and ice cold, and she stayed under it until her skin turned splotchy, as if through the work of enduring discomfort she might put herself back together. Then alone in the jerry-built washhouse, shivering, she dabbed her body with paper towels.

She was back in bed when Miguel and I returned.

We'd brought her a sandwich. "You asked us yesterday for vegan options."

She'd forgotten this. She unwrapped the tinfoil and took a bite. Peanut butter and Nutella. Without mentioning that Nutella wasn't vegan, she said thanks and set it down. She learned from us about a stadium collapse in St. Louis and listened to our commentary on it, passively accepting our company. It occurred to her that only recently she would have found this conversation exhausting. She would have been tormented by the impossibility of gauging each speaker's sincerity and by her inability to persuade people of her own. I said it was so strange what things had become, people trying to go about their days and dying in such numbers, and she disagreed but said nothing.

The church lights dimmed, and people went to sleep (or at least to bed) at the suggestion of FEMA officials with guns. Kids were called inside. Some chose protest. There was a loud crack, but it was just a rerun of last year's World Series playing out on the Shell. This season had been cancelled. Miguel and I took bedrolls near Winnie's cot. Miguel's tablet, propped against a folding chair, played an old documentary in which Ayla Amsler-Fitzgerald, between salacious clips of her

Love Dirty tour, came out about her struggle with depression. Winnie listened to us gab over the whole thing—me wanting to view the doc as a gesture of repentance for AAF's career-long promotion of narrow beauty standards in jingoistic action films and fast fashion ads, Miguel dismissing her as vain, another entertainer who tried to sell her struggle in exchange for more publicity. "*My Struggle* by Ayla Amsler-Fitzgerald." We both laughed and fell asleep halfway through, while Amsler-Fitzgerald continued dancing and screaming at stagehands, and coyotes howled at the Shell, and Winnie lay back, wishing for quiet.

The hours passed.

She heard the spruces brushing arms outside.

She remembered waking up in the hospital in San Francisco after her electrocution. How everything had been stiff and pale.

She thought about the note that she had written for her mom in Nevada. It would never be read, she believed. And she was glad for that now, as it embarrassed her. She pulled out her phone and, that night, composed a different note. This one, however, would not go only to her mom's Patientlink inbox. Instead, she scrolled through her contact list and added her aunt and uncle. She added Chip Knoepffler and the board of BodyThink. She added the faculty of Attainment Academy.

She added every political campaign that had ever spammed her, every brand that had ever sent her a request for feedback, be they monitored email addresses or not, she added Patientlink customer service. Her building superintendent. Her librarian. Her doctor from the burn ward. The UCLA chancellor who had frittered away her cohort's funding.

She added everyone to whom she, Luna, and Nat used to send activist emails, fond and hostile—social media commentators and Ayla Amsler-Fitzgerald and Victor Bickle.

She added the whole generation of people who at one time or another filled in the role of parent to her, or could have. And she staged the message so that she could send it in a few days' time, once she was sure that she was ready to go.

The Shell

Barely three months after the Switch-On, the Shell cracked. It was a loud crack, a million fibers of steel and copper tearing in a straight line, three nautical miles long over the Pacific, near the equator, about twenty degrees south of Hawaii. All along the laceration, screens exploded in a shower of neat glass pebbles, but they did not fall to sea. They bobbed and rolled against the concave ceiling, toward the crack, through it, and then fell upward, into space.

"That's it," said Kiko Alexandra. "There goes life as we know it."

Fez allowed herself a pause to collect her thoughts, but this would be cut in post if it seemed affected. "It's just one Shell district broken," she said. "And we want to be clear to all our listeners, the Santiago Commission says there are currently no evacuation orders—"

"Because they know," said Kiko Alexandra, "that extra circuit traffic is just gonna accelerate things. I'm seriously scared. Like, I woke up this morning feeling—" "We're all a bit scared." "What is the right way to do the podcast today, if there is a right way, I don't know." "I think if we just document our honest take, which is what this is, that's what you're all listening to—" "Document? For what? You understand which way the Shell broke?" "It's not totally confirmed." "It broke outward." "It's just one district, and we're waiting for a report, so we'll be able to talk more about that next time, in our next episode, which we're planning a conversation with special guests Morning Makeup. If you're scared and you want answers, you're in good company. Even on the news, people right now are trying to figure out what's going on . . ."

* * *

The contractor for the district in question was (typical luck) CWC—a fact brought to Imani's attention by a dozen simultaneous phone calls and a rap on the door of her corner office.

"Come in."

Her assistant entered. She made a small face, probably at the Calming Ocean Breeze air freshener with which Imani was developing an unhealthy relationship. "How bad is it?"

Imani said, "A twenty-kilometer breach at least. The South Pacific Upspout is spilling water back into the ocean. They're going to evacuate most of Polynesia. And as far south as Bora Bora the screens are grayed out."

"What are we telling the press?"

"I don't know," said Imani. "What did Simteca tell the press when their Pacific C.D. lost power last week?"

"They denied it."

"Denied that the Shell was dark? How?"

"They just denied it. 'We deny it.'"

Imani looked out the window beside her, which, like everything in the office, still felt like Cromwell Grant's rather than her own. No matter how much she redecorated and drenched in Glade the office of CWC's Chief of Communications, it refused to abandon loyalty to its old master. Out the window, other skyscrapers too grand to rebuild stood parallel to Aviation Tower, their frames being pulled together by contraccelerator plates on every floor, but down below on Earth, which sat orthogonal to the building, everything appeared to lean. Streetlights and telephone poles bowed as if caught in an invisible gust, as did pedestrians struggling to keep their balance. Cars honked. A runaway football bounded down the seemingly flat sidewalk. Imani had to grip the window frame in order to prevent the city she navigated every day—now observed from a certain distance— from making her sick.

She looked up and tried to really imagine what the world was coming to. The Shell, at its high altitude, spun faster than objects on the ground. Its pillars were built to support its massive weight with the help of some centrifugal force. They weren't built to cling *inward* to what had effectively become a centrifuge working to cast the Shell into space. And if this, this full inversion of gravity, was happening up there, then what if it really was only a matter of time before effects equally strong were felt on the ground? The Commission's models said it would start at the equator. Weightlessness, then a drift, straight up; and the more everyone hurried onto circuit vessels trying to flee, the worse it would get, until it'd spread to the poles. Towns would tilt and tilt, and then all of a sudden, they'd be dumped off the face of the Earth. Into the sky. Imani thought of her husband and son.

A phone rang. She started for no reason and was annoyed. Hadn't she gone offline? She had; the phone wasn't hers.

"I'll get it," her assistant said and dug into a cardboard box full of CWC phones left behind when Imani inherited the office. Her assistant found and silenced the offending phone. Then it lit up in her hand with another incoming message. As soon as the holographic image emerged, she flung it. "Ew, ew!"

"What?"

"Who even has these numbers?" she asked and Imani shook her head, she didn't know, as the phone lay on the floor, white light shooting from a crack down the center. "Someone just sent us a picture of his dick!"

Cromwell Grant pulled up his swim trunks, already forgetting whom he had just sexted. He stumbled out of the bathroom onto the pool deck of John Sugar Jr.'s villa. The pool lapped around models' waists in the neon Shell light as they splashed to a DJ's bleeps and bloops. Grant searched for any familiar face. Gravity was below 60 percent *g* in this warm clime, and middle-aged men were doing spin-flips. "Where's the candy man?" he shouted to no one.

The pool surface turned red. Like blood. The red Shell shining down announced, "For the next generation, and their experiences, look to China Circuit Group." Grant booed, swatted the air away from his face, and staggered through a group of women who all looked like his wife.

(Ex-wife.)

"Where's the candy man?"

Where was anyone? Where the hell was he? He was on some Caribbean island, but he couldn't remember which. San Andrés or Santa María or the Koch Sanitation Base. How did he get here? How the hell was he gonna get home?

(To his hotel.)

He reached the bar, wrenched by narcotic thirst, and ordered a "Vera and tonic."

"Vera?" asked the catering-company barman.

"Gin, you muppet. Learn to speak English." He poured his own. The distance between him and his hands spread like putty.

He sunk into the pool, his kimono flowering around him like a powerful aura. His gin tasted like chlorine. His thirst dodged every sip. Some Spanish girls toasted behind him, "Arriba. Abajo. Al centro. Pa' dentro!" People's voices seemed to be coming out of other people's mouths. Who the hell were all these grockels? As soon as he found the candy man, John Sugar Jr., he was going to kill him.

"Zur Mitte. Zur Titte. Zum Sack. Zack zack!"

His head slid below the surface. Cool quiet. A rainbow forest of scissoring legs. He belched bubbles, and water snuck up his nose, burning like gin. A lighting shift turned his knees green, kimono gray. It recalled an anorak. Victor Bickle had ruined his life. Bickle was the reason he lost his job, his stock, his reputation. Bickle, leaking private emails, had precipitated his divorce. CWC might be suing Bickle at his behest, but he wouldn't rest at seeing Bickle broke. He wanted Bickle dead. That's right. Bickle would be next. But first he was going to kill John Sugar Jr.

Someone heaved him out of the water, then toppled buoyantly
backward, while Grant landed supine on the stone deck. Bleep-bloop
shook the ground. Two or four or six heads eclipsed the brilliant,
wasted sky.

"Where's the candy man?" Grant coughed.

"Scusi?"

A woman was extolling the benefits of Mastercard on the Shell,
but clouds got in the way. He heard Sugar Jr.'s voice across the pool
and lurched up. Atop the stairs, silhouetted by houselights, Grant's
old friend and mentor stood abreast his wife (he had a loyal one, that
jammy git, or a tight prenup) delivering a toast in his insufferable
Bojangles' Chicken 'n Biscuits accent, ". . . entire evening would not
be possible without the generosity of Tencent Holdings."

"Out of my way." Grant dodged around the pool and ascended
the steps three at a time to catch Sugar Jr. moments after his toast
concluded, while everyone was returning to their drinks.

"Why'd you let them do it, schattenparker? You sold me out!"

Sugar Jr. turned around, head first, then shoulders, then legs. "Not
this again."

"You said you'd shield me. You said no one on your board would
get the sack."

"Cromwell, how long do you think it's been since we last had this
talk? I'll tell you. It's been three minutes. You're gone-zo, my friend.
Here, take two of these."

Grant ate two yellow pills. "Did you say you're getting paid by
Tencent to throw this party?"

"Of course I'm getting paid," said Sugar Jr. "You think I'd have
all this fun just for kicks? We just bought our polar bunker home in
Punta Arenas and Sue-Anne wants a new kitchen. CWC forced me
out too. Look, Cromwell, go home."

"I *lost* my home in the divorce, you . . . you pommy."

"D'you need a place to sleep?"

"Where's Victor Bickle?"

"Oh, Bickle ain't *here*."

"I'll crucify him. I'll show him why they called my office the Calvary."

"Haven't you gone after that poor man enough? Between you and me we both know he didn't have shit to do with CWC's data breaches. That organization was always leaky as a Brit coming off Indian lunch buffet."

"Fuck you," said Grant. "No one gets away with recalcitrating in my department." (Imani Handal's department.) "He'll pay. Jeff in Legal is still loyal to me!" He canted backward. Someone caught him. He fell forward again, getting in Sugar Jr.'s face. "You know what I did to him that last day in my office? I told him he had a daughter!"

"Cromwell, sit down. Get some Gatorade in you."

"You should have seen his pathetic face. Oh, it was worth his salary! He believed it. As if a dudka like him could sire kids. I had Noah retrieve that woman's medical records before we ever interviewed Bickle, back when we were making sense of his Columbia scandal. The bitch had a daughter alright, but it wasn't his. We got the paternity test. That's how I win, you see—I always make sure to know the people around me better than they know themselves. I know *you*, John! I win and always will, I toy with my prey. Victor Bickle wasn't a father—at least not with that Lynx woman, maybe he got his dick wet after I made him a star. I made him . . ."

"What's he on about?"

"You remember Noah?" said Grant. "Whatever happened to that little rim-slurper? I'd have thought he'd slurp his way somewhere by now . . ."

"Cromwell, come back."

He fell, practically headlong, down the stairs and back into the pool. Once heaved out again, he let himself into Sugar Jr.'s house, where a circle of chaebols ate tacos and played *Slot Cars* on the big screen. He stumbled through the house, depressed by the contraccelerators, dragging his soaked kimono until he tripped out the other end.

Onto the front lawn. The party music reached him through a low-pass filter. "Lemon-emon-ems!" the Shell screamed through thick clouds. In the shadow of a palm tree, Grant heard the fervent whimpering of his youngest son.

"Charlie? Is that you?"

He crawled nearer. The lawn beneath him seemed to swell. He peeked over a hollow decorative boulder and saw to his delight, not his son, but two teenage caterers with their khakis dropped to their ankles, furtively making it.

They climaxed quietly and left in a flurry of reproachful whispers. Grant collapsed, feeling unresolved. He was exhausted and battered into the boulder by the waves of all he hadn't done. Yet. Hadn't done yet. He would never give up. People had always underestimated what he was capable of. What pain he was prepared to endure. When in his thirteenth year, his delicate mother had moved them to the crumbling council estate in the concrete hinterland of Northwest London, where balcony women in brassieres fumigated their lungs and advertised their misfortunes day in and out while their cultureless issue beat Cromwell for the capital offense of proper elocution and habiliment, he did not cry for his old house. Nor did he give himself over to the brutes like his submissive older sister did. He'd always been able to bear what others couldn't. Even before then, when his father (the magnetic heart of his childhood, the philanderer) kicked them to the curb, Cromwell watched his mother's breakdown with bland disgust. He would live to see his manhood disseminated across screens around the world. The world is harsh, he knew even as a child, but it cannot hurt you; only your brain's reaction can do that. If you let it. Don't let it. There was no glory, let alone joy, in the inability to withstand. Those who thrived in this world would not be the whingers. They'd be the ones who could keep working while others screamed that the house was burning down. The ones encircled by a ring of water. The islands, like him. Saint Grant.

Wind shook the palms. Where were his uppers? He could handle more. Those yellow tranquilizers, or whatever they were, from Sugar

Jr. had made him maudlin. He dug through his wet pockets until he pinched a gooey clump of pill capsules. Their imprint codes had rubbed off. He ate them all and rolled over to see the house. The music went bleep-bleep-bleep, and he chanted along, "Bleep! Bleep!"—not catching on when the song ended and adding one additional bleep all his own. The douchebag solo. On the Shell, they decried the failure of the Shell. They talked about the end of the world. Nothing new! Infant Grant had been lulled to sleep by clamor that the end was nigh—well, let it come once more! Let the world do its worst. His house? His job? Is that the best it could do? He would be buggered and blagged, beaten and bruised, left high and dry, and he would endure. He would be kicked in the face, punched in the balls, forced to fly coach. Subjected to hours on end of royalty-free Shell programming, spit on, and then shot. He would be lobotomized and dismembered, catheterized and colonoscoped, disencumbered of liquid assets, executed by inexperienced headsmen, and put through puberty twice. He would be consigned to Jesus, he thought, wringing his kimono sleeve into his mouth, chewing it for moisture, despite the dirt and chlorine, as the pills desiccated his veins. Or consigned to capitalism: conscripted into janitorial labor. Divorced. Driven over, then reversed over, then driven over again, and embalmed for schoolchildren's ridicule. Strung up for posthumous execution and struck by lightning. Stabbed. Drowned. Granulated. Tied down by smaller men and poked in the eyes. Given a suite of electronic devices and then, just when he got used to them, have them all, without warning, updated to newer software. He would be made to say goodbye to his boys for two weeks every two weeks, for the remainder of their childhoods. Torture him. Defenestrate him. Parade him around like a Trojan prince. Bloody hell, he spat into the webby waters of his mind as the overdose did its gruesome work. Insult to injury, smart upon smite, everything dear in the world could come crashing down, but Cromwell Grant would never surrender.

DAYS OF 2 HOURS

A few minutes after Grant died, as if to clear his passage to heaven, the Caribbean Shell tore open. News of this second rupture reached me through the screens above the church parking lot, where even more arrivals to Keber Creek (who were put up in walk-in shipping containers that now ran down the street and into the woods) gathered to play games, barter, and watch the evening programs. The Shell screens had been dimmed to divert power. Their light reached the Keber Creek encampment with about as much luminosity as a full moon on a misty night, and it was strange to remember that just beyond, there might in fact have been a full moon, or even the gleaming sun. Following this second Shell breach, water had poured down on the Dominican Republic. Thousands were missing. Fox News interpreted maps of Santo Domingo and interviewed a woman who'd been separated from her children on the overrun flight to Haiti. The American president was expected to speak about the response in Puerto Rico, while his austerity was blamed in an onslaught of posts by Puerto Rico's governor. I watched the politicians argue, and I couldn't slow the nauseating slide my government had been making for some time now in my mind, from a state (in every sense of the word) to a mere agent.

Like bugs, circuit vessels darted between white and black patches of screen, their *pops* drowned out by hammering inside the church, where occupants were installing locks to protect themselves against nocturnal theft from the hundreds of newer refugees arriving each week. Officials with guns watched them and neither assisted nor intervened. They maintained a border around the refrigerated FEMA trucks parked in a clearing of crushed aspens. I noticed one official, a sharpshooter, stationed in the church belfry, surveilling the woods.

He was able to stand on the ladder, leaning into it backward.

The ground had started to tilt noticeably even in Keber Creek.

"... *Oh my goodness, and you can hear the noise on our feed, that is air just ripping out of that opening ...*"

"What do you think will happen?" asked Miguel, his neck craned.

I didn't know. It felt like something I'd always anticipated was finally here, but it wasn't at all as I'd anticipated it. I was cold and ready to go back inside, but I watched the news, trying to force everything they said to sink in—repeating to myself that developments were unfolding, which, despite their speed, strangely could not be undone. The Shell was breaking outward. The pipes weren't going to hold. The skies and seas would be torn up, and as we moved things out of the path of destruction, we'd spin our planet faster and faster until everything flipped, as it was already doing. The incontrovertibility of the situation remained vaguely implausible to me, and yet it seemed (a horror) the truth: The world had been capable of rapid change all along, and our grandparents, and then our parents, and then we ourselves had changed it for the worse.

Maybe the destruction would stop before reaching Keber Creek. I didn't know. Games flashed and whirred. Children were gambling over food vouchers, and weed smoke wafted across the lot. There was a rumor that some of the newcomers to the camp were selling guns. There were also rumors of gang rapes in the washhouse at night, which I had no reason to believe, and didn't. As far as I could tell, people were just cold and hungry and, at worst, starting to succumb to the ease of public urination. I watched a family of four try to play cards without taking off their mittens. They'd told me they received FEMA vouchers after their teetering apartment building in Tulsa was condemned.

Most families kept to themselves. A man fished a phone line from the trash while speaking to a journalist from the *New York Times*. He said he came from Louisiana—he'd lived through the pre-crash Acadiana floods, he'd rebuilt his house two different times in the past ten years, but now his whole town was sliding into the Mississippi River Delta. I myself had spoken to the *New York Times* journalist the other day. She had asked me how many people were in the camp. I'd been hoping she could tell *me*. She went off to count the containers, which fit like puzzle pieces amidst what trees hadn't yet been bulldozed. Between them hung lines of fairy lights strung with drying clothes, and on the narrow paths occasional motorbikes roused spirits from the dust. I was the only Keber Creek local who kept volunteering at food distribution—Ashtyn and her friends now came into town only to pick up supplies they carried home.

Most days I walked home with Ashtyn to change my clothes and see my mom, who was usually in the kitchen watching the news. She looked okay. Somewhat rested. In an hour there, I would watch her take five sips of coffee, and we'd exchange almost as few words. She asked me when the refugees would be leaving. I told her I didn't know. I didn't sleep at home, now that Miguel had joined me in Keber Creek. My mom refused to meet Miguel, and I hadn't the spirit to try to change her.

The night that the Shell broke, I crawled into my bedroll on the dusty hardwood floor of the church. Miguel was in the bathroom, and I read on my phone that the markets were in freefall.

"Tanner," someone whispered. I sat up to see over an empty cot. It was Winnie.

"Hey," I said.

She asked how Miguel and I were. "Tired," I said. "It's amazing how tiring it can be to do so little."

Her smile was nice to see. Earlier that day, I had gotten worried about her. I had seen her outside the washhouse surrounded by a gang of teenage boys who'd made a name for themselves stealing phones and reselling them from their container. (The authorities seemed aware of this racket but didn't know how to respond except with notices admonishing people to watch their personal items.) When I saw them cornering Winnie against the washhouse wall, I approached. Winnie was speaking back at them with quiet insistence. I asked what was going on, and they all turned and said it was none of my business, and Winnie walked away. She seemed okay now, though, sitting cross-legged on her cot. Her sweatshirt (ALL YOU NEED IS LOVE. AND COFFEE) was pulled over her knees.

I asked if she was doing alright.

She said, "Still here."

And then I got a chill. There was something familiar about her gaze.

At the time, I thought what I recognized was a glimmer of myself, or something common to the generation to which she and I (however different our paths) both belonged. Something impressed on her by the circumstances of our particular historical moment that had also, through my journey toward comprehension, been impressed upon me.

That may have been partly true, but now I believe there was something else I saw in Winnie that night. Of course, I'll never know if I actually identified this or if, like so much that happened along the periphery of my life, it appears to me only uselessly in hindsight, but I can't help thinking that the shiver that ran up my spine in that moment carried a recollection of the tearful woman I once saw in Bickle's office, telling him to leave her alone.

I should have said something to Winnie then, something to try to know her, and through knowing, hold her in a space where she might understand that she belonged. But all I thought to do was chuckle and say lamely, "I'm glad." She looked through me, surveying all the people huddled in the church, people drying their feet before pulling on socks over socks to keep warm. She rolled over and buried her head in her pillow.

Miguel arrived and we got under the covers. Eventually most people fell asleep. Miguel said "descansa" and was shortly snoring, leaving me to lie awake on the hard, sloped bedroll. I heard Winnie whimpering, as she did most nights, talking to her mother. Usually I tried to block her out, less for my peace than for her privacy. Did it occur to me that she needed someone to hear? The someone oughtn't have been me. It ought to have been her parents, and I found myself wondering where they were. I wondered if they regretted the world they'd left her. I wondered if any of our parents did. Nonetheless, it was I that heard her, whether I pretended to block her out or not. As hours slipped by, her whimpering faded into my own semiconscious eructations of anger, arguments I held in my mind with childhood bullies and senators on the news, my parents, and CWC . . .

The next day, the Shell over Keber Creek lost signal. Every few minutes, the sky flashed white, then returned to bars of dull orange. Miguel and I manned one of the food distribution tables that evening. It was cold, and people queued in blankets, trudging up Main Street, which had become something of a hillside to the church steps. Miguel asked "cheese or peanut butter" of each, an official handed them their sandwiches, and I stamped hands. Occasionally one of the Spanish-speaking families Miguel had come to know would reach the front of the line, and he would ask also how their kids were and sneak them extra chips. One child proffered a hand so cracked by eczema that it hurt to see it stamped. Another refused to take off his mittens. There was a girl who asked to stamp herself. Her father eventually said okay that was enough, and thanked me. The father was young, and I wondered if he had a partner and where they were. A woman asked for an extra sandwich, and the official said no, and she said she understood.

There were two sisters who spoke only Russian. After receiving their stamps, the elder said unexpectedly, "Thank you, Tanner." There was the *New York Times* journalist, who lingered beside the table to chat with an official about the lack of hot water. A confused old man returned four or five times to ask Miguel what the heck was wrong with the sky. Ashtyn came with her friends. The official gave them enough sandwiches to take home.

"Are you going to come over?" she asked me. I said I was too tired tonight.

She talked to Miguel awhile. They talked about an old TV show they both used to like.

The teenage boys who had been bothering Winnie came to the table stoned. They asked for barbecue sauce like they'd gotten the day before and set me on edge when they wouldn't accept Miguel's answer. The official scared them off. I felt sorry then, seeing them retreat without dinner. The young, straight couple behind them kept quiet. There were people of all ages wearing headphones who just pointed, peanut butter or cheese. Siblings ordered for siblings. Some people said they'd take either, whatever was more helpful. A woman, after waiting through the whole line, heard the options and passed, but her husband took peanut butter for her just in case she changed her mind.

Those of us who slept in the church decided to rotate our bedrolls forty-five degrees so our heads would be uphill. It took twenty minutes, but was done without any dictator or discord. I hoped it would allow me a full night's sleep.

The breaches in the Shell had still not been repaired. China's president was trying to negotiate a joint venture of various army corps of engineers, but the US refused to join. People read the news on their phones in the church after lights-out, making the rafters blue and distant. Families whispered about family matters.

"Have you been able to get ahold of Bickle this week?" Miguel asked.

I held him from behind, as tightly as I ever did when we were boys just beginning our twenties. I ran my fingers down his chest, along his hips, over his penis, which was cold, and between his thighs. "No," I said. There were a lot of people we hadn't been able to get ahold of in the past week.

"I hope he's okay."

"I wrote him. He didn't respond," I said.

Birds scampered on the roof.

I said, "I miss him."

Miguel squeezed my arm. "You were important to him, minou."

He rolled over.

"I'm glad we're back," he said.

"Me too," I said and felt myself choking up. I started to talk, then closed my mouth. I wanted him to see my tears so he would know how much he meant to me, but it wasn't worth crying right then. There were enough tears, probably even right there in that church. Mine could wait.

"Promise me we will never hurt each other again," he said.

I pressed my face into his neck.

"Whatever happens, at least between you and me, it will just be easy from now on."

"I hope so," I said, so softly the words almost stayed in me. "I hope so, minou."

One by one, the lights at each bedroll went out. I rubbed Miguel's hand, receiving squeezes every few minutes, which seemed to be his way of saying he was still awake, even though he wasn't really. Somewhere a woman was humming. She must have thought no one could hear. It was an old-sounding song with a slow, erotic melody. Several times it stopped, as if it was the other instruments' part, and then one time it stopped and that was the end. Snores collected over the sleeping, who dreamt of flower buds hung over puddles, and offices, and brackish ponds where people passed their lives, lives by other names. Here and there someone suppressed a cough. A child whispered. The floor was hard. It is a strange sorrow that I have never gotten used to, bedtime. The quiet and the being left to one's thoughts. I didn't notice that from Winnie's cot there was, for the first night ever, no whimpering. There was from Winnie's cot that night no noise at all.

I scrolled through silent videos on my phone, reading the subtitles: reactions to the president's use of the word "apocalypse." I learned from one video that apocalypse doesn't really mean the end of the world. In Greek, "apocalypse" means an uncovering or unveiling; it means something brought into view.

After a long time, I put my phone away and got up to use the bathroom. I peed with the lights off, but then turned them on to wipe the seat. At the wash counter, I wet a paper towel and wiped away other people's toothpaste stains. The mirror showed me gaunt in my pink Forwards Foundation shirt, which I wore only for sleeping. I pushed back my hair. I used to hate my red bangs. I picked up paper towels from the floor, replaced the toilet paper where it was low, even tightened the hinge on one of the stalls with a coin from the windowsill, which I took in my pocket.

Heading back, I happened to peek up the ladder to the belfry and found it unlatched; no one was there. I decided to climb up—it was tall, five stories—and I pulled myself through the trapdoor.

That high, the air smelled less of propane and fetid containers than down below, more of greenness and nothing. The Shell, catching an errant signal, came momentarily to life with rumbling ju-ju drums and actors demonstrating the percussive stamina of Domod aluminum pots—"Domod akesee!"—but soon dissolved back into static. There was space for me to pull myself onto the ledge and dangle one leg, which in the moment seemed worth dirtying my pajama pants for. Containers stretched down the road. Tree branches touched like bucks at play. I sat beneath the brittle lights, remembering clear London evenings when a glimpse of the moon would just break your heart. I could almost feel the world spinning and the belfry holding on.

I was startled from my reverie by the sound of voices downstairs. I brought my leg in. There was some disturbance. People were waking up, asking what was happening. I picked Miguel's voice out of the crowd. Down below, Miguel was straining to remain calm, telling Winnie to lower the gun.

Signals

VB: "Hello, Luna?"

LT: "I still haven't found her. I'm sorry. She's not answering my calls."

VB: "It's okay. Listen—"

LT: "There are too many people missing since the seawalls were breached. No one's even taking reports anymore. We're supposed to be evacuating the Bay, and I don't know if I should be leaving without her or what."

VB: "No, Luna, listen. I think *I* know where Winnie is."

LT: "You do?"

VB: "I got an email from her. The subject is 'Notes from the Federal Service and Relief Center at Keber Creek.' The rest I don't understand, but I think she went back to where we're from. She doesn't seem okay. I think you ought to go. If I can make it on a pod, I'm going too. I'm going to try to get there as quickly as possible."

END OF DAYS

It was becoming clearer, the design of order and chaos in the world, in Winnie's mind. Sitting alone in the bathroom, she had taken deep breaths, thinking about the curve you can't see up close. The line is chaos, the circle is order. Soon she could be outside. That evening, she had hit send on the mass email she'd composed. Her note. She was ready to die. She really was.

Wasn't she?

It was strange to feel the gun against her belly, a smooth, metal other stashed in her sweatshirt. She'd gotten it from the boys by the washhouse. A handgun, she didn't know what kind, whether a Smith & Wesson or Glock or whatever. She had to look up how to use it. She thought about the metal bullet changing from a part of the gun to a part of her. She thumbed her nose ring. What did it mean to be her? In her fever, she'd been taken by surging thrusts of dissociation for so many hours that when she came out, the visual plane remained flat. She couldn't remember what it was like to compile the world around her "correctly." She didn't know how she could even get out of bed and talk to people. She could do it, but the people were just data now. Odorless, flavorless, synthetic info, like code. Like an app, rushing to IPO. Like a gene. Her genes. From gen to gen. She had tried for so long to make sense of it, but it had all been senseless. Not like the gun. The gun was solid against her belly, inside her sweatshirt that was out of ideas.

She thought she heard the bathroom door opening. It scared her into leaving her stall, and though there wasn't anyone at the door, she didn't stop her momentum into the hallway. She passed the water fountain. She ought to go back to the bathroom, she thought; she shouldn't bring the gun where everyone else was sleeping. But it would look suspicious to turn right around, so she went to her bed. It creaked. The walls of the church loomed in their southward cant. She tried not to let it bother her that her feet were dirty on her bed. The gun was small in her lap. She lifted it. She put it in her mouth. There was no electricity, just death. She removed it.

A few hours earlier she had charged her headphones, thinking she might want music when the time came. She remembered this now. Now that those hours were over and the time had come. They chimed a full battery sound when she put them in her ears, but unable to think of anything to play, since all the music she knew seemed to be about someone else, she took them out again. She could hear the wind but not feel it. The gun's slide was louder than she expected, like knuckles cracking, and it didn't scare her except that she was scared of waking people. She knew that what she was planning to do would necessarily disrupt others—they'd hear the shot and find her in the bathroom—but she didn't want to disrupt them any more than she had to. She would have done it outside in the woods were she not so afraid of the soldiers. No, her plan was as good as it could be. She would wait a minute then return to the bathroom, and that would be that.

"Tanner?" someone whispered. It was Miguel. He groped the empty space beside him, and watching him, she felt pity. The muzzle of the gun had a smooth ring the circumference of her middle finger. Miguel sat up.

He looked at her.

"What is that?" he said.

Frozen, she stared at him.

He stood. "Winnie, give me that."

She didn't move. He repeated himself louder, and others sat up too. The closest people started murmuring, asking Miguel what was going on.

The word "gun" traveled like its own kind of bullet from ear to ear. Whispering turned to urgent hissing: *get the children out*. A man fumbled with the lock on the front door.

"Give that to me, Winnie."

They were afraid of her. They thought she would hurt them. She raised the gun and he stepped back. She slid off her cot and reversed toward the bathroom, bumping into a woman who was hurrying for the door. The water fountain hummed. Everything was foggy. Miguel told her to put the gun down. His voice contained less fear than aggrievement. The first people outside shouted for help.

Winnie dropped the gun, turned, and hurried down the hall. She reached the bathroom door but found herself trapped. Instead she made a right and started climbing up the belfry. The rungs were rough like damp sandpaper. She climbed quickly, unsure whether she'd be followed.

Officials had gotten inside and were asking where she'd gone. Miguel said it was okay. They appeared at the bottom of the ladder.

"Come down and lie on the ground," they commanded. They asked Miguel what her name was and started using it. She was almost at the top; the ladder went on and on. The whole belfry leaned in gravity's slow failure.

"We'll shoot," they threatened.

But she ignored them, fleeing as if for her life. She shut the trap-door underfoot.

Outside, she could feel the wind so strong it almost hurt. It was like flying, being up there all alone, or so she thought, deafened by the air in her ears and her own heavy breathing. She climbed atop the railing, readying herself to jump. Trees held out open arms. Lit at all angles by the sky on standby, they formed a crackling horizon of jagged lines in ash and black. She looked down at the sloping lot five stories below. Would that be enough to end it all? Everyone was now outside watching. Suddenly, she thought of her mom, and she didn't know if she wanted to go through with it. She didn't want to die in the middle of all of them. The last thing she wanted was more messiness. She just wanted to see it all neatly concluded.

"Come back down. We won't shoot," said the state.

She was mumbling "okay" when in a flash of white static she saw, at the edge of the crowd, apparently just arriving at the scene, Luna. And beside her, Winnie could have sworn, stood the CWC spokesperson Victor Bickle.

Then from behind her, a figure in the dark, I reached out. I touched her shoulder. "Winnie," I said. She leapt and spun around, losing her balance.

"Whoa," I said.

The railing collapsed, and she plunged at the Earth.

○ .

Freefall.

She felt her organs floating as they rushed her into the first-aid container. Feet clanged. People crowded. And while the pain squeezing her was not totally unlike others she had experienced in her life, it was by far the worst. There were tubes pumping fluid up her nose, Luna hyperventilating, the paramedics saying that with full gravity and flat ground, the girl might well have died.

I stood in the corner, unable to stop shaking. Victor Bickle was stammering about the email he'd gotten. Saying that Winnie's mass-messaged "Notes from the Federal Service and Relief Center at Keber Creek" was completely unintelligible, just a bunch of "O"s or one long moan, he didn't understand it, it must have already been too late.

When he searched for it now to show Luna, he realized for the first time that there was another message from Winnie's email address in his inbox. It wasn't newer but older. It had been sitting in his inbox for years, unread.

Dear Dr. Bickle, it began. *You don't know me, but I am a high school sophomore originally from the same town as you. I am writing to express my concern about your messaging on behalf of CWC, whose conduct creates economic, health, and environmental damage around the world. I really hope that you will please consider . . .*

The chatter was loud in Winnie's ears, and she squeezed her eyes shut, but still felt like she was floating. She imagined herself levitating off the vacmat and floating up through the clean surgical lights and the layers of corrugated, anti-graffiti corten steel, up to the tips of trees, where she could see the structures and figures of the camp in miniature. Imagining herself at eye-level with the mountaintops, she watched the pods launch and fall across Alaska, across Canada, and on barges that littered the southward-streaming sea. And then the pods didn't fall anymore but flipped, onto their heads, and just kept—

Rising. Almost like Rapture. She imagined everything rising. She saw the disintegration of the Shell. Toothy smiles in the sky shattered, their jingles fading out through daylight's blue expanse. As water gushed from torn support pillars, people debating contracts and tariffs spun off with their scooters, trash, and ambition. She rose in her mind, and the horizon strained. It curved.

Beneath her in the roaring wind as she rose, containers became encampments became geography. Concentric systems of chaos and order bloomed in her widening perspective. At thirty thousand feet, all those circuit vessels, which had refused to fly in any but the same direction, crashed in midair. At sixty thousand feet: the crack-up of the Shell. And then space. And it was as if the noise of some broken machine suddenly stilled. A new depth of silence. What had it been like to live at that critical time when all the world was more malleable than the human heart, she couldn't say. But she could see the shape of that bright, sorry world, assembled below her, growing smaller and smaller.

Acknowledgments

The best companions are those who bring out the best in you. My companions at New York University's creative writing program shaped my artistic sensibility, and I owe special thanks to friends who gave me feedback and advice on their own time, including Nolan Capps, Jamie Walters, Willie Watt, August Thompson, Nikita Biswal, Omer Friedlander, and Alex Kapsidelis. Danya Soto, Fernando Al Assal, and Michael Wang helped me with foreign languages. I was lucky to have a lot of creative friends growing up, and I'm particularly indebted to Eli Ruffer, who lived with me while I finished this book and from whom I stole a few jokes herein.

Peter Blackstock draws out the best in a writer. He inspired many of the most intelligent ideas in these pages and steered me away from my dumbest ones. Thank you to the whole team at Grove Atlantic for saving me from countless embarrassments: Sal Destro, Mike Richards, Michael Mah, Margaret Moore, and Miranda Hency caught innumerable errors in the manuscript; Deb Seager, John Mark Boling, Natalie Church, and Rachael Richardson's adeptness hides my own lack of media savvy; Jeff Miller, Dan Rembert, and Gretchen Mergenthaler distilled the book's vibe into their striking jacket image, which, among its many achievements, manages to make the open sky feel claustrophobic; Emily Burns not only guided the publication process but also kept me company when I showed up alone at a party.

Dan Kirschen and Abby Okin keep me calm. Dan's extraordinary decency creates an environment where people can be their most dignified selves, a rare thing in New York.

Riva Hocherman has filled my days with purpose and given me an occupation in which I'm constantly learning. My great group of friends at Holt make me excited to go to work, and I'm a much more cheerful person for that.

Thank you to my teachers, Rachel DeWoskin, Dan Raeburn, Rachel Cohen, Sergio Troncoso, Darin Strauss, John Freeman, Uzodinma Iweala, Hannah Tinti, David Lipsky, Nadifa Mohamed, and Jeffrey Eugenides. Jonathan Safran Foer has shown me how to become an adult without either losing my curiosity or letting it distract me from the important things in life. His example has meant, for me, permission to be such an adult.

My parents have always supported my interests. A writer of any age couldn't ask for more enthusiastic editing or readership than my crayon-drawn "Harry Potter pop-up book" received from my parents. My brother, Jack, is as magnetic off the cuff as I labor to be on the page. He reminds me that levity isn't so bad. My grandmothers, Sandi and Lynn, gave me my sense of humor. Brad and Allison Levin welcomed me into their own readerly family.

And Tess, who read countless drafts of this book, was patient with me when I wasn't patient with myself. So much of this book is a translation of the love you've brought into my life.